# The Car

*Ali*

*This book is for those who've been burned too many times before.*

# Chapter 1: Dead Tired

S he was just one hour from a long, lazy weekend with nothing more taxing than some early Christmas shopping and a good nap. She nearly made it.

As Fridays often were, today had been a washout. Following on from a devilishly early start, the newly minted Detective Chief Inspector Elsie Mabey had spent eight hours sitting around at Snaresbrook Crown Court only to be told that she wouldn't be needed today because the Crown Prosecution Service had dropped the case.

That sort of thing always happened to Elsie. If there was even the slightest chance that something could go wrong, it usually did.

She was keen to put the case, a run of the mill domestic spat turned violent, well behind her. Over the last seven and a bit years she'd seen dozens of these garden variety deaths. Husbands killing wives, gang members stabbing each other, and more overdoses than she could count. Thankfully, her days of being second-in-command were now over – as long as she passed probation.

By the time she got back to her new office in New Scotland Yard, her eyes were beginning to glaze over. The Met's personnel files on her new team members were on the desk right in front of her, but she couldn't bring herself to read through them.

After a hotly contested appointment process, command of Murder Investigation Team 18 was hers and with it came the large office she now found herself in. The room was in dire need of redecoration. For now, it housed a splintered old desk, three battered chairs, and several boxes of the outgoing DCI's personal belongings which still hadn't been taken away. If he didn't collect them soon, she'd bin the lot.

Personalising her office, however, would have to wait. Elsie was still on the graveyard shift, the worst possible assignment in her view because it made it impossible to keep to a proper sleep schedule. It meant she would be tasked with investigating whichever deaths came in between six pm and six am. Officially, her first on-call period had started a few moments ago. In practice, she hoped not to be given a case until after her team had had a chance to gel.

Tonight was the most important meet and greet yet as Elsie had saved meeting her new team for last. The final three members of Murder Investigation Team 18 that she had to meet were her detective inspector, the man who would deputise for her in her absence as well as the two detective sergeants who would do the donkey work on any investigation. Elsie opened her office door to find one of them missing. The two women were chatting away and only fell silent when Elsie cleared her throat.

'Sergeants Knox and Matthews?' Elsie said. 'Where's Detective Inspector Stryker?'

'I saw him leaving, ma'am,' the younger one said. She had the unblemished skin and cheeky dimples of someone in early adulthood set against a bulbous nose atop which sat a pair of round horn-rimmed glasses that were too large for her face.

'When was this?'

'No more than a few minutes ago. He seemed to be in a hurry.'

Strange, Elsie thought. She put it from her mind for the moment. 'Then we'll start without him. Come on in.'

Knox threw herself down into the chair with a thud while Matthews was far more graceful. Elsie took her seat across the desk from them. It was her first time being on the boss' side of the table. She was used to following orders and now she somehow had to manage a team that she knew very little about.

Before she could say anything, her iPhone buzzed angrily as it vibrated on the desk, the glint of a green WhatsApp notification visible out of the corner of her eye. She switched it into silent mode and then tucked it in her handbag.

'Sorry about that. It's been one of those days. The CPS chucked my case out because the witness wouldn't testify. The poor thing was terrified. I'd have thought the CCTV was enough to try, but then I'm not a lawyer.'

She was rambling and the other two were letting her. The older one, DS Patricia Knox, was pushing forty and looked even older. Her bloodshot eyes, wispy grey hair and nicotine-stained teeth contrasted sharply with the Met's crisp uniform. It was anyone's guess as to how she had gone this long without following the usual "up or out" career trajectory of the Met. She leant back in her chair, tilted her head to one side, and just watched as Mabey babbled. Something about Knox was off. What was a woman with twenty years of experience doing serving as a sergeant? Elsie had skimmed her disciplinary file which had been surprisingly light for such a long-serving member of the force. She appeared to have been demoted for "disciplinary issues" only weeks ago.

DS Georgia Matthews was the polar opposite. Where Knox was dumpy, squat, and obviously the oldest woman in the room,

Matthews seemed childlike with glasses that made her eyes look like saucers, a slender figure and a nervous disposition evident from the way she shifted in her seat.

'First things first, welcome to the team. I know a bit about you both, but why don't you tell me what you think I need to know. Why don't you go first, DS Matthews?'

Before Matthews could say a thing, Knox butted in. 'Look, Mabey, can't we go down the pub? I booked us a table for six at The Three Dragons. I invited Seb.'

Elsie looked at her scathingly. To suggest the pub was one thing. To interrupt a direct question was outright insubordination. Elsie ignored her and pressed on. 'DS Matthews, please continue.'

'I've just finished officer training.'

Elsie had read that in her file. She was as green as an officer could be. 'Ah yes, you did the graduate scheme. Remind me again what it was that you studied?'

'Physics and history.'

She'd read that too. Matthews wasn't just any grad either. She'd managed a double first which put Elsie's own upper second-class honours degree to shame.

Knox drifted away, her attention focused on the window rather than on the conversation.

'Patricia, what's your problem?' Elsie asked. 'You've been off ever since you walked in. Let's hear it. If there's a problem, I want to get it out in the open so we can deal with it now.'

No wonder her file noted "disciplinary issues". Knox appeared to have no respect for Elsie's authority.

Knox tensed up. 'Nobody ever calls me Patricia, alright? Not Patty or Pat either. It's Knox, no more, no less.'

Her tone was terse, clipped. Elsie decided to confront the obvious elephant in the room – it had to be more than simply a table reservation at the pub. 'Why have you got a bee in your bonnet, Knox?'

'Nah, it's nuffink.'

'It's clearly not nothing. Out with it.'

'Look, love,' Knox said. 'Leave it out, yeah? You don't wanna go there.'

'Out with it, Sergeant Knox.'

'You really wanna hear it?' Knox said with a sneer. 'Fine. You don't deserve the chair you're sitting in. You're too young, you ain't got the experience, and there were far better candidates. You only got the job because of who your father is.'

That stung. It wasn't the first time the accusation had been thrown at her either. Her father had, up until only a few years ago, also worked for the Homicide Command. He'd even written some of the Met's training manuals. So far in Elsie's career, it had been impossible to escape his shadow. Elsie felt the vein in her temple throb as her temper rose. It took all her restraint not to reach across the desk and strangle DS Knox. She forced herself to calm down, her voice icy.

'Knox, I'm going to say this once, and once only. I earned the right to lead this team. If you disagree, tough. The reality is I'm in charge and I'm not going anywhere. This is my team, not yours. If you can't live with that, the door is over there.'

Without hesitating one heartbeat, Knox leapt to her feet, took Elsie at her word and stormed out. The door slammed shut behind her and an awkward silence filled the room. Elsie was fuming. She forced herself to breathe in and out slowly.

Matthews looked at Elsie as if to ask permission to go after her friend. 'Ma'am,' Matthews said. 'She doesn't mean it. I know she's just frustrated. Let me go after her, calm her down.'

'Get going then,' Elsie said. 'Tell Knox that she's got until Monday to apologise or start looking for a new job.'

Matthews closed the door gingerly behind her. Elsie slumped over her desk and wrenched her glasses from her face. The world immediately blurred away and her eyelids became lead weights as the shutters came down. Tears had begun to form in the corners of her eyes. This hadn't gone the way she'd wanted. She'd been in charge for less than ten minutes and the team had already fractured. It didn't help that she was so damn tired that she could easily drop off in her chair.

The iPhone buzzed for the nth time and Elsie could ignore it no longer. She forced her eyes open and blearily squinted at the screen before stabbing at it with her thumb. As she squinted, the WhatsApp message swam in and out of focus. *Still on for dinner, beautiful?*

She bolted upright. Sometime between breakfast, when she'd packed her make-up bag into her handbag, and now, her date had completely slipped her mind.

With a couple of swipes, she opened the calendar entry. Her date was expecting her at a fancy gastropub in Mayfair. A little pretentious for a first date, Elsie thought. It was, however, nice that someone wanted to impress her. She retrieved her make-up from her handbag so she could make a bit of effort for her latest suitor, an accountant called Raj, who she'd found online.

She'd long since given up on finding Mr Right, and was now willing to settle for Mr He'll Do. Ever since she'd turned thirty-two, she'd found herself becoming less and less picky as the tick-tock of the biological clock grew ever louder. She began to apply her make-up starting with a thin layer of foundation.

As well as the make-up, she needed to dress smartly but not too formal. A little cleavage but nothing too slutty. The top hanging on the back of her office door would have to suffice. It was a black V-neck top with a little sequined bow on the shoulder. As she put it on, she ruminated over tonight's date. Raj seemed nice enough if a little forthright: it had taken him less than five brief messages to suggest dinner. Elsie supposed there wasn't much point waiting until they'd exchanged missives for months. There was only so much you could learn about someone online after all.

In all honesty, she wouldn't normally give a guy like him a chance. He was an accountant. How exciting could he be? The thing that swung it in Raj's favour was simple: he'd taken the time to read her profile rather than greet her with a generic *"Hey"* as if being monosyllabic and vague were sexy and mysterious. But was merely unobjectionable really enough to sustain a whole evening of chit-chat?

It was tempting to cancel given the day she'd had. She thrust that thought from her mind. A promise was a promise, and a girl had to eat. It really wasn't a huge burden to swing by the pub on the way home. If she skipped it, she'd just go home and crash, and regret it in the morning.

It would have to be quick though, only a main course and maybe dessert. She wasn't worried about being prudish, it was just that there was no way she'd keep her eyes open much longer than that. The mere idea of a protracted first date – let alone sex – was far too exhausting to contemplate.

Come on, Elsie, she thought, cajoling herself onwards. *It's Friday night. Don't waste it.*

She gently applied mascara to her eyelashes, applied a veneer of red lipstick, and checked out her handiwork. Not bad for a woman who'd just spent almost ten hours straight in court. The sound of a fist rapping smartly at her office door wrenched Elsie's attention away from her task.

'Come in,' she called out as she snapped the eyeshadow closed. The door opened to reveal a behemoth of a man with broad shoulders, a chiselled jawline, blue-black hair tinged with grey, and eyes that locked straight onto hers.

'Detective Inspector Stryker, how nice of you to finally show up.'

Sebastian "Seb" Stryker was the third and final transferee to join her intrepid Murder Investigation Team. Until Monday, he'd been somewhere up north investigating the source of cheap methamphetamine appearing in schools and colleges; his old boss had wanted him gone pronto, and so he'd been dumped in Elsie's lap. He was a mystery too. Why had he been dropped like a hot potato? There was a hint of urgency in his expression and yet when he spoke it was with a calm, collected voice that instantly put her at ease.

'Big date planned tonight, boss?' He casually looked from the travel make-up mirror on the desk to Elsie's lightly made-up face. She seldom wore much more than mascara and a little foundation. 'Who's the lucky man?' he said.

For a moment, she debated telling him to mind his own bloody business. Unfortunately, he had caught her, if not red-handed, red-lipsticked. 'I'm supposed to be going out on a random first date but I'm not feeling it,' Elsie said.

He looked relieved. 'Then maybe I'm not the bearer of such bad news after all.' He paused for breath, letting the silence hang just long enough to arouse her curiosity. 'They've found a body.'

That got her attention. 'When?' she demanded.

'Just after six,' he said. 'Minutes after our on-call shift started. You weren't responding to my calls, so I thought it best to come and get you.'

She glanced at her phone. She had six missed calls which had come in while her phone was on silent. All were labelled "Sebastian Stryker". She deflected. 'You should have gone to the crime scene.'

'I did,' Stryker said, flashing her a lopsided smile. 'It's secure, the woodentops are keeping guard, and they've got half a dozen PCSOs on crowd control, not that many people are out in this weather. We just need you on-site. I assume the rest of the team have been paged. Patty Knox and Georgia Matthews might even be there already.'

Elsie doubted it. Knox had stormed out in such a mood that Elsie half-wondered if she might never see her again.

If Stryker had had the time to secure the crime scene and get back again within the hour it had taken for Elsie to meet Knox and Matthews, then change and do her make-up, it stood to reason that the crime scene had to be nearby. Straining against the urge to put her head back down on her desk, she hauled herself to her feet and shrugged on her coat.

'What happened?

'You won't like it.'

# Chapter 2: The Front Doorstep

Churches and church towers designed by Christopher Wren were dotted around London. The crown among them, a stone's throw from the City itself, was St Dunstan in the East. It had stood atop Dunstan's Hill, in one form or another, from 1100 right up until the moment that the Luftwaffe struck. Despite the damage, the bombed-out remains, Elsie thought, evoked the atmosphere that Wren would have wanted, a beautiful, calm place of solitude. Floodlights had been haphazardly arranged around the perimeter by the first bobbies on the scene, illuminating the church walls against the night sky.

Elsie wasn't a religious woman, and yet the thought of a murder happening here left her feeling numb. Her initial task was a simple one – walk the perimeter, and make sure that the first officers on the scene had put the cordon in the right place. Best practice was to start wide just in case, and that meant tape running right around the perimeter of St Dunstan which would normally draw a lot of curious onlookers. This evening, the police had been lucky. Either the public had been chased off, or they were cowering from the December downpour. It felt like it had been raining for a week straight.

Looking up at the bomb-damaged outer walls, Elsie could see, touch and feel the very real damage that the Luftwaffe had inflicted upon London. Satisfied that the perimeter was in the right place, she approached the security cordon where the uniformed officer on duty, a man Elsie didn't know personally, looked her up and down and then smirked as if to mock her for being overdressed. One of his eyebrows, which were thick like baby caterpillars, arched in the most comical fashion.

'Do share the joke,' Elsie said. She shot him a withering glare, and he averted his gaze.

Unperturbed, Elsie proceeded to duck under the security cordon. St Dunstan was split over two levels with sprawling palm trees that seemed to mock the cold weather simply by being there. The body was in the lower section of the garden. As Elsie walked, she messaged Raj with a short and simple cancellation.

*Sorry, I have to work tonight. Duty Calls.*

He had seen her dating profile which clearly advertised that she was a policewoman, and so he ought to understand that emergencies and cancellations were part and parcel of her career. He needed to be able to deal with that like a grown-up, a hurdle many men had fallen at in the past. She debated adding an extra line suggesting they reschedule and then decided against it. If Raj were keen, he could suggest another night. He might not have much luck. If this was another "Lady Killer" victim then Elsie's schedule was about to get really busy, really fast.

There was a profound loneliness to the police life. In spite of all the activity around her, Elsie had nobody she felt she could always rely on except for dear old Dad. Where better to be lonely than in a crowded city whose inhabitants were so desperate to avoid each other that they'd walk past a person – or a corpse – sooner than they'd stop and help?

Stryker trailed in her wake. A goofy smile suggested he'd glanced at her phone while she was messaging Raj. When she looked over accusingly, he feigned nonchalance but there was a trace of a smile in the corners of his eyes. Once they were beyond the blue and white tape of the inner security cordon, they found themselves in the main courtyard. The total absence of a roof let the rain pelt down upon the courtyard, and the wind whipped through forcing Elsie to tuck her hair behind her ears to keep it out of her eyes. In the centre of the courtyard, eight wooden benches were set out in a circular pattern. Rubbish was strewn around the benches, especially cigarette butts, evidence of the thoughtlessness of the Londoners who came here to eat lunch. It struck Elsie as cutting one's nose off to spite one's face. For those office lackeys who worked in the surrounding monoliths, St Dunstan was a respite from the concrete jungle, and so to despoil it with crisp packets and cigarettes was disrespectful and self-defeating. Tonight, the tranquillity of the place – an oasis between the hustle and bustle of Fenchurch Street a stone's throw to the north, and the Tower of London humming with tourists just to the east – had been shattered. Engines stood idle, humming away just out of earshot beyond the church boundary.

Elsie couldn't remember the last time that Homicide Command had camped out in a church. Of course, she didn't know much about what the other Murder Investigation Teams were up to at any given moment.

Working homicide investigation was exhausting. Whenever a case came in, she'd work every hour under the sun until it was solved. For a cop who suffered from debilitating tiredness, the night shift was living hell and it was almost a relief to find a body and start working more sociable hours. Her illness was properly called *Myalgic Encephalomyelitis* though the media always erroneously called it Chronic Fatigue Syndrome. Elsie also called it CFS in her mind, not because it was the right term but because she could spell it.

As she was still on the graveyard shift, her new team would no doubt pull the same awful cases she'd been working on for years: the bloaters pulled from the Thames, dead sex workers and the sulphurous corpses of the homeless.

Nobody really cared if she got justice for them because they didn't have family that cared enough to harass the police for progress reports, nor enough clout to go to the press. The bloody media didn't give a crap unless the victim was famous, attractive or died in an unusual way, and ideally, they wanted all three.

The body came into view as Elsie approached the bench.

'Told you that you wouldn't like it,' Stryker said.

She didn't. Murder was always bloody and horrible but the death of someone so young, so innocent-looking, was as abhorrent as cases got.

This victim was a newspaper editor's wet dream. She wore a long white wedding dress that would have been pristine if not for the rain which made her look a little like a drowned rat. Like the first victim, she had been posed on a bench facing south as if she were sleeping. She lay on her side, her arm under her head as if it were a pillow which caused her Chestnut-brown hair to cascade gracefully down her shoulders. At first glance, it appeared that she had simply stopped for a nap. It was the unnatural stillness which struck Elsie. She kept expecting to see the girl exhale, stretch and sit up with a yawn. Instead, her body lay exactly where the killer had left it, the movement of the rain contrasting sharply with the lifelessness of it all.

'Looks just like the photos of the first crime scene to me,' Stryker ventured.

Elsie wagged a finger in his direction. 'Let's not get ahead of ourselves. This could be a copycat.'

The details of the first murder had made front-page news up and down the country. A young black woman had been stabbed through the heart, dressed in a black lace gown, and left on one of the three wooden benches at the heart of Chelsea Physic Garden. The press had been fascinated by the idea of a sartorially astute killer roaming the streets of central London, posing his victims in their Sunday best and leaving them on display in public places. Even just one known victim had been enough for the killer to gain notoriety. Nicknames sprang out of the woodwork in short order: The Dressed to Kill Murderer, The Poser, and The Lady Killer. The last one had stuck. It had even trended as a hashtag. Elsie hated the nicknames. They glamorised murder and made the crime about the criminal rather than the victim. The need for justice gave way to the need to sell as many newspapers as possible. No doubt the talking heads on breakfast television would soon be talking about this victim too. If it weren't the same killer, Elsie needed to prove it post-haste before the rumour mill ran away with the facts.

'Really?' Stryker mocked. 'Both women, both beautiful but lacking make-up while wearing an over the top dress and they've both been posed lying down as if they're asleep. That's oddly specific if it isn't a serial, boss.'

He had been in London for all of five minutes, and he already thought he knew better than she did. 'I'm not saying it isn't,' Elsie said. 'I'm saying don't jump the gun.'

Even as she said it, she privately had to agree with him. It was almost certainly the work of the same killer. The two crime scenes were strikingly similar. Both dump sites were quasi-public, both were leafy and picturesque, and both had wooden benches arranged in a circle at the centre, and as Stryker had been quick to point out, they were both part of the "young and beautiful" demographic that so often drew the attention of serial killers.

The girl on the bench was tiny, easily a foot shorter than Elsie, and her diminutive stature was almost childlike. Neither her head nor her toes touched the end of the oak bench upon which she lay. To be fair, nearly every woman looked like a dwarf compared to Elsie's six-foot stature, but this victim was particularly tiny.

Elsie stepped closer to the victim and then crouched down low. With porcelain-perfect skin, and wide-set cheekbones so sharp that Elsie could cut herself, the victim was bound to make the front page and stay there until the case was solved or went so cold that it ended the career of the Senior Investigating Officer in charge.

Serial murder was a far cry from the "simple" domestic violence kills, street brawls and overdoses she was used to investigating. If she could keep hold of this case, it was a golden opportunity to prove to everyone she'd earned her promotion, and prove to herself that she really was as capable as her peers.

That was ample reason not to immediately label it a serial murder. If she did, the Senior Investigating Officer for the first murder would probably take over, consigning her to a lifetime of looking at dead hookers.

'No sign of the pathologist,' Elsie said, eying Stryker accusingly as if it were his fault that neither forensics nor the pathologist were in attendance an hour after the first page had gone out.

Stryker held his hands aloft as if to defend himself. 'Not yet,' he said. 'It *is* a Friday night.'

She rolled her eyes. 'Of course, it is.'

Not only were Friday nights the busiest generally, but Friday was also poker night. Top brass from Homicide and Serious Crime Command plus some of the boys from HOLMES, Forensic Services, and the Coroner's Office met to gamble away the week's overtime and trade war stories. It was *almost* exclusively an old boy's club. There was just one female card sharp who played regularly, and she was one Valerie Spilsbury, arguably the Met's finest forensic pathologist.

Spilsbury was the exception that proved the rule. She, together with the current commissioner of police of the metropolis, were held up as shining examples of women in the Met as if a couple of appointments undid years of discrimination. It was, in Elsie's opinion, pure tokenism. Appoint a woman here, a black or Asian candidate there, and suddenly the Met's publicity shots were filled with glossy photos of a diverse smiley little group.

Digging beyond the press photos the past quickly became the present. The Met's men's rugby team had an astonishing number of the top brass within its ranks. Virtually all the other Murder Investigation Teams were headed up by middle-aged white men. Despite having once played in the final of the World of Poker Championships in Paris, Elsie had never been invited to play in the Friday night poker game.

Elsie forced such thoughts from her mind; it was all unfair, but she could do nothing about it except prove that she was as good as any man, and that meant solving the crime right in front of her. Her eyes traversed the crime scene around the body. The victim's clutch bag – an elegant but impractical silver Jimmy Choo affair – lay beside her. The fact that no one had nicked it was testimony to how few passers-by there were this evening. It was weird – St Dunstan was often busy, but tonight the combination of darkness, frigid weather with high winds whipping through, and a police perimeter, had seen off all but the most determined of gawkers. Sometimes the bystander effect kicked in too; nobody wanted to get involved, instead, they preferred to hustle along with their heads bowed against the wind. Nothing to see here, guv.

Stryker gestured at the bag. 'Could be something useful in there, boss.'

He said it just as she was thinking it. It was odds-on that the bag would contain some form of ID and getting a jump on identifying their victim could be critical. They both knew they ought to wait for the pathologist. Standard Operating Procedure and all that malarkey. But SOP had already gone out the window. Spilsbury hadn't bothered to show up as quickly as she ought to have and the Scene of Crime team wasn't here yet either. The golden hour was slipping away and so too was the killer. The longer it took to start the investigation, the less likely it was they'd be able to find witnesses who could accurately remember what they saw, find CCTV before it was overwritten, collect samples that would otherwise be contaminated, or even find a criminal who had not yet left the area.

Caution was fine when there wasn't a ticking clock. Today, deciding not to look in the victim's handbag could mean missing a time-sensitive clue. If they did, it would no doubt still be Elsie's fault later on. It was a damned-if-you-do, damned-if-you-don't choice, and Elsie hated waiting on other people.

'Let's do it,' she said. 'Full gloves and everything goes back exactly where it came from.' *No harm, no foul.*

Once she had donned plastic gloves to prevent contamination, Elsie carefully picked up the designer bag and unclipped the fastening to look inside. There were house keys attached to a garish Gucci pearl keyring, an assortment of condoms, all ribbed for her pleasure, and an array of make-up (despite the victim's unpainted face).

'What's she got?' Stryker asked.

'Nothing much of interest yet,' Elsie said. 'Apart from the designer gear, this could be any woman's bag.'

Digging to the bottom, Elsie found a brand-new iPhone with its plastic screen protector still in place, and lastly, a handful of cards. They included a plastic photo card driving licence which clearly showed the victim's face, two debit cards and half a dozen credit cards. That many cards seemed totally superfluous. Elsie's own purse contained only one debit card she used for nearly everything and a backup credit card just in case. She tried turning on the phone. Nothing.

'Dead?' Stryker said.

'Yep,' Elsie confirmed. 'Don't suppose you've got an iPhone charger with you?'

He was already delving into his pockets before she finished her sentence. He had no end of them, each filled with different knick-knacks that he placed on the ground at his feet. Elsie felt a twinge of jealousy; why didn't they make women's clothing with proper pockets?

'Aha!' he cried. 'There's the blighter.' He handed over a small power bank which had an Apple lightning cable attached to it. Elsie cast a quick glance towards the archway where they'd entered in case the pathologist had appeared, and then tentatively plugged the phone in to charge. A neon-orange light began to glow immediately.

Elsie gestured at the phone. 'How long will it take to charge?'

'For enough juice to turn on? Less than ten minutes. The bank has enough power to charge it fully but by then the pathologist might have deigned to make an entrance.'

She nodded and turned her attention back to the bag. It was real, not one of the knock-offs she'd seen at the dodgy markets by Camden Lock, and had to be worth hundreds of pounds if not more. The debit cards inside indicated that the victim was one Layla Morgan and that she banked at SQ Private Bank.

'She must be loaded,' Stryker said, seemingly reading her mind.

While she waited for Layla's phone to come to life, Elsie produced her own phone from her pocket and Googled to find the requirements to open a bank account at SQ Private Bank. The page took forever to load. When it did, she felt her jaw drop. That was a lot of zeros. She turned the screen to show Stryker.

His jaw dropped too. 'Are they missing a decimal point?'

With a shake of her head, she locked her mobile. How the other half lived! She had thought she was doing okay in life – in charge of her own team, a homeowner (albeit of a small one bed flat a long way from the nearest tube station) and not yet a crazy cat lady at the ripe old age of thirty-two. If it weren't for the chronic fatigue, she'd be winning at life. But seeing how much money this woman, this child, clearly had access to, made her mind boggle. She'd seen people like it wandering the streets of London before, touting their Harrods' shopping bags full of designer swag and getting their weekly groceries from liveried footmen at Fortnum & Mason's, but this dead girl made it all seem less abstract. It was almost as if she and the victim lived in parallel versions of London. They walked the same streets, took the same cabs, and yet lived lives that would never normally intersect. It seemed the victim had it all: youth, money, and looks.

'Think she'd miss the bag?' Elsie joked.

'I'm sure it'd suit you, ma'am.'

Ma'am? A little part of her died inside at the idea she was no longer a 'miss'. 'That's boss ma'am to you, Inspector Stryker.'

He grinned sheepishly. 'Sorry, boss.'

There was still no sign of the pathologist or crime scene manager's team. This too was par for the course when you ran the least important team in London. Elsie was half-tempted to send her father a message. Despite the fact that he'd retired from the Met, he still had more influence than she did. One call from him would expedite things tremendously. She sighed. She needed the help but asking for it would only serve to reinforce the rumours that she had piggybacked his legacy.

The clock was ticking. Every minute was another minute that the crime scene was bathed in rain, trace evidence literally going down the sewer drains. It was just her luck. Whenever something good happened, there was always a fly in the ointment, a run of bad luck that had followed her ever since she'd come down with glandular fever as a teenager.

'Sorry, what?'

'I was saying,' he repeated patiently, 'd'ya reckon this'll get punted over to one of the other teams, boss? If it's a serial killer, shouldn't DCI Fairbanks get first crack?'

He wasn't giving up on the serial killer angle. Elsie wasn't surprised that he knew of DCI Fairbanks. It was impossible to miss the old codger strutting around New Scotland Yard. Fairbanks looked like a column of flab with a face perched atop it. It was a travesty he'd let himself get into that shape. Elsie had seen pictures of his glory days up on his office wall, and he'd been a handsome man once. Worse still was his abysmal solve rate. He might have snaffled the first victim by luck but Elsie was damned if she'd let him get his paws on this case. She shook her head vehemently.

'Fat chance,' Elsie said. 'This one's mine.'

'But boss—'

She shot him a withering gaze. '*As far as we know* this is not a serial murder, understood?'

He acquiesced, not that he had any choice. He might have been a big fish in the small pond that was West Yorkshire Police but down here he was a rookie with no influence. Elsie might suspect a serial killer, she might even believe it to be true, but until evidence backed that up, the case was hers. She needed this case. She needed the chance to prove, once and for all, that she'd earned her command. Solving a case like this was the only way to quash the rumours, to quieten the snide remarks.

Such high-profile crimes were a double-edged sword. While success would redeem her reputation, failure would forever condemn her to working the graveyard shift. A tiny voice at the back of her mind screamed out that she should hand it off to DCI Fairbanks. It was the easy way out. If she let him have the case, she'd have no risk of failure, no media spotlight to deal with, and nobody comparing her to her father. Her team was too green, too new. The safe choice beckoned.

# Chapter 3: Spilsbury

The echo of a hacking cough announced the pathologist's belated arrival. Elsie hastily stuffed the victim's mobile into her pocket so she wouldn't see the orange light. The coughing grew louder and louder until Dr Valerie Spilsbury appeared out of the darkness. She was a curmudgeonly old woman, grey and hunched with a face that was all wrinkles surrounding large eyes made even bigger by her designer Tom Davies glasses. The doctor looked comically small next to Stryker. It would have been easy to assume that her height and age reflected her ability. It was a mistake that nobody made twice. Spilsbury spared little time for the detectives and forensic scientists with whom she had to work. She had her favourites – they all did – but Elsie was not among them.

'Doc,' Elsie said by way of greeting. Spilsbury didn't even glance at her. She barrelled past at elbow-height as if the corpse could wait no longer.

'Move aside,' she said with a wave of her hand. 'I can't have you contaminating the crime scene any more than you inevitably have.'

Elsie's nostrils flared angrily. Every bloody time it was assumed that she was incompetent because she was young and she was a woman. Never mind that the doctor had had to deal with the same prejudice once upon a time. Perhaps that was it; Valerie Spilsbury had risen above the bile and so she had contempt for anyone who couldn't follow in her footsteps. What hurt the most was that Spilsbury was right. Elsie had broken protocol by going fishing in the victim's handbag. Elsie bit her tongue, though she arched an eyebrow at Stryker from behind the pathologist's back. He managed a wan smile in return.

By now the pathologist was poring over the body with rapt attention. She leant in so close that she was almost but not quite touching the body. Elsie could hear the pathologist's laboured breathing as she watched her breath rise in the winter air. It was the sort of bitingly cold night that made Elsie long for thick woollen mittens, and a warm log fire to retire to. If she closed her eyes, she was transported back to the Chesterfield, in the window overlooking the garden of her childhood home. It was her reading nook, her sanctuary where Mam would bring her hot chocolate, and she missed those days sorely. She shivered as she looked at Spilsbury dressed in an overcoat that looked paper-thin, and wearing nothing more than sterile gloves on her tiny weather-worn hands.

The doc worked methodically, and even Elsie had to grudgingly admire her efficiency. She progressed from sense to sense, first taking in how the body looked, both up close and within the context of her surroundings, then pausing as if to listen to the corpse which struck Elsie as a fruitless exercise. She'd asked about it once, and Spilsbury had claimed to be able to hear the decomposition, even smell the slow process of putrefaction. Such things turned Elsie's stomach.

Spilsbury muttered to herself as she worked, still oblivious to the detectives waiting for her to provide a time of death. The heavy breathing stopped suddenly, and then Spilsbury sniffed the air as if she were a dog.

A giggle escaped Elsie's lips at the thought of the vaunted Doctor Valerie Spilsbury with matted fur and a wagging tail.

Spilsbury's head snapped around towards her so fast that she wouldn't have been surprised if she suffered whiplash. 'What's so funny?' Spilsbury demanded.

She shrugged, stifling the urge to laugh. 'Nothing.'

The pathologist turned away and dug an oversized camera out of her bag with which to take photos of the body in situ. It was a task that ought to have been delegated. Elsie watched as the body was thoroughly photographed from every angle. The doctor worked quickly, the single-lens reflex mechanism of her full-frame camera snapping with a clack over and over again. Every passing moment was another opportunity for evidence to degrade.

Once the photography was out of the way, the doctor pulled out a long thin thermometer that ended in a wicked point. She eyed the victim as if deciding where to stick it.

'Can't decide if you want to put it under the tongue or up the bum?' Stryker joked under his breath.

Unfortunately for him, Spilsbury heard him.

'Name?' she demanded.

He glanced at Elsie as if he expected her to leap to his defence. Instead, Elsie shrugged. When Spilsbury asked a second time, Stryker told her.

'Mr Stryker, I will assume you're new to the Met, and I will give you the benefit of the doubt *once*. Is that clear?

His head dropped, and he stared at his feet.

'Yes, ma'am.'

'Right, then come closer.' She beckoned him with a gnarled index finger. 'This,' she held aloft her thermometer, 'is the most important tool I own. Do you know why?'

He eyed her warily. Was it a trick question?

'To take a corpse's temperature,' he said.

'Indeed,' the doc said. 'And why do we want that?'

'Time of death,' he said much more confidently this time.

Spilsbury nodded appreciatively. 'You're not a complete idiot then. Back when I started, we used a rough rule of thumb, bodies cool at roughly one point eight degrees Fahrenheit per hour.'

'Not now though,' Elsie chimed in.

'Quite,' Spilsbury said. She turned to her bag, withdrew a small laptop and set it upon the ground. 'These days I use a Bluetooth thermometer that feeds into my laptop so I can consider more variables. Any idea what those variables could be, Mr Stryker?'

He looked around the courtyard. The rain was still pounding down as it had been on and off since they'd arrived, and it brought a chill with it that would no doubt affect the forensic timeline. 'How cold it is out?'

'That would be one such variable. There are many. Everything from ambient temperature to the size of the body, air pressure, salinity, and whether a body has been dumped will cause differences. If this isn't the primary crime scene, then we don't know what the conditions were like where she was murdered. These may be minor variations with no meaningful impact on the forensics or they may throw off the timeline. Now, did I hear one of you say you think that this might be a serial?'

The pathologist had to have impressively sharp hearing to have heard them talking about that.

'Maybe,' Elsie conceded cautiously. 'Maybe not.'

'Those are the options.' Spilsbury crossed her arms as she spoke. To Elsie she looked like Sister Mariana, a nun who had taught her as a child and had assumed a very similar position whenever she was unamused.

If sexual assault were a possibility, then proper procedure dictated that the pathologist couldn't use a rectal thermometer lest she contaminate the evidence.

Spilsbury glanced from one detective to the other and then gave a little shrug. 'Can't chance things,' she said cheerfully as she stabbed the victim's abdomen with her thermometer. The spiked end of Spilsbury's thermometer slid almost effortlessly into the body. It was obviously a procedure that the doctor had done a thousand times before, and the disinterested look on her face reflected that. Where Elsie naturally recoiled from even looking at the corpse, Spilsbury handled it dispassionately.

'How long's she been dead, doc?' Elsie asked.

The doc seemed to be working it out in her head.

'I'm not putting a number on it.'

'Why not?' Stryker demanded. 'Can't you just subtract her current temperature from normal body temperature, and then divide it by two degrees Fahrenheit or whatever you said it was?'

Spilsbury didn't budge. 'First, it's one point eight degrees, not two. Secondly, it's nearly freezing so doubtless she'd have cooled quicker than usual. Humidity, body mass, etc., they all matter too.'

'Then give us a ballpark, doc,' Stryker retorted.

'No,' Spilsbury said firmly. 'And watch your tone if you don't want your first murder case to be your last. One more outburst and I'll be putting in a formal complaint.'

Elsie threw her hands up in surrender. Her new protégé was proving more trouble than he was worth. 'Doc, Stryker's sorry, aren't you, Seb?'

One glance at Elsie's face and he knew he was outnumbered. Contrition dawned upon him. He thrust his hands into his pockets, the spitting image of a spoiled schoolboy caught with his hands in the biscuit tin.

'Sorry,' he mumbled.

Spilsbury ignored him and turned her attention to Elsie. 'You've got a body dump here. There's visible livor mortis.'

Sure enough, her lower limbs were covered in red-and purple bruises. 'How's that impact our post-mortem interval?' Elsie asked.

'That alone says she's been dead for two hours minimum.'

A quick glance at Elsie's watch proved the same. They found the body hours ago. 'Any more than that?'

'Fools guess. Experts know their limits,' Spilsbury said. 'I need to check the nearest weather station. Until I know the temperature, wind speed, and humidity, I can't give you more than an educated guess, and I never guess.'

Elsie couldn't help but parrot Stryker's question. 'I know it's not possible to say definitively, but it would be valuable to have *some* idea of the timeframe. I'll take your educated guess over a complete absence of information any day.'

Spilsbury sighed. This was a battle she knew she'd never win. She held up her hands in defeat.

'The only thing I can tell you are the odds. It's probable that she's been dead for a day or more,' Spilsbury said, though she sounded less certain than her words indicated. Perhaps it was Spilsbury's famous poker face, or perhaps she was simply unwilling to stake a thirty-year career on a hunch. 'There's no sign of rigor,' she continued. 'Someone has taken the time to pose her on this bench, and it would have taken them a while to get this dress positioned so elegantly.'

The thought set Elsie's mind racing. Someone had *posed* the body? If it were a serial, and the first victim had been posed too, that detail hadn't made it into the newspapers. Elsie made a mental note to check the Met's own HOLMES 2 database. 'Are you sure, doc?'

'Almost certain,' Spilsbury confirmed. 'Don't quote me on it until after the autopsy though. I've no visible cause of death. Let's get the body bagged and transported to the mortuary. Do you want to be present? I should be able to start at around nine o'clock tomorrow morning.'

It was a tempting offer. Elsie cast a glance at the reticent Stryker.

'As you two are getting on so well, Stryker will come watch,' Elsie said. 'Like you said, it's his first murder investigation, and he needs to learn, don't you Stryker?'

The doc grimaced, and Elsie knew she had set the cat among the pigeons.

Faced with an entire morning with a man she clearly disliked, Spilsbury's prim and proper façade broke. 'You've got to be kidding me. Fine. He can come, but he'd better not puke in my autopsy room.'

With that she spun on her heel, and then stalked back the way she'd come, leaving Elsie and Stryker standing in the rain. Echoes of her footsteps – and the accompanying hacking cough – faded into the night.

Once she was sure no one was watching, Elsie pulled the victim's phone out of her pocket, and then placed it gingerly under the victim's thumb.

It didn't unlock. The screen read *Enter Passcode. Your passcode is required to enable Touch ID.*

She swore, and then shoved the phone into an evidence bag. Elsie mulled over her options – canvass the area, babysit the crime scene manager whenever he or she arrived, or look up the victim's address. The victim had a driving licence in her purse so Elsie decided to start with the last, easiest, task. After she'd done that, there was scant more she could do on-site. If St Dunstan in the East wasn't the primary crime scene, she had to find out where the victim had actually been killed, and the victim's home seemed as good a place to start as any. She made her decision.

'Stryker, the crime scene's all yours. When our crime scene manager gets here, make sure the body is bagged, then crack on with the general canvass. If Knox and Matthews bother to show up, I want them going door to door, and I want copies of any CCTV recordings within a quarter of a mile. Got it?'

'But where are you—'

'Do you understand or not?' She wasn't about to explain herself to the cocky detective.

'Got it,' he said reluctantly.

'Call me if you find anything inceptive.'

Confusion furrowed his brow as if they didn't think about inceptive evidence up north. They probably just called it meaningful or something else equally vapid. No doubt he would Google the term the moment he was out of her sight.

'And, Stryker?'

'Yes, boss?'

'Welcome to the Met.'

# Chapter 4: Life Interrupted

Annie Burke knew it was going to happen. She'd spent the whole day tidying up around the house compulsively putting everything away just how she liked it. A place for everything and everything in its place. That's what her parents had drilled into her. This was her long-awaited weekend off with her hubby, Sam. The champagne was chilling in the fridge, a fresh lasagne was in the oven, and the table was set for two.

Her mood had varied throughout the day. Something about the anticipation felt like a first date complete with butterflies in her stomach. She loved the romance. Sometimes though, she felt like she was in love with being in love and not in love with Sam.

She'd nearly finished preparing dinner before the call came in from the area forensic manager. 'Not tonight, please,' she'd pleaded. 'It's my wedding anniversary.' It was no use. The boss didn't care if she'd been married eight years today. It didn't matter that she had an elaborate dinner planned, and rose petals scattered across the bed. It didn't matter that her husband was on the way home from the airport having been away in Asia for almost a month. It didn't matter that tonight was their last chance saloon, the night she'd pinned her hopes on to rekindle it all, to find that spark they'd once enjoyed.

It was much the same as when she'd first got married. Her schedule ruined everything, and he demanded more. She could be called at a moment's notice and was duty-bound to respond. Such was the life of a crime scene manager working murder cases.

When a body was found, and she was the only crime scene manager on the duty roster dumb enough to answer the phone on a Friday night, she had to go. If she didn't then evidence could be lost. The first few hours were critical. She had no choice.

Dinner had been abandoned – not for the first time – and an apology note left on the table for Sam. Their reconciliation had waited months if not years already. Another day or two couldn't hurt, could it?

It was nearly eight o'clock when her taxi pulled over on St Dunstan's Hill. The road ahead was blocked by squad cars, and her police colleagues loitered on the pavement awaiting her arrival.

'Sixty quid please, love,' the cabbie called over his shoulder. *Sixty pounds?* It was daylight – or rather evening – robbery.

Not more than a second after the cabbie spoke, Annie grimaced and shut her eyes as she groped for the purse that she knew wasn't there. She'd been in such a rush to grab her kitbag that she'd left it on the kitchen counter. When she didn't move, the cabbie repeated himself, this time more loudly with an edge to his voice causing the hair on her neck to stand on end. The taxi door was still locked; Annie wondered how unsafe she would have felt had they not been parked next to two police cars. She rolled down the window, and a man she presumed was the new guy on Murder Investigation Team 18 approached with an expression of curiosity on his face.

'You're Mr Stryker, right?' Annie had been texted by the Senior Investigating Officer that one Sebastian Stryker would be waiting for her at the crime scene.

'Guilty,' he said with a lopsided grin. 'Call me Seb.'

'Seb, I'm in a bind. I was in a rush and forgot my purse—'

Before she could finish her sentence, he thrust his hand into his trouser pocket and fished out his wallet.

'Say no more,' Stryker said. 'It happens to the best of us. What's the damage?'

'Sixty quid,' the driver grunted.

'*Sixty quid?* Where'd you drive her from? Nottingham?'

'Look, mate, that's what it says on the meter. Don't like it, take it up with the Mayor of London. I'm sure he'll give a shit. Now, you going to pay up or shall I turn the meter back on?'

Stryker scowled but still handed over three crisp twenty-pound notes that looked like they were fresh off the printer. The cabbie unclicked the passenger door locks.

'Mind giving me a hand with my kit?' Annie asked as she stepped out onto the pavement. As well as a large police-issue holdall, she had a bundle of boards ready to lay on the floor so that footfall wouldn't contaminate the scene.

Stryker grabbed the stack of boards. He stumbled under their weight.

'You alright there, Seb?'

He flashed a forced smile. Typical man. 'Nothing I can't handle,' he said.

Once the mildly delayed cabbie had been paid, he reversed full throttle to escape the artificial dead-end created by the parked police cars and then sped off with his tyres screeching as if he couldn't wait for his next fare.

Annie turned to her rescuer. 'Thanks, Seb. Send me your bank details, and I'll square us up tomorrow morning, I promise.'

'Forget it,' Stryker said. 'I'll stick it on expenses.' He flashed her a smile, and then added, 'Elsie won't care. I assume from the kitbag that you're with forensics.'

She nodded. The enormous bag she dragged along must have weighed a ton as it was laden down with everything that she needed from luminol to camera. Within minutes of arriving, while Stryker lumbered along behind her and asked questions machine-gun style, one after the other, she changed into her forensics suit, put on gloves – two pairs as required by law – and then began laying boards down at the edge of the crime scene.

'Bit late for that,' Stryker said. 'The boss wanted to get a move on.'

Her jaw dropped. She knew he'd been on-site – his footprints were visible in the mud – but to admit having broken procedure was astounding.

'Look, Seb, this might be your first rodeo,' Annie said sternly. 'But it isn't mine. You want to catch your killer and get a clean, safe conviction then you have to follow my rules. No access without proper suits, no touching the body, and I get first crack at the crime scene. Do we understand each other?'

The cheeky smile vanished. A brief nod signalled his acquiescence.

'Right, then you go do your job. I'll do mine.'

STRYKER FUMED, NOT at Annie Burke, but at himself. He ought to have known that the crime scene was sacrosanct. He was stuck in the middle. He agreed with the rules and didn't yet know how much they could be bent before they broke. Elsie's argument that the killer could be nearby was powerful in the moment but was now less urgent as Annie imposed order and logic upon the crime scene. He watched her and wondered just how much evidence would be left once the rain had finally stopped. Judging by the slick grey stone underfoot, any trace evidence was probably in the gutter by now.

'What're you looking for?' he asked Annie as she continued to beaver away.

'Inceptive evidence.'

He looked at her blankly. They kept using that phrase, one he'd never heard in his life. Google hadn't been much help either. She took the hint.

'I'm looking for stuff you can use right now like a gun or a knife, or blood drops trailing across the ground. Anything we find now can be expedited – assuming your boss doesn't mind the expense.'

'When will you know if we've got anything?'

'Thankfully it's not a Sunday so if we find trace DNA, you're looking at about a nine-hour turnaround with the national DNA database.'

'What's wrong with Sundays?'

'They're closed,' Annie said. 'No idea why. Now can you step back – a little further please – that's it, just the other side of that wall.'

Stryker kept stepping back through the archway and up the steps until Annie was completely out of view.

'Are you messing with me?' he called out from the upper level of the garden. 'Is this like sending the newbie out to buy tartan paint?'

'Nope,' Annie said. He heard ruffling. Presumably, Annie was searching through her bag. If she were following proper procedure – and he had no doubt at all in his mind that she would be – then she'd have to start by photographing the crime scene.

He stepped forward to sneak a peek and saw the glint of a camera lens.

'Annie, don't you normally stand in the corner?'

She turned in the direction of his voice and saw him peering around the archway to watch her work. 'It used to be done that way. That's the old method of photographing a crime scene. Now we do it this way.'

He watched as she put a wide-angle lens – marked "28mm" – onto a tripod at the centre of the crime scene. She walked around the wall to stand next to Stryker so she wasn't in the shot.

'Now I just press this button,' she said. The moment that she did, the camera began to rotate through three-hundred-and-sixty-degrees. 'It's like your phone's panorama feature but better.'

Stryker smiled appreciatively as she returned to the lower level of the garden. 'Can I come back?' he called after her.

'Nope,' Annie said loudly. 'I've got work to do.'

So that was how it was. He didn't blame her. He already felt like he was getting under her feet. With a huge crime scene to process – and no sign of reinforcements on the way – she needed to crack on alone, and he had to do likewise.

# Chapter 5: One Too Many

His encounters with Annie and Doctor Spilsbury had left Stryker feeling like the proverbial village idiot. His first day working for DCI Mabey had been a big adjustment from life in Yorkshire, and it only got worse when he heard the unmistakeable click-clacking of high heels along the rainswept alleyway, more than one pair by the sounds of it. Then he heard two women giggling far too loudly. When he proceeded to look just past the security cordon, he found Patty Knox and Georgia Matthews stumbling along, obviously tipsy. The former swayed on her feet, drool running down the corner of her mouth while Matthews held her up.

Knox looked at him curiously as if trying to work out if she knew him. Without any warning, Knox flung herself towards him, her handbag flying wildly and upending its contents all over the pavement. He realised she was going to fall just in time to leap forwards. He caught her awkwardly, his arm taking the brunt of her weight. She looked up at him as if it were his fault that she had tripped.

'Bloody hell,' Stryker muttered. Matthews stooped to gather Knox's belongings just as a lipstick rolled into the gutter, through the grate and into the drain below.

'Bugger,' Matthews muttered as she stuffed everything back in haphazardly. Her movements were slow and uncoordinated. Stryker suspected that she'd had a couple of drinks. Tipsy, not drunk, unlike Knox who was so far gone that she was now leaning heavily into him, clinging onto his arm for dear life.

She poked him in the chest with a yellow calloused finger. 'You,' she slurred. 'I know you!' She twisted to look at Matthews and waved off the handbag that Matthews was trying to return. 'Don't I know him, Georgie?'

'You do, Knoxy, you do,' Matthews said. She was merry, but not slurring-her-words. His hunch that she'd had two or three was on the money.

Stryker watched them talking to each other, his own presence superfluous, and exhaled deeply, trying his best to stay calm. First, the boss ignored his calls, then he messed up with the crime scene manager, and now he had to deal with drunk colleagues. Could today get any worse?

'I see we've been to the pub,' he said. 'How many have you had?'

'Bottles?' asked Knox. She squinted at her hand and began to fold down fingers. 'One... two...'

Before she could get to three, Stryker held up a hand. 'Girls, you can't be here while you're under the influence. Go home, drink loads of water, and get a good night's sleep.'

'Go home? Why would I do that?' Knox swayed on her feet. ''tis early yet, pretty boy. Why don't you come back to the pub with us?'

'Sure,' he lied. 'Let's grab a cab, shall we? Where is it that you live, Knox?'

'Putney way, handsome,' she said. 'But don't you get ahead of yourself, alright?'

It took Stryker real restraint not to puke. He led them back towards the main road and flagged down a cab.

'After you,' he said as he held the door open. Then he whispered to Matthews, 'Get her home. Look after her, won't you?'

Matthews, who was still clutching Knox's handbag, nodded her thanks as she clambered in.

'A proper gentleman!' Knox said. 'Ain't had one of them in a while, have we Georgie? I call dibs.'

The two women were clearly as thick as thieves.

'Did you two already know each other?' he asked with one hand on the still-open door.

'We did,' Matthews said. 'Did my placement with Knox and Fairbanks. It's so nice to see her again.'

That explained the unspoken camaraderie that Stryker was missing out on. He closed the door behind the girls and leant down to the front passenger side window.

'Driver, Putney please,' Stryker said

'You ain't getting in?' The driver said in a thick Scottish brogue. 'Your friends look like they're going ta puke in ma cab.'

'They won't,' he said with little conviction. He flashed his warrant card. 'Police business.'

It sounded even lamer than he'd expected.

The cabbie laughed at him. 'Right, and are you going ta pay for cleaning ma cab, Mr Officer Sir?'

Stryker felt for his wallet. Sixty quid to help Annie out, and now this. It was just as well he'd visited an ATM this morning in anticipation of a big Friday night on the town. 'How much?' he demanded. He had yet to get used to London prices. Cabs seemed to operate a racket whereby prices leapt at evening and weekends, not that the alternative was much better what with Uber's bewildering surge pricing.

The cabbie stared at Stryker's wallet as if trying to work out how much he could afford to pay.

'Hundred quid, and if the plastered one manages not ta puke, I'll give 'em back half.'

Fat chance he'd see that fifty quid ever again. Once the last remnants of his wallet were gone, the cabbie sped off with DS Knox near catatonic in the back. Hopefully, Matthews was sober enough to get Knox home without causing any more trouble. He just needed them as far away from his crime scene as humanly possible. This was the sort of unprofessional crap he'd left Yorkshire to try and avoid.

Time to do the best with what he had.

# Chapter 6: Travelling Unseen

He turned on the spot, St Dunstan's Hill suddenly quiet. He shivered as the rain pelted down. The lights around the crime scene seemed almost ephemeral in the darkness. No doubt Annie's team would soon be swarming all over the site looking for the tiniest trace of the killer. He didn't envy them that task. Back when he'd been investigating drug smuggling, the forensics were much easier – take a sniffer dog out, see if it barked. Some sniffer dogs could be trained to bark on command, and that always worried him as it undermined the whole point of using them. Annie's task was to find the proverbial needle in a haystack. If anyone could find it, he knew it would be her.

Stryker ran through a checklist in his mind. How did the killer get in, how did they get away, and how was it that nobody saw them dragging a body through central London?

The answer to the first would likely answer the second. It was the third that posed the biggest challenge. There were roads running around the perimeter of St Dunstan. The nearest road to the dump site ran down the eastern edge near where he'd parked earlier.

The killer had to have driven to the dump site. There was no way in hell that someone had lugged a body off a train at Fenchurch Street or ambled through the universally detested underground station at Bank with a body in tow. Even in London, nobody was that wilfully blind.

The corner of an office building at the southern end of the road offered some respite from the downpour. Stryker took refuge in front of its revolving door and then pulled up the Met's London traffic map on his phone. The light of his phone cast a dim glow over the nearby red, black and white City of London bollards. When the map had loaded, he centred the map on St Dunstan in the East. He didn't know London too well yet but even he could see that the best way of getting into St Dunstan unseen would mean approaching the City from the east. From the traffic alerts within the mapping app, he could see that the roads were gridlocked to the west. It would take serious balls to sit in a bumper-to-bumper queue with a body in the boot.

To the south, there were numerous ANPR cameras on Tower Bridge which ruled out that approach. The east was the only way in. If the map was right then so long as the killer avoided coming in on the A1203 from East Smithfield or the A13 through Whitechapel, it was possible to drive all the way to St Dunstan without driving past a number plate recognition camera.

It would have required extensive research on the killer's part to find all of the cameras, map them and then plot routes in and out of St Dunstan in the East that didn't go past a single camera. While Stryker had access to the Metropolitan Police's internal ANPR map, the general public didn't. Could the killer have known which roads to avoid?

Once again Stryker turned to the internet for answers. One quick search for "ANPR camera map London", and, to his disgust, he found a Google Map belonging to a pro-privacy campaign group. It listed the locations of hundreds of ANPR cameras in London. A careful criminal could easily use this to stay off the grid while driving. Worse yet, if he marked each of the cameras as a traffic hot spot, his phone's mapping app would find the camera-free route in seconds. He opened up the Met's own map to compare and found it eerily accurate as if someone on the inside had let slip where the fixed cameras were installed.

As Stryker had suspected, simply avoiding the 'A' roads was almost enough to miss every camera in the area. A simple route down Fenchurch Street onto Leman Street and then out east via Shadwell would do the trick. As long as the killer circumnavigated the Limehouse tunnel, they could be well beyond the cameras and blend into the traffic within ten minutes.

Private CCTV was another matter. There was no centralised map which meant Stryker would have to traverse the streets on foot. It wasn't his favourite task. He knew that many security cameras would be fakes, many more would be poor quality, and even where footage did exist it might not be willingly surrendered. The team would have to run down every lead, talk to every shop owner, call every third-party security firm and make sure that they left no stone unturned. The quiet hum of the main road to the south was punctuated by the occasional thwack as Annie continued to lay down the boards to protect the floor of the crime scene. The noise echoed off the buildings.

This was familiar territory, the simple dogged procedure of an investigation. Just last year he'd had a case where a shop owner had volunteered footage from the camera outside his shop. The camera had been angled to cover the front of the shop. On the edge of the frame, it was possible to see a narrow slice of the road. That gave Stryker a hobbled view with which he'd managed to pull a partial number plate for each and every car that drove by. It was the kind of slow laborious task that seldom yielded results, but on that occasion, it had proved that the man in the dock had driven his Saab right past the shop. While it wasn't enough to find the criminal, it was enough to nail him in court by making a mockery of his alibi.

Tonight, Stryker wanted to approach the investigation in the same way. He'd walk a slow spiral radiating out from the crime scene, and for every camera he'd take a photo of its location, write down the name of the business which it appeared to be guarding, and drop a Google pin on his phone to record the GPS location. That would give him a hit list to return to when they opened in the morning.

It should have been straightforward. The nearest proved anything but. It was on the same building which he'd taken shelter under, less than fifty feet from the revolving door. It pointed due north along St Dunstan's Hill towards Great Tower Street. From the lack of a red light, Stryker didn't think it was on. The office had loosely boarded-up windows, and an 'office space available, from 500 to 20,000 square feet' sign prominently displayed at the top of the building.

Perhaps that was how the killer had managed to dump the body without being seen. There were no occupants looking out over St Dunstan. These offices were usually bustling as it was prime land in the heart of zone one, but the recent recession, combined with soaring business rates, had hollowed out many of central London's skyscraper office blocks. Was that merely fortuitous or did the killer have local knowledge?

Technology was making Stryker's job much harder than it would have been in bygone years. Before the internet, he could have happily assumed that such knowledge meant a local perpetrator. With the rise of websites offering property to rent, it was no longer the case. A careful criminal could pre-empt many lines of enquiry with a bit of diligent planning.

'Oi!' a voice called from the darkness. 'Clear off!'

Stryker turned. The voice appeared to be coming from the front door to the empty office block. A homeless person?

He squinted into the darkness. Beyond the pallid light cast by the lamppost above him, Stryker could make out a figure in the darkness. He stepped towards it, his heart rate rising in anticipation of a confrontation.

The speaker was a gruff, bearded man dressed in just jeans and a T-shirt despite the rain and cold. He was still dry so he couldn't have been outside for more than a minute. Big eyes, one of which stared off to the side in the most unnerving fashion, locked onto Stryker.

'Who're you?' Stryker demanded.

The man puffed himself up and bellowed back in an accent that Stryker couldn't quite place. It was neither northern nor Irish nor Scots, but some weird amalgamation of the three. 'Who am I? Who the feck are you? I saw you looking through me window.'

His *window*? Stryker glanced at the gap between the boards, then back at the big man. If that was what counted as a window in London, he might have to return to Yorkshire after all.

'You squatting here?' Stryker said. He stepped closer still. As his eyes adjusted to the light, the man's dirty blond beard glinted in the moonlight. He didn't look much like any of the squatters that Stryker had met.

'Naw,' the man spat. 'I live 'ere. Now clear off before I call the fuzz.'

Stryker rolled his eyes and reached into his pocket for his freshly printed warrant card. It was pristine and official-looking unlike his old one for West Yorkshire Police which was faded and looked a little like a library card. He flashed it to the man.

The man's expression flipped from angry to panicked. 'I ain't a squatter, honest, guv'nor. I'm a property guardian.'

His accent was so thick it sounded like he said "proper tea garden". Stryker scrunched up his face until the penny dropped that he meant property guardian. Property guardians weren't a thing up north, as empty offices were usually damp and derelict, and often inhospitable. In London's ultra-prime bubble, property guardians lived in temporarily empty offices and other buildings to prevent squatters and criminals moving in.

'You here earlier tonight?'

'Aye,' he said. 'I was. This gon' take long? Want to step inside away from't rain?' He mock-shivered to emphasise his point.

As the wind howling made it hard to hear the man, Stryker was only too happy to accept the invitation. He followed him inside. The front door was locked with a pin code which the man shielded from view with a hairy hand.

Stryker didn't know what to expect inside. It was obviously an office building but without its occupants, it felt more like a warehouse full of dusty, unloved desks and bundles of cables.

'Upstairs,' the gruff man said cheerfully. Being inside had immediately lifted his mood.

There was a lift, and Stryker moved to hit the call button.

'I would na if I were ye. Empty building, innit? Don't want to be stuck in t' lift with nobody around t' get us out.' He bounded up the stairs two at a time, Stryker trailing in his wake.

The man climbed effortlessly. By the sixth floor, Stryker was starting to feel it in his legs, and yet his host bounced along as if his shoes were sprung.

The top floor looked much like the ground except for the absence of tables and chairs. A large mattress, which had seen better days had been thrown in one corner. Next to it were two suitcases, both open, piled high with what appeared to be everything the gruff man owned: gym clothing, towels, and tighty-whitey underwear. There were two suits on top of the pile, both very smart, and next to the cases was an array of smart leather shoes. There was even a fake Breitling Navitimer sitting inside one of the shoes.

'Not bad, eh, this place? Two hundred quid a week, and I get to use their old projector for me movies.' He beamed, and proudly cast a hand towards an old office projector that sat atop a pile of cardboard filing boxes. It was pointed at a blank wall.

He crouched down and sat at the foot of the mattress which was covered by a thick, quilted duvet. The man patted the spot next to him as if to invite Stryker to sit down. Now that they were inside with proper lighting, Stryker realised that the man was not half as handsome as he had appeared in the moonlight. What had appeared to be flawless skin revealed tiny indented scars, a telltale hint of childhood chickenpox. Stryker shuddered. The man's lazy eye stared creepily out the window in the direction of the crime scene.

'No thanks,' Stryker said. 'I'll stand. What's your name?'

'Suit yerself, big man,' he said. 'Rekshun, Andrew Rekshun. Me friends call me Drew.'

Stryker pulled his notebook from his pocket and wrote the name down. 'Have you lived here long?'

'Not long,' he said simply.

'How long is not long?'

He gave a sharp intake of breath and then paused as if counting. 'Four months on Sunday. 'Spect they'll be wanting me t' move on soon.'

'Move on?'

'Aye. Sooner or later, someone'll want t' rent this place as an office again, and I'll be off t' next one.'

'Sounds stressful. You said you were here tonight?'

'All evening,' Drew said proudly. 'Been working on me novel. Want t' read it?' He leapt up to fetch a copy of the manuscript from the nearest suitcase.

'No, thanks,' Stryker said far too quickly. Drew's face grew dark. 'I mean I'm on duty. Otherwise, I'd love to.'

His damage control was too late. So much for the rapport stage of the interview. He cut to the chase.

'A woman was murdered, and her body dumped nearby tonight. Did you see anything?'

'Might have,' Drew said. He waved the folder containing his manuscript around. 'It's a crime novel, ya know. Be real good to get an actual copper's opinion.'

'After I solve this case, I might have time to help,' Stryker said. He had no intention of actually reading whatever drivel the man had thrown on the page.

Drew's smile returned. 'Then yeah, I think I did. I heard a car outside.'

'That's not unusual, is it?'

'Naw, but it was loud. Thought I heard a boot slam. Didn't pay it much attention mind you.'

'You didn't investigate at all?' Stryker asked. Drew had come quickly to the front door when he'd noticed Stryker peering through the window.

'Nah. I was up here,' Drew said, leaning back and surveying his domain. 'I was on me way back from the khazi when your shadow crossed me window. I looked through the slats 'n' yer little cherub face appeared.'

'So you didn't see anything?' Stryker said.

'Didn't say that, did I? I looked out when the boot slammed a second time. Saw a car speeding off.'

Stryker's eyes lit up. 'What make was it? What colour? Did you get a registration plate?' Dreams of solving the crime in record time came to Stryker as he asked his questions at his signature rapid-fire speed.

''Twas blue, I think,' Drew said. 'Or black mebbe. Not a car person I'm afraid, 'n' I only saw it fer a split second.'

Stryker slumped, deflated. Blue or black. That was half the cars in London.

# Chapter 7: Home, Sweet Home

Elsie hadn't been surprised to see such a swanky address on Layla's driving licence. Layla lived in leafy Fulham, a suburban part of west London dominated by yummy mummies in yoga pants, and dreamy daddies donning papooses. Elsie supposed the upmarket address went hand in hand with Layla's SQ Private Bank debit card.

Nearly three-quarters of an hour after finding the address, Elsie pulled into the right road. She cursed the precious time they'd lost waiting for the damned poker game to finish. It was well after sunset and Elsie had to squint through the darkness to make out the house numbers.

As she drove past home after home with Christmas trees in the window and lights around the eaves, she muttered "number twenty-eight" under her breath. One house even had a giant inflatable snowman up on the roof where it swayed in the wind. The sole exception to the merriment was Layla's home. It was a broad semi-detached townhouse set over three floors with a single driveway out front with nothing parked in it. Elsie swung in and killed the engine immediately. Once she was out of the car, she glanced back to admire her parking. Perfect.

There were no lights on inside number twenty-eight. The curtains in the front bay window were drawn tight, and Elsie could see a wedge of leaflets stuffed halfway through the letterbox.

The key was chunky and old-fashioned, probably original, and a perfect match to the equally old-fashioned keyhole. Elsie twisted it forcefully to unlock the door which creaked slowly open as it met the resistance of a small pile of junk mail. Once she was inside, she fumbled around in the dark for a light switch. A sickly yellow bulb, the old energy-inefficient kind, flickered to life with a low hum.

Mess. Mess everywhere. The façade of a beautiful home had given way to what Elsie's mum would have called "Marylebone chic", a house which looked beautiful on the outside but was decrepit on the inside.

No doubt it had once been a handsome family home. A layer of dust covered the hallway. Even the pile of leaflets from pizza companies and estate agents on the hall table had a thin film upon it. It was as if the victim hadn't really lived there at all. A door on Elsie's right was cracked open. She peeked through and could see a living room with two torn-up sofas, but precious little else. For now, she ignored the lounge and progressed down the hallway. Stairs on her left rose towards the first floor.

The hallway was the long and narrow kind, typical of these old Victorian terraces. Wooden boards creaked underfoot as Elsie gingerly navigated towards the rear of the house, every step kicking up a small cloud of dust.

'Ah-ah-ahchoo!'

Nobody had been in this end of the house for a long time. At the far end of the narrow hallway, Elsie found the kitchen, a tiny galley-like space. She shivered as she entered the room. It was draughty in the way only an old, unloved house could be. The sink was piled high with mismatched crockery. From the smell, Elsie knew that it had been there a while. She pinched her nose and drew closer. There was mould everywhere – black, green and brown. How on earth anybody lived like this was unimaginable.

Elsie beat a hasty retreat down the corridor, this time heading for the stairs. As she ascended, she noticed there was less dust here as if there had been greater footfall upstairs than down.

The bannister was worn, and Elsie was reluctant to lean on it lest it give way. There hadn't been much work done to the property in some time, and it wouldn't surprise her to learn that the fixtures were as old as the house. At the top of the stairs, she found a small bookcase on the landing. It was a young woman's bookcase full of life-affirming tracts on being a modern woman, with a scattering of romance. The books were arranged by the colour of their spines rather than alphabetically or by subject. While it was pretty, it would be almost impossible to find a specific book without searching extensively. It spoke of a mind preoccupied with form over function.

To her left, Elsie found a bathroom. This was much cleaner than the kitchen with bright spotlights that flickered briefly. The LEDs certainly weren't original; Elsie could see a circular patch of plaster infill where the original ceiling rose had once been. As dilapidated as the downstairs had been, someone had taken the time and money to modernise the upstairs. The bathroom counter had a large sink on one side. On the other, boxes were piled up almost to the ceiling. It seemed that Layla Morgan was a make-up addict with plastic tubs filled to the brim with more cosmetics than Elsie had seen in her life, much of it unopened and left inside Sephora-branded shopping bags. Evidently not only did the victim have good taste but she was also well-travelled; the nearest Sephora store was probably in Paris. Layla had amassed such a collection that Elsie doubted it could have been accrued in just one trip. The contrast was readily apparent. The victim had lived in a pricey postcode, had been well travelled, banked with the most prestigious of banks, and enjoyed the finest of luxury make-up, yet she had lived in squalor. Elsie turned her attention to the chipped sink and an enormous mirror hanging above it. There were motivational messages scrawled all over the mirror in lipstick. Love yourself. Tomorrow is a new day. Fake it until you make it.

Confident that the bathroom had little else to reveal, she went in search of the master bedroom. Three doors – and three obviously unused bedrooms – later, she finally stumbled into an opulently oversized master bedroom that dominated the third floor. It was here that Layla Morgan had evidently spent the overwhelming majority of her time. As Elsie eyed the sumptuous bed, she wished she could teleport herself home and lay her head on her own pillows. It was barely eight o'clock in the evening and she was already ready for bed. Not that a nap would help. That was the nasty thing about chronic fatigue syndrome; she woke up just as tired as when she went to sleep.

Gone were the musty smells and the peeling paintwork. Here everything was without compromise. Layla's taste erred on the Versace-esque with Baroque gold leaf wallpaper and oodles of old dark wood which only worked thanks to the outrageously oversized bay window. It was stylish in a very brash, overstated way. If it had been Elsie's place, she'd have gone for a lighter touch to make use of all the natural light. The bay windows opened out to the south. Elsie could just imagine how the daylight would stream through to make the gold wallpaper sparkle. The overstated style screamed money and lots of it.

The wardrobe cemented this opinion. Virtually all the clothing within it was designer. From established labels such as Gucci and Jimmy Choo through to the cutting edge of the London fashion scene, every piece was well chosen with a rainbow of colours and styles that gave no clue as to their owner's tastes. The one thing that they all did have in common was size. Everything was tiny. Layla Morgan was a very slender English size four, and the variety of international labels reflected that; size zero on the American labels, size thirty-two on the European scale. It was a punishing wardrobe that would rarely permit a glass of wine or a slice of cake.

'Who were you, Layla Morgan?' Elsie mused aloud. The young woman had lived a very solitary life. There were no photos, no mementoes, and no signs of friends or family anywhere in sight. Every surface in the bedroom was clean but for a little dust which might have been tracked in from elsewhere in the house.

Perhaps the most striking thing about Layla's home was the absence of any sign of a man. Here she was, young, beautiful, and stylish, but with no sign that any man had ever made it into her bedroom. There were no men's shirts in the wardrobes, no stray cufflinks on her desk, and the bathroom down the hall was free of men's deodorant. Perhaps she preferred women? Elsie pondered. The neatly hung size four clothes could belong to two similarly pint-sized waifs. Again, the bathroom pointed the other way; there had been only one toothbrush in the cabinet.

The desk drawers were the first place that Elsie found a hint as to who Layla was. Like Elsie, she had stuffed documents away out of sight and out of mind. The top drawer was full of glossy magazines, the kind that were more advertisement than content with vague sales pitches for perfumes that offered no clue as to how they smelt. Nothing of note there. Elsie wasn't going to judge a woman for picking up a trashy magazine or ten. The second drawer was much more interesting. It was chock full of crumpled receipts, invoices, and bank statements, none of which were recent. Elsie plucked out one of the bank statements, decanted it from its envelope, and began to read through.

'Blimey!' Elsie muttered as her eyes scanned through page after page of line item accounts. There were payments in – albeit few and far between – but it was the "Out" figures that astounded her. Layla Morgan was spending a fortune on clothes, shoes, and international travel. Her outgoings were those of a movie star while her income was akin to that of a road sweeper. Elsie checked a few more statements to see if the earlier months were the same. As she worked backwards, she found the balance figure growing. It seemed that Layla had once been in possession of a good fortune which had slowly been eroded by gregarious spending. Perhaps, Elsie mused, she'd inherited both the house and enough money to open an SQ Private Bank account.

At the very bottom of the drawer was a moleskin notebook with "In" and "Out" figures for every day going back for years. At first, Elsie thought that these numbers too were part of Layla's financial records, but the numbers were much too high – approximately fifteen hundred in and fifteen hundred out every single day. She might be spending fifteen hundred quid a day, but she sure wasn't earning that much. Elsie was stumped until she noted that each daily total was be made up of three numbers. It was only then that the penny dropped. One number for each of breakfast, lunch and dinner. Layla had been compulsively counting her calories, and, judging by the years and years of numbers, she was obsessed with her weight. It lined up with the waif-thin corpse and the much-too-slender clothing in the wardrobe. Layla was the kind of woman who thought that if thin was beautiful, thinner was even better, and she'd taken it to the extreme. With just a few pounds more on her frame, she would have been genuinely stunning. Elsie struggled to reconcile the gaunt, bony frame of the dead girl with a modelling career. Surely the industry didn't expect models to be *that* thin?

Something wasn't right. It felt as if Layla had never had a single visitor. No friends, no family, not even an address book and certainly no landline telephone for it to sit beside. All the post had been of a business nature – bills, adverts, and correspondence from HMRC. Usually finding next of kin was a cakewalk. It wouldn't be this time. They'd have to go back to the old standby of obtaining the deceased's phone records and looking for who Layla had called the most. Elsie made a mental note to delegate that job to Matthews. She hated dealing with phone companies as they almost always demanded a warrant which was a pain in the backside to sort out. No magistrate would refuse. It was just a lot of very boring paperwork that was now within Elsie's prerogative to delegate. Formal death notification needed to take place as soon as possible.

As Elsie backtracked to the hallway, she took in the cavernous space. It was almost empty. Only a bookshelf lined the wall, and that too was nearly empty, unlike the smaller bookcase that Elsie had seen on the stairs. Elsie couldn't imagine knocking around such a huge house all on her own with not so much as a cat for company. She certainly wouldn't buy such a grand old home just to live in on her lonesome, and if she'd inherited it then it would surely be on the market post-haste especially if Layla was as broke as her bank statements suggested. She added "research Layla's homeownership" to Knox's to-do list. Who knew when Knox would deign to show up to work? Knox was going to be a pain to manage as she had no interest in being a team player.

There was only one way to deal with that: Elsie had to give her the dross work with clearly defined outcomes, the work which was either done or it wasn't. If it didn't get done, Knox would be fired post-haste. There was no point carrying dead weight on the team for any longer than necessary. Perhaps Elsie should have seen it coming; there was a reason the rest of the Murder Investigation Teams hadn't wanted her.

Elsie trekked back down the stairs and once again took in the musky, dust-ridden atmosphere on the ground floor. Officially Layla Morgan was an aspiring model for the most glamorous fashion brands on the planet. Unofficially, Elsie thought, she was a broke pretender with anorexia living off what appeared to be a fat inheritance while feigning success.

Confident that the house had little more to yield tonight, Elsie pinged Stryker, Knox and Matthews a group message summoning them all to an early morning meeting at eight o'clock sharp. For tonight, Elsie thought with another yawn, it was time for the tiredness to win.

# Chapter 8: The Major Incident Room

I t took Elsie three alarms to get up that Saturday morning. Had there not been a pressing case to attend to, she'd probably have stayed in bed until her back hurt or her stomach growled, whichever came sooner. It was neither the mobile phone alarm nor the sunrise clock that finally roused her, but the "backup" alarm, a radio which came blaring into life at six thirty on the dot summoning her from the comfort of her duvet to the hallway where the radio sat upon a high shelf. When she could ignore it no longer, she dragged herself from her bed and then got ready as fast as she could. The office was a half an hour's drive from her home in Muswell Hill, a journey usually punctuated by roadworks and endless traffic. For once, she had a clean run, arriving only ten minutes after she'd intended to. Perhaps the other denizens of North London were, quite sensibly in Elsie's opinion, having a lie-in.

The clock read ten past eight, and, despite Elsie's slight tardiness, the others were nowhere to be found. A no-show on Knox's part wasn't unexpected. The others had no such excuse. After double-checking that she had, in fact, sent the eight o'clock meeting details to the rest of the team, she fetched herself a large cup of instant coffee from the vending machine, pulled a face the moment she took a sip, and then busied herself with setting up the new incident room. The space she had to work with was dire. The admin staff who kept the building up to snuff had refurbished this floor only last year, and yet still the dim, flickering strip lights remained. Elsie hated the pallid glow they cast over the windowless room.

The only thing the space had going for it was square footage. An incident room needed to be big enough to accommodate the many individuals who would be coming and going as the investigation ramped up: the finance manager, the receiver, the action manager, a document reader, two or three people to deal with indexing and registering evidence, an IT tech to deal with HOLMES support, researchers, analysts, a file prep officer, a typist and a disclosure officer. The list was almost endless. The major incident room as it was properly called, or MIR, was like a start-up with a hum of activity in the background from beginning to end. Today was the calm before the storm.

She glanced to the far wall, a good forty feet away. It was studded with boards long since pinpricked with a thousand little holes from the documents which had been pinned to it over the years. When full, the boards would be covered in photos, documents, and anything else the team thought could be useful for the investigation. Elsie made her way to the board in the corner and pinned up a few blank sheets so she could jot down her initial thoughts. She'd have one of the junior officers digitise them later on so that everything was on the central computer. To the casual observer, the paper-based wall might appear old-fashioned but for Elsie, it was a way of collecting her thoughts in one easy-to-peruse place. Staring at a wall of evidence was much less tiring than sifting through dozens of digital folders containing the same information and it was easier on the eyes too.

Working from the top left of the board she marked down the name "Layla Morgan" and then pinned up printouts of everything they had found out so far. There wasn't much. Overnight,

Annie Burke had uploaded photographs of the crime scene to the HOLMES 2 database. Elsie flicked through Burke's initial report stifling a yawn. The headline discovery was a cotton thread snagged on a bush near the eastern entrance at approximately six feet above the ground which Burke thought could be important. If the lab showed the cotton was consistent with the wedding dress then they knew which side of St Dunstan the killer entered, and they could approximate the killer's height. The physical strength required was suggestive of a male killer; few women could lug a body over their shoulder. Even if they could, that really didn't narrow down the suspect pool; few women killed, and fewer still stabbed their victims. This felt like a straightforward crime of passion. The victim had been stabbed through the heart. It screamed jilted lover to Elsie. Why else would the killer go to the extreme of posing Layla in a wedding dress?

Until they officially had the definitive cause of death from Valerie Spilsbury, Elsie was on a go-slow. This was the phase of the investigation that her dad called "getting the ball under control". The energy of Friday night had fizzled out, and now Elsie had to manage *everything*. She had to manage her own team, that was a given, but she also needed to manage the press and the myriad support personnel collecting, processing, and logging evidence. Perhaps most important of all she needed to manage expectations. This wasn't going to be solved overnight given that Burke's investigations had found precious little other evidence.

First order of the day was to get through the autopsy, rush the initial lab work, and notify next of kin. She'd dispatched Stryker to attend in person, and he ought to have something before midday. That didn't excuse Knox and Matthews' non-attendance. Two blue ticks on WhatsApp confirmed that they had all seen Elsie's message. That was outright insubordination which Elsie needed to nip in the bud. She had expected someone on her new team to challenge her, she'd just expected that someone to be DI Stryker. A man having trouble with working for a strong woman was to be expected. Knox, however, was an old hand and ought to know better.

Next to the Layla Morgan board was a second which remained blank. Elsie desperately wanted to fill it with details from the last "Lady Killer" murder victim, that of Leonella Boileau, the woman who had been dumped in a black ball gown two weeks ago and had been all over the news ever since.

If she did officially connect the dots, she as good as admitted that this was a serial, and then she'd have to give Fairbanks the lead on the Morgan investigation. If it were a serial – and Elsie's gut instinct said it was, no matter what she'd said to Stryker – then those details would inform how she ought to proceed.

Without committing anything to print, Elsie reviewed the historical crime on her laptop. Leonella Boileau had been found in Chelsea Physic Garden. The similarities were immediately apparent. Leonella, or "Nelly" as the newspapers had nicknamed her, was young, beautiful, and she'd been left lying on a bench with her arm tucked under her head as if she were sleeping. Like Layla, Nelly had been dressed to the nines.

That was where the similarities ended. Layla was Caucasian, of minute stature, thin, and had been posed in a wedding dress. Nelly had been taller, though not nearly so tall as Elsie, and she was black, curvy, and had been posed in what appeared to be a one-off black lace gown. Looking at the crime scene photos, there was a sense of déjà vu that Elsie couldn't shake. The scenes were too similar for comfort, but they didn't fit the sort of pattern Elsie expected. Serial killers, in her limited experience, tended to select within the same demographics. More often than not their victims were women. Assuming this was a serial killer, they appeared not to care about race or height. That struck Elsie as off.

Perhaps then, Elsie mused, it was about access. While the autopsy results for Layla Morgan weren't back yet, the older report for Leonella Boileau indicated a personal kill. Nelly had been stabbed through the heart just once. Her killer had managed to get up close and personal and kill her without needing to strike twice.

Nelly had to have known her killer. She trusted them enough to get close. Elsie could tell that Nelly's killer had been significantly taller than her from the angle of the stab wound in the autopsy photos. Odds-on they were looking for a killer who was at least five foot ten. That narrowed it down to about a third of London.

The killer had to be strong. There were no drag marks around either crime scene which meant the victims were cleanly carried. Even with a fireman's lift where the killer could sling his victim over a shoulder, it took some serious physical strength to move the lightest of adult bodies. Elsie flicked through her iPad to find out how much Layla Morgan had weighed. She was the smaller of the two victims coming in at a mere five foot three. Her weight was listed as forty-seven and a bit kilograms or one hundred and four pounds imperial.

Leonella Boileau, at five foot seven, had to be a bit heavier. Again, it screamed a tall, strong man. Or a team. Elsie couldn't rule out a duo killing together. Two could move a body with relative ease. Did that fit with the thread being found six foot off the floor? Elsie struggled to imagine a pair carrying a body at that height. Forensics would be able to rule it out easily enough; two killers would leave two sets of contact evidence.

She didn't know how long she'd been staring at the incident board thinking. It was long enough that she regretted taking another sip of her coffee.

'Yuck,' she muttered. It was long cold. Where on earth had her team got to?

While she continued to wait, she absentmindedly scrolled through social media on her mobile. It was a mistake she made all too often. It was supposed to be a place to connect with old friends, keep tabs on old enemies, and remember when her third cousin's second child's birthday was.

Instead, it was an endless pit of despair. She scrolled lazily with a thumb, only to see oodles of wedding and honeymoon albums, engagement announcements, and baby photos. Faces from the past – friends, family, colleagues – floated up to smile at her mockingly. Each happy snapshot stoked the green-eyed monster, and Elsie found herself falling slowly into the pit. These people had it all. They had what she wanted – the family, the loving partner, the successful career. What did she have? A sarcastic "good in bed" T-shirt to celebrate her unparalleled ability to nap?

'Don't judge people by their Facebook statuses, boss,' Matthews said. She had appeared from nowhere while Elsie stared at her screen. 'It isn't real, boss. They're just posing like for the camera like. If you compare yourself to that, you'll never be happy. People don't post when they're feeling lonely or blue, do they? Here.'

Matthews proffered a tissue from her purse. It was only then that Elsie realised her eyes must have watered, smudging her mascara down her cheeks. She snatched the tissue and turned away, desperate to pull herself together. Why on earth was she so emotional today?

When Elsie turned back towards Matthews, her expression had hardened. She no longer had it in her to chastise Matthews for being late to the meeting. Instead, she asked where Knox was.

'She's off sick, boss.'

An unconvincing lie. Elsie knew that Knox had a reputation for the drink. It was probably why Knox had ended up joining Elsie's band of misfits. She wanted to give Knox the benefit of the doubt. More than once she'd heard her father say that the numbness that the bottle brought was a siren call for many officers after a long week. Too seldom did officers seek help for the stress of the job, and it was rarer still for appropriate support to be given. To show weakness by asking for help would be a death knell. If you admitted you needed help – and Elsie knew that she herself needed help too – then you'd never be trusted with a proper case again.

But was this a drinking problem or an attitude problem? The former deserved understanding and help, the latter was disrespectful. Everything so far said that Knox fell into the latter category and for that she would pay.

'Then you'll have to cover the jobs she ought to be doing. I'm going to need you to find her next of kin and to tidy up the boards in the corner,' Elsie said. 'But first, take a seat, and then tell me what you found out last night.'

Matthews gulped.

'Spit it out.'

Her face turned ashen, and she averted her eyes. 'We didn't make it, boss. Knox and I that is.'

Elsie's fingers gripped the edge of the desk she was leaning against until they turned white.

'Why on earth not?' she growled through gritted teeth.

Matthews hung her head. 'We'd had a few too many drinks. Knox really wanted to celebrate the new team of ours...'

I'll bet she did, Elsie thought. Knox was proving to be the disaster that Elsie had expected. Her insubordination was bad enough but dragging down the rest of the team was unforgivable.

'Boss, I—'

Elsie cut her off. 'You what? You thought you could just ignore a page summoning you to a crime scene? You didn't think to call me and tell me you were inebriated?'

A logical voice in the back of her head backed her up. It was worse than simply ignoring the page. The girls had to have acknowledged the page otherwise the computer system would have automatically notified Elsie that her pages had been ignored.

Matthews cowed as Elsie ranted. 'It's even worse than I thought, isn't it? You acknowledged the page and then didn't bother to show up. You know the rules – don't answer the page if you're not capable of responding. It's that simple. We've got cover in place exactly for this kind of scenario!'

'But, boss, Stryker said—'

'*Stryker said*? On what planet does Stryker have any authority here? This is my team. You report to me and me alone. Not a man who has been on this team for less than a week!'

Elsie spun and turned to face the incident board. 'That victim, Layla Morgan, right there at the top. That's who you're letting down. The first few hours are crucial. By skipping work, you might have let her killer get away.'

It was Matthews' turn for the waterworks. Her mascara turned into rivers of ink streaming down her cheeks, and she buried her face in her hands. As Elsie watched Matthews sob, her anger ebbed and she sank against the table, defeated.

Matthews looked up. 'Sorry, I'm sorry, okay? I didn't want to go to the pub anyway. I just... Knox is like a big sister to me. I did my placement with her and Fairbanks.'

She was just a kid. An overgrown child with no self-confidence. Elsie's anger quietened down. It would do no good to destroy Matthews' self-confidence entirely. Her anger would be redirected at the woman who deserved it. 'Everyone gets one mistake,' Elsie said. She jabbed her index finger towards Matthews. 'Make a second error and you'll be looking for a new team, got it?'

'Got it,' Matthews said. She straightened up. 'Oh... by the way, I brought us all breakfast.'

Elsie's eyes flicked towards the table nearest the door. Sure enough, Matthews had stopped at Gail's bakery. That was why she had been a little late – apology bagels.

'Make yourself useful. See that big board at the back? I want a map of the crime scene up there showing the most likely approach to the dump site. We need to know how the killer managed to appear in central London with a dead body in tow without being seen.'

It seemed impossible and yet the evidence was incontrovertible. The body was there, and there was no sign of the killer anywhere nearby. Just how had he got Layla Morgan's body to St Dunstan in the East?

# Chapter 9: Dead on Time

Parking at St Guy's hospital was dreadful. Stryker ended up abandoning his car in an overpriced car park by Butler's Wharf and making his way to the mortuary on foot. If he'd known parking was going to be this bad, he'd have taken a taxi from the office instead.

The hospital was home to the renowned Department of Pharmacy & Forensic Science. Working under contract with the Met, the department had been responsible for helping to massively improve the murder "solve rate" in London. It was an exciting trip for Stryker. He'd never had the opportunity to really get stuck into the forensics while working drug busts, so today was his first time swapping the intractability of reading people for hard science.

Spilsbury started dead on nine o'clock as promised. A porter had pointed him in the right direction, and, after donning the appropriate plastic clothing to avoid contamination and health risks, Valerie Spilsbury had let him in to watch.

She said little, her beady eyes fixed upon the body bag containing Layla Morgan. An assistant lurked behind her, and then, at her command, stepped forward to open the body bag.

Layla looked waxier than the night before. The stiffness, or rigor mortis in her limbs had gone entirely, and with its passing, she had turned completely floppy. The grimace that Stryker had noticed on her face at the crime scene had disappeared, and he began to wonder if he had imagined it entirely. He watched as the assistant struggled to shift her out of the body bag and onto the cold metal of the mortuary table. Once Spilsbury was satisfied that the autopsy could begin, she turned to speak to Stryker in a voice which was muffled by the mask over her face.

'Mr Stryker, I will permit no uninvited questions while I work. Keep quiet, watch carefully, touch nothing. Do I make myself clear?'

'Yes, ma'am.'

She nodded and then turned her back on him. For the next two hours, he knew that she would ignore him entirely. That was what he'd heard from the other detectives.

The bag was left in place for the first part of the post-mortem. Under 10x magnification, Spilsbury looked over the entire body inch by inch. Her approach reminded Stryker of a grid search working left to right then top to bottom. It took forever. Every now and then, Spilsbury paused to take a sample. Hairs were removed by tweezer, dust by what looked like a fancy version of Sellotape. This trace evidence would be rushed to the lab in case the killer had left so-called "contact evidence" on the body.

Once she was satisfied that she had collected all available trace evidence from the body whilst it was in situ, she stepped back from the table. Her assistant stepped forward once more.

Spilsbury broke the silence. 'Every contact leaves a trace, Mr Stryker. Oh, don't look so surprised, I do talk. If Fairbanks told you that daft rumour that I must always work in silence, more fool you for believing him. It's only him I can't stand talking to.'

Locard's Exchange Principle was so fundamental that, even in Yorkshire, they covered it as part of the forensic training all detectives were mandated to undertake. His new colleagues at the Met probably thought he was some sort of idiot farm boy. He'd have to work doubly hard to dispel that myth. He watched as the assistant photographed the body using an enormous camera that was mounted in a frame attached to a hinged arm. It looked cumbersome.

The assistant saw him looking. 'It's to keep the shot in focus,' he explained.

Before Stryker could make a quip about stating the obvious, Spilsbury scowled at her assistant. 'Just because I talk through the autopsy, it doesn't mean you can.'

He shot a guilty grin at Stryker as he deftly pushed and pulled the frame around taking whole-body shots first before zooming in on the face. As he worked, the images were transmitted wirelessly to a computer in the corner which flashed up each picture. It was this monitor that Spilsbury watched like a hawk.

'Right, that's enough, Terrence. Thank you.'

The camera frame swung out of the way, and Terrence busied himself taking the camera back out of its mount. He placed it on a bench at the far end of the examination room and then stepped back again to allow the boss to get to work.

'Now, Mr Stryker, this is the bit where green detectives often get queasy, and it's only going to get worse from here. Can you handle it?'

His mind screamed no, he couldn't handle it. A bit of blood was one thing, but the mere idea of yanking the innards out of a corpse turned his stomach. He nodded anyway. 'I'm not a newbie.'

There was an evil glint in her eyes that suggested she knew something he didn't. 'Drug busts don't prepare you for the smell that's going to hit you. There's a bin in the hallway if you need it.'

His neck whipped around to look through the tiny window in the door to see where the bin was, just in case he did need it, and he realised that he'd been played. There was no bin.

She tried and failed to hide a smile as she continued. 'I'm going to start wide, narrow down to look for the details and then widen out when I give my conclusion. Today is going to be a bit unusual not that you'll appreciate it when you've got nothing to compare it to. What I'm going to be doing today is a combined virtual autopsy, or virtopsy, with a traditional medicolegal autopsy.'

He demurred for a moment, knowing that he was about to ask the obvious question, and then he did it anyway. 'What's the difference?'

A derisive headshake met his question. 'Unlike a traditional autopsy, a virtopsy is non-destructive. I'll be running the body through a combination of computerised tomography and magnetic resonance images scans.'

'So?'

'So, Mr Stryker, I can build up a three-dimensional model of the body. This is a brand-new technique which takes lots of flat images known as slices and then builds up those slices so I can render the body on-screen in three dimensions. That lets me move through it with the click of a mouse. Anything out of the ordinary will stand out like a sore thumb, and if this case is murder then the defendant's solicitor will be able to instruct their own expert to verify my findings which saves a lot of my time.'

'You're taking pictures *inside* Layla Morgan? And then stitching them together into a great big three-dimensional mishmash? Magic!'

'And then, alas, cutting her up anyway.' Spilsbury sighed heavily. 'Home office rules, you know. The tech might be there but the civil servants will take a few decades to catch up.'

He said nothing. Whatever response he gave, Spilsbury would once again shoot him that look that made him feel like the child being told to sit in the corner of the room.

As she had at St Dunstan, Spilsbury leant in close to the corpse and sniffed. It was like watching a hipster in a third-wave coffee shop hunched over their pour-over sniffing for the slightest hint of the crisp apple and butterscotch promised on the tasting notes.

'All the senses must be considered, Mr Stryker. What I can smell, what I can feel, these are just as important as what I can see.'

Stryker managed a wan smile. 'Best start working on a scanner for smells then, eh?'

Without missing a beat, she replied, 'That's what mass spectrometry is for. Now, see here where the skin on the wrists is marked. What does that tell us?'

He leant in close, taking in the subtle asymmetrical marks on the victim's wrists, and then ventured a tentative guess. 'That the killer pinned her down?'

She tutted. 'Not a bad guess. No. If she had been pinned, we'd see much more marked bruising. This is subtle. It suggests that the killer massaged the joints post-mortem.'

'The killer... massaged a corpse? Is that a fetish thing?'

'I've seen it before,' Valerie said, waving her hand expansively. 'It's not a sexual thing. In order to pose a body, the killer had to manipulate the limbs. Normally that would mean being quick enough to do so before rigor mortis set in, or else waiting for it to wear off. The only other way is to massage the body to break rigor.'

'Doesn't that give us our timeline?'

'In theory, it probably means the killer dumped the body during the normal rigor window. It could mean we're dealing with a forensically aware killer.'

'Right... right...' Stryker scribbled the words "forensically aware killer" in his notebook. 'Does that mean a doctor, a nurse, a cop?'

'Or simply someone who takes the time to Google these things,' she said in a mockingly cheerful tone. 'They're not state secrets.'

He scribbled in his notebook once more and then paused. 'Can I ask a really stupid question?'

'Another one?'

He pouted. 'When I saw the body at the crime scene, it looked like she was grimacing in pain. Now she's not. Was I imagining it?'

'That's rigor for you,' Spilsbury said. 'She wasn't grimacing because of pain. When adenosine triphosphate levels spike, muscles contract. This can show as a frown or grimace on a corpse. Now that rigor has worn off, the frown is gone. Now, what was your stupid question?'

She laughed heartily at her own joke, a wheezy rasp that sounded as if it came from someone who'd been chain-smoking nonstop for several decades.

'You said all the senses... can you hear a corpse too?'

She beckoned with one finger. 'Come and put your ear near her and find out.'

It was only after he stepped forward that she burst into laughter again. 'Good lord, you are green. No, generally you can't hear a corpse. Occasionally gases will escape that you can hear.'

The next step was the most humbling. The assistant stepped forward once more to make surprisingly short work of removing and bagging Layla Morgan's dress. Once her modesty was stripped away, Stryker averted his eyes and busied himself studying the wedding dress that was now enveloped in thick plastic to prevent contamination.

It was older than Stryker had initially thought. The dress had a dirty hemline, and some of the fine detailing was beginning to show wear. It was old-fashioned too with a beaded lace bodice that stretched right down to the hips, and a long train that went well past the ankle. At size six it was markedly larger than Layla was. Elsie had told him that the dress was dated and cheap, especially in comparison to the clothes she'd seen on the victim's Instagram. Perhaps it was. He opened his phone to have a look for himself. He found her handle easily with just her name. @LushLaylaM had an enormous following and so appeared right at the top of the search listings. Despite that, she had remarkably few likes or comments. As he flicked through her Insta life, he came to the conclusion that the dress was just wrong. It didn't fit with the hedonistic, modern lifestyle in her photo stream. Layla was obviously unmarried – there was no sign of a ring on her finger in any photo nor were there the telltale untanned bands of a recent divorcee. She was pictured with dozens of people, presumably her friends. Duckface pouts abounded as did arm's-length selfies which were orchestrated to titillate and tease. Layla was a hottie, and she knew it. Why on earth had she been wearing a wedding dress when she was dumped unceremoniously on the bench in St Dunstan church?

'Why?' he said in a barely audible whisper.

'Why what?' Spilsbury said. She turned her attention away from the body which she had been combing over while he fixated upon the dress. 'Oh that. I wondered why she was wearing a wedding dress too. I take it she wasn't getting married on the day she was killed.'

'Not as far as we know. I'd have thought an imminent wedding would have been obvious.'

'I wouldn't know, never had one,' Spilsbury said. 'But if I were you, I'd call her local church and see if they published banns announcing upcoming ceremonies.'

It was a solid suggestion which Stryker resolved to check as soon as he could. He had a feeling there was an equivalent for civil ceremonies too, a notice period before a wedding could go ahead. There was little doubt he would find nothing – if Layla had been engaged then Elsie would have found signs of a man all over her home.

He looked at the pathologist curiously. He had assumed the lack of a wedding band on her hand to be the result of an abundance of caution. It wouldn't have been wise to wear jewellery while doing an autopsy after all. He had just assumed that there was a Mr Spilsbury given her age. Then again, it wasn't much of a surprise. Apart from her Friday night poker game, Spilsbury seemed to work around the clock. It would be incredibly hard to have time for a family as well as such a demanding career.

While they talked, Spilsbury beavered away. She plucked hair samples, scraped the victim's fingernails, and took swabs in case of sexual assault. There was no respect for the privacy of the dead. Now that he looked, cause of death was so obvious that the whole charade was pointless. There was a great big stab wound right through her chest just left of the centre. Someone had stuck a dirty great knife through her heart. The modus operandi was identical to the murder of Leonella Boileau a little over two weeks ago. If it was a serial, no doubt he'd strike again, and soon too. It was common for serial killers to accelerate, the time between murders getting shorter and shorter as their thirst for blood grew until they lost all control and got caught.

'Isn't this all a bit superfluous? Even I can see that she's been stabbed. She can't have survived that, can she?'

She paused for a moment to make eye contact. 'Rules are rules, Mr Stryker. I do what I'm told, and then we don't have disputes in court later. Yes, you're probably right that the stab wound is the cause of death.'

With that, she turned back to the body and began to carefully pry open the victim's fist. 'I once found a scrap of paper in a victim's clenched fist that turned out to be a bill for a restaurant dinner that she'd had a few hours before her death. The man she'd been out on a blind date with had assaulted her, and her dying act was to make sure the police realised he was her killer. You never know what might be relevant until you find it.'

The body was washed next, and every scar on Layla's body photographed. Recording Layla's corpse for the world to see struck Stryker as even more intrusive. Curiously the pathologist worked clockwise radiating from the outside of the body in. It was unlike the left to right approach she had taken while Layla was clothed. He asked why.

'Because I can,' she said simply. 'Either is legally permissible. I get bored.'

There was little to document. A few marks indicated the body had been dragged around post-mortem. There was no petechial haemorrhaging nor was the cartilage in her neck broken which allowed the pathologist to rule out strangulation. It appeared the only perimortem injury was the stabbing. There was no sign of a protracted struggle. Stryker couldn't imagine trusting anyone enough to let them get near him with a knife. Perhaps Layla had suffered a deer-in-the-headlights moment and frozen on the spot, unable to stop her assailant.

Stryker glanced at his watch. He was as bored by it all as Spilsbury was, and he'd only been there for an hour. 'How long's this going to take?'

'Not much longer. Everything so far is consistent with the Boileau case as you no doubt suspected.'

'Then it is a serial!' Stryker said. Elsie would have to surrender the case to Fairbanks, and he'd get the rest of his weekend back. Thoughts of Sunday morning rugby surged in the back of his mind. The Met had a team he desperately wanted to join, and this was his first opportunity to join them for training.

'Not for me to say,' Spilsbury said. 'I can only tell you if it's consistent or inconsistent.'

Her tone was bored, detached, and professional. They could have been discussing virtually anything. 'How're you so... *clinical*?' Stryker asked. 'Doesn't seeing death every day get you down?'

'It's that or quit. I could get bogged down by emotion. I see dozens of bodies a week, many victims of brutal stabbings, fires, and abuse. If I let it get to me, I'd never make it through the day. All I can do is focus on the families. They need to know what happened. I owe them that much. After that, justice is up to you.'

'No pressure then.'

'Right, enough of this. Down the hall.'

'Eh?' He looked puzzled as the pathologist's assistant wheeled the body out the door. Where on earth were they going?

'We've got the best tech in existence here at St Guy's, and I'm going to use it,' Spilsbury said. She kept up a brisk stride, her right hand resting on the edge of the trolley to help steer it. 'The court system might be stuck in the nineties, we're not. If I can make this new process part of the standard operating procedure, I can guard against errors in future cases. You might be right that this time we don't need it. That data is just as valuable as it helps to show when a virtual autopsy is worth doing, and when it isn't.'

Her comments left Stryker in contemplative silence. She obviously had an agenda to push. If that meant he got better data to work with than normal, he was all for it.

The procedure was simple enough. Once they were in situ, the pathologist began to place reflective marks on the body.

'Think of these as reference points,' she said. 'We're going to take scans from all sorts of angles. These markers let us work out how those images relate. Got it?'

'Like stitching together a panorama in Photoshop?'

'Exactly, but on a three-dimensional level. You can watch it come together on that screen.'

For the next hour, Spilsbury and her assistant took photo after photo. To do it she used a "locator" device. 'I'm using this,' she said, 'to define the resliced plane. Every scan shows a different depth or slice of the body.'

She dragged the device, which looked like a laser gun, across the body. Each time she rotated it through ninety degrees, and then dragged it back. Again and again, she scanned. Each time a few more dots appeared on the monitor in the corner of the room.

Shallow views, then deeper views. A foot pedal switch let her see inside the body. Eventually, she was satisfied. The whole body had been rendered. She moved across to the computer next to the screen and switched the view around.

'See how I can now zoom in on any part of the inside of the body? Every millimetre has been mapped. I can see where the knife went through her heart. More importantly, another pathologist can too. It means the courts don't rely just on my expertise but can test and verify my conclusions.'

'Well done!' Stryker said. He straightened up as if to go. 'When will I get your report?'

'Hold your horses, Mr Stryker,' Spilsbury said. 'We're nowhere near done yet. Don't you remember me saying I have to follow the Home Office guidelines?'

'What now?'

'Now we've got to cut her open, and make sure our virtopsy results are the same as the real autopsy.'

His stomach rumbled. It was going to be a long day.

# Chapter 10: Review My Ex

Despite Knox's non-attendance, Elsie and Matthews had spent a productive morning working through a few of the more mundane tasks before their midday meeting with the Crime Scene Manager.

Before they'd left, Matthews had quickly sketched out a map of the crime scene for the wall while Elsie had tried – and failed – to read through Annie Burke's forensic report one more time. The report was so dense, and Elsie's fatigue so overbearing, that she hadn't been able to stand the thought of spending all day staring at her monitor. The bright white screen had made the floaters in her eyes – a "minor" part of the CFS – dance in and out of her vision in a most distracting way.

Instead of sitting in a stuffy incident room, she had decided to return to the crime scene early. She wanted to spend the extra time trying to work out how on earth the killer had managed to get in and out of St Dunstan in the East without being seen by a single witness.

Elsie and Matthews parked up on the pavement outside the Walrus and Carpenter public house, a few minutes' walk south of the crime scene and then headed up on foot, Matthews desperately trying to keep up with Elsie's long strides. Elsie had to suppress a smirk every time the younger woman broke into a jog to do so. Sometimes, being freakishly tall had its advantages.

'Boss?' Matthews called after her in a breathless voice. 'Can we talk? Before we get too far?'

Elsie stopped abruptly. 'If this is another apology about Friday, save it. I was angry – justifiably so, I might add – but now I want to draw a line under it.'

There was little point crying over spilt milk. Matthews looked as if she might just burst into tears again.

'It's about Knox, actually,' Matthews said. 'I wanted to apologise for her too. She's not usually like this, you know.'

This was a new one – a junior DS making excuses for a woman almost old enough to be her mother.

'It's not you who ought to be apologising.'

'I know that, boss,' Matthews said, 'but you don't know the context. Knox was promised a promotion to detective chief inspector as soon as a spot came up. That was six months ago.'

*It was absurd. Knox had just been demoted for disciplinary reasons. She couldn't possibly have been on track for promotion six months ago.* Curiosity got the better of her. 'What happened?'

'Honestly? I don't know. She and Fairbanks had a blazing row – I heard muffled yelling coming from his office – and the next thing I know, she's the same rank as me. Until a month ago, she was Detective Inspector Knox – she's been on the force for a decade and a half and she's solved more murders than...'

'Than me?' Elsie demanded.

'Well, yeah.'

'I'll tell you what I told Knox. If you don't want to serve under my command, walk away now. There's a reason I'm leading this team. I'm the best woman for the job, and we're going to solve this case or die trying. Are we on the same page?'

'Yes, boss.'

'Then keep your nose out of things that don't concern you. If Knox wants to apologise, she need only walk into my office and do so.'

The scene looked markedly different in daylight. Today, tourists thronged around the edges of St Dunstan, many of them asking the uniformed officers stationed around the perimeter why they couldn't visit the famous church garden. The blue and white police tape ought to have been a bit of a clue, Elsie thought.

The winter sun gave the atmosphere a crisp, clean feel – Christmas was in the air and so everyone was wrapped up tight under thick coats, woollen mittens and patterned scarves – the sort of clothing that made it all too easy to conceal a knife as the killer must have done.

The cordon was still in place as they approached in unamiable silence, and a different officer greeted them – yesterday's numpty was nowhere to be seen. Perhaps he too had gone AWOL. Elsie signed the crime scene log, donned her protective clothing, waited for Matthews to do likewise, and headed past the tape. The rigmarole of plastic shoe covers was pointless now that the whole of St Dunstan in the East had been combed over by the scene of crime officers. Putting the forensic booties on was just for Matthews' benefit. Elsie didn't want to be responsible for getting her into any bad habits.

Once they were back in the lower garden, they could see a chalk outline marking where the body had lain on the bench.

Fresh eyes might not yield very much, and Elsie's were far from fresh after a fitful night. Her only hope was that the morning light would help them spot something they'd missed in the darkness. Until Stryker and Spilsbury were finished with the autopsy – which ought to be any moment now – there was little Elsie could do but try. She had asked the crime scene manager to attend to run through the initial findings. It was five to twelve, and they'd agreed to meet on the hour. If only Elsie could keep her eyes open.

'...results.'

The words pulled Elsie out of her funk. Matthews was looking at her expectantly.

She pulled a confused face.

'I said: "when do you think we'll get the autopsy results?" Seb ought to be done by now.'

'Soon, I'd imagine. No doubt Inspector Stryker will get in touch as soon as he knows what's up,' she said just as her phone buzzed.

'Speak of the devil,' Matthews commented. Her own phone buzzed moments later as if Stryker had group-messaged the whole team. Out of the corner of her eye, Elsie caught the glimmer of a smile as Matthews unlocked her phone.

'Quit grinning,' Elsie said sharply. 'Think of the optics.'

It wouldn't do for one of the Met's finest to be photographed smirking at a crime scene, especially when they were investigating such a sensational murder.

'Sorry, boss,' Matthews said sheepishly. 'But look – he's *so* cute!'

Matthews turned her screen towards Elsie.

As curious as she was, Elsie didn't even look. It was obvious she was chatting to a fella on work time.

Elsie scowled. 'Put it away, or I'll take it off you.'

She ignored Matthews' protests and unlocked her own mobile. The message wasn't from Sebastian Stryker. The phone had buzzed because of a WhatsApp message. Raj. Again. At the risk of looking like a hypocrite, she quickly swiped down at the top of her screen so that she could read the message from the within the notification without opening the app.

This time his message read:

*How about having that dinner tonight? I won't let you get away from me this easily.*

'Creepy,' Matthews said. She had clearly snuck a peek at Elsie's message. 'I went on a date with a guy like that a few weeks back. He was like so lovely at first, and then the moment I didn't give him what he wanted, he turned into a right psycho.'

For a fleeting moment, Elsie wanted to yell at her not to peek at her screen. Then curiosity got the better of her for the second time in one morning. 'How'd you meet Mr Wrong?'

'Review My Ex, obvs,' she said.

It was the same dating app that Elsie was on, a fact which surprised neither of them. The app had gone viral earlier in the year thanks to a very unusual premise. Users were encouraged to review their exes and say what did and didn't work for them. One woman's rubbish was another's treasure. Better yet, the first six months were free for women, and Review My Ex claimed that most women found their ideal man long before that arbitrary deadline. Raj's reviews said he was "intense", "overly generous" and "a bit old-fashioned". None of those sounded like deal-breakers to Elsie.

'What're your reviews like, boss?' Matthews asked. Then, without waiting for permission, looked her up on the app. 'Ooh, that's harsh. "No work-life balance", "unreliable, cancels frequently", and "extreme emotional swings". Men can't half be harsh, eh, boss? I had one dreadful ex say I "looked crap without make-up". Says more about him than me, though, doesn't it?'

Elsie was saved from swearing by the arrival of the crime scene manager, Annie Burke. Her ECCO Chelsea boots echoed against the path in the most reassuring manner, and the woman herself did not disappoint. She wore a grey Karen Millen belted overcoat which hugged her hourglass figure. She had a Michael Kors bag slung over one shoulder which she opened the moment she stopped to retrieve an iPad Pro.

'Miss Burke, I presume?' Elsie said. 'I'm Elsie Mabey, and this is Detective Sergeant Georgia Matthews.'

'Mrs... for now anyway,' Annie shot her a wan smile. 'Call me Annie.'

'I was expecting someone in a lab coat, not someone quite so stylishly dressed,' Elsie said.

'I'm afraid your call caught me short. I was about to have a belated anniversary lunch with the hubby. It was supposed to make up for last night's abandoned dinner. That's twice now this case has ruined my plans.'

'Sorry about that,' Elsie said. She flashed a wan, knowing smile. The job took a lot away from them.

Annie waved a hand dismissively. 'It happens. Now, if you ladies would follow me, I'll walk you through my findings. There isn't much to tell, I'm afraid.'

They followed Annie through the crime scene. She didn't lead them straight to the spot where Layla had been dumped but instead started at the road on the eastern edge. She flicked the iPad screen as if searching for something, and then turned it towards them to show a single long white thread magnified so much that it appeared almost like a ribbon undulating across the screen. Annie turned away to point towards the east.

'On that bush here, right next to the eastern entrance, I found this tiny thread snagged on a bush approximately one hundred and eighty-two centimetres above the ground.'

Elsie stifled the urge to roll her eyes. If that was Annie's idea of a ballpark figure, she'd hate to see what Annie was like in the lab. It was the same thread Elsie had seen in Annie's initial report.

It soon became apparent that Matthews hadn't read the report. 'It's like just a thread though, right? What's the big deal?'

'The silk is consistent with the dress that your victim was wearing,' Annie said. Her voice sounded patient, almost teacher-like, though her expression was strained as if she were frustrated at having to deal with a non-scientist. 'I've sent it to the lab for confirmation. I'm waiting to hear back but it looks like this is where your victim was carried into St Dunstan.'

'Nice work.' Elsie nodded appreciatively.

'If you think that's impressive, you just wait,' Annie said. 'From the height at which it was found, we can deduce that the body was carried over the shoulder of the killer.'

Matthews leapt in before Elsie could. 'A fireman's lift?'

'Exactly,' Annie confirmed. 'If I'm right – and I usually am – then we can deduce from the height of the snagged thread that your killer is well above average height, somewhere approaching two metres tall. It also suggests a single killer working alone as two men wouldn't carry a body at shoulder height. In my experience, a team would carry a body closer to hip height as it's much more manageable.'

Aha, Elsie thought. She'd had the exact same thought. 'I figured as much. One psychopath killing women and dumping them in public gardens is a push, two would be phenomenally unlikely. But I think your numbers are off.'

'Never,' Annie said. Her tone was so certain that Elsie began to doubt herself.

'Think about it,' Elsie said. 'The body wasn't in rigor when it was found so it would have been a literal dead weight. If the killer were smart, he or she would have distributed that weight evenly so the body would have crumpled over the shoulder from the midsection. The thread is from a wedding dress – one with a puffy, billowy skirt.'

Annie looked pensive. 'I suppose you could be right...'

'The thread was approximately six foot off the ground—'

'A hundred and eighty-two centimetres,' Annie reminded her.

Bloody metric. Elsie did the maths in her head. 'Right, so that's about six foot. We think the body would have been laid over the killer's shoulder. What's the average man's shoulder height? Anyone know?'

Matthews immediately Googled it. 'One thousand, four hundred and forty eight millimetres.'

It was like an auction in precision. They'd leapt from inches to centimetres to millimetres.

'Feet please,' Elsie said.

'Four-foot nine give or take.'

About a foot under the average man's height. Elsie thought. 'Then even the tallest men are going to have a shoulder height in the region of five-and-a-half-foot.'

'So,' Matthews said, 'the rest of the height had to come from the dress billowing in the wind?'

'Exactly,' Elsie said. 'We don't know how windy it was at the precise moment the killer walked by. We know that he or she's reasonably tall – that much is obvious from the fact that Layla Morgan was carried in – but beyond that, we're making an educated guess.'

'That's all on you,' Annie said defensively. 'I'm following the evidence. How you extrapolate that data is none of my concern.'

'It is when you make a leap like "perhaps two metres tall",' Elsie said. 'But we all read into things a bit much now and then.'

Annie nodded glumly as if she were angry with herself. 'Sorry,' she said tersely. 'We have to follow the evidence. I extrapolated too far.'

The sudden contrition was a departure from the businesslike demeanour she'd exhibited so far. It seemed that Annie worked best when she was on solid ground. Like so many of her colleagues, she clearly wanted to follow the evidence but didn't have a detective's knack of considering it in the context of the people involved. Elsie knew she herself often swung too far the other way. 'Don't worry, it happens. I read your report about the thread on HOLMES. What else do I need to know?'

In truth, Elsie had merely skimmed the summary of Annie's report. The full report was so long that trying to scroll through it maxed out her laptop's RAM and caused it to slow to a painful crawl. What was worse, her brain was taxed just as much. Trying to wade through ultra-technical forensic reports while half-asleep had sent Elsie into a stupor. The bloody chronic fatigue syndrome had a lot to answer for. It was at moments like this that she wished there was something, anything, she could do to reset her brain. The laptop could be turned off and on again. Her brain couldn't be.

'There are two inconsistencies you won't like,' Annie said. 'There was trace evidence on the dress – fibres of some kind – which I've sent off to the lab. More importantly, I found a number of unknown DNA samples on the dress, and of course, there are hundreds of DNA samples all over St Dunstan itself.'

That hadn't been in Annie's report unless Elsie had missed it thanks to her foggy brain. 'What kind of samples on the dress?' Elsie demanded. 'Contact transfer?'

Annie nodded. 'Yes. The dress had hairs on it inconsistent with the victim's own hair – we had a mix of blonde, brunette and black hairs. They're all with the lab.'

Elsie chewed the end of her finger as she thought. 'Long hairs?'

'Indeed,' Annie said. 'Didn't look dyed either from a cursory glance under a microscope... not that I'm venturing a definitive opinion on that front. My gut says they almost certainly came from three different women, maybe more. I sent them off for urgent analysis.'

'What did they find?'

'Nothing yet. You'll know as soon as I do. I'm hoping there's a bit of root left – couldn't see much in the rain so bagged and tagged the samples and left them to the lab to deal with.'

'That would be a pain.' No root meant no DNA.

'There's always mtDNA,' Annie said. 'While there's no nucleus in a hair shaft so you can't run a Y-DNA or autosomal test, mitochondrial testing still works. If you can find the mother of the person that the hair came from then we can get a match.'

Fat chance of that.

'Anything else I need to know?'

'Nope, but could you do me a favour?' Annie said. She rifled through her purse.

'What?'

'Give Sebastian this.'

She plucked out sixty quid in used notes from her purse and held them out.

Elsie looked at her quizzically.

'He'll know what it's for.'

# Chapter 11: Dad

It was nearly nine o'clock when Elsie plonked herself down on the L-shaped sofa that she usually spent all of Saturday curled up on with a good book and a bottle of Chianti. It was good to be home, tucked up safe and sound in her cage well away from the frantic pace of the incident room. The afternoon had gone badly – it had been wasted requisitioning all the funding she needed for the investigation – and her evening had been even more tortuous. Her date had gone as badly as she'd expected. Raj had been an outright letch. Within minutes of taking her seat opposite him at London's renowned Rules restaurant in Covent Garden, he had begun to slowly drag his leg against her own. At first, she gave him the benefit of the doubt. When she leaned back, he leant forward closing down her personal space. Before dessert, she'd made good on her excuses and left.

Maybe Matthews was right. Maybe the men on Review My Ex were pigs. Who voluntarily signed up to a website that encouraged everyone to slag off their former partners? You did, Elsie, a little voice in the back of her mind said as she made it home. She never could resist a freebie, and the idea of going into a relationship forewarned about a suitor's foibles meant no nasty surprises. She'd once come home early to find her then-partner trying on her Victoria's Secret underwear. What was worse was that he looked better in it than she did.

She needed to vent which meant talking to the one man who had her back no matter what. He answered the FaceTime call after several rings.

'Hi, Dad,' Elsie said as his image appeared in low resolution on her iPhone. Her father was still stuck on an ancient iPhone 4 and refused to upgrade before it physically fell apart. 'You look awful.'

It was true. His hair was unkempt, and there was less of it than in years gone by. Dark bags under his eyes made him look perpetually exhausted. Even his skin had a sallowness to it that made him look much older than his sixty years. He sat at the partner desk in his office that Elsie remembered so fondly. It was a huge oak thing off of a ship and had been the perfect place for games of hide and seek.

'Nice to talk to you too, Boop,' Dad said with a smile that was all teeth. 'Keeping well? Haven't heard from you much this week.'

'I've got a murder case, a proper one.'

'My girl!' he cracked a toothy grin.

'Fancy a remote cuppa to celebrate?' Elsie had in mind a big mug of steaming loose leaf tea, maybe a digestive biscuit, and a chance to pick Dad's brains and make sure that she did this thing right.

On the screen, she could see him wrench himself from his seat and shuffle gingerly towards the kitchen. She did likewise though she opted for a fruit tea rather than her dad's choice of builder's tea.

He spoke loudly to be heard over the sound of the kettle boiling. 'Nice to see they're letting you loose on more than just the manslaughter and infanticide cases now. What've you got? A domestic?'

He was referring to the most common category of murders. Domestic killers ranged from a spouse killing their significant other to a child murdering a parent, and everything in between. Spousal murder was the Met's bread and butter. Those cases were less about the investigation and more about doggedly compiling and logging mountains of evidence so that the case was watertight at trial. In Elsie's experience, the watertight cases never got that far as inevitably the defendant would plead guilty in the hope of a lighter sentence. The Ministry of Justice encouraged early guilty pleas because it saved money by offering an "early plea discount". It was as preposterous as it sounded, but thankfully that hare-brained scheme didn't cover the few crimes which carried a mandatory life sentence.

She shook her head. 'Not sure, don't think it's domestic.'

'Robbery? Sexual gain?' he prompted again. She could see a vein in his temple throbbing as the cogs began to whir, his eyes twinkling with that old detective's spark.

'Dad, you're retired,' she said, almost pleading. 'You know the doctors said you've got to take it easy what with your blood pressure and all.'

He leant forward in his chair, his eyes dancing. For the first call in forever, he seemed his old self. 'Oh, come on, Boop, I'm quite safe here in my office. Can't hurt to just talk, can it? I practically wrote the handbook after all.'

It was true. He had authored several chapters in the Met's *Murder Investigation Manual*, a fact which had not escaped those Elsie had trained with, and one which had not helped combat her reputation for trading on her father's name.

He continued to rattle off the different types of murder, almost word for word, from his own manual. 'Gang, confrontation, jealousy, revenge, reckless attack, racially motivated... what're we dealing with here, Boop?'

He had not yet mentioned the last category of murder, the kind that Elsie knew could make or break a new DCI's career, the so-called "unusual cases": serial murder, mass murder and terrorism. It was hard to get the experience necessary to be allocated such cases. The Met operated on the principle that to investigate a serial killer the senior investigating officer had to have experience of investigating serial killers. It was a nice idea in principle – no family wanted a rookie investigating a relative's death after all – but it soon fell apart in the cold light of day. The unusual cases were so rare that virtually nobody had any experience. It was why Elsie needed this case. If she solved one, she'd be a shoo-in for the next unusual murder, and then, in no time at all, she'd surpass even her old man's reputation. It was the quick way out of the doldrums and onto a career path that would see her investigate the most interesting, unusual and dangerous of cases.

'Possibly none of those...' she paused, his use of "we" ringing in her mind. It was bad enough for her colleagues to *think* she needed his help. Now he actually *was* helping, and, much to her irritation, she still needed him despite having attained the rank of DCI years younger than he had. She swallowed her pride. 'I *may* have two connected victims.'

'Two?' Dad echoed. 'You've got your first serial?' He beamed, his grin widening so much that he was a caricature of his usual bombastic self.

She cocked her head to one side and shrugged. 'Maybe. Or possibly a copycat. The thing is, I only pulled the second case.'

'And so, you've got to hand it over.'

A notification flashed up on her phone indicating that her tea had been steeping for the required three minutes. Once the tea strainer had been removed, Elsie made a beeline back to the sofa with her mug in hand. She kicked discarded clothing out of her way as she went. This week's workload, combined with the unrelenting tiredness, had put paid to any chance of doing the domestic chores. She made a mental note to make sure to put a load on before bed otherwise she would have to go to work in the morning wearing a bikini and her finest woollens, the last of her clean clothing. 'But,' she said, 'it's not *definitely* a serial...'

He pursed his lips and glared at her the way he used to do when she was a child. 'Don't be daft, Boop. This is me you're talking to. Do you think it's a serial?'

Four times in one conversation. He never used her childhood nickname this much.

'Yep,' she said, suddenly glum at the prospect that her big case was about to be snatched away.

'Then you've got to follow the rules,' he said. 'Who's the SIO for the first case?'

'DCI Fairbanks.'

He gave a sharp intake of breath. 'That old fool's still going? God help us all.'

'Still want me to hand it over?'

'I'm 'fraid so. You can't run your cases effectively in isolation, and even if a dimwit like Fairbanks is in charge, the best chance of getting justice is by handing it over and letting him run both cases together. Now, no more work, how's progress on Operation Grandson?'

*Not this again.* She rolled her eyes. 'About as far along as I've got for the last ten years. Had another dreadful date tonight.'

He coughed, apologised, and then said, 'He can't have been that bad?'

She didn't want to say it outright. Raj was a letch who just wanted her for sex. Instead, she rambled on about the many other reasons he was a douchebag. 'He spent the whole date trying to impress me with how incredible his life was, how much money he had. He kept rabbiting on about his holidays here and there, his latest car, and his amazing job. Not once did he ask a single question about me, about what I wanted, about who I am. Sorry, but your grandpa days will just have to wait.'

'You're being too hard on yourself, Boop.' There was a sadness in his eyes she couldn't quite put her finger on. 'It'll happen sooner or later. I don't want to put a dampener on your Saturday night. Want to go back to telling me about the case after all?'

'Sure,' she said cheerfully. 'I've got a woman found dumped in the old church at St Dunstan wearing a wedding dress that was much too large for her despite the fact she appears to have lived a man-free existence.'

'Not engaged then?'

He had jumped to the same conclusion she had, the same conclusion that Stryker had spent the afternoon disproving by searching both church and civil records for notification of intention to marry. 'No chance. The best evidence we have is a thread suggesting the killer is tall, six foot two plus. On the other hand, trace fibre evidence on the dress comes from several women. Can't imagine there's a six foot two Amazonian-height serial killer with a dress fetish on the loose. God knows if I let

Fairbanks have this, he'll run with whatever theory lets him do the least work possible.'

He guffawed heartily. 'He hasn't changed then. So, what do you think happened?'

'I think our killer is a man, physically powerful, and that he managed to drive to St Dunstan in the East, lug a body from the road to the bench, and then get out of central London without anyone seeing him and without tripping a single CCTV or AN-PR camera.'

'Boop, in my forty years on the force, I never once pursued a criminal that clever. There's always a clue. It's just not possible to be the invisible man in the way you're describing.'

'That's where the evidence is leading me.'

'No way,' he said with a shake of his head that caused his grey-flecked beard to swing from side to side. 'It's an insane theory – and your first proper murder to boot. Make sure you get a EuroMillions' ticket tonight. I hear it's a rollover.' He gave a hearty laugh that quickly became a hacking cough. He waved off her concerned look.

'Fine,' she huffed. 'What do you think happened?'

He coughed again, this time the coughing lasted a full thirty seconds.

'Dad, are you alright?'

'Fine,' he said, almost too quickly. 'I'm just going to grab a glass of water. BRB.'

'For God's sake Dad, you don't *say* "BRB".' It was no use. He was long gone.

Echoes of coughing sounded across FaceTime. By the time he was sitting back down in his office in front of his iPhone,

Elsie was convinced something was up. 'Are you sure you're okay, Dad?'

'Yes, yes.' He waved a dismissive hand. 'Where were we? Oh yes, your serial killer Amazonian. Absurd. Totally absurd. Run me through how your evidence got you there again, slowly this time. I'm an old man, you know.'

She did. She went through every last detail so far, leaving nothing out.

'Have I taught you nothing, Boop?' he said. 'Remember Occam's razor. Always assume the simplest explanation is most likely to be true. That blonde hair could have come from anywhere. It could be someone the victim knows, someone the killer knows or someone who tried on the dress in a shop once. It could even have blown in on the wind. St Dunstan in the East is a high traffic area, and any defence counsel will explain away the hair without breaking a sweat. You're fixating on the wrong thing and you're missing the bigger picture.'

In a heartbeat, she was a little girl again, suffering through one of Daddy's lectures. She set her jaw, and said tersely, 'What do you think you're seeing that I'm not?'

'The first vic, the one that the papers are calling Nelly, she got stabbed through the heart, didn't she? I assume your second victim is the same.'

'Yes,' she said. Stryker had called before her date to confirm that, and the formal autopsy report would be added to the incident room board first thing in the morning.

'It screams love and betrayal to me. Not only stabbed, but through the heart, and, given the lack of defensive wounds, both victims knew their killer. Who're they dating?'

'I had the same thought, Dad. The trouble is, Layla Morgan didn't have a man in her life, and nor did Fairbanks note anything about a partner in Boileau's casefile either.'

What she didn't need to say was that Fairbanks' file was wafer-thin in contrast to the man himself.

'Bull,' Dad said, slamming a meaty fist on the desk in front of him. 'There's a boyfriend or husband behind this, you mark my words.'

'I'm open to the possibility, Dad. No doubt Fairbanks will be too. I'll pass on your thoughts to him tomorrow. Now,' she said with a yawn, 'I'm going to have to turn in. It's been a long couple of days and I'm shattered.'

'Alright, Boop. Sleep tight. I love you.'

He hung up before she could say "I love you too". And yet, it was so bizarre he'd said it at all. Dad never said he loved her. Why was he being so affectionate?

# Chapter 12: Digital Footprints

When Matthews arrived early on Sunday morning, the Yard's hot-desking area was dead. She picked a desk near the break room for easy access to the mud that passed for coffee around here and settled in for a long morning. It took her only a few moments to arrange her desk precisely as she liked it. The slightest mess irritated her so her breakfast – granola, diced fresh fruit and yoghurt – was arranged in three identical plastic tubs ready to be combined.

This work wasn't strictly on the clock as the boss hadn't authorised overtime. There wasn't much point if the case was going to be passed over to DCI Fairbanks anyway. That wasn't a bad thing – Fairbanks had far more experience as did the rest of his team. The idea of Elsie's team investigating a serial murder for their first case together terrified Matthews. It would be far less risky for them to cut their teeth on a simpler case that wouldn't kill her nascent career. The last thing she wanted was to start her first out-of-training gig with a blemish that wouldn't go away.

She needed to keep her nose clean and prove she had done everything she reasonably could have. If things went to hell, Matthews wasn't going down with the sinking ship. That was why she'd come in so early.

The killer couldn't have picked a better time to kill.

Everything moved at a snail's pace at the weekend and Sunday was even less productive. Even the DNA database team didn't work Sundays. Without access to resources at the weekend or a proper budget, DCI Mabey had two hands tied behind her back. Matthews wanted to find something she could contribute – something tangible, something with paperwork to prove her worth – so that if the case did go ahead, she was pulling her weight... and if it didn't, she could point out that she tried her best to steady a sinking ship.

The obvious place to start was Layla Morgan's web presence. DI Stryker had found one tiny facet of it on Instagram under the handle @LushLaylaM. What he hadn't done was a proper deep dive into every footprint that Layla had left around the web.

Because they already knew who Layla Morgan was and where she lived, Matthews had a great data set to work with. She started a fresh document and wrote down everything they already knew.

*Name: Layla Priscilla Morgan*
*DOB: 05/03/1995*
*Address: 28B Kingwood Road, Fulham. London*

From those scant details, Matthews could hit up the most obvious databases for more information: the electoral roll, 192.com, and Experian. They confirmed what she already knew; Layla had never moved house.

It only took one little bit of extra information to spider out. She Googled the username @LushLaylaM. Not much came up. It appeared that Instagram was Layla's sole social media account. That couldn't be true. A woman that young who had never posted a drunken selfie or unflattering photograph? Her entire web presence had been curated so as to convey an air of success, sophistication and money of which she really had precious little. Layla seemed to live by the mantra that the boss had seen scrawled on her bathroom mirror – Fake It Until You Make It.

There had to be a "before" footprint, a hint of who Layla Morgan had been as a teenager. Everything that came up on Google was less than two years old as if Layla Morgan had sprung into existence sometime during 2017 without having been photographed before then.

The earliest Insta photos were less polished, the kind of mirror-selfie shots that every woman takes. The difference was Layla had been vain enough to share hers online. Matthews clicked the "images" tab in Google and then clicked the little camera logo. Two options popped up, one to search for an image by a web URL and the other to upload the image.

Matthews picked the former and searched for the first photo that Layla had ever uploaded to Instagram. This sort of search would show where else that photo had been used on the web. It was a simple, cheap way to find someone online and it almost always worked.

Bingo. Layla had posted the image all over. There was a post on Reddit, the world's largest forum, asking for feedback on her make-up. Matthews added that username to her document. Facebook showed an account on which the photo had been a profile picture. The rest of the account was locked down – Layla had set it to private so there was little to be found there.

Then there was an old Myspace profile. It had long since been abandoned. Thankfully, Layla wasn't among the users hit by the infamous server migration data loss scandal. Photos had been posted for several years going back to Layla's childhood. Even then she had been a poser, standing aloof from the crowds. Back then she hadn't been quite so skinny and she looked much better for it. Anorexia had taken a heavy toll as the years wore on. Interesting but not actionable intel.

Back to Reddit. Layla had posted for years. There were memes aplenty, vapid comments that weren't worth reading and hundreds of posts about make-up and modelling.

What stood out among the dross were Layla's comments about anorexia. Not only was she suffering herself but she touted her services as a "ProAna Coach" on a "Thinspiration" subreddit, offering to teach others how to keep to infinitesimally small calorie limits. It made Matthews sick. The idea that those suffering from what was, in her opinion, a mental disorder banding together to not only survive anorexia but to promote it... it boggled the mind.

Some of the comments she replied to were horrendous. One teenage girl had written:

*"I hate my body n bcoz of it, I hate myself."*

Layla was one of dozens of users to pop up and offer to "coach" these young ladies.

These people genuinely thought of anorexia as a lifestyle choice rather than a life-threatening disorder. Layla had found a community of like-minded individuals, each wanting to be reminded on a daily basis how "fat" they were so they could "stay strong". The self-loathing was indicative of something bigger, perhaps depression or low self-esteem. No wonder Layla had fallen prey to a serial killer. She was uniquely vulnerable and needy. She had been quick to help others degrade themselves, to further entrench mental illness. Matthews' sympathy evaporated. Perhaps Layla wasn't quite the innocent-in-white that the dress suggested.

Working backwards through the comments, Matthews found one in which Layla mentioned that she kept an online "Thinspo" journal. She'd even linked to it.

Matthews clicked through to a blog entitled "Thinspo Layla, One Girl's Journey to a Beautiful Body."

There was post after post. Some were numbers like the in-out figures that DCI Mabey had found in her journal. Others were photos of her meals. Still more were photos of her getting thinner and thinner, each captioned with a message saying how fat she felt.

Occasionally, she paid tribute to her own Ana Coach. Many of the commenters – presumably other young girls – asked who her coach was. Matthews didn't think that Layla's "coach" was the killer – the posts were the better part of a decade old – but she couldn't stop herself reading on.

Layla had responded to one of them.

*"He's an older guy. He hasn't got anorexia himself but he's helped LOADS of girls achieve their Thinspo Dreams. I send him daily pics of my scales as well as body checks. Some are in my underwear and some are nude so he can see me from all angles."*

Yuck. Layla had been seventeen when she'd written that. Wherever girls showed vulnerability, there was always a creep ready to step in and take advantage of that. Layla hadn't just been perpetrating the ProAna problem, she'd been victim to it first. Matthews wondered just how many girls were perpetuating this vicious cycle.

She carried on reading.

*"If I miss my targets, he gives me punishments. He's very strict. He makes me humiliate myself for him so I won't mess up again. I know it's a weird relationship but it works. I've lost ten kilograms since he started coaching me. Accountability really helps my Thinspiration."*

It got worse and worse. Matthews dreaded to think what the punishments entailed.

Layla Morgan hadn't just become a victim.

She'd been one for a *very* long time.

# Chapter 13: The Choice

It took Elsie until nearly midday on Sunday to find DCI Fairbanks. He was in the Soldiers Rest just across the road from his Stratford abode. He was having lunch alone, though looking at the sheer volume of food piled up on his plate, Elsie could have been fooled into thinking he was feeding a family of four.

The pub didn't feel like the right venue to be handing off a case of this magnitude. To so casually pass it over meant giving up on Layla Morgan and Leonella Boileau thus consigning Nelly's family to the anguish of a half-arsed investigation. Elsie couldn't deny that it was a relief though. An investigation this big needed experience, a strong team, and even then, it was the sort of case that could end a detective's career if it went awry.

'Mabey!' he guffawed over a mouthful of roast potatoes. 'Finally come to see what all the fuss is about, eh?'

The fuss he referred to was the legendary all-you-can-eat roast dinner. It was a miracle that the pub hadn't gone bust giving Fairbanks his fill of lamb, pork, and chicken plus all the gubbins for a mere twelve pounds.

'I'm afraid not,' Elsie said. She took the seat opposite him and leant back. When she spoke, her words were deliberate, measured. 'Evidence has come to light linking my investigation into Layla Morgan's death with your investigation into the death of Leonella Boileau.'

'Hmm, Boileau, Boileau.... Remind me again which one that was?'

His tone was that of a man trying to remember a point of trivia. As soon as he'd finished speaking, he stuffed another forkful of fatty pork into his mouth. Before he'd even chewed once, he delved back in to reload his fork for the next bite. It was like watching a starving man eat a proper meal for the first time in years.

How he couldn't remember a victim as memorable as Leonella Boileau was mind-boggling. While it was true that each Murder Investigation Team had around a dozen open cases at any given time, Elsie couldn't believe he'd forgotten one of the most unusual murders ever committed in London.

'The girl in the black dress over in Chelsea Physic Garden.'

He chewed his pork for an eternity and then spat the last of the gristle into a napkin which he put on the edge of his plate. 'Oh, the darkie. What about her?'

Elsie gritted her teeth. The ease with which Fairbanks could throw out a casual racist slur summed up his character.

'The pathologist believes the same person killed again on Friday night,' Elsie said, forcing herself to keep her voice steady. She stared straight down her nose at Fairbanks not to intimidate him, but to avoid looking at the plate in front of him. 'I'm here to notify you that I'm surrendering the case to you.'

'What utter hogwash. Rags like *The Impartial* might think we've got a serial killer running around London sticking women in fancy frocks and posing them in gardens, but nobody in their right mind could countenance such nonsense. You've been had, lass. It's a mistake your father would never have made.'

Anger boiled up inside her. Would she ever escape the shadow of the great DCI Peter Mabey? Every time she made progress in her career, someone, somewhere had to compare her to dear old Dad. They had to insinuate she'd traded on his name for her command whether deliberately or not. If she ever did solve this case, no doubt they'd still find some way to turn her success into a negative. The first homicide she had solved – a relatively straightforward death by dangerous driving case – was met with comparisons to her dad's first case. Of course, Dad had landed a murder on his first try, and so whatever she managed to achieve would always be worthless by comparison. He cast a long and seemingly inescapable shadow.

Still, she forced herself to remain calm. If she showed her anger, Fairbanks would know how much he could get to her, and so easily too.

She folded her arms across her chest. 'The details of the first murder were highly publicised. The similarities so far could indicate a copycat. That said, I think it best that the same team runs both cases regardless.'

'Sounds like a waste of my time,' Fairbanks said. 'You do it.'

Her fingers gripped her arms so tight that her knuckles began to turn white. She wanted the case, but not like this. Not if it meant *he* won. 'That's not proper procedure, *sir.*'

'So?' he mocked. 'You've got no chance of catching this guy, and I've wasted as much time as I'm going to on a mulatto. There are more important cases that demand my time. You want to waste the next six months of your life then go for it, but mark my words, all you'll ever prove is that you aren't half the detective your father was. All you're good for is demonstrating that we tried. You tick that box, and the rest of us can investigate the crimes that really matter.'

The temptation to punch him grew ever stronger. For a fleeting moment, she imagined her fist striking right between his piggy little eyes, and the fat man's chair toppling backwards and him tumbling to the floor. At the end of the table, the glint of a heavy glass water jug caught her eye. Before she could even think about the consequences, she found herself reaching for it. It was nearly full and heavy with it. Her arm moved without thinking, and she watched it in slow motion as if watching someone else take over for her.

Time sped back up, and she upended the jug over Fairbanks, drenching him so thoroughly that his shirt clung to his rolls of fat.

'You bitch!' he spat. 'I'll have your warrant card for this!'

In a heartbeat, her doubts evaporated. The risks be damned, she could do this. It didn't matter that serial murders were exceptionally hard to investigate. It didn't matter that her team was greener than an unripe banana. It didn't even matter that Fairbanks' own botched initial investigation would significantly impede her ability to get justice for Boileau. It was her challenge and she knew how to live up to it.

Elsie leant forward, her face towering inches above his. 'Try it. Try it, and I'll tell everyone exactly why I did it. I'll tell them what a useless, fat, racist, waste of space you really are, and you know they'll agree with me. You're not half the man my father is, and, in case you haven't noticed, Chief Inspector, I'm not a man. No matter my shortcomings, I'm twice the detective you'll ever be, and I will get justice for these women, you mark my words.'

He was welcome to snivel to the Directorate of Professional Standards for all she cared. He could even go and try to complain to dear old Dad, not that it would do him much good.

She was her own woman, with her own team, and she knew she would solve these murders or die trying.

# Chapter 14: Two Dead Ends

Now they had two cases to investigate, the incident room seemed to shrink as the detritus of the combined operation grew beyond control. Reports, photographs, and diagrams littered every available surface waiting to be pinned up on the boards. The room hummed as support staff buzzed around like flies, adding little but making the room so unbearably hot that the stench of unwashed armpits hung in the air. What Elsie needed was space to think, to sleep, and to cogitate. She couldn't show weakness lest she undermine her leadership, and the fatigue was growing worse with every passing hour. Physical sleep deprivation had compounded her fog until her caffeine-drenched brain could no longer focus.

'Boss?' Stryker called out. 'The printer's whirring again.'

It had barely stopped all morning. Everything had to be printed, read, sorted and logged. They were swamped with documents from forensics, from the pathologist's lab, and a transcript for every hoax tip that had come in via the switchboard. Every sensational murder brought out the nutters; those who tried to confess to every crime, the psychics predicting things that any old idiot could guess, and the conspiracy theorists who thought the government was behind every crime. The team, except for Knox who was still AWOL, had assembled to sift through everything, and all were waiting with bated breath for the DNA results.

A deluge of support personnel was required to deal with it all. The finance manager, two evidence clerks and half a dozen other support staff doing God knows what all beavered away in the background as Elsie worked.

She picked up the latest printout, saw the heading "Sample SDEDec07A081", which was the reference code for unknown contact fibres founds on Layla Morgan's dress, and called for hush.

As she did, the door opened. Knox slunk in. She loitered in the doorway, her head in her phone. She was oblivious to Elsie's glare.

Stryker cleared his throat. 'The results, boss?'

She gave the printout a quick scan. 'It appears we have fibres on Layla Morgan's wedding dress that are consistent with those found on Leonella Boileau's lace gown.'

If she had hoped for a reaction, she didn't get it.

'So?' Stryker asked.

'So,' Elsie said. 'It is indicative of a serial killer.'

'I'm not following. They're just random fibres. Couldn't they have come from anywhere? I'm not sold on either of your theories. This could be a one-off murder by a woman. There are women my height about. It could be a copycat for all we know. Annie used gender-neutral terms all the way through her report so why are we assuming it's a man?'

He looked so dubious that she'd have to show him.

'You're right to be sceptical. But you're wrong on this one,' Elsie said. 'The killer is almost certainly a man. Women your size might exist – I'm one of them after all – but women just don't have the physicality. But don't take my word for it. Inspector

Stryker and Sergeant Matthews, would you kindly join me at the front of the room?'

They traipsed up, glancing at each other with bemusement. While they obligingly waited, Elsie snatched her iPad off the conference table and opened up the photos of the dress. With a swipe, she cast the photos to the room's projector which hummed to life and projected a flickering image on the wall behind her.

'This is the dress that Layla was found in. As well as the obvious fact that it's at least two sizes too big for her, it's also quite...' her brain seized up, the word eluding her '... billowy. It puffs up so that anyone who wears it could easily knock things off tables around them without realising. Matthews, I want you to pretend you're wearing this dress.'

'Right...' She looked unconvinced and mockingly ran her hands over the contours of an imaginary dress.

'And you're dead.'

Matthews obligingly fell to the floor with a thud. She looked up at Elsie with a grin before squeezing her eyes shut and letting her neck go limp.

'Sergeant Matthews, I want you to let all your limbs go as floppy as possible. Dead people can't hold their own weight. Now, Inspector Stryker, I want you to pick her up and put her over your shoulder.'

He looked at her as if to question her sanity. 'Get on with it then,' Elsie said with a smirk. He shrugged, stooped low and paused as if trying to decide how best to lift her, and then grabbed her around the waist. He hauled her up onto his shoulder with relative ease.

Matthews was about the same size as Leonella Boileau's five foot seven frame so she was the perfect proxy victim. Her body draped over his shoulder with her legs on one side of him and her torso on the other. It seemed like an obvious way for a body to be carried, and yet Matthews was distributing her body weight evenly which made it much easier for Stryker.

'Limp, Matthews, remember that you're dead.'

She flopped, her limbs dangling, and Stryker staggered under the undistributed weight. Without Matthews helping, his job became much harder. Elsie knew it was the difference between carrying a child who was awake versus the cumbersome nature of lugging around a sleeping child, just on a much bigger scale.

'Now, imagine you're carrying Matthews for the hundred and fifty feet from the nearest road to the bench where we found the body at St Dunstan in the East, maybe even a little more. Sounds pretty painful doesn't it?' She looked at the grimace on Stryker's face and decided to really ram her point home. 'In fact, don't imagine it. Pace the room for me. Back and forth for a hundred and fifty feet or so.'

Elsie was beginning to enjoy herself. Stryker huffed as he carried Matthews back and forth. After a few short minutes, he was sweating profusely.

'Alright, that's enough. Anyone still doubt that it was a man who carried Layla Morgan?'

Despite being a behemoth of a man, Stryker had visibly struggled to carry Matthews' weight. It was inconceivable that a woman could pull off such a physical feat. Elsie was stronger than nearly every woman she knew and she'd never have managed to carry Matthews for more than a few feet.

Nobody raised a hand. One issue down. Now for the snagged thread from the wedding dress that Annie had found a hundred and eighty-two centimetres off the ground.

'Now, imagine that big billowy dress with the wind whipping through. Every gust would have caused the dress to move and flow in the air. I don't think the thread height gives us much information – our little demo here shows that. The wind could have whipped the dress up, increasing the height of the fibre, or gravity could have dragged it down during a quiet moment.'

'How,' Stryker panted, 'does this relate to the common fibres you're on about?'

'Simple,' Elsie said. 'Contact transfer. The pressure from the body would make textiles more likely to rub off you and onto Matthews. By the same principle, the fibres we've got are likely to have rubbed off the killer's shirt at the shoulder and been transferred to the victim's dress while she was carried. The fact that we've got two victims, both with similar fabrics, suggests our killer carried them while wearing the same coat.'

She'd checked with Annie that it was plausible when she'd signed off on the expense of analysing the fibres. The crime scene manager had replied with nothing more than a journal article entitled "The Transfer of Textile Fibres During Simulated Contacts" published in the Journal of the Forensic Science Society back in eighty-two. Luckily, the conclusion was in the abstract so Elsie didn't have to wade through the whole thing.

He picked up the printout from where Elsie had left it on the desk. 'Hardly DNA, though, is it?' Stryker said. 'Surely, they made more than one coat, shirt, whatever from... *polyester*?'

'As Annie will no doubt remind us, it's merely consistent.'

'There's also sweat at the same point,' Elsie said.

'Which doesn't connect the two murders, does it? All that proves is that carrying a body is hot, heavy work.'

She nodded. 'There are DNA samples we haven't analysed. Something is likely to be in there – our killer had extensive contact with the dresses. Getting definitive proof – either way – is our number one priority.'

'I agree,' Stryker said.

'Good because I need you to chase, chase, and chase the lab for confirmation of a DNA match. I need it yesterday. I don't care what you have to do to get it moving. Beg, borrow, steal whatever resources we need – and then send the bill to DCI Fairbanks. He'll be only too pleased to see Leonella Boileau get justice. Got it?'

He nodded.

'Then get going. Call them now. If nobody answers, call back. Just keep calling.' In theory the turnaround time was nine hours on any day except Sunday when the team behind the police DNA database took time off. It struck Elsie as daft that it wasn't yet a round-the-clock service. Criminals didn't take Sundays off, Elsie had worked Sunday. The boys in forensics might argue that they were only two hours into the working day on a Monday morning – and no doubt had a backlog to get through after taking it easy on Sunday – but it didn't cut the mustard in Elsie's book.

Once he was gone, she turned her attention to her sergeants. The room still felt claustrophobic and both women knew that Knox was about to get a rollicking.

'Sergeant Knox, I think you owe me an explanation.'

Knox looked around the room. While Stryker was gone, the room was still abuzz with support staff.

'I was ill, wasn't I? 'Nuff said.'

It most certainly was not enough said. 'You're going to have to do better than that, Sergeant Knox. You've been absent since Friday and we all know you were drunk.'

'Tha's my prerogative, innit?' Knox said.

'Not when you answer a page acknowledging it and then fail to show up.'

'I didn't.'

'Didn't what?'

'Fail to show up. I was there, wasn't I, Georgie? Seb said we could go home.'

He did *what?* Elsie turned her ire on Matthews.

'You told me you didn't make it.'

'Err...'

'The truth, Matthews, now, or I'll fire both of you.'

'Wouldn't do that if I were you, love,' Knox said. 'I was off sick. Can't discriminate against me for being ill now.'

'Got a doctor's note?' Elsie demanded.

Knox shook her head. 'Don't need one. I can self-certify for five days. That's the law.'

Elsie floundered. Knox might well be right. 'Regardless, what do you mean you were at the crime scene? Matthews?'

Matthews took a step back as if afraid of being caught between Knox and Matthews. 'We'd had a couple so when we got there... well, Seb – Stryker – said we couldn't be there.'

Words would be had with Inspector Stryker. 'Why on earth did you acknowledge the page? You both ought to know the rules. If you're not in a fit state, don't reply and it'll be escalated to the backup rota. You left me short of manpower at a critical time. Consider yourselves on probation. Last chance – yes, both of you. Now, sit down and help me.'

Knox glared back at her but still took a seat as far away as it was possible to be within the confines of the incident room. Matthews followed her like a puppy.

'Time for you to prove you're worth keeping on this team,' Elsie said. 'What ideas are you two bringing to the table?'

They looked at her in silence for a moment. She stared back, confident that one of them would feel so awkward that they would be compelled to volunteer something.

'Boss, if it is a serial, what about geographic profiling?' Matthews said tentatively.

It wouldn't work. Geographic profiling was the idea that a serial killer started their spree close to home, and then spiralled outwards as he or she became more comfortable. The problem, and in the circumstances, it was a *good* problem, was that they only had two data points to use. Fewer victims was never a bad thing.

'Nice thought, Matthews. Sadly, geographic profiling isn't likely to yield much with just two victims. Both murders so far are central London, and while we can probably rule out the killer living right next to the crime scene—'

'Nobody shits where they eat,' Knox said. Billericay born and bred, Knox had a way with words surpassed by none.

'Quite,' Elsie said, barely concealing her disdain. 'Nobody lives in Chelsea or the City anyway. Our killer must have driven in, and that screams suburbia. We're more likely to find our killer in Hornsey or the Isle of Dogs than we are in Holborn or Sloane Square.'

'Hey, what about a psychiatric profile? See what kinda lunatic we're looking for,' Knox suggested. 'The man who did this,
he's defo a headcase. If we know what *kind* of head case then that
oughta help.'

Elsie looked from one to the other. Perhaps they weren't as
useless as she had initially suspected. 'A psych profile is a good
shout. We need some groundwork to be done before that because Fairbanks is bound to have messed up.'

'Damn right he will have,' Knox said. 'Prick couldn't investigate a D and D in a brewery.'

'You know him well then,' Elsie said. She decided to give
Knox a test. Failure would justify firing her.

'I need you to run down everything in the Leonella Boileau
investigation. Assume nothing. Reconfirm the witness statement
in Fairbanks' report, check everything for inconsistencies and
unpursued leads. I want to know what our victims have in common. Maybe they went to the same gym, got their hair done at
the same hairdressers, or drank at the same clubs. Look through
the bank statements that I found at Layla Morgan's home then
cross reference them against whatever Fairbanks dug up on Nelly
Boileau. Look for anywhere they both spent money. Chances are
their lives overlapped somewhere, and that's where we'll find our
man.'

'That's a lot of work.'

The comment elicited a far-too-sweet smile from Elsie.
'You'd best get cracking then, hadn't you, sergeant?'

'What about me?' asked Matthews.

Elsie considered what to do with her. She too was an unknown quantity, and there were few tasks Elsie could risk del-
egating if they weren't going to be done to her own high stan-

dards. 'Can you find out what expertise is available to us, please? Forget in-house profilers, they're booked out for months and time is of the essence. See if you can find a post-doc researcher at one of the universities willing to consult on this case. Get me a few quotes to run past the finance manager.'

From the other side of the room, the finance manager waved. Matthews' task was make-work really, a test to see how reliable she was when given a task. Elsie needed a profiler, that much was true, but she knew which one she wanted and nobody else would do. Knox headed out without further objection, and the conference room fell silent.

'You got it.' Matthews rose and began to gather her things. Her iPad Pro, phone, and thermos went into her bizarrely oversized bag. She tucked each into a compartment except for the thermos which she clipped to the outside before slinging the lot over her shoulder.

'One thing before you go,' Elsie said. 'I need to talk to you privately. Could everyone else give us the room?'

# Chapter 15: East Meets West

When everyone else had vacated the incident room, Elsie stared at the crime scene layout sketch on the far wall. It had caught her eye during the meeting. Something about it was off. Elsie traipsed the length of the incident room to take a closer look and immediately realised what had been bugging her.

'Walk me through this map,' Elsie said. She beckoned Matthews over and stared at the wall. The map that Matthews had sketched was beautiful. It had been done on her iPad using an Apple pencil and then printed out. There was one problem. It was plainly wrong.

Matthews looked puzzled as she approached the map. 'What 'bout it?'

It was hard not to laugh. The error was so egregious, and yet Matthews was utterly oblivious.

'Where's the church?'

'There,' Matthews said. She pointed at the right-hand side of the map. 'St Dunstan in the East.'

'Uh-uh,' Elsie said. She was waiting for the penny to drop at any moment. 'And where have you drawn the eastern entrance?'

'Here,' Matthews said. She looked at Elsie as if she were talking to a child. She was pointing at the left-hand side of the map – the western edge of the church boundary.

Elsie exhaled and shook her head in disbelief. 'And what's wrong with that?'

'Nothing.'

She handed Matthews a blank sheet of paper from the conference table and held out a pen. 'Matthews, draw me a compass.'

As she scribbled away, she muttered under her breath. 'North... south... east... west...'

The finished drawing was inverted in the same way that the diagram of St Dunstan was. Matthews had mixed up east and west.

'You've swapped east and west. East is on the right-hand side of the map,' Elsie said gently. 'Shouldn't the eastern entrance be on the right of the church?'

'No, boss, it's St Dunstan in the *East*.'

She said it with such conviction that Elsie wanted to believe her. Matthews made it sound like the church was the eastern edge of existence.

'Open your iPad for me.'

She did.

'Now type in St Dunstan on Google Maps, and zoom in.'

Elsie tapped her foot impatiently until Matthews gasped.

'Ohh...'

'Oh indeed. Does this happen a lot?' It would explain why Matthews had never stayed in a team for more than a few weeks. She'd been bouncing around the Met since she'd joined despite holding a first-class degree from Cambridge. She ought to be on the fast track to promotion.

'It's not right, boss,' Matthews said. 'Think about it. You always say "north, south, east, west", right? And you write left to right... so....'

Elsie didn't know whether to laugh or cry. She tore the sheet off the wall and screwed it up into a little ball. 'Redo it, get it right this time, and put it back in place by the end of the day. Do that, and we'll say no more about it.'

There was the hint of tears in the corner of Matthews' eyes. She turned away, dabbed at her eyes with her sleeve and turned back. 'Sorry, boss. I can't help it. This always happens... and I feel so thick if I tell anyone...'

That explained a lot. Poor Matthews. Elsie's mind whirred. If she made these mistakes and Elsie didn't catch them, it could cause major issues. On the other hand, Matthews deserved a fair shake of the tree, and it wasn't insurmountable.

'If you're confused in future, ask someone. This is the sort of silly mistake that makes us all look terrible but we can avoid them. What I need you to do is run everything by someone else on the team just to make sure. Can you do that?'

Matthews nodded.

'Then get going. And burn this.' Elsie held out the screwed-up map. Matthews took it.

'Thank you.'

Elsie winked. 'What for?'

MATTHEWS KICKED HERSELF. She often mixed up left and right, an old mistake, one that she usually caught. The east-west confusion was an extension of that and she hated that she hadn't caught it before the boss had noticed. It easy to fix. She'd drawn it digitally and mirroring the image was child's play. Once she'd redone the map, she pinged it over to the wireless printer down in the incident room and made a mental note to pin it up later, then turned her attention to finding next of kin. She was sitting in the hot desk area of New Scotland Yard among the hum of other detectives working or pretending to do so. When she plugged her laptop into the dock the Met's secure login screen immediately flashed up on the monitor prompting her to slowly peck away at the keyboard. She had yet to master the art of typing with more than one finger per hand, and so resorted to slowly hunting down and pecking the keys in the most deliberate of fashions.

The first thing she tried was strictly by the book as she looked up who else had been on the electoral roll at Layla's address. Any adults living with her were likely to be family or, failing that, know who her closest relatives were. She typed the address and hit search.

Nada. Nobody else was currently registered at Layla's address. She texted Knox to ask what she ought to do next. Seconds later, her phone pinged.

Knox's message read, *kid, cn u chk historical rcrds?*

It took her a moment to decipher the message. 'Ohh... check the historical records.'

Bingo. This time, it showed that Layla Morgan used to live with Denise and Francis Morgan, both of whom had lived in the property up until the year before last. At that time they'd been in their late sixties. Matthews presumed that Denise and Francis were mum and dad, and if they were still alive then they were next of kin.

A quick search revealed no further addresses for Denise and Francis Morgan, and so Matthews resorted to the old standby – Google.

Within seconds, an obituary popped up. The pair had died in a light aircraft crash eighteen months ago. That explained how

Layla had such a beautiful house in a sought-after part of London – she'd inherited it. Perhaps inheritance also explained how she had a bank account with SQ Private Bank. Layla wasn't successful enough as a model to earn that on her own.

The next task was the one that Matthews had been dreading – calling Layla's mobile phone company and asking for a copy of her recent calls. Whichever numbers she called most often were likely to belong to family or friends, and that might lead to next of kin.

The frustrating thing was that the press had already jumped the gun. God only knew how they'd found out who the victim was so quickly. Layla Morgan's photo – stolen from her Instagram profile – had been splashed across the front pages even without a name. It was odds-on that the next of kin already knew she was dead.

Matthews found the number for the O2 switchboard and punched it into the phone. She hated using landlines. Who used such old-fashioned tech these days? It just felt so awkward.

She hit the dial button.

'Welcome to O2, your call is important to us. For your pay-as-you-go balance, press one. For billing and other enquiries, press two. For...'

Matthews kept pressing the hash button over and over. If the phone tree thought she was hearing-impaired, she might get forwarded to a real person.

This was going to take a while.

# Chapter 16: The Profiler

The man Elsie had driven twenty-one and a half miles to meet lived and worked alone. His house was well outside central London, and, since his official retirement, he refused nearly all visitors. Thankfully, he was particularly fond of Elsie. He had been her godfather since she was ten months old which was probably why he'd agreed to work one last case. The great Burton Leigh would help her by profiling the Lady Killer.

His house was up on the hill, tucked away behind wrought-iron gates which opened to admit her car only after he himself had had the chance to watch her through a camera. His years liaising for the Met on unusual murders had rendered him paranoid, and so the gates shut behind her almost before she was through them.

Once Elsie had parked the car, she stepped out onto the driveway where the gravel underfoot gave a loud crunch. Her eyes watered as the cold air struck her. She made a dash for cover, the imposing oak front door cracking opened almost immediately, just far enough for Bertie to poke his head out.

'Come in, come in,' he said, his tone frantic. 'Hurry up!'

She squeezed through the doorway only for him to slam it shut a split second later. Before he could stop her, she enveloped him in a hug.

'Geroff me, girl!' he muttered. When she eventually released him, she smirked. Now that she could see him without a door in the way, he looked older, his hair thinner and flecked with grey and white, his beard as unruly and unkempt as his clothing. Since Auntie Diane had left, he'd gone a bit feral.

'Good to see you, Uncle Bertie,' Elsie said. 'It's been a while.'

'You're one to talk. I'm always here.'

It was true. He let the Waitrose delivery guy in once a week and saw the occasional patient by Skype. Other than that, his only social contact were the far too rare visits from Elsie or her father.

'Seen my dad lately?'

Bertie turned ashen. 'Visited him the other day.' He led her along the main hallway as they talked. Wood panelling lined the walls, every ridge thick with dust. The whole house needed a thorough clean. They eventually reached the orangery at the rear. From here Elsie could see right across the hills and back towards north London, though without any of the biggest landmarks in sight it could be almost any slice of suburbia. The cold blue hues outside contrasted sharply with the warmth of the orangery's underfloor heating. It was one of those cosy places that enveloped and stifled. No wonder old Bertie rarely left.

'*You* visited *him*? I thought you hated leaving Griffin Lodge.'

'Sometimes I leave,' he said defensively. 'Sit, girl, sit. Tea? Coffee? Port?'

*Port at this hour? Old Bertie had been retired for far too long.* A lead crystal decanter on the sideboard was half full of the stuff, and, if Elsie sniffed, she thought she could detect a hint of it in the air as if he had been indulging before she'd arrived. 'Just water for me,' she said.

He muttered as he made a beeline for the kitchen. 'Thank God, I haven't got any milk in anyway.'

She raised an eyebrow. 'You looking after yourself, Uncle Bertie?'

Only the sound of him running the tap broke the silence. She stared out of the window, admiring how the light played on the trees. London was where everything happened. It was where the people were. It was where the work was and it was dirty and cramped. Here was different. Hatfield was a lovely place to retire to, especially if you had a Jacobean mansion to potter around.

Bertie shuffled back in with a jug of water, two glasses, and a plate piled high with a variety of biscuits.

'My favourites are the chocolate Hobnobs,' he said as he set the plate down in front of Elsie. She knew that all too well. Whenever Auntie Diane hadn't been looking, he'd sneak the Hobnobs from a Kilner jar which he had hidden at the back of the cereal cupboard. He only shared them with those he particularly loved.

Learned, vaunted, and respected, Burton Leigh PhD was still, well, *weird*. There was no other way to describe his eccentricity. If Elsie hadn't known him for three decades, she might think he was losing it.

'This on the books?' he asked. 'I could do with the money.'

'Sorry,' Elsie said. She meant it. If she had the budget, she would put everything through properly. As it was, the initial funding allocated to the investigation was barely enough to do the legal minimum. She couldn't afford to spend the thousands it would take to pay for a full psychiatric profile to be worked up, not with the spiralling DNA testing costs associated with the myriad samples collected at St Dunstan.

He sat down on the chair opposite with a thud. 'You mentioned a serial. This the Lady Killer? Don't look surprised. Even

I watch the news every now and again. What do you want to know?'

She chewed over a Jammie Dodger as she thought. What did she want to know? Everything. She wanted to know what kind of man would kill two women. She wanted to know how anyone could pose a body so coldly. She wanted to know how he dared to drive into central London without worrying about being seen while dumping a body on a bench in not one but two of London's busiest public gardens.

Above all, she wanted to know why. Why did two women lose their lives to this monster? What was it that drove him to murder?

'Why?' she rasped simply.

He leant back as if to consider the question. 'Why indeed,' he mused. For a moment she could imagine him sitting there with a white cat on his lap, Bond villain-esque as he contemplated the Lady Killer.

'Money, fun, anger, and jealousy,' he said finally. 'Those cover the vast majority of murders. Serial killers are like any other killers in that regard.'

'But different in others?'

'They tend to be thick,' he said plainly. He paused to pour himself a glass of water and then topped up Elsie's glass. 'Serial killers are usually one to two deviations below the average IQ. Killing one person is high risk and with every subsequent victim the pressure will escalate. Getting away with murder takes luck, skill, and confidence. Being thick helps – they think they can get away with it. The rest of us know we probably wouldn't get away with it which is why the threat of life in prison works.'

'Dunning-Kruger?'

'Yep. Stupid people don't realise how thick they are, smart people do. If you know your limits, you know it's too risky. It isn't that smart people don't have a violent streak – we all do under the wrong circumstances – but we weigh up the risks and rewards more accurately. That leads to lower levels of violent crime as education levels rise.'

'How does that help?'

'Your killer isn't normal, and that bothers me,' Bertie said. 'Less intelligent killers use simpler murder methods—'

'Like stabbing you mean.'

'Yes, like stabbing. In that way, the Lady Killer is very much a typical serial killer. Where he or she differs is in the execution. Stupid people don't get in and out of central London with a body without being seen. The contradiction between simplicity and elegance doesn't sit right.'

'Could he have got lucky?'

'Once perhaps,' Bertie said. 'Not twice. Your killer had to have been planning the murders for some time. I assume from the report you emailed me that the automated number plate recognition has drawn a blank.'

'Correct.'

'Then the killer knew he had to avoid the cameras and he knew how to avoid them. That is not reflective of a typical serial killer.'

It sounded as if he didn't think the two murders were connected at all. 'Then what am I dealing with?'

'Either you're dealing with the luckiest moron to ever cross paths with the Met, or...' His voice trailed off as if his thoughts had meandered.

'Or what? Give it to me straight here, Uncle Bertie.'

Bertie crunched a ginger snap. 'The positioning of the body rules out money in my mind. I can't rule out a hedonistic or sexual component. I read the autopsy report that you emailed me. The way the killer plunged the knife straight into each victim's heart suggests you're being taunted by a highly intelligent serial killer who is driven by a sense of inner rage. He's angry enough to want everyone to see his handiwork. That's why he's posed his victims in public the way he has.'

'Are the benches significant?'

'Perhaps, though why they would be, lord only knows. Something is driving me mad. There's an inconsistency in the crime scenes. Your killer is arrogant enough to use the most public dump sites imaginable. He didn't faff at the crime scene. It was careless snagging the dress which contradicts the planning required to get in and out without being seen. It just doesn't gel.'

'Adrenaline is a hell of a drug.'

He nodded. 'That it is. My point is your killer has mixed the recklessness of a knife-wielding murder with the planning required to pose a body in zone one without being seen. Why has he dressed them up? Why has he chosen gardens with benches? It's an exceptionally high-risk strategy.'

'They're police heavy areas too.'

'Quite,' Bertie said. 'So there are four reasons to dump the bodies the way he did. Either he didn't care about the risks, was oblivious to them, or he thought the benefit was worth it.'

'That's only three reasons.'

'Very good. Number four is that he had no choice. He could have a compulsion that stops him from being rational.'

It sounded plausible. The police dealt with more mental health issues than the public knew. Elsie had heard junior colleagues complain that much of the time they spent on the beat was wasted triaging mental health problems rather than solving crime. 'What would drive such a compulsion?'

'It could be driven by physical attraction like the BTK killer over in the States. Dennis Rader picked his victims based on how much he fancied them.'

Bind, torture, kill. Rader was a textbook example of the kind of crazy that Elsie hoped never to come across. 'Moving on,' she said quickly.

'Some killers use their victims as proxies. In their mind, the victim isn't the victim. They're imagining an ideal victim, and the body in front of them is just a proxy to take their place.'

'Like a killer who wants to murder their ex, but they can't so they kill someone who looks like her?'

Bertie nodded. 'Pretty much. Perhaps the bench represents a place of significant trauma for the killer. Or maybe he's just lazy and it was easier to dump the body on the bench than the floor. Revenge is a simple primer. Think of Robert Hanson.'

He named another American serial killer. Hanson had taken his victims prisoner, released them, and then hunted them down.

'Any sign the victims were stalked? Text messages? Emails?'

They still hadn't managed to crack Layla Morgan's iPhone. Elsie bumped that task to the top of the team's to-do list. 'Nothing yet. Can't rule it out.'

'And then there's the "because he could" sort of killer like Gary Ridgeway. Sometimes just being able to do something and get away with it is enough.'

The sheer range of evil scared Elsie and this time even Occam's razor wasn't helping. Psychology was just so messy. She checked her own notes on her phone for the scenarios she'd outlined before driving over.

'Your killer is losing control. He couldn't wait a fortnight before he struck a second time. You know what that means.'

Bertie let the ticking clock hang in the air. It was five minutes to midnight. Serial killers never stopped at two and they always got quicker as they lost control.

'How long?'

'A week I'd say. Maybe less.'

The imperative to find the killer grew and with it, the pressure on Elsie intensified. She felt a knot form in her throat thinking that at any moment some poor girl could be slaughtered and left on display like a doll.

Perhaps though, it was really one kill disguised as a series. Her father had seen that before. 'Can we rule out the possibility that the killer has picked a strange modus operandi just to mess with the investigation?'

She expected the answer to be a firm no, that such a psychopathic approach was impossible to disprove. He surprised her.

'I think so,' Bertie said. 'The level of hatred required to stab someone through the heart is astounding. That doesn't strike me as a clean, dispassionate way to kill. It is possible the killer is a sociopath pretending to be an obsessive anger-driven compulsion killer... but that sort of wheels within wheels logic will give me a headache and I already feel drained.'

He looked it too. In just the half an hour that they'd been chatting, his skin had grown sunken, waxy, and grey.

Elsie leant forward to pat his knee. 'Are you okay?'

'I'm old!' he cried. 'But it sure as heck beats the alternative.'

# Chapter 17: Most Called

Thanks to persistent pestering on the part of DS Matthews, Layla Morgan's phone network had given up a list of her most frequently called numbers without having to resort to a warrant. The telephone that Stryker was assigned to investigate belonged to an unregistered pay-as you-go mobile phone. It was just his luck.

He swung by the Met's Digital, Cyber and Communication Department to see what they could do about finding who owned the number.

The IT liaison assigned to Mabey saw him coming and quickly focused his attention on his screen as if he thought that his in-ear headphones would save him from being accosted. Fat chance. Even at this distance, Stryker could see that he was playing some sort of card game. That was leverage he could use.

He approached the tech from behind and yanked one of his earbuds out. The man spun around in his chair and leapt to his feet as if to berate Stryker for such insolence. He cowed the moment he saw how tall Stryker was.

'Hi,' he said with a smile. 'I need to trace a pay-as-you-go phone. Can you do that?'

'Naw, mister, not without you filling in form two two eight B—'

Stryker tutted. 'You're such a stickler for the rules, huh? Aren't there one about running unvetted programmes on the Met's system?'

He had no idea if it were true. It made sense in his head. Not only did the video game represent a waste of police time, it was also a security risk. Who knew what code it could contain?

'Err... sorry, you said mobile phone?' He sat back down and turned his attention to the monitor, hit alt F4 on his keyboard to close his game, and ran a programme that Stryker didn't recognise, and certainly didn't have access to. 'Let me sort that for you now. Then we cool?'

'We cool,' Stryker said. He felt like he was talking to a teenager even though the greasy-haired man in front of him had to be pushing forty-five. 'Here's the number.'

The tech looked at the screen, and then, quick as a flash, had typed it into his terminal. 'I'm Ian by the way.'

'Stryker.'

He turned away from his monitor to face Stryker. 'No way! That's such a cool name. Why'd my mum have to go and call me Ian? Such a boring name.' He tapped away at his keyboard. 'Huh, it looks like your phone is unregistered.'

*Duh.* 'I know that. I told you that, didn't I?' Stryker hoped he didn't look as frustrated as he felt.

'Naw, you just said pay-as-you-go,' Ian said. 'So, what I can do is search for it online.'

'Tried that.'

'Guess you're not as much of a jock as you look then.' Ian stroked the fuzzy patch on his chin that passed for his beard. 'I could triangulate it if the phone's on. Lemme try that.'

He swapped from the database over to a map which showed all of the mobile phone masts scattered across London. There were thousands. Each had a circle drawn around them.

'Each circle represents the optimal range of each tower,' Ian said. 'But that's in perfect conditions.'

He clicked a button and the circles shrank.

'What're the smaller circles?'

'Typical coverage taking into account average British weather at this time as well as the background radiation the city usually generates. What I'm going to do is see which masts your number has connected to. Then from the strength of the signal, I know how far, roughly, it is from each mast.'

'And then you triangulate to tell me where the phone is.'

It was simple mathematics. A stronger signal meant quicker responses to radio pings and that strength was predictable enough to nail down a location to within a few feet.

'Right,' Ian said. He typed far faster than Stryker ever could, the spring-loaded keyboard underneath his fingertips clicking and clacking rhythmically as he worked. 'Uh-oh.'

'What?'

'Your phone is on, that's the good news.'

'And the bad news?'

'It's somewhere in Milan.'

# Chapter 18: Trace

The boss refused his request to pursue the mobile phone to Milan saying it "wasn't realistic" and that "they couldn't afford it". Don't ask, don't get, Stryker thought. He drummed his fingers against the steering wheel impatiently. Traffic was especially bad this morning despite the fact that he was driving away from the crowds. Nothing was going his way today.

Instead of letting him go to Milan, Mabey had ordered him to keep chasing the lab results from Annie Burke's plethora of samples. He'd already done the paperwork, emailed to chase the lab and left half a dozen phone messages. Nobody had called him back so now it was time to try in person. Mabey had asked him to bill it to Fairbanks which he felt a little uncomfortable doing. Nevertheless, the chain of custody logs were updated to reflect Mabey's request and forensic services purchase orders were submitted to the independent body which oversaw DNA analysis.

The UK National Criminal Intelligence DNA Database, or NDNAD as it was called in the force, had been operational since ninety-five, a fact which had surprised Stryker the first time he heard it. Back then, it was nearly empty. Now it had millions of DNA samples, all taken from criminals and crime scenes.

As every police officer who had tried using it knew, the system had two flaws, one major and one minor. Since the Protection of Freedoms Act in 2012, samples belonging to those who were acquitted and to those who were never formally charged had to be deleted with no exceptions.

That meant Stryker could only really use the database once a criminal had been otherwise identified. It was great for catching offenders that didn't see the error of their ways, but anyone who wasn't convicted essentially had a free pass simply because they weren't on the database. If Stryker could find a first-time offender by other means – through witness testimony or CCTV footage for example – then he could use DNA to confirm the suspect was at the crime scene. What he couldn't do was use the DNA database to identify them in the first place because their DNA wouldn't be in the system. It was a win for civil liberties and a royal pain in the backside for him.

For Stryker, DNA was a means to an end. The fact that the cowards at the Crown Prosecution Service almost always wanted a forensic slam dunk barely entered his consciousness.

The minor flaw was less of a problem. It was too expensive. Even a DCI as moneyed as Fairbanks would never be able to sign off on testing every sample at a scene as big as St Dunstan. Annie's report had stated that the number of unique DNA samples left at the church was in the low thousands. Hundreds of people had sat on the very bench the victim was found upon.

Mabey didn't know it yet, but Stryker had been taking an online course in forensics ever since he knew he'd be transferring to the Met. He wasn't quite as thick as Valerie Spilsbury had made him feel during the autopsy. He didn't need to be up to Annie's level, he just needed enough of a grounding, and it seemed his reading so far had left him in good standing. Just this morning his breakfast literature had been a report about the new DNA-17 standard that had been adopted, a technique almost as impressive as its enormous price tag.

Now forensic scientists looked at sixteen markers plus a gender identifier instead of six, the error rate had dropped so far that finding an unrelated match (which Annie called an "adventitious match") was one in a billion. Even the late legal theorist William Blackstone would surely approve of that and he was famous for saying "better that ten guilty men go free than one innocent man be incarcerated".

Stryker scoffed. Money was now the barrier to justice. He parked his newly assigned BMW outside the London headquarters of the National Policing Improvement Agency, the public body responsible for managing the database.

Part of Elsie's cost-cutting had been simple triage. She and Annie had worked together to prioritise only those samples which were most likely to yield results and kept the rest in storage. She gave priority to the samples which tested positive for amelogenin, a marker only found on the Y chromosome. That one simple measure meant that they could halve the number of necessary tests by homing in on the men. It was an educated gamble based on Elsie's demonstration during which she'd made him pick up Matthews and walk back and forth for a-hundred-and-fifty feet. He'd only just managed it despite being a habitual gym monkey.

Then Elsie had homed in on the samples which had been from the route between the killer's chosen entrance on the eastern edge and the bench. That got rid of many of the samples belonging to the general public.

All of that still left them with 242 distinct samples, and, in Stryker's mind, it still rested on the assumption that the snagged thread was from the dress, that the killer didn't plant the thread as a bit of misdirection, and that the killer had actually left the contact fibre evidence on the dress that they were assuming had been transferred from his clothing. If the killer were, it was entirely plausible that he could have staged the crime scene or worn gloves.

Stryker didn't know exactly how much it was all going to cost. He knew it was in the thousands rather than the hundreds despite Elsie's careful planning. It was funny how numbers became ephemeral as they grew larger. He'd just as easily believe that a DNA test cost five hundred pounds as he would a thousand pounds. Both figures sounded plausible. How did they price up these sorts of things? The numbers appeared to have been plucked from the air.

It wasn't like there was an open market to compare the prices to. Commercial genealogy services existed and they were a hundred pounds or so. Stryker had made the mistake of buying a DIY genealogy kit last Christmas. His mum had turned as white as a sheet when he'd explained how they worked. Two awkward weeks later, he knew two things. First, he was of British descent. *Quelle surprise.* Second, he had a half-brother and a stepdad, not a brother and a father. He wasn't looking forward to this year's festivities and he couldn't opt out of Christmas. There were festive lights and trees everywhere. Around nearly every street corner, carol singers not only got in his face to sing to him but expected him to pay for the inconvenience to boot.

As he wended his way through the reception, he was reminded of this by plastic snowmen, a gaudy fake tree, and a huge tub of Celebrations chocolates sitting on the reception desk. He approached the receptionist and cleared his throat to try and get her attention.

'Ahem! I'm here to enquire about the status of several DNA tests.'

She finally looked up, listless and bored but clearly unhappy to have had her solitude interrupted. He forced himself to flash her a winning smile. Despite the approaching holidays, she looked as miserable as he felt. He could understand that. Christmas could be tough.

'Name?' she asked.

'Sebastian Stryker.'

'And, pray tell, Mr Stryker, do you have an appointment?' Her tone suggested she knew the answer.

'Well, no, but—'

'You've got to have an appointment.' She handed him a business card. 'Here, call this number and they'll sort you out. I can't do it from here.'

'How long do you think it will take to get an appointment?'

'This time of year? Hmm... four to six weeks.'

He wanted to swear. That would mean no way to chase the DNA results until after Christmas. The secretary had already turned her attention back to her laptop. Stryker eyed the security gate ahead of him and the lift on the other side of it. The barrier was barely waist-high. Sod it, he thought. He spun on his heel and ran towards it.

And promptly tripped. He landed face down on the marble floor and swore loudly. The thud he made as he landed drew the attention of the receptionist. She cracked a grin so wide that Stryker could see all of her back teeth.

'That. Was. Epic.'

Stryker grimaced, his lip curling upwards, raw and bloody. He pulled a tissue from his pocket and dabbed at the split lip. It came away stained red. 'Uh, thanks.'

'Hey, you're the one that ran on a marble floor,' she said. 'Didn't you see the sign?'

Now that she mentioned it, he had noticed a wet floor sign on his way in.

She walked around the desk to help hoist him up to his feet. 'What did you think you'd achieve anyway? The lift needs a security badge, you daft ape.'

'Oh,' Stryker said.

'Look, who're you here to see? I'll call and see if they can fit you in.'

'Like I said, I need to chase some DNA evidence for a murder enquiry.'

'Murder?' she said. 'Who do you think we are?'

He was beginning to feel less sure about his trek. 'Don't you handle the DNA database?'

'Yeah, we do, but we don't process any evidence here. SCD 4 do all that. If we haven't given you a match, it's because the ERU hasn't processed it.'

He held up his hands. 'ERU?'

'Don't you know anything? The Evidence Recovery Unit. You must have heard of 'em? Part of the Specialist Forensics Service. You sure you're a copper? Let me see some ID.'

He flashed his newly minted Metropolitan Police warrant card and mumbled something about being new to the force. She shook her head and took pity on him despite his stupidity.

'Right, why don't you give 'em a ring and see if they can speed up your samples. My brother-in-law works over there. Tell him you know me – my name's Bertha by the way – and I'll make sure you're at the top of the pile, okay, love?'

Three frustrating hours later, he had his first results. The dresses from both crime scenes had multiple DNA samples on them. There was one DNA sample in common that had been found on both dresses which confirmed what Elsie had believed as soon as she saw the less-definitive fibre evidence.

The DNA sample in question wasn't in the Met's National DNA Database. As they expected, it belonged to a man. No surprises there.

The killer had left his DNA behind at both crime scenes. They had him.

Now all they had to do was find him. Before he killed somebody else.

# Chapter 19: The BFF

The most called number stayed in Milan until Wednesday morning when it disconnected from Wind Tre, an Italian mobile phone network. It was in Malpensa Airport at the time, northeast of central Milan. If the owner of the phone was heading home to the UK, and the fact that it disconnected from the Wind Tre network at almost exactly the same time as a flight left suggested it was, then it was odds-on that Layla Morgan's closest friend or relative was on flight RYA332 from Malpensa to Heathrow and would land one hour and fifty minutes after departure.

Thanks to a quick heads-up from Ian, the uber nerdy tech who was now Stryker's BFF, Elsie was able to be there to meet the plane. A stout, dour man from the UK Border Agency had met her in the short-term car park and escorted her right past security and onto the tarmac so she could wait for the plane. The wind whipped through her as she stood patiently until the plane had landed and rolled to a stop less than fifty feet away. She still didn't know who the number belonged to before she arrived, but the moment she saw the passengers start disembarking, she had a sneaky suspicion that it might be the woman roughly her own age who descended down the plane steps with the elegance of a dancer. Despite the frigid weather, the girl from the plane was dressed in little more than a dress with a silk scarf wrapped around her neck. She looked runway ready rather than jet-lagged and strode confidently towards the gate. If she wasn't a model, she ought to be. It had to be her.

Just in case it wasn't, Elsie planned to ring the phone and listen out for a ringtone. As she dialled, she hoped the owner's phone wasn't on silent otherwise she'd have to stop every passenger until she found it which wouldn't make her very popular.

Her hunch paid off. The lithe woman's phone rang seconds after Elsie hit the dial button. As Elsie approached, the woman answered in a childlike voice that grated like nails on a chalkboard.

'Hello? Ugh, if it's you again, stop calling me, you weirdo.'

Elsie approached her slowly. 'Everything okay?'

She sniffed and looked up at Elsie. The woman was tall by normal standards and seemed perplexed to meet a woman even taller than herself. 'No. Someone keeps calling and saying nothing. It's like so creepy.'

Up close, the woman wasn't half as attractive as she had looked from a distance. Now the trim figure appeared unnaturally waiflike, the face frozen as if it had been paralysed from Botox injections, and she wore enough make-up to last any normal woman a month. Forget foundation, this woman had built the entire house.

'I'm afraid that one was me,' Elsie said. 'DCI Elsie Mabey, Metropolitan Police. And you are?'

'Étoile.'

Elsie rolled her eyes. 'No, your real name.'

The woman fished a passport out of her clutch bag and held it out with the photograph page facing Elsie. Her name really was Étoile. As Elsie read the name, she flashed back to being in French class as a teenager. Étoile meant "star". It was the kind of moniker that suggested class and elegance. The child in front of her was pompous and presumptuous. She'd clearly adopted it to try and present herself as more than she was.

'It's like a mononym like. I changed it proper and everything.'

'Like Prince,' Elsie said. Or Voltaire, she thought. Not that the woman in front of her would get the reference.

'Nah, like Twiggy,' Étoile said. 'She's a model too... well, she was, like fifty years ago or sommat.'

Twiggy couldn't be that old, could she? She'd been big in the sixties. Elsie quickly did the maths and realised that Étoile couldn't be too far wrong.

'Okay,' Elsie said. She resisted the urge to ask Étoile her birth name. It wasn't important. 'Étoile, would I be correct in saying that you know Miss Layla Morgan?'

'Why?' Étoile said, her tone suddenly sharp. 'What has she done this time?'

This time? Elsie let it lie. 'Are you family?'

'No,' Étoile said. 'Her family's all dead as far as I know. Her mum 'n' dad are gone like and she never had no siblings.'

'Aunts? Uncles?' Elsie began to run down the priority list for next of kin.

'Nothing. She made a big deal of being all on her lonesome at her parents' funeral, couldn't shut up about it like. Look, I got a taxi to catch.' She made as if to barge past Elsie who responded by extending an arm to block her path.

It seemed there was no family member left alive to identify the body which meant it had to be a long-standing friend. It appeared the only *friend* that Layla had ever had was standing right in front of Elsie, and she didn't seem friendly in the least. 'I'm afraid not. I'm sorry to inform you that Layla Morgan is dead.'

Étoile didn't seem surprised. 'Is that like why she didn't come to Milan?'

She'd stopped trying to push her way through so Elsie lowered her arm and then gestured for them to walk towards passport control. Étoile had flown in on a budget airline which meant that the terminal was a long walk from the plane. 'Was she supposed to?'

'Yep,' Étoile said with a firm nod. 'I'd booked a twin suite and everything. Well, our agent did. I'd rather have had my own room... which I guess I did in the end.'

Twin *suite?* Elsie thought, a pang of jealousy shooting through her. Not even a twin room. Elsie had neither the money for a suite nor a friend to share it with. It was a bit weird that Étoile had flown no-frills while splashing the cash on a Milanese hotel. In Elsie's experience, Italian hotels weren't too friendly on the purse.

'Did you often travel together?'

'Sometimes,' Étoile said. 'I set her up with my agent. That's like totes why she even got the audition. He keeps sending us out for the same stuff.'

'Not worried about the competition then,' Elsie said.

'As if, that skank couldn't steal my thunder if it struck her dead.'

So disrespectful. Elsie looked at Étoile incredulously. 'Aren't you sad your friend is dead? You've known for less than five minutes and you're already disrespecting her memory.'

'I guess. I'm... sorry?'

It was a question rather than a statement.

'Where were you on the night she died?'

'Hang on... you don't think I had anything to do with it? She killed herself, didn't she?' Confusion reigned on Étoile's face before the realisation that Layla had been murdered dawned. 'No way! She was murdered? Cool!'

Elsie stopped dead in her tracks. *Cool?* She stared at Étoile and the younger woman stepped backwards with a cowed expression.

'Where were you on Friday night?'

If she were guilty, Elsie would have expected some sort of a reaction. Instead, Étoile acted as if she got asked for an alibi all the time. She simply checked her iPhone's calendar and then turned to show Elsie the entry. 'I was travelling and then landed in Milan at like three that afternoon.'

Sure enough, the screen read '*Audition, Milan*' all day and showed an address somewhere in the backstreets of the *Quadrilatero della Moda*. Elsie made a note of the details just in case. It was a compelling alibi.

'What were you in Milan for?'

She shouldn't have asked. Étoile launched into the details at a million miles an hour, her enthusiasm undeniable. 'It was for this new silk manufacturing company. They're launching these new scarfs. Think Liberty of London but even nicer if that's even possible. I've wanted to work with them for ages and so did Layla. Their stuff is to die for.'

Despite her enthusiasm, only her lips moved. Her forehead remained totally still. Elsie had to force herself not to react.

'Layla wanted to work for them? I thought you said she had no chance?'

It was too obvious. Étoile struck Elsie as callous, unsurprised, and she might even have benefitted from Layla's death. The model hesitated for a moment before answering. Elsie just watched her, letting the silence sit heavy between them until Étoile felt compelled to say something, anything just to fill the void.

'Well, yeah. She was supposed to be there. They wanted a whole range of heights and body types. She isn't my competition. We're just not in the same market, not that she'd beat some of the girls out in Milan. They're like almost as gorgeous as me. When Layla didn't show, we just thought she'd finally realised she's not in our league. The poor thing said she was running out of money. It was silly that she'd spend her money flying out for something she was never ever going to get.'

For the moment, Elsie ignored the money thing. If Layla had been heading for the infamous bankruptcy court in Carey Street then Knox ought to be able to find that out as she'd already been tasked with confirming the source of Layla's money and home.

'Why wouldn't she get it?' In Elsie's opinion, Layla was better looking than Étoile by far.

Étoile snorted. 'Have you *seen* her? That girl had no hope.'

How rude, Elsie thought. So much for them being friends. 'What was wrong with her?'

It took Étoile an enormous effort to avoid reeling off Layla's many perceived flaws. 'Look, she's nice okay. But she's too thin. Modelling totes isn't ProAna anymore and she's a tiny little thing. Was a tiny little thing. There's demand for like so-called alternative models. She could've done that sort of work. She just wasn't tall enough or pretty enough to go mainstream and the silk scarf gig was like really really big league.'

It was a bit rich for Étoile to criticise anyone else for being too thin. She herself was so slender that it would easily be possible to wrap two hands around her waist and have the fingers meet. Elsie far preferred her own physique, a little curvier like real women and still slim enough to pass the police fitness exams without skipping a beat.

'Did you get the gig?'

Her question was met with a languorous shrug. 'Who knows? I should get a call either way in a day or two. I'd be surprised if I don't.'

Elsie wanted to retch. The sheer arrogance was mind-boggling. Instead, she forced the conversation back in the right direction. 'Did Layla have a man in her life?'

'If she did, she kept it quiet.' She looked as sceptical as she sounded. It was almost as if she truly believed that Layla had been so unattractive that it would have been impossible for her to find a partner.

'Or a woman?'

'Hah. No. She definitely liked men.'

Just to be sure, Elsie asked about a wedding. It had been Uncle Bertie's big theory. 'No fiancé then?'

Étoile pulled a face. 'God no. There was no way Layla could have kept that quiet. She was a right blabbermouth.'

Elsie bit her tongue, looked at the motormouth in front of her, and smiled politely.

'I'm afraid you'll need to come down to the station and give a formal statement.'

'But I'm due to fly out to—'

Elsie cut her off. 'She was your friend, right? This won't take long. Besides, if she hasn't got any family you get to identify the body.'

As Étoile picked up her bags, her expression brightened. 'Oh... I think she might have like a cousin or something somewhere? Maybe you don't need me after all.'

'The more the merrier,' Elsie said. 'Come on, let's get you through passport control.'

# Chapter 20: Trust but Verify

Drudge work. That was what it was. The jumped-up little tart who'd taken over Murder Investigation Team 18 was such a hypocrite. She knew she was trading on Daddy's good name. Once upon a time, Knox had served under then-Inspector Peter Mabey. He'd been alright, unlike pretty much every boss she'd had since.

She didn't feel guilty for calling in sick. After a decade and a half on the force, she'd earned her first proper sickie. She needed the time to think about how to get back on top. The DCI job ought to be hers. This Mabey girl was a train wreck waiting to happen. Elsie was inexperienced, overworked, and far too young.

Knox knew she deserved the job. She was long overdue a promotion. One dodgy disciplinary hearing – not even her fault – and she'd been cast aside like yesterday's supper. The new boss was almost a decade Knox's junior and her inexperience was self-evident. Mabey had given Stryker nearly all the good work leaving Knox to dig through the paperwork with Matthews. The sheer cheek of it. All her experience and here she was sat next to one woman almost young enough to be her daughter and working for another.

Even Matthews wasn't talking to her. It seemed she thought Knox was a bad influence. So what if she'd planned a bit of team bonding on Friday night? How was she to know that some woman would get herself murdered just as they sank their third round of mojitos? It was just plain unfair. Despite condescending to leave her beautiful office and come into the incident room in search of company, Knox had to work in silence without even a bit of chit-chat to break up the day. The task ahead of her was especially dull as she had to find Layla's money. It ought to have been easy. Any home as nice as hers in the London borough of Hammersmith and Fulham, one of the swankiest in West London, would easily be worth a couple of mil once it was tarted up a bit. The only problem was she didn't own the place, a fact that immediately became apparent when Knox looked up the house on the land registry's website.

She elbowed Matthews and pointed at the screen. 'Look, Georgie, the vic didn't even own her own house. She didn't rent it neither.'

Curiosity was enough to break Matthews' silence. 'Go on, tell me, who owns it then?'

'They do,' she said and pointed. Matthews leant forward to squint at the screen.

'Who on earth are Meyer & Griffith LLP?'

Google came to their aid. Meyer & Griffith LLP were a solicitors' firm that operated out of a post office address in Old Street.

'I've seen this before though,' Knox said with a knowing tap on the side of her nose. 'They're trustees, ain't they?'

The young woman pulled a face. 'You what?'

'Trustees, love. It's a swizz the rich tossers pull to avoid paying inheritance tax. Hand your house over to a trust, live in it all the same, and when you pop your clogs, your kids get the house and the taxman gets shafted because technically the house hasn't changed hands so there's no tax to pay.'

What she didn't tell Matthews was that she'd benefited from a trust herself. It hadn't been much, but it had meant that her first divorce wasn't totally ruinous. Her scumbag ex couldn't touch the flat. His face hadn't half been a picture when he'd found out. There he was in open court, suing for divorce and dreaming of a big payday, and wham, that little bombshell had put paid to his gold-digging ambitions.

'Blimey!' Matthews said. 'One rule for us and one for them, eh?'

'The rules always favour the rich, love.'

'What's this mean for our victim?'

Knox paused to let the photos of Layla's home float into her mind: beautiful but worn and dated. 'Well, she couldn't flog the house. And she didn't spend much keeping the place in good nick. If I had to guess, I'd say she was broke.'

'But she had lovely stuff in her house!'

'Having well nice stuff and earning enough to keep having nice stuff are very different concepts, Georgie. If she inherited a nice wad and then blew the whole lot, she could look like a rock star and still have nought more than tuppence to her name.'

It was a weird situation. Layla Morgan looked every bit the successful socialite and model. Her Instagram was filled with photos of her partying at London's swankiest spots from the sub-terranean tiki bar of the stars to the legendary Raffles nightclub on the King's Road in Chelsea.

'But didn't she bank at some fancy pants bank?'

Again, Matthews was right. The victim had been carrying her debit card on the night she died, a fact which had helped rule out robbery as a motive. Mabey had found a number of bank statements. The account number on those statements matched the one on Layla's debit card.

'Problem is, Georgie, we know she *did* have money. What we don't know is if she's *still* loaded. She's been spending it as if it's going out of fashion. Could be the well's run dry.'

It was obvious money wasn't Matthews' bailiwick. It simply wasn't something she thought about. In the months that Knox had known her, Matthews had given up her life story. She'd gone from her parents' home in Hampshire on to Cambridge, stayed there for far too long living in halls, and had then moved to London to join the Met's grad scheme. She'd never had to think about money, never had to plan or budget beyond the basics. Her life was simple, mundane, and easy with it. She was, in Knox's opinion, so thoroughly cosseted that she may as well have lived in a nunnery.

Knox held out her hands, exasperated. 'It's like this, love. Layla obviously had some money. I'd bet my life she inherited it because she clearly earned fuck all as a model. She burned through her dough faster than it came in to show off and keep up wif da London social scene so her inheritance wouldn't have lasted forever now, would it? Her Insta shows her chucking her wonga around ta try 'n' buy her way ta success. It didn't work.'

'But look,' Matthews said, producing photocopies of Layla Morgan's bank statements from a folder, 'she's got literally tens of thousands in all of these.'

A quick glance at the statements confirmed it. Layla had been minted for a while. 'Those statements are all well old, love. The most recent one is for just over two years ago. If you look at them in order, her bank balance has been in freefall ever since her parents popped their clogs.'

'Why doesn't she have any recent statements?'

It was a good question. Why had Layla Morgan kept older bank statements, but not a single printout covering the last year or two?

'Maybe she closed her account?' Matthews suggested. 'Should I ring around and see if any of the other banks will admit to having her as a customer?'

'That's not impossible,' Knox said cautiously. 'But if I was a betting woman – and I am – I'd say that she probably just switched to online banking.'

It was the simplest explanation. Now Knox had to prove it. She was tempted to just call Layla's bank and ask nicely. That might be a waste of her time. Banks like SQ Private Bank were notoriously secretive and guarded their client's privacy like a tiger with a new-born cub.

'We're going to have to get a warrant, Georgie. Want to come down to the magistrates' court with me?'

Matthews beamed. 'Sure!'

# Chapter 21: The Dream Team

Knox and Matthews were off looking at what Layla Morgan had been up to in life in the hopes of tracking her whereabouts in the days leading up to her death so Elsie turned her attention to the first victim, Leonella "Nelly" Boileau. She'd asked Annie and Stryker to join her in a tiny breakout room two floors above the incident room. It was cramped but at least it had a window and a table large enough for four. Elsie got there first so she could sit facing the Thames while the other two were less fortunate in having their backs to the river.

Annie had reviewed the forensics from the first crime scene. She had Fairbanks' paper-thin report in front of her. She scowled as she riffled through it.

'This,' Annie said, 'is a bodge job.'

Her face was contorted into a sneer and she looked to Elsie for agreement; alas Elsie hadn't yet read all the forensic reports. There were simply too many to deal with.

'How so?' Elsie asked.

She shouldn't have asked. Annie began to reel off the errors she felt Fairbanks' team had committed when Nelly had been murdered. 'He only authorised enough funding for a handful of DNA samples sent to the lab from the dress, he didn't request a toxicology report on the victim's blood, and no analysis of the victim's phone was undertaken. They did the bare minimum and haven't followed through. It's like Fairbanks didn't even care.'

'He doesn't,' Elsie said bluntly. 'But we do. How can we make this right?'

'Got a time machine?'

It was, Elsie thought, an unfair shot across the bow. Mere days into taking ownership of the Boileau case and she was already being punished for Fairbanks' failure to investigate properly. No wonder he hadn't made progress. He'd done diddly squat.

'I get it, you're pissed off. I am too, but I didn't run the first case. This isn't on my shoulders or yours. We can't undo what's been done... Help me make it right. If we catch Layla's murderer, we get justice for Nelly too so let's focus on what we have got, not what's been missed, and you can scream bloody murder at Fairbanks when we've caught the bastard who did this.'

The chair screeched backwards as Annie stood to offer a handshake. She extended a handshake with a look so formal it almost made Elsie laugh. 'Deal.'

'Let's run through what little they did get,' Annie said once she had sat back down. She flipped up her laptop and spoke as if reading from her notes. 'The body of Leonella Boileau was recovered quickly after death. The pathologist determined that she'd been stabbed in the heart with a short-bladed knife with a smooth edge. Unfortunately, the wound was too generic for that to give us anything useful and the scene of crime officers didn't find a knife anywhere in the vicinity.'

Sensing that Annie was about to run through page after page of notes, Elsie cut her off before her monotone reading could become too soporific. 'Something we can use, please.'

'I was getting there.' Annie's tone was terse. 'Let me lay the groundwork first.'

'What I think the boss was saying,' Stryker said, 'is that we've read the report so we don't need a recap of absolutely everything. We just need to know what you think is salient.'

Newly mollified, Annie closed the laptop and spoke more naturally. 'The black dress that Nelly was wearing had DNA on it.'

'Yep, I proved it matched the DNA sample on the wedding dress from St Dunstan,' Stryker said. Now that they had a DNA match, the fibre evidence was irrelevant.

Annie waved him off dismissively. 'Not that.'

He looked like he'd been slapped. 'What then?'

'There were multiple DNA samples on the black dress as well as hair from multiple women,' Annie said. 'It must have been worn a few times at least for the quantity of DNA transfer I found and it's quite an unusual dress.'

It wasn't unusual for an off-the-peg item of clothing to have contact DNA on it. Dresses were worn, handled, bought, and returned all the time. This dress was much too nice for that sort of high street manhandling. Stryker looked from Annie to Elsie and back again; he clearly didn't understand the significance of it.

Elsie turned to him. 'Annie's report mentioned the type of lace it was made of,' she said. 'If you Google "Leavers Lace", you'll see how ridiculously expensive it is. It's only produced in minuscule quantities.' She turned back to Annie to check that the forensic specialist was on the same page as her. 'Is it fair to conclude it's a one-off bespoke piece?'

'I think so,' Annie said. 'Perhaps if you call the designer, you might be able to trace the person who bought or commissioned it.'

It was a good shout. It was an easy task for Elsie to delegate. 'Stryker, get on that now.'

'Okay, boss,' Stryker said. 'But before I go, can I run you through something?'

Elsie's eyes had begun to shut on their own accord, the tiredness circling once more. She could do with bringing this meeting to a close and going home. The worse the fatigue was, the shorter her fuse. Every little thing niggled and she'd be best off hiding on her own away from the world. As she couldn't do that, she nodded. 'Have at it.'

Stryker folded down Annie's laptop to make room for his own and perched it precariously at the very end of the table where all three of them could see it. It showed a large map of London zoomed in so that St Dunstan was at the centre. 'I've been mapping routes in and out of both crime scenes by car. The killer had to have driven in as there's no other way to plausibly move a body into central London, and a witness saw a blue or black car speeding away from St Dunstan.'

'Hold on! There's a witness? What witness? Why am I just hearing about this now?'

'Didn't seem important, boss,' Stryker said. 'All he heard was a car boot bang and a blue or black car speeding off. No big deal.'

She stood up and jerked a thumb towards the hallway. 'Outside. Now.'

When they were outside, Elsie shut the door behind them and motioned for him to follow her down the corridor out of Annie's earshot, and then let rip.

Her voice was low, but there was no mistaking the venom in her tone. Flecks of spittle flew from her mouth as she went at him, all guns blazing. 'What the hell do you think you're doing, Stryker? How on earth is a witness not important?'

'Well, he didn't witness much, did he? It was only a car and he didn't even see it for more than a moment.'

His smug grin disappeared at the sight of her unrelenting scowl. 'That's not for you to decide,' she said tersely. 'I want a full statement from you about your encounter with the witness on HOLMES by tomorrow morning – on your own time, not mine – and if you ever do this again, you're out. Now find out who bought that dress and how it ended up on the victim.'

'But boss, what about—'

'No buts,' she said. 'Get out of my sight.'

She spun on her heel and headed back inside.

# Chapter 22: Dirty Money

She knew it was wrong. She knew she shouldn't. She was doing it anyway.

The offer had been too tempting. Five thousand pounds and only she would ever know about it. A life-changing sum and all for a bit of information that was going to come out sooner or later anyway. The Lady Killer would be in the news whether or not she handed over the folder that was ensconced in the bottom of her handbag.

As she surfaced at Holborn Underground Station, she pushed her way past the lawyers, tourists and students jockeying for access to the Central and Piccadilly lines, and then made a swift turn to the east along High Holborn. Lost in her thoughts, she nearly walked straight into the market seller who camped outside Krispy Kreme to sell fruit and veg to passers-by. The journalist she was on her way to meet had asked her to swing by *The Impartial's* glass-fronted office building on Fleet Street. That request was much too risky and so they'd compromised on meeting in a nearby pub.

The Knights Templar was situated halfway down Chancery Lane where legal London merged with the newspaper publishers based to the south. She made it in record time, her heart thumping. The pub was part of the infamously cheap Wetherspoons chain and it was heaving. Judging by the age of the crowd, about half of the clientele were students. Baby-faced drinkers crowded around the bar with a smattering of suited and booted professionals, mostly men, sprinkled among them.

Vaulted ceilings gave the place an airy, upmarket feel. At the end of the bar farthest from the entrance, grand stairs led to a raised area away from the crowds clamouring for their next round of drinks. She made a beeline for the back and found herself poking her head into little nooks and crannies. At the very back, sitting with his back to the wall, where he sat tapping his foot impatiently, she found her contact.

'Mr Porter?' she asked. Her tone was tentative and she glanced around furtively as if expecting to be ambushed by Professional Standards at any moment.

Porter nodded and gestured for her to take a seat. 'What've you got for me?'

With a slender, manicured hand, she unclipped her handbag and pulled the folder free. Wordlessly, she slid it over to him. The surface of the table was sticky with the residue of cheap beer and even cheaper food.

He pushed his glasses up to focus through the lower half of his varifocals and then thumbed through the papers in a plodding, meticulous way. It seemed as if Porter was actually reading rather than merely scanning the contents. All the gory details were in there. The autopsy reports for both victims, forensic proof that it was a serial and even a copy of the HOLMES case file.

'Two and a half.'

She reached out to grab the folder back, but he pulled it away from her.

'We agreed on five.'

'I said it was worth up to five thousand,' Porter smiled. 'This isn't.'

'I need five.'

'Then I want more. These notes indicate it's a serial. He's not done yet; he's going to strike again. I want everything before it leaks. Get me that and then you'll get the rest.'

He stood, delved into his pocket, and tossed a jiffy bag towards her. She caught it, the heft of a wodge of notes landing in her outstretched palm.

'Not that you've got much choice now, have you darlin'?' Porter said with a smirk. 'If you want me to keep this little exchange quiet, you'd best keep sending information my way.'

And then he was gone.

# Chapter 23: Ring Ring

Stryker sang cheerfully as he fetched Layla Morgan's iPhone from the evidence locker. Dozens of cameras watched his every move from every conceivable direction as he scrawled an illegible squiggle on the release form in front of him. Where West Yorkshire Police had used a secure but informal evidence locker, the Met was professional and businesslike throughout. The man behind the counter, whose name tag read Amit Malhotra, scrunched up his face in disapproval at the Disney tune.

Not even the hint of a smile. The morose evidence clerk slid the bag containing Layla's phone across the opening in the plate glass.

'Cheers, Amit. Choir practice same time next week? I'm thinking me, you, and chubby old Fairbanks. With my baritone and your monotone, we could sing some glorious harmonies – if you ever find your voice that is.'

Before Amit could reply, Stryker was gone, his laughter echoing back down the corridor behind him as he left Amit scowling at his back. He leapt up the stairs two at a time until he found himself in the seclusion of the breakout room. He was on the third floor, well away from the hustle and bustle of the incident room, and he had space to breathe, to think, and to try and get into Layla Morgan's iPhone. He knew that the boss had already tried a few times. It wasn't the victim's birthday, nor was it 1234, 9876, or any of the other really common pin codes. He thought for a moment and then punched in 2308. The twenty-third of August had been her parents' wedding anniversary. It seemed like a good shot.

Immediately an error flashed up:

*iPhone is disabled*

Underneath that, in a smaller, all lowercase font, it read:

*try again in one hour*

'Bugger,' Stryker cursed. Time to take a late lunch. He slipped the phone back into the evidence bag from whence it came and shoved the whole bag into his jacket pocket.

AFTER A BRIEF SOJOURN to the open-air food market around the corner in Strutton Ground, Stryker returned to the office with his favourite lunch. He hadn't expected to find the Middlesbrough-inspired delicacy anywhere in London and so he'd almost plumped for the melt-in-the-mouth pulled pork burrito that Elsie had recommended. The unmistakable 'boro twang of a stallholder touting for business had drawn him further in where he'd found it – Parmo.

One bite was all it took to take him back to childhood. Breaded chicken had been slathered with a layer of gooey béchamel sauce and then topped with parmesan before being grilled until crispy. Heaven.

It was so good that if he'd been at home, he'd have licked the packaging clean.

'Damn, that smells bloody good!' Knox said. 'Wanna go halfsies?'

He quickly snatched up a tissue from his desk and dabbed at the corner of his mouth. He hadn't realised that he had an audience.

'You snuck in quietly,' he said over a mouthful of Parmo. 'And no, I'm not sharing. Buy your own lunch. You still hiding from DCI Mabey?'

'That's a bit harsh, Seb. You were gazing off into the distance as you ate and I stomped in with all the grace and elegance of DCI Fairbanks after four double bacon cheeseburgers and six pints of pale ale. What on earth is that monstrosity you're eating anyway?'

'Food of the gods, Knox, food of the gods. It's Parmo. Think fried chicken meets lasagne. If you're from the north and Parmo isn't your go-to meal, you're not a proper northerner.'

'Thank fuck I'm not a northerner then,' Knox said. 'I'd rather not have a heart attack before I turn forty.'

'Thought you already had,' Stryker muttered. 'What is it you want anyway?'

'To tell you to hurry up and look busy. Mabey should be out of her meeting with the finance manager any moment now and, from what I saw through the window, she's in a hell of a mood. I'm going to get out of her way before she starts yelling.'

It was the perennial problem, money or the lack thereof. The less they had, the further it had to go. Everything got squeezed: longer hours, fewer lab tests, and more arguments with those holding the purse strings.

'Our overtime will be fine though... right?' He looked at her pleadingly as if it were her decision. She couldn't resist teasing the newbie.

Knox smirked. 'Don't count on it.'

'What've you been up to?'

'Just got back from the mags,' Knox said as she perched herself on the end of his desk. 'Thought the mare wasn't going to give me my warrant for a while. As if there was ever any doubt that we'd need to look at Layla's bank records. I should have been in and out in minutes. Instead, she wasted ages lecturing me on *privacy*. Privacy in a murder investigation. Madness, eh, Seb?'

He looked up at her. Knox was far too old to be a DS. He desperately wanted to ask why someone so obviously competent was beneath him in the pecking order. He didn't dare.

'So,' he said instead, 'what did you find out?'

'Our victim didn't have tuppence to rub together. Like I suspected, she'd been spending like a madwoman for years and it caught up with her in September. She's been in debt since, and let me tell you, her lender is none too happy about it. When I told 'em that she didn't even own the house, they went ballistic so I hung up the phone on 'em. Without a house to seize they're left holding the bag for Layla Morgan's debts. I think it was a point of pride for 'em, not that a few grand will dent their profits much.'

'Where's she been spending the dough?'

She handed him a printout. 'Take a gander.'

She'd been spending money everywhere. There was the usual array of big-name shops – Harrods, Liberty London in Regent Street, Jimmy Choo, plus some more mundane purchases at the likes of Selfridges and John Lewis. The bigger problem was the clubs. Tens of thousands of pounds at the swankiest places in town: Cirque Le Soir, Raffles and Mahiki. Then there were the plethora of charges from Uber. Miss Layla Morgan thought herself too important to join the rest of London on the Underground or on the bus.

'Excellent taste, bugger all income,' Stryker said. 'Not a great combination.'

'And the cash too. She liked to flash the paper money about.'

Stryker had skimmed over the ATM withdrawals. The amount that Layla habitually withdrew grew progressively smaller over time – five hundred quid a time on the oldest statements then three hundred and then, most recently, a mere fifty pounds per withdrawal. The withdrawals were erratic and infrequent so it was no wonder that they hadn't been noticed straight away amongst the myriad restaurant and shopping charges.

'We didn't find any cash at her home, did we?' he asked.

'Nah, not a penny in her purse.'

'Killer might have taken it.'

They hadn't seriously been considering robbery as a motive. She still had her iPhone, her handbag, and her jewellery on her. Cash was much easier to steal. It was virtually untraceable.

'I'd nick it, wouldn't you?' Knox said. 'In for a penny, in for a pound. Not much point getting squeamish about a few quid if you're willing to stab a woman through the heart.'

Her logic was irrefutable and yet something didn't gel. If the killer were, as Dr Burton Leigh's report suggested, compulsive, then stealing was much too logical, too opportunistic. Perhaps the victim simply hadn't been carrying any cash on the night she was murdered.

He rifled through the pages Knox had handed him. She still had the most recent statement. 'When was her last transaction?' he asked.

'Two days before we found her at St Dunstan.'

'Doesn't that strike you as odd? This woman took a private hire car everywhere she went. I can almost imagine the route that her car would have taken between the shops she bought things from. Look at this. On the fourth of September, she took an Uber from Fortnum & Mason to Nobu where she ate dinner. That's a five-minute walk, tops. Layla Morgan was a lazy so and so. And yet she didn't take an Uber when she left her house for the last time. We know she wasn't killed there – the scene of crime boys have been all over it and found nowt but dust for their trouble, so that leaves us with two questions—'

'Where'd she go and how'd she get there?' Knox interrupted sharply.

'Right.' Again, Stryker was struck by just how quick off the mark Knox was. Why on earth wasn't she more senior?

'If she doesn't ever walk anywhere, then chances are someone gave her a lift.'

Her eyes twinkled, a mix of rheumy yellow and excitement. She was clearly thinking along the same lines he was. Could her murderer have picked her up?

'Let me check something,' Stryker said. He opened up the ANPR map he'd used at St Dunstan and homed in on Layla Morgan's home way out west. If there were number plate recognition cameras in the vicinity then maybe they could find out who had given her a lift.

'Damn.' Nothing. Not one camera for at least two hundred yards. The nearest was on a major road and so would pick up thousands of cars a day. Might as well pull the list anyway just in case something showed up. It seemed the killer drove a blue or black car so that would cull a good half of the list. He pinged a quick email to Ian down in the Digital, Cyber and Communications Department and cc'd in DCI Mabey so she could sign off on the spending.

'Mabey's coming, look busy.' Knox gathered up her papers and made off at ninety miles an hour in the direction of the stairwell.

'Hey!' Stryker called after her. 'Grab me a cup.'

It was too late.

As Mabey's footsteps grew louder, Stryker pulled the iPhone back out of his pocket and put it on the desk. The phone had to hold the answers. Every bit of Layla's life was digital and her phone was the key to it all. He scanned down his list of pin codes. 2828 was next on his hit list – her house number repeated twice. He tried it.

A red warning flashed up. Pin try number nine was wrong.

2301 was next. January twenty-third, her late mum's birthday.

Wrong again.

Before he knew it, the phone began to wipe itself.

'Shit shit shit shit shit!' Stryker said. He put his finger on the power button, trying to force Layla's phone to turn off. It didn't. The phone was forcibly deleting every bit of data it had ever contained, an optional security measure that Stryker had never expected to come up against. Worse still, the boss' shadow loomed over him. He hastily shuffled the papers on the desk so that Layla's phone was underneath and prayed that Elsie hadn't seen him do so.

'Everything alright, Stryker?'

He looked up. 'Uh, yes, boss, I'm fine.'

'You don't look fine. You look flushed,' Mabey said. 'What's stressing you out?'

He had to think of a lie and fast. 'I've got to be in Yorkshire tomorrow afternoon. I've got a case I'm supposed to be testifying in... Should I ask them to reschedule?'

'It's a bit late to be asking now, isn't it?' Elsie put her hands on her hips. 'What sort of case is it?'

He racked his brain, trying to think of the most plausible case he'd really worked. This lying thing was damned hard work. If only he hadn't been so stupid. Any old answer would have been better than "I've got be in court". It was so easy to disprove. 'Racketeering,' he said, hoping that he hadn't taken too long to reply and made his deceit obvious.

'Then the Serious Organised Crime Boys won't like it if you mess them about. Go, but come back as soon as possible. Think about taking the train so you can sort some of your paperwork on the way. I know you're well behind on that front. And don't even think about sticking around for a cheeky pint. I need you back here post haste.'

He nodded. 'Got it, boss. I shan't be gone long.' *Especially not for a fictional hearing.*

'Have you seen Knox?'

'You just missed her.'

The moment that she was out of earshot, he scooped up his things, stuffed Layla's phone back into the evidence bag and made a beeline for the place he should have gone all along: the Digital, Communications and Cyber department.

# Chapter 24: Bling Bling

The victim's spending confirmed that she had planned to go to Milan. She'd booked to fly out on British Airways going business class from Heathrow to Malpensa. The tickets were surprisingly reasonable, a mere £297.54 for the round trip including baggage. It back up what Étoile had said and established beyond doubt that Layla had been due to fly out to Milan on the Friday that she'd been found which was consistent with Spilsbury's assertion that Layla had been dead for around a day before she'd been found.

Now that she'd secured Layla's bank records from SQ Private Bank her last three statements were spread out on the left-hand side of Knox's desk. Despite being unfairly demoted by Fairbanks, she still had her old office which reflected her former rank of detective inspector. The title was gone, the big empty office a stark reminder of what she'd lost. It did, however, allow her the luxury of space to work. She'd also managed to get bank statements for the earlier victim, Leonella Boileau, and she'd had only to ask Nelly's building society nicely for those, no warrant needed. She spread the most recent three statements top to bottom on the right-hand side of the desk so that the statements for each woman were side-by-side. She could now compare September with September, October with October and November with November.

Each line item represented one transaction. Some were detailed showing exactly what had been bought and where, while others were bereft of specifics and impossible to decipher. Knox hoped to find something in common between Nelly and Layla but the two women couldn't have lived more different lives. While Layla had spent and spent, Nelly had been her polar opposite. Nelly had been frugal to a fault, her penny-pinching such that her monthly outgoings were in the low hundreds and so her meagre bank balance had been climbing month after month right up until her death. It looked like Nelly had been saving up for something. A deposit perhaps? Or a car? There were no charges for insurance, not much spent in supermarkets, and only the odd restaurant charge, usually a cheeky Nando's or a MOD Pizza which Nelly enjoyed no more than once every other month. It was reflective of an austere lifestyle. Nelly's monthly spending would barely cover one night on the town for Layla.

As much as Knox hated to admit it, she had to agree with Mabey. The victims' paths must have crossed somewhere. Knox was sure of it. The killer had picked these two women for a reason. They were physically dissimilar in nearly every way. Nelly was black, Layla white. Nelly was tall, Layla short. The contrasts went on and on. Where Layla was an upper-middle-class socialite enjoying all the trappings of zone one living, Nelly barely ventured out of Croydon.

The only things that the victims appeared to have in common were age and beauty. Both were in their mid-twenties and both were objectively attractive. Beyond that, they didn't shop in the same places, didn't share a gym or hobby. They lived almost as far apart as was possible within the limits of Greater London. Nelly's home in Croydon was a world away from Layla's upmarket Fulham address.

Particularly lacking was spending in the days before their deaths. It was par for the course for Nelly not to spend but very unusual for Layla. All she'd spent the day before her death was a whopping twelve pounds via contactless payment at a place called "Katz Klawz" which appeared to be her local nail salon. Katz Klawz only appeared once on her bank statements so it wasn't a regular appointment so far as Knox could tell. Perhaps then she was primping and preening for a reason. Could she have been headed out to meet a man?

While there was scant information about Layla's movements, there was even less about Nelly. Fairbanks hadn't even bothered to canvass beyond her immediate neighbours. The file on her death was as thin as he was fat and devoid of meaningful content. His team had notified her next of kin –her mother – and then done very little. A family liaison officer had been assigned to the case but their work had been hamstrung by the lack of progress. Knox knew from experience that it was heartbreaking to tell a family member that they had no new information to share over and over again.

There was only one thing for it. Knox was going to have to do some old-fashioned leg work. If she could find a big enough map of Greater London, she could put a pin in the map for every transaction the two victims had ever made. Red pins would mark Layla's spending – Knox would need several boxes of those – while Nelly's would be in blue. Perhaps then Knox would see somewhere they'd both been, some connection between them no matter how tenuous.

But before that, she needed a drink.

# Chapter 25: Nelly

At the time of her death, Nelly Boileau still called the same tiny house she'd grown up in home. She'd never even moved out of the smallest bedroom on the third floor. Like many young women her age in London, she still lived with her mother. She had died before she had had a chance to spread her wings and fly the nest.

Elsie found the Boileau residence easily enough. It was at the end of a row of Victorian terraces on Ashling Road, a stone's throw from the tram stop, and only a few minutes' walk from the recreation ground.

Sombre black curtains hung in the front window. They were drawn tight as if to exclude the outside world. Elsie had to knock on the bright blue front door several times before it was answered.

The woman who answered was the spitting image of Nelly. She was tall, broad, and had the same hauntingly beautiful brown eyes except for the fact they were bloodshot, a sure sign that she hadn't slept properly for weeks. Despite that, she was immaculately made-up and her clothing was nothing short of stunning. She wore a long dress that covered her from head to toe offset with a jacket, which Elsie recognised as a "karakou", which was emblazoned with gold sequins that depicted a floral pattern running its length. The same pattern was traced around the cuffs and elbows while black fabric underneath contrasted against the gold to create an elegant, mature look. To top it all, she wore a thick golden necklace with loops leading down to a beaded pendant.

'Mrs Beya Boileau?' Elsie asked. 'I'm Detective Chief Inspector Elsie Mabey. May I have a few minutes of your time please?'

She didn't move. 'Mabey... Mabey... where is fat man? He was supposed... supposed to come back. He promised me weeks ago.'

'DCI Fairbanks is no longer leading the investigation into your daughter's death,' Elsie said. A hint of relief came over Beya Boileau's face. 'I'm the new senior investigating officer.'

'Then in, in, come in... in out of cold.'

She spoke in a disjointed way as if picking her words carefully. She was Algerian like her daughter and her voice was slow, melodious, and soothing with a Gallic accent that was unmistakably French.

The house was surprisingly clean. Perhaps Beya had filled her days with dusting and sweeping ever since her daughter's death. She took Elsie through to the kitchen which overlooked a tiny walled garden. The sink was empty as was the drying rack. Elsie wondered if the older woman had been taking care of herself.

'Mrs Boileau, are you eating?'

It was, in retrospect, far too forward.

'Oui, oui. My friends, my neighbours. They bring me food... since it happened. Look, look.'

Beya opened the fridge door to reveal dozens of containers, a mismatch of colours and brands. It was a lot of food. Elsie said as much.

'They won't listen. I tell them. I say no more. Still, they come. Day after day. More food than I have seen before. I gain weight.'

It sounded wonderful if a smidge smothering. Elsie couldn't imagine having that sort of support. Out here in Croydon, there were still pockets of community. By contrast, her own home in Muswell Hill felt isolated, the sort of lonely isolation that can only come with being lost in a crowd. She loved the area. It was full of lovely restaurants and she had both Hampstead Heath and Alexandra Palace on her doorstep so there was no lack of greenery to go ambling around. What she was missing was what Beya took for granted – a community to turn to when in need.

'It must be nice to have so many people who care.' Her tone was more wistful than she had intended. Beya's expression softened, her demeanour switching almost imperceptibly from grieving to mothering.

'Miss Mabey, it is nice. East Croydon is where the broken, the lost, and the poor come. We make our life here... we have no one and nothing else to turn to... so we look after each other.'

Beya turned away and put a stove-top kettle on to boil. She shuffled over to the corner where glasses were stored in a high cupboard. Beya had to stand on tiptoes to reach. Two tiny glass cups were set by the stove. She cast a quizzical look in Elsie's direction as steam began to erupt from the kettle.

'Milk, no sugar for me,' Elsie half-shouted over the whistle.

Whatever tea it was, it smelled amazing. When Beya put the glass in front of her, she got a waft of mint.

'Maghrebi tea,' Beya said. 'Forgive me... the lack of ceremony. I fetch the pastries.'

The name of the tea rang a bell. Elsie had seen it on one of those Saturday morning television shows. It seemed to be a mix of syrupy sugar water and little pellets of mint that unfurled before her eyes. She took a sip, finding it soft and sweet, almost delicate.

Delectable pastries were served on a small silver tray, each morsel no more than a mouthful. They were almost too sweet when combined with the tea.

When they had supped a little, Beya set her glass down purposefully and exhaled. 'So, Miss Mabey, how goes your investigation?'

'It's a work in progress,' Elsie conceded. 'I took over from DCI Fairbanks on Sunday. I'm trying to get up to speed. I hope you don't mind me taking up your time today. I called your family liaison officer but he said you weren't answering the phone.'

'I didn't feel like the chit-chat,' Beya said drily. 'As for my time, it is, how you say, invaluable. I have more time than I know what to do with.'

Elsie didn't correct her mistake. She clearly meant that her time was worthless, bereft of meaning without her daughter. There were photos of Nelly everywhere, her smile lighting up whichever photo frame that she found herself in. Noticing that Elsie had emptied the tiny glass, Beya poured a second. This time it was stronger, a bitter note coming in behind. Now Elsie understood why the tea was served with pastries, the drink needed the contrasting sweetness.

'My Nelly, she loved this tea. Three glasses. The first, sweet. The second, warming and strong. The third... well... you wait.'

Elsie wouldn't have to wait long. Her second glass was almost empty and Beya snatched it up though she didn't immediately refill it. The final steeping of the tea was a distraction that Beya fixated upon.

'Tell me about Nelly,' Elsie said.

'She was a good girl,' Beya said. 'The night that she went, I lay awake in my bed. I wait and I wait for the jingle of her many keyrings. I wait for the key to turn in the door. Usually, it is like clockwork. That night I heard everything, every fox mewling, every door slam, every blow of the wind.'

'What time was she usually home by?'

'Midnight,' Beya said. 'Nothing good ever arrives from being out after midnight. That was our understanding. Nelly was a good girl – a sweet girl – and London is not a sweet place at night.'

'What did you do when she didn't come home?'

'I text her. Then I text her again. I got the green label. It was not like her not to call or text if she was delayed. Look.'

Elsie felt a pang of sympathy for the older woman as she watched Beya flick through her phone's inbox. Nelly had been her only regular correspondent. Until Nelly's death – which had brought out a deluge of well-wishers – Beya had received virtually no messages from anyone else. Just as Beya had said, Nelly was predictable. Every message was signed off with "JTM Maman".

'It means "I love you, Mum." She stay true to her heritage like that.'

Tears were beginning to form in the corner of Elsie's eye. Whether that was genuine sadness or merely a result of her CFS which always made her more emotional particularly at certain times, Elsie didn't know. She quickly pressed on.

'What did you do when she didn't come home?'

This was one thing she had gleaned from the logs. Fairbanks' notes said that Beya had waited a full twenty-four hours before calling Nelly in as a missing person. By that time her body was already in the mortuary. The twenty-four-hour waiting period was a myth that cost lives every year.

'Eventually, I fell asleep,' Beya said. 'I tossed and I turned. And she wasn't there in the morning.'

For a moment, Elsie furrowed her brow. Green label? It took her a moment to realise Beya meant the message had gone through as an SMS text message rather than iMessage. At the point Beya had texted, Nelly's phone was either dead, on Airplane Mode, or out of 3G reception.

'Do you know where she had gone out to?'

'She like to go to the clubs. Not to drink. My Nelly never like the booze. Instead she just like to dance. Sometimes she go to the clubs in Soho where the men don't bother her.'

It was plausible. Elsie wasn't a fan of heavy drinking either. 'Was there anyone in Nelly's life who she didn't get on with? A boyfriend perhaps?'

'Oh no, no boyfriend,' Beya said sadly. 'The poor girl found the same curse I did. She is tall and broad. Men here do not like that. She had many first dates and far too few seconds.'

'But she was dating.'

'Oh yes, she always trying. Like all you young people, she found them online.'

Her laptop had been seized by Fairbanks. His report hadn't mentioned any dating sites. 'Do you know which websites she visited?'

'No, no, not on the laptop. On the phone. She was always on her phone. She hid it from me, but I saw the smile, the smile only a man can give. Many times, she smile... and then heartbreak.'

Elsie felt like she'd been punched in the gut. Nelly was only a few years her junior and had already tried and failed.

'Which app was it?' Elsie showed Beya her own phone which had the usual array installed. Bumble, Tinder, and Review My Ex were all in a folder. The older lady arched an eyebrow.

'You too?' Beya pointed at the screen. 'That one, the yellow and green one.'

Review My Ex. No surprises there. Everyone seemed to be on it. Accessing the victim's mobile had just become the top priority. Hadn't Stryker said he was going to sort that out days ago? As Elsie fumbled with her phone to send him a chaser, Beya poured the final glass of tea. Elsie snatched it up without thinking.

'Yuck!' she grimaced. After steeping for so long, the brew was horrible.

'Bitter no?' Beya said. 'Like death. Too much of a good thing. Just like this conversation. Miss Mabey, I am tired. Is there more you need today?'

'Not that I can think of. I'll keep you updated.'

'I am sure you will,' Beya said. Her tone said she didn't believe it.

IAN WAS FINISHING OFF his second bag of flaming hot Cheetos when Stryker found him hiding in the small galley kitchen that belonged to the Digital, Cyber and Communication Department. If the contents of the bin were anything to go by, the techs lived off of junk food – microwave burgers, ramen and sweets.

The greasy-haired tech turned at the sound of Stryker's voice. 'Never heard of the whole five-a-day rule, Ian?'

Ian smirked. 'Five what? Pot noodles? Chicken and mushroom flavour counts for one, right? King size for two?'

'We do pay you enough to afford real food, don't we?' Stryker said. 'If not, I'll buy you an apple. I'm generous like that.'

'Buttering me up, eh?' Ian said. 'You need a favour, don't you?'

Stryker held out the evidence bag containing Layla's mobile. 'Save my bacon. I've managed to wipe this iPhone. Can you recover it for me post-haste?'

It couldn't have been more than a second before Ian returned the bag with a dismissive wave. 'No can do, big man.'

'Can't or won't?' Stryker demanded. He could deal with won't.

'Can't,' Ian said. 'It's as good as gone. You've tried too many times. The data is long gone. Finito. Kaput. Dead as a—'

'Alright, alright, you've made your point. When you say "as good as" ... that means it's not totally gone, doesn't it? Is there anyone who can get data off it?' A better tech perhaps? Stryker thought scathingly.

Ian hemmed and hawed. 'It's not theoretically impossible... but it may as well be. Fear not, young Stryker. I have an idea.'

'If this is about me and you going to Namco Funscape after work, you can stop asking.'

He'd asked three times now. The last time had been in the men's bathroom where Stryker couldn't even walk away. Ian was persistent. Stryker had to give him that.

'It wasn't!' Ian pouted. 'Though that place rocks. They've got dodgems, arcade machines...'

'Ahem, your idea, Ian. Now.'

'This is one of two phones, right? I saw on HOLMES that you've got Boileau's too. I know nothing's been done with it 'cause Fairbanks hasn't sent it down to us and it's an older iPhone unlike Layla's.'

'Which means?'

'No automatic deletion.'

There was a catch coming, Stryker knew it.

'But,' Ian said, confirming his suspicions, 'you'll have to try and guess manually. One every five minutes.'

Stryker ran the number. Ten thousand combinations, twelve an hour. 'But that'll take me—'

'Eight hundred and thirty-three hours unless you get lucky early on.'

Stryker swore. 'Can't you do it?'

'You wish.'

# Chapter 26: Leaks

By six o'clock, Elsie was flagging and had to call it a day. The incident room was still buzzing when she headed home, desperate for a fluffy pillow and a steaming mug of tea. Information of dubious quality had been flowing in all afternoon on the Met's tip line and every single one had to be investigated thoroughly. If something had even the slightest merit, it was logged, assigned to a member of the extended team and then vigorously investigated. It was never-ending drudgery which was best left to those at the bottom of the food chain. Despite the tips, nothing new had come to light during the time she'd taken to visit Beya Boileau. The siren call of her bed grew louder as she descended to the lobby.

On her way out, she nodded dozily at the elderly Welsh night guard. He leapt off his perch by the front door and waved her down before she could cross the lobby.

'Might want to take the Richmond Terrace exit tonight, ma'am.'

'Why?'

'There's a bit of a stir outside.' He jerked a thumb towards the front door. 'I think the fourth estate are waiting for you.'

She squinted out the window but couldn't see a thing. 'Journalists?'

'Aye, with cameras, ma'am.'

'Cheers, Ted.'

Richmond Terrace ran right down to the A3212. Elsie made it out without being caught and flagged down a cab. She'd have to leave her car where it was for the night. The journey to Muswell Hill took the better part of an hour and by the time the taxi turned into her road, it was tipping it down again. She'd hoped the rain and the winter cold, exacerbated by the winds which whipped between the old Victorian houses, would keep the tabloids at bay. She was wrong. The glint of a long-range camera lens caught her eye just as the taxi slowed down outside her house.

'Keep going!'

'But we're here, ma'am.'

There it was again, ma'am. It made her sound so old. She ignored it. 'Just keep going. Drop me off on Colney Hatch Lane.'

It was the nearest main road, thronging with traffic. She paid the cabbie and then hopped out by Woodberry Crescent. The smaller road looped back down south. She kept up a brisk pace, her eyes peeled for any sign of journalists. What had they found out that was worth tracking her down for? It was one thing to find them camped outside New Scotland Yard. There was almost always one sensational crime to report on. The fact they'd followed her home meant it was her case and there could only be one that might be worth the trek – The Lady Killer case.

She decided to forgo going home. Her dad's place was only a mile away. She could hole up in her childhood bedroom until the storm had passed. By the time she arrived, she was sopping wet and shivering. Her eyes were closing of their own accord and she half-wished she'd stormed past the journalists while saying "no comment" over and over again.

When she knocked on the door, nobody answered. It was odd. He rarely left the house these days and so for him to be out in the evening was troubling. It was nearly freezing out and the pavements were slippery with black ice. Dad wasn't getting any younger.

For a moment, she wondered if the spare key was in her other handbag. Thankfully she had it with her, tucked in amongst a barrage of unneeded receipts. She let herself in to find the house was barely warmer than outside. Someone had turned the heating off.

'Dad? You home?'

Her heart began to beat faster as horrible scenarios flooded into her mind – he'd passed out in the bathroom, dead in his bed, or on the stone kitchen floor.

'Dad!'

She went from room to room, checking them in much the way she would a crime scene. Each time she didn't find him, a little voice shouted "Clear!" in the back of her mind. Nothing downstairs. She proceeded up the staircase, the fourth step giving that familiar little creak that had been the same since she was a girl.

The upstairs was deadly quiet. The bathroom was empty, not a soul in sight. 'Dad!' she called out again. The last room to check was the master bedroom – his room – and she tiptoed in quietly as if she weren't supposed to be there. Nothing.

Where on earth had he gone? His house was empty and the heating was off in the middle of winter. She sat on the edge of his king-sized bed and looked around the empty room. Shivers ran down her spine. She called him, hoping that he had his mobile phone to hand, her mind conjuring up images of him fallen in a gutter or run over.

'Pick up, pick up, pick up.'

He answered on the fourth ring.

'Boop? Everything okay?'

'Where are you, Dad?'

'In bed.'

'Uh-uh, I know you're not. I'm sitting on your bed right now.'

Busted.

'I'm... out.'

'Where?'

'Can't a man have a bit of privacy?'

Not when he lies to me, Elsie thought. It wasn't like him at all. 'Dad, this really isn't funny. I've got a dozen journalists camped outside my flat, and I don't know why, and now you're off playing silly buggers.'

He went quiet. 'It happens, Boop. It means someone got a scoop on your story and they're going to ambush you with it. Something juicy too if there's a dozen of 'em camped out.'

'How do I find out what it is?'

'The quickest way is to walk outside and let them ambush you. Just stay calm and say no comment all the way. They'll get bored quick enough.'

'And the way that doesn't involve throwing myself to the wolves?'

'Call Hamish.'

It hung in the air like lead. Hamish Porter was one of *The Impartial's* editorial staff. He also happened to be Elsie's ex.

'You know I can't.'

'Then go talk to the press. Or wait until tomorrow when they'll print whatever they've got with or without you and give the killer time to get ahead of the leak. If you confront this head-on, you've got a chance to use it to your advantage. Boop, you've got to be proactive, not reactive.'

His voice was gravelly, almost pained. 'Dad, tell me what's up with you.'

'Can't, Boop. I've got to go. Dinner time for me. I've got a smoking hot woman in uniform waiting just for me.'

'Dad! Why would you ever tell me that?'

He chuckled. 'Bye, Boop. Feel free to stay at home if you want to take the easy way out.'

He hung up, leaving Elsie alone with her thoughts. *A smoking hot woman in uniform?* The thought of her elderly father out on a date made Elsie retch.

'Damn it,' Elsie said. He was right. She had to close down the story. She had to call Hamish Porter.

# Chapter 27: The Impartial

Despite the late hour of her call, Hamish agreed to meet her after he finished work so long as she was willing to head towards his end of town. He chose to meet at VQ, one of the few truly twenty-four-hour restaurants in London. It was on the Fulham Road, a stone's throw from his flat in Gilston Street. He worked late – often past midnight – but tonight he had managed to get out of the office by ten.

She took an Uber, enjoying a brief period of shut-eye on the way that ended far too soon when the driver gruffly announced their arrival. She thanked him, quickly gave him a five star rating on the app, and headed into the restaurant.

As was his habit, he had taken a booth right at the back where pendulum lamps swung overhead. Elsie shuffled in, her knee brushing against his as she sat down opposite him.

'You look good, Els,' he said. His lopsided smirk said he'd missed her.

She managed a wan smile as she stole the line that he usually said to her. 'You look tired.'

He had once joked they ought to have T-shirts printed that said "Tired, hun?" and "Always" so they could stop having the same conversation time and time again. He really did look exhausted. There were dark bags around his eyes, his chin was studded with at least two or three days of growth, and his clothes looked like they were allergic to the ironing board.

In front of him was a stack of pancakes slathered with what appeared to be Nutella and fresh strawberries. Hamish was a stress eater. He always had been.

'Still eating healthily, I see.'

At least he had the good grace to look bashful about it. 'Sorry I ordered without you. Long day, no time to stop for food. Let me flag down the waitress for you.'

His left arm flailed wildly.

'No, don't, I'm not hungry.' She was too slow. A bushy-haired waitress sauntered over to take her order.

'Could we have a jug of tap water please?'

The waitress looked thoroughly unimpressed to be summoned so enthusiastically for a simple jug of water. When she returned, she slammed it down on the table causing droplets to spill over the top. A slightly dusty glass was placed in front of Elsie.

'Grim,' Hamish said. He leant over to wipe it out with a napkin, and then, pronouncing it clean, handed it back.

Elsie ignored the jug and the still filthy glass. 'You know why I'm here, right?'

'Yup.' He nodded. 'The Lady Killer. You want to know who leaked it all.'

*Who leaked what?* 'First things first, I need to know what you've got.'

'What's it worth?'

She leant back as far as she could in the confined booth. It hadn't been built for people her height. 'What's it worth? Are we horse-trading now, Hamish?'

'Yes,' he said simply. 'I've got something you want. You need me. Tell you what, let's call it a favour. I'll call it in when I need something.'

'Not happening. You didn't come and meet me just to taunt me.'

'No, I came for the free dinner.'

A small laugh escaped her for the first time in days and the tension flooded out of her. Cheap was the one thing Hamish Porter was not.

He smiled, flashing those immaculately white teeth that must have cost him a fortune. 'Worth a try, wasn't it?'

'It didn't work when we were dating and it certainly won't work now. I'll pay for my tap water, you buy your own dessert. Now spill.'

She knew he was going to. He had to. Though they hadn't worked as a couple, they could work as friends. He'd even given her a glowing summary on Review My Ex. If she knew Hamish at all, he wasn't here to barter titbits. It wasn't his style.

'Sorry, Els, I'm afraid that I don't know who your leak is. All I've seen is what everyone else has seen – photos of your incident room wall. The resolution isn't bad. I'm guessing your leak used a smartphone camera.'

*Crap. Someone had taken photos?* She summoned up an image of the long wall in her mind, desperately trying to work out what was on there that might be worth it for the press. It was too fuzzy, too indistinct. A summary of the pathologist's report was up there. So was a summary of Annie Burke's. Beyond that, they really hadn't found a smoking gun.

'I'm drawing a blank here, Hamish. It's outrageous that someone has taken a photo – and mark my words, they'll pay when I find out who – but surely none of this is worth camping outside my flat for?'

'Your killer, his DNA. You haven't found a match yet have you?'

'No,' Elsie said. 'He's not on the database.'

'But you do know it's a serial killer.'

She had to concede that one. 'Hardly a state secret.'

'Right, but you know your victims were both socialites too, right? Both loved to hit the big nightclubs.'

Beya Boileau had only mentioned that Nelly liked to dance occasionally. She'd implied that Nelly went to the gay bars of Soho to avoid men pestering her. The image that Beya had painted of Nelly was that of a studious, shy, geeky girl. Perhaps parents were the last to know what their children were up to.

'Why on earth do you think that?' Elsie asked. Beya had been pretty vociferous in Nelly's defence, saying over and over again that "My Nelly is a good girl, I tell you, a good girl.".

Hamish stopped smiling as if he didn't want to be the bearer of bad news. 'Rumour has it that Channel 4 found Nelly's ex. He's set to go live on breakfast television, a tell-all about her sordid love life, how she cheated on him, yadda yadda yadda.'

'That's bullshit!'

'Perhaps,' Hamish said. 'But it sells and you can't libel a dead person. Don't you love the law?'

'Who is he? I need to get to him before he goes live.'

'Wish I could help you, Els,' Hamish said. 'I really do. All I know is they're filming his segment live in the morning so you'd best be up early. They're an efficient bunch over at Channel 4, they'll probably have him in make-up by five o'clock. Sorry I can't give you any more to go on.'

Great. Another night going to bed late, getting up early, not that it would have made a difference. CFS meant that no matter how much Elsie slept, she still felt as if she'd run a marathon. The life of a policewoman. 'You'll tell me if you find anything else, right?' she asked, failing to stifle a yawn.

'Of course. Night, Els. Take care of yourself.'

# Chapter 28: Live on Air

The glass-fronted building was less than a mile from New Scotland Yard. It wasn't worth trying to find a parking space in the heart of Westminster even at this ungodly hour and so Elsie parked up at the office where she found Stryker waiting for her by her assigned parking space. So much for her plan to meet at the studio on the dot of five.

'Good morning!' he said far too cheerfully.

She looked at him bleary-eyed. 'It's quarter to five in the morning.'

'The early bird catches the worm. I take it you couldn't find anywhere to park near Channel 4 either.'

She'd have rolled her eyes if she had had the energy. Here she was, zombie-like and shuffling along as if holding an invisible Zimmer frame, while he was bouncing on the balls of his feet. It was doubly impressive that he was so jovial when he'd have to trek up to Yorkshire and back later. 'Shut up, Stryker. Just walk, would you?'

'Need to find a coffee en route?' Stryker asked.

It was no use. While there were plenty of decent coffee shops around – her local go-to, Iris and June, was almost en route – none would be open.

'Let's just get there and find out who this guy is.'

'Any guesses what he's going to say?'

'Something sensational, I imagine. It's morning television. Sometimes the shock factor is just the thing to wake up their viewers when it's dark and cold outside.'

They ambled along the oddly named Perkins Rents in amicable silence only punctuated by the click-clack of Stryker's Loake boots on the rain-slicked pavement.

The studio was easy to find. A giant three-dimensional sign announced the building to the world. At first, it seemed like a mishmash of pieces of metal that made no sense to man nor beast. The pieces only lined up when standing on the corner of Chadwick Street directly in front of the main entrance. Doing so revealed the depth of the sculpture. The constituent parts of the installation aligned perfectly to reveal the iconic "4". Behind it, the building was a relatively squat five storeys high with a red television antenna poking skywards from the right-hand wing. It was all glass and brushed aluminium. Even at this hour, Elsie could see people scurrying around within.

'That,' Stryker said. 'Is really cool.'

It was impossible to disagree. 'Come on,' Elsie said instead, 'let's go find Nelly's ex and get the scoop before the nation knows more than we do.'

In the vague expectation that Elsie would do him a favour in return someday, Hamish Porter had called in a friend of his to help get Elsie and Stryker into the building. The friend in question was a security guard for the TV studio who had been told to expect their arrival so, after a brief examination of their warrant cards, Elsie and Stryker were allowed through the metal detectors and into the main building.

They still didn't know the name of Nelly's alleged ex. Hamish had simply known that he was due to do a tell-all live on breakfast television this morning and that the studio was likely to start all the prep for the morning around five. Nelly's ex was around somewhere, possibly already in make-up or a green room rehearsing whatever he had to say.

Two wings led off in opposite directions. One corridor seemed to be much busier than the other.

'Let's follow the crowd,' Elsie said. 'Say nothing until I do. We don't have a warrant, we're here because they let us in and they could throw us out just as easily.'

The corridor went on for miles. The names of presenters were painted on the doors nearest the entrance while the doors further in had temporary placards affixed to them as if the occupant would change by the day or even the hour. They had to be getting close.

Staff bustled along. They were far too busy to pay much attention to the strangers in their midst.

'Boss,' Stryker whispered. 'Stairway at eleven o'clock. Sign says "Screening Room & Central Studio". Our man could be sitting down there miked up and ready to tell all.'

They found the studio easily. It was enormous and very modern. The centrepiece of the room was an austere white zigzag-shaped table. There was one chair on either side of it and a Mac-Book Pro on top of it. Two video walls lined the studio, each made up of six screens that were easily as wide as Elsie was tall. The screens were already on, the TV studio's logo slowly revolving in a rainbow of colours. The lights gave the subterranean space a bright, light and airy vibe that Elsie hadn't expected.

'Where is he?' Stryker whispered.

The seats were unoccupied. There were people moving in the background adjusting lights, checking boom microphones, and sweeping the floor.

'Excuse me,' Elsie said to the nearest cameraman in her most authoritative voice. 'Do you know where our six am set piece interviewee is?'

The terminology was a total guess. She ran the risk of looking like an idiot but the cameraman still answered.

'In the green room?' His tone was scathing as if it were so obvious a child ought to know. Elsie followed his line of vision towards the back of the room well away from the stage where a tiny sign marked "Green Room" hung above the door. She strode past him as if she belonged, acutely aware of being watched as she swept towards the green room at a brisk pace. Stryker followed hot on her heels.

Through the door was an exceptionally small green room yet there was nothing green about it. A circular sofa dominated the room with televisions on the walls surrounding it. Each TV showed a different view of the studio that they'd just come from.

A young man in his twenties stretched out languorously on the sofa, his feet up as if he were at home rather than in a television studio. Elsie resisted the urge to bark at him to move his feet – it wasn't her sofa. The man was dressed in a hooded jumper that was two sizes too big, cargo trousers that were equally oversized, and the whole look was topped off with a solid gold chain that looked like it belonged on a nineties' rapper. If he had been properly dressed, he might have been handsome.

Beside him, there was a mug of steaming coffee which smelled divine. Elsie felt a twinge of jealousy. She could use a coffee right now.

'Are they ready for me already?' the man asked. He sat up, looked Elsie up and down, and then wolf-whistled. 'I guess this face don't need no make-up.'

'I didn't realise it was already Halloween,' Stryker said.

The man leapt to his feet and squared up to Stryker. 'You what, mate? I'm the main mofo I'll have you know.'

'Nah,' Elsie said, 'you can't be. You're not the one who dated Nelly Boileau, are you?'

He turned, puffed out his chest, and then smiled. 'Fo sho. That girl was ma hoe for going on a year.'

The man beamed at Elsie as if it were an accomplishment. 'What's your name?' she asked.

'Vito.'

'You're Italian?' Elsie asked. *That explains the long, dark eyelashes and winter tan.*

'Half,' Vito said proudly. 'My papi was from Naples.'

Elsie sat down and motioned for Vito to sit with her. She leant forward conspiratorially, deliberately ignoring Stryker. 'When was it that you dated Nelly?'

'Til Christmas,' Vito said. 'That's when that slut decided to up and leave me.'

'Nearly a year ago then. Why are you on TV today?'

'To tell the world what that skank was really like.'

'What was she like?'

'She was a nasty, lying, manipulative shrew who no man can tame.'

Stryker arched a disbelieving eyebrow at Vito.

'What you looking so surprised at, pretty boy?' Vito said. 'I know Shakespeare.'

Before she lost his attention, Elsie wrestled the conversation back to Nelly Boileau. 'What was it she did that was dishonest?'

'It'd be quicker to ask me what she did that was real. That girl manipulated everyone in sight. Even her own mama. She tell everyone that she this nice, Christian girl. She was this butter don't melt angel in front of everybody else. With me, she was crazy.'

Stryker jumped in before Elsie could. 'Then why did you date her?'

'Crazy be good, man,' Vito said, 'for a little while anyhow. You know how it is. We'd snort some blow, hit downtown, drink at the nicest places.'

They had him. He'd openly admitted to doing blow in front of two police officers. If all else failed, Elsie could now haul him back to the station and keep him there long enough to run down this double life that Boileau had been living.

'How,' Elsie interrupted his reminiscing, 'did you afford that?'

'She was a sugar baby. Some rich white dude in Westminster gave her jewellery, money, even a car.'

'And you didn't mind?'

'Mind? Are you insane?' Vito said. 'Of course, I didn't. So long as she wore a condom, I didn't give a rat's ass. I got to live the high life. An old geezer got the occasional blowie.'

'And now she's dead.'

'Yeah.'

'You have anything to do with that?' Stryker asked.

'I told your producer I didn't already,' Vito said. He still hadn't twigged that he was talking to the police.

'Just to be sure, where were you the night she died?'

He was on the defensive immediately. 'None of yo bidness. We gon do this interview or not? I'm hungry.'

Stryker flashed his warrant card. 'It's literally my business. Now talk.'

Panic lit up Vito's chiselled features. 'I don't even know when she died. And I don't keep track of my days, see, so even if you tell me, I don't know.'

'So, you don't have an alibi,' Stryker said.

'I don't need one!' Vito said. 'I didn't kill nobody. Do I need a lawyer?'

'Not if you haven't committed a crime.'

Vito turned white as he realised that he'd just bragged about doing coke to two police officers.

'You can't do this, man,' he said, turning to Elsie to beg. 'You told me you were a producer!'

'Nope, you assumed I was a producer. I said nothing of the sort. You can have your lawyer if you want one. I'll happily take you out of here in cuffs right now. The morning news will get an extra juicy segment that way.'

'Or,' Stryker jumped in, switching to the role of good cop, 'you help us out here. We want to find out who killed her. You obviously knew her better than her mum. Point us in the right direction. Do that, cancel this TV segment and we'll both have mysterious amnesia about the cocaine confession.'

'Blud, I can't. They'll want their money back... and I already spent it.'

'How much was it?' Elsie asked out of sheer curiosity.

'Five Gs.'

Five thousand pounds to smear a dead woman's reputation. It was easy money for a toad like Vito.

'What'd you buy with it?'

'I paid Ma's rent for a few months.' His eyes were puppy dog-like and the tears forming in the crescent of his eyes appeared genuine.

'Tell me everything now,' Elsie said. 'And I'll do what I can. If I can avoid walking you out in cuffs, I will. Just be quick because the actual producers will be in here for you at any moment. I want specifics. Who was she a sugar baby for and how did she meet him?'

'She met men online, yo. I don't know all their names. At first, it was just this one lonely old geezer – I think he suggested it – and then she started looking for them. She'd send out hundreds of flirty messages on every dating site under the sun.'

'Including Review My Ex?'

'Duh,' Vito said. 'How could she not use it, yo? It's like the biggest app going. Most dudes would back off after a while so she started asking for money earlier and earlier in the chat. I thought that'd scare the guys off.'

'Did it?'

'Some. It got rid of the guys who usually flaked. She asked them for what she called a "deposit", yo. How wack is that? She ask 'em for money up front to prove they were serious.'

Ingenious. It was like those email scammers who deliberately filled their messages with ungrammatical and illiterate verbiage. Those stupid enough to fall for the con carried on reading while everyone else was filtered out.

'Efficient,' Elsie said. 'Did many fall for it?'

'Loads. Nelly was a hot piece of ass and she knew it. She pulled that sweet and innocent routine so often that I think she started to believe in it. She'd tell them she needed money for tuition, for rent, for food. Whatever story worked, she built on it.'

It sounded like more work than a real job. 'How on earth did she keep track of all the lies she told?'

The question elicited a small grin. 'She kept notes, yo. She filled up a little black book, thought it was all literary and shit. Pages upon pages, one for every dude stupid enough to fall for her lies.'

'Were you in it?' Stryker asked.

Vito's face fell. 'Yeah man, right at the beginning too. Bitch got me good.'

'How did she do that, Vito?' Elsie said.

'She...'

'She what?'

His head drooped, his eyes closing as if to shield himself from the pain. 'She told me she was pregnant. She told me it was mine. I loved her, yo. I thought we were set for life.'

'And it was someone else's?' Stryker asked.

Vito looked up, his big blue eyes blinking as tears began to roll down his cheeks. 'There was no baby, man. She just lied to get me to pay for shit. She told me she was getting clean, that she was going to stop hustling. All that was a lie too.'

The nurturing part of Elsie wanted to believe him. She nearly did except for one simple fact. Spilsbury hadn't mentioned any signs of drug abuse at the autopsy and Doctor Valerie Spilsbury was never wrong.

'Three weeks ago, Vito.'

'Huh?'

'That was when she died,' Elsie said. 'Where were you then?'

'At my ma's down in Croydon, yo. We were celebrating.'

Stryker looked sceptical. 'Celebrating what?'

'Her seventieth birthday, man.'

'Can anyone vouch for that?' Stryker said.

'My whole family. Ask my ma, my pa, my cousins, anyone.'

'When was this, Vito?' Elsie asked.

'Early. I picked my cousin Zoe up from school at like twenty-five past three and then we headed over to Ma's.'

'Did you leave at all?'

'Naw, I live there. I slept in 'til midday on Saturday. It was my worst hangover in like forever.'

Vito was innocent – of murder at least. Assuming his alibi checked out, and Elsie was sure it would, he was a long way away on the night that Nelly Boileau was dumped in Chelsea Physic Garden.

'We'll check that,' Stryker said.

'I know man, go ahead. Can I go now?'

'Yep, straight to New Scotland Yard,' Stryker said. 'Stand up, turn around, hands behind your back. You're under arrest for possession of a class A substance.'

She debated stopping him as he began the mandatory police caution. It wouldn't hurt to shake Vito up a bit. He might remember something in the cells that would be more useful – and at the very least, it kept Nelly's sordid story out of the media for a few more precious hours.

'You do not have to say anything. But it may harm your defence if you do not mention when questioned something which you later rely on in court. Anything you do say may be given in evidence.'

Now they just had to get off the premises before Channel 4's security team realised that they'd just arrested the morning's star guest.

# Chapter 29: End Run

Layla's neighbours were keeping schtum. No matter how many of their doors Knox knocked on this morning, nobody admitted to knowing a damned thing about Layla Morgan's life. Nobody had seen friends coming or going. None chatted with her in the street. They didn't even pay attention to the parade of Ubers that must have come and gone at all hours of the day and night. It was as if she existed in a vacuum, her entire life a series of photographs staged for Instagram with no substance or reality behind them.

In the days since the boss had visited, the crime scene boys had swept the house from top to toe and found nothing, not one unexplained DNA sample. Notably, there wasn't any booze in the house. Something about that set Knox's hair on end. Layla's Insta depicted a party girl, a socialite, someone trying to climb the ladder and become a social media influencer. Her web presence was confident verging on narcissistic. In every photo her hair and make-up were Photoshopped to perfection.

Knox wanted to try something different. She had Layla's credit card records. That gave her a vivid picture of what Layla's final days were like. Knox had debated running down the various clubs that Layla had frequented the weekend prior to her murder. It was possible that she met someone there. If Knox didn't already know Fairbanks was utterly useless, she would have assumed his team had covered that angle. Running down the details of Layla's nightlife would be a last resort. Many of the clubs that Layla had frequented were enormous super clubs, the biggest of which topped twenty-five thousand square feet spread over multiple floors. The sheer volume of people that Layla could have come into contact with – most of them high and/or drunk to boot – would make showing her photo around the clubs an exercise in futility. Knox had spent her youth in London's most notorious club, Fabric, wandering its labyrinthine hallways, getting blind drunk and regretting it all the next morning when she woke up next to a troll. Nowadays she still drank but the manhunting had become less fruitful with each passing year. In any case, flirting with men wasn't Layla's modus operandi. She didn't seem to take men home, nor did she have any drug paraphernalia lying around. It was as if she dabbled in the club scene just to pose for Instagram, not truly partaking of everything that London had to offer after midnight.

There was something about the victim that simply didn't make sense. On the one hand, the notebooks and papers that they had found in her home gave the impression of a young woman struggling with anorexia, presumably grief-ridden at the loss of her parents and spending vast quantities of inherited cash. That side of Layla was impulsive, out of control, and on a downward spiral.

On the other hand, her life was on an upward trajectory in the months before her death. The most recent bank statements showed that she had reined in her spending to almost normal levels. The way she portrayed herself on social media was carefully curated to be on-brand. Surely that mask, that perfect varnish, had to slip every now and then.

As the Met's standard Trace, Interview, Eliminate strategy had been a total bust, Knox had to think outside the box. The usual approach to these sorts of inquiries – and Knox had deputised for Fairbanks in hundreds of them – was to get every possible suspect in the pool, prioritise the suspects and then go and talk to them. Take out the obviously innocent, pursue whatever leads arose. With a dearth of witnesses and suspects, Knox fell back on an even older technique – retracing her victim's steps. It was an extension of the map-plotting work that she'd done days earlier. By putting every transaction on the map, Knox could reconstruct where Layla had gone, which routes she'd taken, which streets she'd walked. If she used that information, she could retrace her steps and see what Layla had seen, go where Layla had been. It was slow, laborious, methodical work.

The very last transaction ever recorded on the victim's debit card was at a nail salon. There wasn't a similarly timestamped charge from Uber or Addison Lee so it was safe to assume that, for once, Layla had travelled by Shanks' pony.

It took her just eight minutes to get to the salon from the station walking at a brisk clip in light of the winter chill ripping through the street. The neighbourhood was upmarket, full of young mums pushing babies in designer pushchairs. Katz Klawz felt oddly out of place. It was part of an older mixed-use block with flats above the retail unit. There was a stark contrast between the shabby chic exterior and the glossy white interior that would have been at home in a Tesla showroom. Knox made her way inside, a bell above the door jingling as she entered, and looked around. On her right, the barstool-height nail bar was white-on-white, obnoxiously bright and faultlessly cleaned to showroom perfection. Chandeliers sparkled overhead, the light reflecting off the marble underfoot. Along one wall, six rows of identical bottles of nail varnishes showed off a rainbow of possible colours. There was a harsh smell of acetone in the air masked by an overpowering grapefruit diffuser which was on the far end of the nail bar.

There appeared to be just one technician on duty, an elegantly dressed young Asian woman who spoke with a Thai accent. Knox could hear someone else moving around beyond the door marked "Staff Only".

'Do you got appointment?'

'No, 'fraid not—'

'No walk-in, we very busy.'

Knox looked around at the half-dozen empty seats. 'I'm with the Metropolitan Police.'

The woman paled, her eyes flitting towards the Staff Only sign and then back to Knox. 'Sorry. Me no speak English.'

The poor girl looked terrified the moment she heard the word "police". She didn't seem scared of Knox, not in the way that a criminal might when hiding their wrongdoing. The girl's demeanour was that of a victim. Up close, Knox could see that the elegant clothing was frayed around the edges as if it had been worn for too long.

Behind the bar, a large sign read "50% off for Cash".

It was never a good sign. Any predominantly cash-based business that had little trade was a dead giveaway that something was afoot. From Knox's cursory Googling, Katz Klawz had been in business for several years. The place ought to be heaving with regular customers.

Knox mulled over the explanations. The simplest was that Katz Klawz was a front, a money laundering operation that washed drug income so the tax man didn't get suspicious. That didn't fit with the Companies House accounts that Knox had pulled. Katz Klawz only declared a modest profit, barely six figures gross.

Forced labour. Trafficking. That was more likely.

She looked around for any sign of a handler. Then she noticed a tiny blinking red light up in the corner. A nondescript, high-end, security camera was watching their every move.

Knox raised her voice in case anyone was listening and spoke in the posh voice she reserved for the telephone and press conferences. 'I have a big date tonight. Are you sure you can't fit me in?'

The Staff Only door opened to reveal a heavy-set Asian lady who had to be at least Knox's age.

'Hello, Sister,' the young woman said.

The older woman ignored her and homed in on Knox. 'What you want?'

If it hadn't been so serious, it would have been comical. Knox was standing in a nail bar which was open to the public and the woman's tone made it sound like Knox had knocked on her front door at half past midnight.

'I need my nails done,' Knox said. She showed the woman her damaged cuticles.

'Here, here, price list.'

The cheapest option was the first, a fifteen minute "Quick Fix" for fifty quid, or twenty-five after the discount for cash. Knox pointed at it. Seemingly satisfied that Knox was a genuine customer, the older woman turned away to polish the end of the nail bar.

Mindful of both "the Sister" and the camera, Knox took a seat with her back to both. The nail technician pointed at the row of nail varnishes.

'You pick colour.'

Knox perused for a moment, acutely aware that her haggard old hands and nicotine-stained nails made her incongruous in a place like this. Having her nails done was not one of her pastimes.

'Do you think the red will cover up the damage?' Again, she spoke loudly for the benefit of the Sister.

'Manicure first,' the manicurist said. 'Then we see.' The technician began to file the edges of her nails in silence, the Sister glancing over every now and again. Once the bar had been polished to perfection, the Sister disappeared into the backroom once more.

Knox leant in, ever mindful of the camera, and spoke in a hushed voice. 'Are you okay? If you're here against your will, tell me that I need a follow-up treatment next week – doesn't matter what for.'

The hand holding hers began to tremble.

'I can't fit you in next week,' she said and looked towards the door at the back of the property. The Sister terrified her.

'Right,' Knox said. 'That's a shame. I'm sure we can work something out, my schedule is always up in the air. I'm Knox by the way. What's your name?'

'Sumiko. It mean "smart girl".'

'Nice to meet you, Sumiko. I'm wondering if you know a friend of mine. She came here last week. Can I show you a photo?'

'No photo. No photo.'

Even the thought of being seen looking at a photo was enough to terrify Sumiko. 'Okay, her name was Layla Morgan. She might have been a regular.'

'What she look like?'

'Short, very slim, pale white skin, wavy brunette hair.' Perhaps Layla had dyed it. Knox wasn't getting a reaction so she strained to think of something more helpful and her mind flashed upon one of Layla's most popular Instagram posts. 'She had little lotus flowers on her fingers in pink against red.'

'Oh!' Sumiko said. 'I know her. She very famous, no?'

'Do you think?'

'Oh yes, she come in here, always in black cab, always talking about flying here, flying there. I see her Jimmy Choo bags, a different one for every day of the week.'

'You sure they weren't fake?'

As Sumiko moved onto the base coat, she shook her head vehemently. 'No, no. Not fake like ones some of my clients go buy in Camden. They break at seam, look awful under spotlight. This real deal. And miss tip very well. Sometimes fifty pounds for nails.'

Even in a place like Katz Klawz, it seemed that Layla Morgan was desperate to keep up appearances. Matthews was right. Layla lived her life according to the mantra she had scrawled on her bathroom mirror – fake it until you make it.

The Sister reappeared again and Sumiko recoiled under her gaze.

In a nervous voice, Sumiko said, 'Now, you want this just scarlet red or something different?'

'Just plain red is fine,' Knox said. She looked around once more. In the twenty minutes she'd been in Katz Klawz, there had been no other customers. There certainly wasn't any need for two members of staff. The telephone hadn't even rung.

'You guys do custom nail painting too, right? I've got to go back to work after this but I'd love to have some flowers added. Could you sort that out before my big date tonight? I'm free after work.'

'Tonight, I go to other job,' Sumiko said. Her voice wavered as if this were something she dreaded. Then she added in a whisper, 'In Soho. Could you come back? Before six?'

'Is that when your shift ends?' The Quick Fix treatment was nearly up. If she had to get a team from SOCO back here before then, she'd need to get a shift on.

Sumiko nodded.

'Then I'll see if I can shift my calendar around. How's five-ish work for you?'

'I can do that. You pay now. Twenty-five pounds.'

Knox proffered thirty pounds in crumpled notes.

'No, you pay Sister.'

The big woman ambled over and snatched Knox's money wordlessly. She didn't offer change. A thin-lipped smile said that Knox was no longer welcome.

Outside, Knox fumbled for her phone. The Sister was clearly suspicious. Were her suspicions enough to go back and watch the CCTV? Would she know that Knox had identified herself as a policewoman? If so, Sumiko was in danger. Traffickers were known for shuffling their victims around – or worse. If Knox let Sumiko leave for her evening shift in Soho – no doubt a prostitution gig – and didn't follow up tonight then Sumiko would almost certainly disappear for good and it would be because of Knox's visit.

The man she dialled as she walked away answered after just four rings.

'Ozzy? It's me. I need a favour right now.'

# Chapter 30: Better Future Media Limited

Vito had clammed up the moment he had arrived in the custody suite so Elsie had left Stryker to babysit while Vito's solicitor was summoned, and headed to the Old Street Roundabout instead. This was London's answer to Silicon Valley, the so-called Silicon Roundabout where tech firms and start-ups operated out of shared offices and incubator programmes. They offered everything from financial services to online games. The office she had come to see was much larger than most start-ups, occupying an entire building just north of the tube station.

Elsie arrived to find an explosion of primary colours on the outside of the building that belonged to Better Future Media Limited. They were the company behind the now-infamous Review My Ex app which had been responsible for Elsie going on a string of awful dates. Elsie had arrived solo. The team was stretched thin and she couldn't afford to use two people when one would suffice, a logic which applied to her as much as it did to the rest of the team. The weirdness continued inside the building. It was as if the office had been plucked from a child's imagination, everything soft and colourful. Where the reception desk ought to have been, a man lay in a hammock, his eyes closed as if asleep. Behind him was a wall of fabric in a rainbow of colours. Two empty hammocks were strung up on either side of the lobby, unoccupied but for a scattering of throw pillows that made Elsie long to lie down and have a good nap.

At the sound of Elsie's approaching footsteps, the man stretched, yawned and then swung around to sit bow-legged in the hammock in the most awkward fashion.

'Welcome to BFM. What can we do for you today?'

She flashed her warrant card. 'DCI Elsie Mabey. May I speak with whoever is in charge?'

He sucked in a breath of air as if she had asked to borrow the crown jewels. 'Hmm... let me go see for you, 'kay? Take a hammock while you wait.'

Behind the hammock, a gap in the curtains that Elsie hadn't noticed opened up to admit him. She caught a glimpse of two suited men standing in the corridor just inside, their arms crossed, and little white earpieces in. There was security after all.

Elsie settled into the hammock and closed her eyes. It was the perfect spot to take a break. Pop music wafted in from an air vent well above her as the soft supportive hammock cradled her so well that she nearly dropped off to sleep. A simple chair would have been a safer choice. Two songs later, there was still no sign of the receptionist. She idly picked up her mobile, intending only to take it out of Airplane Mode long enough to ask the team for a status update. Almost immediately a succession of messages from Raj came in.

*Hey, what you up to?*

Then:

*I'm busy too. I'll try you later.*

Before she could even flick away the notification, another message appeared:

*As long as ur not wasting my time.*

*How abt drinks tonight?*

*ANSWER ME!*

*Stop ignoring me. BITCH.*
*I'm sorry. I didn't mean that. Dinner?*
*I can see ur online. What did I do wrong?*
*Whatevs, you're not worth my time anyway slut.*

God, men could be crazy. In just a few hours of being offline, he'd gone from the perfect gentleman to budding psychopath. It was just so illogical. Didn't normal people keep normal business hours? She was about to reply telling Raj just what he could do with his offer of dinner when the receptionist reappeared.

'Oh, you use our app too? Having much luck?'

The receptionist was a nosy so-and-so. Elsie cocked her head to one side. 'See for yourself.'

His face paled. It was obvious he'd seen behaviour like Raj's before. 'Just hit the block button. He's not worth your time, 'kay?'

Solid advice, albeit a week too late. The Review My Ex app was crawling with self-entitled narcissists.

'Anyway, Mr Melrose will see you now. Follow me.'

Elsie pushed her way through the curtains to find herself in a narrow corridor that seemed to wrap around the entire perimeter of the building. She passed the two heavies who nodded curtly. The reception was on the southeastern corner of the building and her internal compass said she was heading clockwise towards the back of the building. After the third corner, the corridor opened out into a huge atrium with glass and yet more splashes of bright colour everywhere.

A massive slide dominated the centre of the atrium running down from a balcony around a bullring of glass-fronted offices that encircled the atrium. A skinny, grungy man slid down it as Elsie watched. He leapt to his feet and strode in her direction.

'You must be the fuzz!' he called out as he approached. He was loud enough that everyone in sight turned to watch the spectacle. 'To what do I owe the dishonour today?'

He was cocky, brash, and American. Elsie disliked him immediately.

'Mr Melrose, I presume?'

'That's me, the one and only Adelrick Melrose. My parents were particularly sadistic, you see. Mom was a Scot which is why I got Melrose. Pop, bless his dead cotton socks, was a German with a grandiose sense of entitlement for his son. Adelrick means "noble and regal ruler" which, it turns out, is dead on the money. Welcome to my domain, Detective Mabey. I took the liberty of Googling you while you waited. What brings the Homicide and Major Crime Command to the Silicon Roundabout?'

'We're investigating the death of Layla Morgan. We believe she may have been a client of yours.'

'Almost certainly she was if she were single,' Adelrick said. 'And even if she wasn't, who doesn't love a good shag on the side as you Brits like to say? You're randier than goats around here and I've got the data to prove it.'

'Your data is why I'm here—'

'Thought it might be. Do you have a warrant?'

'No, but—'

'Then I'm afraid we're done here. Legal wouldn't have it any other way and quite right they are too. We store a lot of sensitive data and we take that our clients' privacy seriously. Thanks for swinging by. Do grab a complimentary smoothie from the juice bar on your way out. The lime and chia seed blend is quite delightful.'

Elsie snatched his arm as he turned to go.

'Really?' Elsie mocked him. 'You thought you could give me a smoothie and send me on my way. I can see you're as unhinged as this office is.' She looked up to see the audience in the bull-ring above had grown markedly. The staff watching from the balcony appeared to be uniformly young, mostly men, and all casually dressed. She raised her voice so they could hear her. 'Let's try this again. I'm investigating the deaths of two women, both of whom used your app.'

'Shh, you'll disturb the ambience. Can't you see people are working here?'

Elsie felt her nostrils flare. Anger surged within her. What was with this guy?

'Then I suggest,' she said through gritted teeth, 'you show me to a nice private office where we can have this discussion in peace.'

He relented, beckoning her to follow him. They marched in lockstep towards a lift at the back of the atrium which soared upwards with remarkable speed. Adelrick's office was at the very top of the building above the atrium. Glass abounded in every direction giving panoramic views out over the rooftops. In the middle of the room stood a low coffee table and two chintzy armchairs. It was not a room designed for work.

'Sit down then, Detective Mabey. Tell me what it is I can do to get rid of you. If it is in my power then I shall consider granting it.'

How magnanimous of him, Elsie thought as she sat down, to consider what she had to say. He looked as pleased as punch as if he had handed over the keys to the kingdom.

'Your app,' Elsie said. 'How many users has it got?' This wasn't something they advertised online. Knowing the total user count would help establish whether the victims' use of the app could be mere coincidence.

'In London? Just over a million. Six hundred thousand women, five hundred thousand men. All of them under forty – our cut off age – and none under eighteen of course.'

Elsie knew there were about eight million Londoners, and a third of them were in that eighteen to forty age bracket. Assuming there weren't too many fake accounts, Adelrick had managed to get almost half of all the eligible Londoners to use his app.

'How do you stop under eighteens using the app?'

'You ought to know. You're one of our users, aren't you? We ask everyone for a passport or driving licence scan. They're not easy to fake.'

'Do you run the identifiers?' Elsie asked. Both passports and driving licences had unique identifiers printed on them to prevent fraud.

'No,' Adelrick said. 'We check each document by eye much like a bouncer at a club would. Our goal isn't to make it impossible to cheat. We simply aim to make cheating too hard to bother trying. That is more than we're required to do, you know.'

He was keen – too keen – to suggest that everything was above board. He desperately wanted to come across as offended by the mere possibility of impropriety.

'So, you've never had any cases of age fraud? Or gender fraud?'

'No comment.'

'No comment? Sounds guilty to me.'

He poked a finger in her direction. 'You're here as my guest, Detective Mabey. I suggest you keep this cordial.'

'I am, Mr Melrose. Tell me something else then. How do you get more women than men on your app? Aren't these things usually male-dominated?'

'It's true. Like clubs, a sausage fest will ensue without proper rules. We allow women six months of free membership. That helps us keep the ratios working well.'

*Not discriminatory at all.* 'Is that legal?' Elsie asked.

Adelrick shifted in his seat uncomfortably. 'I'm not a lawyer, Detective Mabey.'

'But you have a lawyer.'

'This is very tiresome,' Adelrick said. 'If you have no more real questions...'

'I need to know who my victims met on your app.'

'Absolutely not.'

'Want me to come back with a warrant?'

'Feel free. It won't do you any good.'

'You think you're above the law?' Elsie made a mental note to check where Better Future Media were incorporated in case that had any bearing on getting a warrant.

'No, I just don't have the information you're asking for. Everything is stored on the client end. We only hold heavily encrypted data and I don't have the decryption keys. If you want to know who your victims were talking to, you simply need to look at their mobile phones.'

'Then I'll do just that.'

# Chapter 31: Delegation or Derogation

'Matthews! Oi, Matthews!' Stryker shouted. He was running at a clip down the main corridor of the fourth floor of New Scotland Yard. Staff lurched out of his way to avoid the lumbering behemoth as he bore down on Matthews. He screeched to a halt before her and doubled over, winded and breathless.

'What is it, Seb?'

'I... have... to go... to court. Need... favour.'

'Sure,' Matthews said. 'What do you need?'

'This,' he thrust an evidence bag at her, 'is Leonella Boileau's iPhone. I've spoken to Ian down in cyber. He says we should just guess the pin. It's only four digits 'cause it's an older one.'

'Four digits... Seb, that's ten thousand combinations.'

'Err, yep, about that. Must dash. Got to be in court in Yorkshire at two and I'm cutting it fine as it is.'

'Fine. I'll do it.'

He beamed. 'Great. One more thing, we've got a fella called Vito down in the cells that was about to blab about our first vic on national TV. See what you can do about holding him for as long as possible.'

'On what charge?'

'Possession – but there's no chance of success. We just need time to find out if his claims have any merit. Look, I've really gotta run. Thanks again!'

Matthews turned to the phone. There were exactly ten thousand combinations and it would take weeks if not months to enter them one at a time. Before she could say anything, he sprinted back the way he'd come, leaping a backpack that had been left halfway along the hall with surprising agility.

She held the evidence bag up. It was an ancient iPhone, the kind that got slammed in the press for struggling to make phone calls as a result of the way the antenna had been designed. The screen showed that someone had already tried to break in. The chain of custody log affixed to the outside of the evidence bag read that it was currently in the possession of DI Sebastian Stryker. Matthews quickly rectified that defect, all the while kicking herself that she let Stryker run off without doing it properly. She'd have to get him to countersign the log later to confirm he'd handed it over.

What Stryker wanted was a miracle. Surely Ian hadn't really suggested that they enter every single possible permutation manually? Maybe Stryker had got it wrong in his rush to dash off to Yorkshire.

Ian was only two minutes away. There was no harm in checking with him before she bricked the mobile and lost any evidence that it might contain. She found the department easily before realising that she had no idea which man was Ian. They all looked the same to her. It was as if every member of the Digital, Cyber and Communication Department had been manufactured somewhere like a toy doll, each with sallow waxy skin, greasy hair and the posture of Quasimodo. Each stared gormlessly at an oversized monitor, earphones on and oblivious to her presence. The room hummed with electricity, hard drives spinning and neon lights glaring in the cavernous basement. It was surprisingly warm which didn't help with the aroma that was a combination of sweaty musk and pot noodles.

Matthews tapped the nearest man on the shoulder and gestured for him to remove his headphones. He did so slowly as if reluctant to speak to her.

'Ian?'

A look of relief washed over him. 'No.' He pointed over his shoulder at the very back of the room at a man who was somewhat older, more weatherworn, and yet still wore a Superman T-shirt. Matthews stalked over to him and called out his name loudly.

'Do... do I know you?' Ian asked.

'DS Matthews,' she said. 'You know my colleague, DI Stryker.'

'Yeah, yeah, we're tight, we are. I think we're going for a beer tonight.'

'Are you now?' Matthews asked. 'That's... interesting. Anyway, Stryker said that you know about phones.'

'I do, yeah. This about the one Stryker bricked?'

Matthews blinked. Ian had to be confused. She had the phone from Stryker in her hand, and it wasn't bricked.

'Huh? Do you mean *this* phone?'

'Err...' Ian looked around as if someone else in the department might come to his rescue. 'Uh... yeah?'

'You don't sound sure,' Matthews said. 'This phone isn't bricked. What did Stryker do?' *Please tell me that he didn't brick Layla Morgan's phone.*

'Stryker? Oh, I thought you said Biker. Different case. What can I help with Miss Matthews?'

'Like I said, I need to get into this phone. How do I do that without bricking it?'

Ian made a great show of looking at the phone as if he'd never seen it before. 'It's an older iPhone.'

'Wow, who'd have known that?' Matthews said, her impatience bubbling to the fore. 'Did it take you years of working in digital forensics to learn how to read the back of a mobile phone?'

It was etched right there on the back, complete with model number. Leonella Boileau had never upgraded past her now-ancient iPhone 4s.

'Alright, no need to be narky, DS Matthews. You're asking me to help you with a drudge task here. I could make you fill out a proper requisition form, you know, do it all by the book.'

He had a point.

'Just tell me how to get in.'

'The Darth Null method,' he said as if this explained everything.

'Right. And that would be...?'

'Usually, these phones make you wait between attempts. Every time you get the pin code wrong, the lockout period gets longer and longer until you're waiting forever. If you try too many times, the newest phones can be set to self-delete all the data they contain to prevent an intruder just guessing pin codes forever.'

'Like Stryker did with Layla's phone.'

'Exactly. But... Shit!'

'You'd already given the game away, Ian. Nice try covering up though. Did you forget that I'm a detective?'

'Yeah, a new one,' Ian muttered.

'Sorry, I didn't quite catch that.'

'Look, he's my mate, okay? He should have brought me the phone – like you did – but he tried guessing.'

'And then left the older phone with me so if the same happened again, I'd be the one to take the fall. What a friend you've got there, Ian.'

He hung his head. 'Sorry.'

'Then make it right. How do we open this phone?'

'What we want to do is enter wrong PINs until it says "disabled for one minute". The next lockout increment is five minutes. The moment that shows, we need to hard power off the iPhone.'

'What's a hard power off?'

'So, you know you usually hit the power button, and then slide the red slider over to shut down? That's a soft power off. We're going to press and hold the power button and the home button at the same time to force the phone to reset.'

'Then what?'

'We're going to wait until the Apple logo appears during the reboot, release the power button but carry on holding the home button for about four seconds more. If we do it right, the password screen will reappear but the lockout timer will be gone. Nifty, eh?'

'Very. How on earth did someone figure this out?'

Ian shrugged. 'Who knows? It's the internet. Some people have waay too much time on their hands.'

'Then do it.'

She handed him the phone. He looked at her nervously but proceeded with the Darth Null method nonetheless.

'Here goes nothing,' he said as the logo flashed up. 'One, two, three, four.'

On four, he released the home button and allowed the iPhone to boot up.

'Yes!' He beamed at her. It had worked.

'Now what?'

'Now you can try as many times as you like. It won't lock you out for good.'

'But I still have to try every combination under the sun until I can get in?'

'I'm afraid so.'

# Chapter 32: The Serious Organised Crime Agency

In the half an hour it took for Knox to return to New Scotland Yard, her contact at the Serious Organised Crime Agency had already commandeered the largest available incident room which was now packed to the rafters with a broad mix of faces, many of them old friends, from SOCA and Forensics, as well as other support personnel. Dozens of chairs faced the front of the room where a projector had been set up with "Operation Broken Chains" staring down at the audience. A beanpole thin man that Knox knew well stood behind a tiny lectern. At the sight of Knox, he smiled and mouthed hi then waved for silence. She settled in at the back of the room, stunned at how many of the Met's finest had been assembled at half an hour's notice and over lunch no less.

Detective Chief Inspector Oliver "Ozzy" Calder waited

'As you all know, the fight against slavery is never-ending. As soon as we close down one trafficking group, another pops up to take its place. There is simply too much money to be made trafficking in human misery.'

A wiry younger man piped up from the other side of the room. 'Cheerful way to start, boss!'

Knox took an immediate dislike to him. He was younger than her, in his late twenties at most. He still had a boyish face with dirty blond hair that flared out which contrasted against a weak, hairless, chin that wobbled as he spoke. It made him look a bit like he had a tousled mop for hair.

'Quiet down, Yohann,' Ozzy said. 'We're not in the business of giving up. This morning Detective Inspector Knox—'

News hadn't spread to SOCA of her demotion then. Knox gingerly raised her hand, wondering why on earth she felt the need to be quite so forward. She was acutely aware when the entire room turned its focus on her, dozens of friends and colleagues holding their breath to hear her mumble, 'Detective Sergeant actually.'

Ozzy's eyes narrowed just for a moment, a mixture of confusion and suspicion.

'As I was saying, DS Knox made contact with a woman this morning she suspects to have been trafficked from Thailand as part of an unrelated murder inquiry. We've been watching several nail bars including the Katz Klawz nail bar for the better part of a year now and this is our first solid lead.'

'Why haven't we made any progress in a year?' It was Yohann again. From the exasperated looks on the faces of the rest of the team, Yohann made a habit of interrupting.

'Simple,' Ozzy said. 'They seem to use a cell structure much like a terrorist organisation. Each nail bar is run by an older woman – usually herself a victim of trafficking – and that puts a layer between us and the real criminals. As soon as we go in, they cut and run.

Yohann piped up once more. 'Where are they trafficking the victims from? The usual?'

By usual, he meant Asia and Eastern Europe. The overwhelming proportion of trafficking victims originated from some of the poorest countries the world: Vietnam, Cambodia, and Thailand. Traffickers lured them with the promise of a better life, seized their passports and then press-ganged them into service. The "lucky" ones endured a life of domestic servitude or back-breaking days toiling in fields picking fruit. The unlucky ones ended up in brothels.

'Is it just recruitment driven?' Knox asked. As well as false promises of employment, traffickers often forcibly abducted their victims, bought them from their families and even seduced them. The last was the hardest to track. So-called "Romeo Pimps" wooed their victims with a surge of romantic affection, grooming their victims so slowly that they were the proverbial frog being boiled alive. Before the victims even knew it, they were isolated from their friends and family, trafficked around the globe, and then forced into prostitution.

'We think this is largely Triad-led,' Ozzy said. 'We know they tend to stick to job adverts because it's low hanging fruit. The poorest victims willingly sign up to be smuggled into Europe or the USA. They often pay for the privilege. Our colleagues on the continent have been trying – and failing – to secure the most porous borders into the Schengen Zone.'

'What's the plan, boss?' Yohann asked.

Ozzy paused and Knox knew he was about to say something unpopular. 'We have to use the victim Knox met with as bait.'

Hush fell upon the room. It was the logical way forward but it meant putting a known victim in danger.

Knox cleared her throat. 'My victim intimated that she was being forced to work multiple jobs. Her day job is for Katz Klawz but she specifically said her second job was "working in Soho". I think we all know what that means.'

Prostitution. The biggest driver of all human trafficking. Victims, almost always women, were dragged to London to service the appetites of London's deviants. The gangs could charge upwards of a hundred pounds per client with each woman seeing dozens of clients every night.

'The plan is simple. Knox is going to return to Katz Klawz for her follow-up appointment to have her nails decorated. When her victim moves onto Soho, we're going to follow. Yohann, you'll be posing as a walk-up client.'

'Wired?'

'No,' Ozzy said firmly. 'There's no point building a case against these victims. I want the handlers. We don't want a tiny win rescuing a handful of women. We want to bring in the madams running the brothels and get them to turn Queen's Evidence. Today isn't about convictions, it's about getting the information we need to stem the flood of victims into the UK.'

'No pressure then,' Yohann said.

'Between now and then, I need comms watching mobile phone activity in the area. Ian, I want you mapping all the cars that go past the ANPR cameras around Katz Klawz. Cross reference that against the ANPR data from previous surveillance efforts, please. Anything that pops up, let me know.'

Ian had slunk down so far in his chair that Knox hadn't even noticed him in the third row from the front. Once again, Knox was struck by how quickly Ozzy had assembled such a diverse group with apparent ease. Was this what it was like working for a competent chief inspector?

At Ozzy's request, Ian straightened up and nodded. 'On it like Fairbanks on chocolate cake.'

'DS Knox, my office, please. We need to get you prepped. Any questions? No? Get to it then people. Time is of the essence.'

# Chapter 33: A Reluctant Return

It had to be any mother's worst nightmare. Children were bound to have some secrets. Elsie knew that if she ever had a daughter, she'd be happy to remain in blissful ignorance. She'd never told her dad half the things that she got up to. It wouldn't have done him any good to know. Perhaps it would have been different if Mam were still alive. Perhaps she'd have listened to Elsie's stories of boys, sex, bunking off classes at college and sipping vodka and coke in the park. They were the sort of follies that practically everyone enjoyed. The only advice Elsie would ever dish out to a teenager would be practical – wear a condom, don't drink and drive, and drugs are addictive so if you have to partake stick to the marijuana.

The secrets that Beya had to hear were far more serious. It was with a heavy heart that Elsie knocked at her front door.

'Miss Mabey! You have news? Come, come. I make the tea.'

Oh God, not the tea again. Beya had bounded off before Elsie could ask for water instead so she gingerly shut the door behind her and traipsed into the kitchen where the smell of baking bread wafted through the air.

'That smells amazing, Beya.'

'You like?' Beya said. 'Have some. I make too much.'

'I couldn't possibly...' Elsie protested half-heartedly. Beya wasn't listening anyway and Elsie knew she'd be leaving burdened with as much bread as Beya could fit into a shopping bag assuming, that was, that Beya didn't hate her after this conversation.

'I spoke to a young man called Vito—'

'That boy no good,' Beya said. 'He come here. He put feet on my sofa. Rude, rude boy.'

'He's made some allegations.'

A dark shadow crossed Beya's face. 'I know. The reporters come ask me if they true.'

She had to ask. She winced as she did. 'Are they?'

'No!' Beya stomped. 'How dare you think my Nelly be like that? Where all this money he say she made? Where all nice things he say she given? Look around you, Chief Inspector Mabey, this is Croydon.'

The kitchen was remarkably shabby in comparison to Beya's attire. Last time Elsie was here, she hadn't noticed that the paintwork was peeling off the walls. The kitchen hob, clean though it was, had seen better days. If Nelly had joined the ranks of the uber-wealthy, her family home hadn't benefitted from the extra cash.

Another pang of guilt. Elsie didn't want to ask the next question either. Sometimes being a detective meant hurting the families of the dead. 'Would you mind if I looked in her bedroom?'

'Go. Go look. When you find nothing, I will be here.'

'Which room is it?'

'Up the stairs, third on the left.'

All the way up the stairs there were photos of Nelly and Beya throughout the years. There was Nelly's first day of school when her face was almost cherub-like, and then, at the top of the stairs, a photo of her dressed up and ready to hit the town for her eighteenth birthday complete with oversized birthday girl badge and helium balloons.

Families reacted one of three ways to a murder. The most common reaction was to spend far too much time in the room of the deceased, weeping for the departed. The second technique was avoiding the room entirely. As the bedroom door was firmly closed, it seemed that Beya hadn't had the heart to go in since her daughter's murder.

The third – and far more extreme reaction – was to renovate the room entirely, destroying any and all evidence of the person that had once lived in it. Beya was nowhere near the moving-on stage and wouldn't be for many years.

When Elsie opened the door, she found a room that was far removed from the little girl in the photograph. There were no pastel pinks here. Instead, the room was dominated by a huge bed, at least a king-sized, made up of an ornate metal frame and a thick, expensive memory foam mattress behind which was a three-panel canvas showing a champagne glass and two jazz musicians. Equally expensive sheets and a silk duvet cover completed the look. The colour palette was rich deep red and plum colours which tied together the walls, the curtain drapes, and even a red wooden divider at the end of the room.

It was stylish, an oppressively dark plush look which was not at all to Elsie's taste, but Nelly had made the room her own. On the other side of the divider was a desk with space for a laptop. Elsie knew that Fairbanks' team would have already taken that in for evidence. A handful of books, all of the "finding yourself" variety, were arranged alphabetically on a shelf high above.

There was no sign of cash anywhere.

Where would Nelly have hidden things in this room?

It was a bit of a conundrum for Elsie. Despite being the only daughter of a police detective, she hadn't had to work hard to elude him. Before she was a teenager, she already knew where criminals hid their drugs and money. She had learned about the Ziploc bag in the toilet cistern, about the drugs taped to the underside of drawers, and even about her father's own favourite hiding places. The great DCI Peter Mabey had once confessed to hiding pocket money from his father by unscrewing the fascia of a plug socket, tucking the money into a drawstring bag inside the partition wall, and looping his stash over the rear of the plate for easy retrieval later on.

It meant that her father had become overconfident. He was so sure that he'd be able to find any contraband that he assumed Elsie didn't have any. When she did eventually decide to hide a pack of cigarettes – which eventually ended up in the bin after the first one made her choke and vomit – she simply stashed it inside her underwear drawer knowing that her dad would never in a million years rifle through her unmentionables. He was barely around with work anyway and Elsie had always been responsible for the domestic chores so it was pretty easy to keep things a secret.

Nelly never had that opportunity. Beya was one of those parents who lived for, and through, her children. Nelly was Beya's sole focus all day, every day. It must have been a stifling environment to grow up in with little chance to grow, to experiment, and to fail.

If Elsie had been brought up like that, how would she hide something from a loving yet overprotective mother? It came down to space. If the allegations that Vito had made were true then Nelly would have needed to conceal drugs, jewellery and money.

Sniffer dogs would find the former pretty quickly. If Elsie didn't have any luck searching by herself then that would be the logical next step. It wasn't ideal though. Poor Beya was traumatised enough and seeing a search team tear the house down in search of her dead daughter's drug stash would break her heart.

The bedroom was nearly empty. There was nowhere obvious to hide things. The mattress had no lumps or tears where things could be put inside. There wasn't any room under the bed because Nelly had stuffed dozens of pairs of shoes under there.

The chest of drawers concealed Nelly's first secret, though what Elsie found wasn't exactly well hidden. Sex toys. Dozens and dozens of sex toys. Elsie slammed the drawer shut as quickly as she'd opened it. There might be something hidden underneath but looking in there again would be a last resort.

Her next stop was the bathroom. The medicine cabinet was largely filled with over-the-counter painkillers, contraceptives and a surprising variety of supplements. Why on earth had Nelly needed so many pills? On the first shelf alone Elsie could see multivitamins, fish oil capsules, St John's Wort and a microwaveable eye mask in a box which bragged that it could stop dry eyes in ten minutes a day. She might have to try that one herself.

She was about to give up except for a little niggle in the back of her mind telling her that there was something somewhere in Nelly's room. She backtracked out of the bathroom and scanned around once more.

Nothing jumped out.

Shoes! Why on earth did she have so many pairs hidden under the bed? The layer of dust on them was so thick that they hadn't been worn for many months so it wasn't simply that Nelly was a shoe addict.

Elsie sat on the floor crossed-legged in order to drag the shoes out, one pair at a time, causing a great cloud of dust to puff up into the air and make her want to sneeze. There were many low-profile shoes – no good for hiding things in – and a couple of pairs of knee-high leather boots. She homed in on those.

They were much more expensive than the kind of boots that Elsie allowed herself to buy though at her height, the choice was limited. Because of her height, she had to buy most of her shoes at a shoe shop in Soho that specialised in selling to transsexuals and drag queens. The shop, which was subtly named *High Heels for Tall Folk*, had no problem stocking a size nine and a half shoe capable of supporting a six-foot-tall woman.

Her 'aha!' moment came when she picked up the nicest pair of boots. They were less dusty than the other shoes and once they were in her hands, Elsie realised that the left boot was markedly heavier than the right. She flipped it upside down to decant its contents. A small bag of white powder fell out. Bingo. Cocaine. There had to be a few hundred pounds worth there. It was enough to make Elsie think that Nelly had been a user but not enough to have been dealing. Elsie pulled out an evidence bag from her pocket, turned it inside out, and bagged the powder. A sample would go to the lab to confirm that it was coke.

Now came the hard part. Beya.

Elsie pocketed the evidence bag and headed down the stairs. Beya was waiting for her at the bottom.

'So?' Beya prompted. 'You find what you seek?'

Her tone was pleading. She was desperate to cling onto the image of the gorgeous little girl pictured on the stairs.

'No,' Elsie lied. 'I didn't find anything.'

Beya broke into a broad, relieved, smile. 'I told you Vito was a bad man. Come, come have some tea.'

# Chapter 34: An Office with a View

Ozzy had a top-floor office with a view right out over the Thames and across the river to Waterloo.

'It's been too long, Knox,' Ozzy said. 'You haven't changed a bit.'

'Apart from the grey hairs,' Knox said. 'I've got a few more lines too. Nobody warned me my thirties would be this tough.'

'It's the stress,' Ozzy said. 'I had my fortieth birthday a couple of weeks ago but I feel like a pensioner some mornings. Don't you miss the good old days of us running around as sergeants? We thought we knew it all.'

'Only morons think they know it all. The older I get, the more I know that I don't know.'

'Can I ask about the elephant in the room?'

She rolled her eyes but nodded anyway.

'What happened?'

'Fairbanks and I had a disagreement,' Knox said simply. When Ozzy motioned for her to carry on, she sighed. 'He made a catastrophic mistake which he somehow pinned squarely on yours truly.'

'That's nothing new. Fairbanks messing up I mean. But why'd he pin it on you?'

Like every good detective, Ozzy was like a dog with a bone. He'd never let it go. Knox glanced at the clock and stalled for time, knowing that she could avoid Ozzy for a while after she'd helped with the Katz Klawz investigation. 'Ozzy, time is getting away from us. We need to be ready for tonight.'

'Fine,' he said, his expression one of pity rather than annoyance. 'I know something funny is going on here. I've heard all the rumours. You can trust me, you know. I'll have your back if you need me to.'

'I appreciate that, Ozzy. But I'd rather just move on. Tell me what you need tonight.'

'Okay, okay. Tonight is simple. I want you wired up and going back for the follow-up appointment you arranged earlier. Ask as many questions you can about how many other women work at Katz Klawz, how long she's been a beautician—'

'Technician. That's what they're called, Oz.'

'Whatever. You get my drift. The more information you can get, the better. I'll be in a van around the corner with Ian. Obviously, you won't have a panic button so if you need reinforcements just say the phrase "What can I do about my damaged cuticles?" and we'll come running.'

'Really? Bit of a long phrase in an emergency. How about "Help!"?'

'You know we'll come running if we hear anything obvious. This is just if you need to be subtle. While you're there, see if you can give Sumiko this.' Ozzy slid what appeared to be a lipstick across the desk.

'GPS?'

'Latest and greatest. It's accurate to within a few feet and small enough to hide inside the lipstick.'

'No way to find it without using it up first then.'

'Exactly.'

'You want me to give it to Sumiko?'

'If you can. No harm if you can't. It just makes everything a bit easier. If we can watch the GPS tracker move, we can line it up with the car in which Sumiko travels. Then we'll be able to look up the owner of the car before we move to intercept. This is an intel-gathering exercise after all, and the more we know, the better the outcome

Knox put the lipstick in her handbag next to her actual make-up. 'I feel like James Bond. Or the female equivalent. Jane Bond? Nah, that sounds a bit naff.'

Ozzy ignored her. 'When you're done, leave and head to So-ho by car but take a roundabout route. You know that safe house we've got in Peter Street?'

'By Westminster College? Dodgy roll-up garage looking place near the walk-ups?'

'That's the one. It should be a good base for wherever these girls are working. It gives us a response time of five minutes or less to anywhere in Soho via motorbike, a bit more if we need a squad car. You know what traffic is like around there. I've asked Yohann to head over now to get ready.'

'You sure we haven't been made?'

The safe house was almost as old as Knox. If the criminals knew it belonged to the police then any operation would be compromised.

'Totally sure.'

It was good enough for Knox. 'Alright, let's do this thing.'

IT WAS HALF AN HOUR before closing when Knox returned to Katz Klawz. Sumiko was still working and the Sister

was loitering nearby, looking every bit as stern as she had done earlier in the day. There were still no customers.

'Hi!' Knox said. She forced herself to smile despite her pulse racing along at a hundred beats a minute. 'Can we put another coat on and then decorate my nails as we planned? I'd like little those flowers, please. You did a great job today but work has ruined them and I want everything to be perfect for my date.'

Before coming in, Knox had roughed them up as best she could.

'Sit, sit,' Sumiko said, her voice pitching unnaturally high. The Sister leered at them.

Knox took her seat. 'I'm so sorry to be a pain but can we put on an extra coat before we do the decorative work? I work in the back of a big restaurant doing the washing up and it's *so* punishing on my nails.'

'No problem. I can make all good for you for tonight.'

The urge to reassure Sumiko was overwhelming. Knox couldn't say anything out of the ordinary while the big woman was watching. How could she tell Sumiko that everything was going to be okay without overtly saying so?

'It's going to be a wonderful night. He's taking me out for dinner.'

'You lucky girl, where you going?'

'Just somewhere in town,' Knox said, picking every word carefully. 'It's a surprise. There's this little restaurant on Wardour Street that we both love.'

The name of one of Soho's most famous streets pricked Sumiko's ears. Knox could see her beginning to breathe a little faster, her face flushing red.

'When you eating? I like to eat early.'

Good girl, Knox thought. It seemed Sumiko understood what Knox was trying to convey. 'Probably half six, maybe seven. They do a lot of early-bird deals. I want to get there before it gets too busy. I hate it when a restaurant is full, don't you?'

'Me too, me too.'

Sumiko deftly finished restoring Knox's nails.

'Can we do those lotus flowers that you did for my friend?' Knox asked.

Sumiko inhaled sharply and looked at the Sister. 'So sorry, no have time for such complicated design today. How about simple flower like one behind me?'

Sumiko pointed to a photo on the wall.

'That's fine. Let's do what we can with the time we've got.'

Knox mentally rehearsed she needed to find out from Sumiko. Ian and Ozzy were listening in from a van around the corner. They were probably cursing her lack of progress right now.

'This is a big place,' Knox said. 'Do many girls work here?'

Sumiko leant forward. 'Many come and go.'

How many? Knox wondered. Was this nail bar a revolving door of trafficking victims?

'Have you been here long?'

'Since summer.'

Five months. That was a lifetime of slavery. Knox felt her jaw tremble as anger flooded through her. She forced herself to stay calm.

'Maybe one day you'll have the chance to run your own place.'

The thought elicited a wan, disbelieving smile from Sumiko who said nothing and continued to apply the topcoat to Knox's nails.

When she was done and it was time to pay, Knox made a big show of putting her handbag on the counter as she fished for her purse. With only the slightest encouragement, her bag toppled over, spilling its contents all over the counter.

'I am so clumsy sometimes,' Knox said as she shovelled nearly everything back into the bag. After a quick glance at the Sister to make sure she wasn't looking, Knox nudged the lipstick towards Sumiko and winked. The bill was quickly settled as the clock ticked towards six, and Knox made a beeline for the door.

'Miss!' the Sister called out. 'You forgot your lipstick.'

Fuck.

# Chapter 35: Out of Place

H e couldn't have looked more out of place if he'd tried. The premises of Quadrozzi Dress Design & Haberdashery on Bond Street were undeniably feminine. The walls were adorned with cream wallpaper with seams of gold tracing floral patterns. The dress selection was mostly wedding dresses with one long wall reserved for evening gowns that ranged from elegant to sleek and sexy. The one thing that every dress on sale had in common was the extravagant price tag. None matched the black lace gown that Leonella Boileau had been found wearing.

A young woman dressed in a smart jacket and skirt combo approached him. She appeared bemused to find a man dressed in khaki trousers perusing their wares. 'Can I help you, sir?'

'Are you the owner?'

'The proprietress is currently with a client, Mr...?'

'Stryker, and it's detective inspector. Could you tell her the police need a word please, love?'

For a split second her eyes went wide and then her shock was gone as quickly as it came. She had an impressive poker face. 'What shall I tell her this is regarding?'

'Murder.'

Her poker face failed her. She scurried off through the door at the back, presumably to find Mrs Quadrozzi. When she hadn't emerged after two minutes, Stryker went after her. As soon as he pushed through the door marked "Private", he found himself in a huge open room with what appeared to be a tufted futon in the middle of it. In an alcove at the back, there was a long gold rail hung with haphazardly placed dresses in a variety of sizes. Stryker assumed that they had been tried on and were waiting to be returned to the immaculate mannequins in the window out front.

'You can't be here!' a voice called out from behind him. Stryker turned, expecting to see the young woman he'd spoken to before. The voice sounded almost identical. He did a double take. The woman in front of him looked just like the receptionist with an identical heart-shaped face, the same lithe figure and even similar attire. But for the grey hair and the telltale sagging skin around the throat, Stryker could have mistaken this new woman for the first. He'd bet anything that they were related.

'Mrs Quadrozzi?'

'Yes, that is me,' she said. 'You are the rude man who scared my daughter with his talk of murder.'

She sounded scandalised as if the mere mention of a crime would ruin the rarefied air of her boutique. Stryker fished in his inside jacket pocket for his warrant card. 'Detective Inspector Stryker, Homicide Command. I'm investigating the death of Leonella Boileau.'

'Terrible, terrible. I saw her in the news...' She bowed her head in reverence before she realised why Stryker was there. 'Detective, are you saying that the dress was one of mine?'

'I am afraid so.'

'No!' Quadrozzi cried. 'The publicity, the bad press... this is terrible! I must call Walter.'

He couldn't help asking. 'Who is Walter?'

'My publicist, he will know what to do.'

The reality of the situation had escaped Quadrozzi entirely. She paced up and down, barely aware that Stryker was watching her like a hawk.

'Mrs Quadrozzi, you have more immediate problems.'

She stopped in her tracks and turned to face him. 'What might those be, Mr Stryker?'

'I need to know who bought the dress.'

'I cannot!' Quadrozzi said. 'Our clients demand the utmost of privacy.'

'Then,' Stryker said slowly, deliberately pausing for effect, 'surely they'd hate for the media to camp out the front? Might put a cramp in your style.'

'Yes... yes... can you keep this quiet, Inspector?' Quadrozzi said. 'I can pay.'

Stryker ignored her offer of a bribe. 'I can try to keep it quiet, just tell me how your dress ended up on my victim.'

'I cannot!' Quadrozzi protested. 'I sold it, and after that, it is out of my hands.'

'Who did you sell it to?'

'I will have to check my ledger...'

'You do that,' Stryker said. 'I'll wait.'

# Chapter 36: Idle Gossip

The investigation was losing steam moment by moment and hour by hour. The clock was ticking as Elsie stared listlessly at the boards in the incident room. If the killer conformed to Uncle Bertie's expectations, he or she would strike again before the week was out. Serial killers almost always accelerated as they lost control.

It had to be a man. Nelly had a whole life that Beya knew nothing about. Perhaps the same was true of Layla Morgan. Nobody existed in a vacuum. The problem was the complete lack of leads.

It was proving no end of trouble to keep the team on track. Knox was continually disappearing to do her own thing and no threat nor inducement could persuade her otherwise. God knows where she was right now. Stryker kept trying but he was too quick off the mark, never thinking through his actions. As for Matthews, she was greener than an unripe banana. The novice was sitting at the end of the table tapping away at Nelly's mobile phone, working her way down a list of four-digit numbers that appeared to be a hodgepodge lacking order or logic.

She'd dreamed of having her own team her entire career and now here she had it and they weren't acting like a team at all. What Elsie needed was to impose order on the investigation. That meant knowing what everyone was doing, why they were doing it and then deciding if it was the best use of their limited resources. The superintendent was already breathing down her neck to make progress on the Layla Morgan case – though, Elsie noted sadly, he didn't seem interested in spending more than a minute discussing Beya's concerns about how Fairbanks had handled the initial investigation into Nelly's death.

'How're you doing?' Elsie asked.

'Amazing,' Matthews said. 'I can't wait for my date tonight-'

'Not personally,' Elsie said, rolling her eyes. 'With cracking that mobile.'

'Oh,' she said. She looked crestfallen. Elsie could see she had the smirk of a woman in the first flushes of a new relationship. Her father called it "girlfriend head", that ditzy state where a woman obsesses over her new beau to the point that it gets on everyone else's nerves.

'Your list seems a bit... random?' Elsie said. Now that she looked more closely, the numbers were all over the show. Some were numbers that Elsie recognised as the most common PIN numbers. Those had all been crossed off. The next section was something else entirely.

'I'm trying the numbers that Nelly is most likely to have used first,' Matthews explained. 'It's not one of the common PINs. Nor is it family related. PIN numbers that refer to dates are common so I'm working my way through those right now. It's taking a while.'

'Okay,' Elsie said. 'How much progress have you made?'

'I've got four lists to work my way through. I'm almost done with this one.' Matthews pointed at the list right in front of her. It had most of the numbers already crossed off. 'This one is in the format day day month month.'

'That would make Christmas twenty-five twelve?'

'Kinda,' Matthews said with a knowing smile. 'While we celebrate Christmas on the twenty-fifth of December, that isn't true everywhere. For example, Orthodox churches in Russia celebrate on January seventh.'

'Which would be oh seven oh one under your system,' Elsie said. 'Our victim is French-Algerian. When do they celebrate Christmas?'

Matthews' smile evaporated. 'December twenty-fifth. But that's not my point. We can't make any assumptions. Odds are that Nelly would have picked something memorable but not something obvious.'

'Presumably, your second list is year year year year?'

'Totally, and then I've got another list for month month year year. If none of that works, I'll have to go through one at a time like Stryker wanted.'

'Hold up a second, Stryker assigned you this?'

'Right before he ran off for his court case. Was I supposed to check with you?'

'It's fine for now, but just let me know in future before you start something time-intensive.' Elsie would have to have a word with Stryker on his return. Elsie couldn't blame Matthews, Stryker outranked her. Leading from the middle of the team hadn't worked as well as she had hoped. Perhaps Dad was right and you could only lead by doggedly staying ahead of the pack.

'Sorry, boss. I'll let you know next time. Is there something you'd rather I be working on?'

'Keep going on this for now. Do you know where Knox has gone?'

'I think she said she had a lead to run down. I don't know what it is.'

Great, Elsie thought. Another loose cannon to rein in. This team of hers was driving her mad. She exhaled deeply, the exhaustion getting to her once more.

'Boss?' Matthews said tentatively.

*What now?* Matthews needed some serious handholding. 'Yeah?'

'Can I ask you something?'

'Spit it out.'

'You look exhausted all the time.'

'That's not a question,' Elsie said, dodging the issue. Perhaps Matthews was more perceptive than she'd given her credit for.

'I Googled your symptoms...'

Of course, she had. There was no way a detective would just ignore it. 'That's pretty rude, Matthews.'

'I'm sorry, boss, I didn't mean to pry. It's just... Well, my cousin's got this chronic illness that makes her tired all the time.'

Elsie mentally ticked off the many things that went wrong with her body on a daily basis – extreme and unpredictable fatigue, check, headaches, check, sore throat, check, dizziness when standing up, check, brain fog, check. Had Matthews cottoned on? The symptoms were quite generic.

'You've got something like that, haven't you?'

'How'd you guess?'

'You're always tired,' Matthews said. 'You get this sort of defocused, glazed-over look in your eyes occasionally.'

Elsie looked at her curiously. Most people couldn't see it. They just saw a young woman in her prime and assumed that she was perfectly healthy.

'I... nobody ever notices that.'

'Don't worry,' Matthews said. 'I shan't tell a soul if you're trying to keep it private though I know Stryker notices it too. He's always looking at you when he thinks nobody is watching. It's kinda cute.'

He was? Elsie hadn't noticed anything unprofessional... 'I think it's time to get back to work. Don't you have a phone to crack?'

WITH ELSIE GONE, MATTHEWS had the whole incident room to herself. The flurry of people coming and going had subsided as the initial energy behind the investigation began to taper off. The good news was that it freed up her Friday night. She'd debated cancelling her plans, but Knox had convinced her otherwise. 'Work to live, Georgie,' she'd texted early this morning. 'Don't live to work.'

While it was solid advice, it was easier said than done, and it rankled hearing it from a woman who had given her everything to the Met. Perhaps that was why Knox was so keen that Matthews didn't follow in her footsteps, she knew how much life in the force could steal.

Mathews absent-mindedly turned over Nelly's phone in her hands. It was older than most, a boring off-the-shelf black colour unlike Layla's rose gold iPhone. It didn't have a case on it and the number of scratches suggested it never had. A hairline crack ran down the top corner of the phone as if it had been dropped at least once.

The battery was at full so it was time to start trying PIN numbers again.

Birthdays were first. Beya Boileau had kindly provided a list of family members that Nelly was close to. Matthews had split them into the day day month month and month month year year format that she'd described to the boss. Beya's own birth date, ninth January nineteen sixty-four had thus become 0901, 1964 and the much-less-likely 0164. Those birthdays were her 'A' list, the most likely to work.

She tried each in turn.

Nothing.

It was a shame Nelly wasn't one of the millions of people who used the most common PINs: 1234, 1111 and 0000 accounted for almost a fifth of PIN numbers. One report that Matthews had read suggested that just sixty-one combinations made up a third of all PINs, and 426 made up half. Repeating patterns like 1212 or 7777 were popular as were numbers that followed a pattern on a keyboard – 8520 sounded random until you realised those numbers formed the middle column of a standard keypad from top to bottom. People were almost always predictable. Unfortunately, Nelly Boileau was not one of them.

Next were numbers with relevance to Nelly. Old house numbers, segments of old telephone numbers, even her high school locker number, were worth trying. Beya Boileau had come through on those numbers too.

It took until Mathews' D list to break in. She gingerly typed each, moving further and further down the list from most likely to least, until an off-the-wall thought came to her – 1962. It was famously the year of Algerian independence and the Boileau clan were French-Algerian.

The phone unlocked.

'Yes!'

It was a clunky old phone. Matthews flicked through the apps. Nelly Boileau had been big on puzzle games. There was everything from Wordscapes to Scrabble. In a discreet folder on the fourth page of icons, Nelly had hidden all the dating apps: Bumble, Tinder, Plenty of Fish and, of course, Review My Ex. Each was locked behind another layer of passwords. Matthews had Googled for each website's password policy and without fail they specified that passwords had to be at least eight letters long, alphanumeric, and have a mix of upper- and lower-case characters. There was no way that Matthews was going to guess that sort of password in the same way she'd worked out Nelly's PIN code. Perhaps Ian could help crack those passwords if given enough time.

The stuff that wasn't hidden behind a second lock would have to suffice for now. The first thing Matthews looked at was Nelly's photo gallery. She hoped to find a visual record of Nelly's life – where she'd been, who she'd been with and what she'd done. If geotagging hadn't been disabled then these photos could be overlaid on a map using the same technique that Knox had used to pin up a visual representation of the victims' credit card transactions.

The photos folder was surprisingly empty. There were virtually no selfies and everything was exceptionally vanilla. There were a few photos of Nelly's family, mostly of her and Beya, an assortment of rainbows and sunsets all over London, and an album of memes and inspiring quotes that looked like they'd been saved from Instagram. Nothing in here matched up with the theory that Nelly was an out-of-control sugar baby with a cocaine habit. From the photos alone, the phone could have belonged to a teenage girl.

The notes section, however, was a different matter. As soon as Matthews opened up the app she found dozens of locked notes. Re-entering the cracked pin code revealed all of them. She had saved explicit photos both of herself and of the men with whom she'd corresponded. Within the notes, Nelly had added comments like "£100 cash gift" underneath which presumably denoted how much the man in question had given her for sending the photo. The allegations were true. Nelly was on the take.

A few taps took Matthews to Nelly's phonebook. Here men were saved simply by initials. Some were simply "M" or "J" while others had the full two initials. Presumably, the monogrammed callers had been in Nelly's phonebook for longer.

It was a huge breakthrough. Any one of these men could be the Lady Killer. Matthews composed a quick email to Ian, the IT tech, with each phone number and asked him again if he'd help crack into the Review My Ex app. Some of phone numbers would no doubt be registered while all of the mobile phones with which the numbers were associated ought to be locatable through triangulation.

DCI Mabey would be delighted with the progress. Matthews couldn't wait to catch up with her. There was a Saturday morning briefing in the team's electronic diary – the second working weekend in a row – and so she decided to wait until the morning to begin the arduous Trace, Interview, Eliminate process using the new suspect pool.

First, she had a hot date.

# Chapter 37: Undressed

It was nearing teatime and Stryker's stomach was growling for his beloved Parmo. The dress had been delivered to an address in Richmond that belonged to one Lady Imelda, the wife of a Russian businessman who was infamous for fleecing the Russian state-owned oil company, Gazprom.

Wherever the money had come from, it had been tastefully spent. Imelda's house had a humble frontage on Montague Road that belied the period features within. She was only too happy to assist the Metropolitan Police with their inquiries. Stryker was whisked through to the open-plan living room which stretched from the front of the house right through the kitchen to a beautiful Japanese garden out the back.

'Lady Imelda,' Stryker said. 'I'm here to ask about a dress you commissioned.'

'A dress?' Imelda said. 'Many dresses I purchase.'

He showed her a photo of the Quadrozzi-designed black lace dress that Leonella Boileau had been found in.

She dropped her head as if ashamed. 'It was my expectation you might come. The dress... it is the one in the news?'

'That's the one,' Stryker said.

'Such a shame,' Imelda said. 'It was a beautiful dress. Ruined now. The lace was flown in special from France. It is rather hard to find now.'

That matched what the lab report had said. The lace was old-fashioned Leavers Lace, a labour-intensive way of making exceedingly fine fabric. This particular fabric was doubly expensive as it was spun from Mulberry silk made by Bombyx mori caterpillars. Expensive, durable, and nearly priceless.

'Could you explain how your designer dress ended up at my crime scene?'

'I gave it away. To the charity shop in town – the one which collects... I forget the name...'

Stryker had to resist the urge to start Googling all the charity shops in Richmond. For such an upmarket residential neighbourhood, there were an awful lot.

'When was this?'

Imelda thought for a moment. 'Months ago. They come to collect.'

'Did they pick it up in a van? Perhaps with a logo or colour scheme on the side?'

'Da, there was a green and white stripe on the side.'

Bingo. Stryker apologised for neglecting the conversation and then used Google Maps to look along the nearby A305 where most of the charity shops were. Bingham Hospice leapt out at him immediately as matching the description. A green and white wave ran along the signage above the door. He showed his screen to Imelda.

'Yes! That is the one.'

'Thank you, Lady Imelda.'

STRYKER SPED OVER, blue lights blazing. The charity shop had officially closed at half past five. He made it there only twenty minutes after closing, and there was still a light on inside.

He parked twenty yards down the road to avoid blocking the T-junction and hopped out. The winter wind whipped right through him as he sprinted from his car towards the shop. The closed sign hung in the window. He banged on the front door.

'Sod off, mate!' a voice called out from within. 'Can't ya see we're closed? We're open again in the New Year. If ye've got a donation, bring it back then, yeah?'

'Police!' Stryker shouted. 'Open up.'

'Yer having a laugh, ain't ya? This is a charity shop, mate. On your bike.'

Stryker pressed his warrant card up against the window.

'Oh, yer not kidding, eh?' The voice was a little less irate this time. He didn't blame the man for wanting to go home and get on with his Christmas holidays even if the rest of the world had to wait at least another week. The locks clicked as the volunteer opened up and beckoned Stryker to come in from the cold.

The charity shop was dimly lit. Second-hand items adorned every available surface. One wall was stacked with hardbacks, another glassware, and another trinkets. Row after row of designer clothing hung on rails that dominated the shop floor. One aisle was given over to Christmas stock, decorations, paper, Christmas cards and the like.

'To what do Bingham's Hospice owe the pleasure, Mr...?'

'Stryker, Detective Inspector Stryker.'

'A fancy detective eh? I take it yer not here about stolen goods.'

'Murder, I'm afraid.'

'Blimey!' the man said. He pulled the shutters down behind Stryker. 'How can we help with that then?'

'I'm trying to track down a dress.'

It sounded stupid even as he said it. There were hundreds of dresses on sale right now, and probably thousands more out back.

'Going ta need a bit more to go on than that.'

'Black silk lace, one of a kind, donated by Lady Imelda. You picked it up from her place around the corner.'

The man nodded at the name. 'Yer in luck, Inspector. I remember that one. Clothing that fancy goes in the window, see? Our man Barney does the pickups and Lady Imelda calls every fortnight or so. Daft woman must spend Monday ta Friday buying stuff, and then Saturday packing it all up again for us... not that we're complaining mind you!'

'Do you know who you sold it to?'

'Not off-hand,' the man said. 'Gimme a mo. I can have a gander at the records.'

There was an ancient PC on the counter at the back of the shop. The volunteer booted it up and logged in. Stryker tapped his foot as he waited.

'Right, so Lady Imelda's a gift aid donor. That means we can claim some extra money from the government whenever her stuff sells.'

Stryker knew that much. It was something like twenty-eight per cent extra. If they were getting even a fraction of the retail value back on Lady Imelda's stuff then it was a significant uplift. 'So you track her donations?'

The man squirmed. 'Sort of. Each gift aid item gets a ticket number so we know who donated it and how much it sold for. We dun keep a list of what was what though.'

'And how many items did Lady Imelda donate?'

'Last month alone... Three hundred and six.' He leant aside to let Stryker have a look at the spreadsheet on the screen.

Stryker swore. That was a lot of clothing. 'Is there any way we can work out which of these transactions was the lace dress?'

'It would have been expensive.'

'How expensive?'

The man thought for a moment. 'A couple of grand, easy.'

'So if we sort these high to low, get rid of any older than two months and then home in on sales over two grand, how many does that leave us with?'

He clicked away at the spreadsheet to do as Stryker asked. 'Fifteen.'

That was more like it. 'Do we know who bought these?'

'Hmm... Six were sold for cash while eight were bought using credit cards. Want the names of the credit card holders? I'm probably not supposed to give them out mind... can you not tell ma boss about this?'

'Of course,' Stryker said. 'I'll be discreet. What about the other buyers?'

'Might be just one cash buyer actually, there's this one guy I always see in here. Total weirdo. I see him every now and again, and every time he's buying women's clothing.'

'Could he have bought the lace dress?'

'Dunno. Maybe. Last time I saw him – a few months back mind – he bought a bleeding wedding dress!'

Stryker bolted upright. 'Do you have CCTV?' His eyes scanned the room.

'Nah, people don't like being seen buying second-hand goods, do they?'

'Suppose not,' Stryker said. 'Can you come down to the station? I'd like you to sit with an e-fit artist and see if we can get a picture of this dude done.'

'Sure, tomorrow morning okay?' the man asked. 'Only I've promised to take the missus out for a movie see.'

Stryker thought about it. Finding a sketch artist would take a bit of time. A short delay overnight probably wouldn't hurt.

'Sure. Nine o'clock. Need a lift to New Scotland Yard?'

'Naw, I'll take the tube. Just ask at the desk for ya? Inspector Stryker, wasn't it?'

Stryker wrote 09:00 on the back of his business card and handed it over. 'See you tomorrow.'

# Chapter 38: Soho

The walk-up in question was hiding in plain sight with a fluorescent sign reading "MODELS" hanging in the little window above the door. Yohann had been traipsing up and down the area between Brewer Street and Green's Court frequented by London's sex workers. He looked like any other punter nervously working up the nerve to ring the bell. He had seen men coming and going for the last few hours. Some were in and out in minutes while others disappeared for hours.

The system was a simple one operated by two members of staff, the prostitute and a maid. It was the latter who dealt with letting in the client when the punter rang the doorbell. If the prostitute was available – or there was somewhere inside for the next John to wait – the maid opened the door. If the prostitute wasn't available, the maid simply didn't answer and the John could carry on to the next walk-up and try his luck again.

A weird quirk of British law meant that these walk-ups weren't illegal per se. Brothels – defined as having more than one prostitute working – were illegal so these walk-ups were essentially studio flats with the girls taking it in turn to work there. There was debate among Yohann's team on how to deal with these prostitutes. Technically the sign could be used for solicitation charges but it was more common to simply use noise and drug laws to shut them down.

In many ways, it was like a game of whack-a-mole. The moment one walk-up was closed, another opened. At any given time forty or so were open to the thousands of men who passed through them every day.

The most serious charges were for those "controlling" the girls, the pimps and madams. This was fraught with problems too. The traffickers were using the "Big Sister" model where earlier victims were made to control later victims. It was a pyramid scheme of slavery which Yohann had seen far too often in his three years with the Serious Organised Crime Agency.

'They're on the move,' Ozzy's voice said in his ear. The tiny little radio looked like a smart hearing aid.

Yohann saw Sumiko arrive. The Sister was nowhere to be seen but another woman trailed in Sumiko's wake carrying a bag. What struck him was how normal it all seemed. Sumiko could just as easily have been nipping out to Tesco to buy milk. There was nothing provocative about her clothing or make-up, nothing to suggest that sex was on sale. She disappeared down an alleyway off Berwick Street.

He followed in time to see the door close.

Ozzy's voice echoed in his ear, the connection rendering it tinny. 'Give it five, then ring the bell.'

Yohann would have except for the drunken stag party coming the other way down the alley. He couldn't let them get ahead of him. He rang the bell.

The second woman opened the door. She was the maid, the fixer, the one who arranged it all. She beckoned him in and then barked at him to close the door behind him. It was cold outside.

A whiteboard was on the wall behind her which showed a handwritten price list that the maid finished writing as he waited. When she was done it read:

*Per Ten Minutes:*

*Straight Sex - £20*
*Sex + Oral - £30*
*Sex + Strip - £50*
*Oral - £15*
*Hand Relief - £10*
*Spanking (given) - £5 extra*
*No Anal. No French Kissing.*
*No Condom = No Service*

Then, underneath, a list of available uniforms was specified. Presumably, that was an added extra too. It was so cheap – as long as you didn't need more than ten minutes – that it was no wonder so many men came to Soho. Yohann pointed to the top of the board. The maid gave him the nod and so he headed upstairs. Payment would be made directly to Sumiko to avoid straying into brothel-keeping with the expectation that Yohann would tip the maid a few pounds on his way out.

He climbed the stairs to find himself on the first floor which housed a tiny kitchen and a shower. This was the titular "walk-up" which, it turned out, led him up another flight to a grotty double bedroom at the top of the stairs. It was as basic as it could be. Black mould gave the room a stale, musty smell while a double mattress lay directly on the floor. As the first John of the evening, he had the unique privilege of seeing it with clean sheets. Curtains were drawn tight against the darkness outside so the room was only lit by a single pallid bulb. By the window, there was a wooden chair that had seen better days. Paint had cracked on its surface as if it were held together by dirt and despair.

Sumiko flashed a smile that almost looked genuine. Only the lack of movement around the eyes gave her away. 'Hi,' she said. She hit the button on a timer which glowed neon red.

'I think you know my friend,' Yohann said.

'Oh, is your friend coming too? That extra.'

'She isn't coming,' Yohann said slowly. 'She's just had her nails done.'

He hoped nobody was listening in. The walls in these walk-ups were paper thin and one wrong move would spook whoever was supervising the trafficked girls. Presumably, that was the Sister. Yohann needed to find out where she was.

Sumiko's eyes went wide as she realised that Yohann wasn't a client. She turned to a tiny stereo that Yohann hadn't noticed and hit play. *Bad Romance* filled the room immediately.

'Full strip, ten pounds extra,' she said loudly as she gestured for Yohann to sit in the rickety chair.

There was a fine balance to be struck between talking quietly enough not to be overheard and loud enough to be heard over the music. 'Who's listening?'

She couldn't hear him. He pointed at his ears. She shook her head, sat on his lap and leant in close.

'Big Sister be nearby,' she said.

'Where?'

'Near,' Sumiko said. 'We use all flats in this street. One at end is where bosses usually are. Maybe Sister there.'

There were six doors going down the street that led to walk-ups. Ozzy and the team would need to hit all of them simultaneously.

'Copy that,' said a voice in his ear. Thank God the mike had been sensitive enough to pick up that conversation without Yohann having to repeat himself.

'How many are in that last flat?' Yohann asked.

'No know,' Sumiko said. 'Usually man plus big Sister. The man drives me around.'

'And they're definitely in there now? Is there anyone else you've seen?'

They needed the Mr Big, the guy behind it all. Arresting a driver and a madam would risk whoever was in charge going underground. Not that they had much choice. If there were six flats with two women apiece – one prostitute, one maid – and all of them were victims then they couldn't leave them where they were.

'No,' Sumiko said firmly. 'Driver and Sister.'

It would have to do. The timer was ticking past nine minutes. He had to get Sumiko out.

'Ready to go, boss?' he asked of the man in his ear.

'Verbally agree to pay for another ten minutes so they don't suspect you, and then take cover. Shit's going down fast.'

'Roger.'

THE RESPONSE TEAM GOT the nod to move in and Knox felt a surge of excitement. . Without hesitation, Ozzy had included her as part of his team. Of course, they'd worked together years ago, when Knox was still a junior DS. Joining Fairbanks' Murder Investigation Team had been a no-brainer it had got her promoted to detective inspector and she'd had the chance to work on homicide cases. While it was a massive career leap, a part of her missed this, the frantic action that went with life in the Serious Organised Crime Agency.

Ozzy had warned her that, any necessary court testimony aside, today's raid would be the last time Knox was involved in the Katz Klawz investigation. The National Crime Agency was chomping at the bit to take over the investigation. It was only the imminent threat to Sumiko's life that kept the case in Ozzy's hands.

Six walk-ups, six targets. Yohann had the first of the walk-ups covered which left the other five to split among Ozzy's thirty-strong team.

'Which are you hitting, Ozzy?'

'The flat nearest the main road.'

She blurted out the obvious question before she could stop herself. 'Why?'

'Sumiko said as much, didn't she?' Ozzy said. 'Think about it. These guys are running half a dozen girls plus at least one nail salon. This isn't a small operation. Someone, somewhere, has to be watching what's going on. Someone is making serious bank on these girls and they'll want to protect that.'

Yohann's discreet bodycam had shown prices starting around twenty pounds per ten minutes. Six girls, a hundred and twenty an hour, working six pm through to two am or so... It was nearly six grand a night before taking into account the nail bar, any income the gang had generated from being paid to smuggle the girls in, or anything else, and these gangs always had multiple income streams in case the police cottoned onto one.

'Then I'm coming with you,' Knox said. 'For old time's sake.'

'Fine with me.'

The team moved quickly from the safe house, each coming out via a separate exit so as not to arouse suspicion. All were in plain clothes though every officer wore Kevlar underneath. In summer, the body armour was hard to hide but now that London was in the midst of a particularly cold winter, it was easy to hide a stab-proof vest underneath an overcoat. The one lingering downside was weight. Knox had put hers on the scales once and was horrified to see it weighed nearly seven and a half kilograms.

The exit that Knox and Ozzy took saw them head through the bowels of the nearby Westminster Kingsway College. They emerged into a hailstorm which was pelting down on Hopkins Street. Two of the other teams would approach from the north, while Knox and Ozzy's route was the quickest, a straight shot down Peter Street and onto the south of Berwick Street.

Ozzy walked briskly but without running. To any casual observer, he was just another Londoner scurrying towards the tube at rush hour. She and Ozzy were the first to make it to the alleyway. Neon lights advertising models glowed in the six windows they were about to hit. The weather gave them audio cover which allowed Ozzy to speak freely to his team over the radio.

He hit the push to talk button. 'Remember, these women are victims first and foremost – even the Sister. Use your kid gloves, don't forget to caution them. Keep them where they are until everyone has given the all-clear.'

Radio beeps came back from each team one at a time by way of confirmation. They were all ready. Teams two through six were to arrest the women within for their own protection but hold off on bringing them out until Ozzy's signal. He wanted time to bring the police vans around without forewarning the criminals that they were being raided.

Ozzy and Knox's target was the first walk-up on the left. The signage here was less overt and the door solid wood rather than glass like the others.

'Eleven o'clock, Oz,' Knox whispered. 'Look up.'

Two overlapping security cameras had been placed under the gutter so that they were barely visible.

They were high-end unlike the grainy black-and-white models guarding the other walk-ups. It looked like Sumiko was right. This place offered the easiest escape route; the scum-bag running the joint had claimed it with a view to saving his own skin should trouble come knocking.

Ozzy thumbed the big button on his radio. 'All teams, get in position ready to go in ninety seconds after my mark.'

The teams had been briefed to mingle with the crowds on the main road until then. Each would slowly circle the area, pausing to admire shop windows, vape or check their mobile as if they too were simply out for a jolly in the Soho milieu.

Beeps came back to acknowledge his orders.

'Want to hit this one first?'

'Yep,' Ozzy said. 'If we've got a trafficker here then hitting the other walk-ups will spook him. I need you around the back, I'll go in the front. Just like old times.'

Fuzzy images of days-gone-by flashed before Knox. Unlike homicide, the Serious Organised Crime lot spent a huge proportion of their time preparing to execute search warrants, arrest violent criminals and engage in foot and vehicle pursuits. It was physically – and mentally – tough. Ozzy was living proof of that. The physical side of things was hard enough. He spent his evenings and weekends in the gym to stay in shape, a task which grew more difficult with each passing year.

'Hang on... Isn't rule one stick together?'

Ozzy grinned. 'Rule zero. Adapt to the situation. Go around the back and radio me when you're there.'

She pursed her lips as she fought the urge to refuse. This was his operation and he could run it how he wished. She nodded and headed down the side of the building. At the back, there was a tiny alleyway running in parallel to the main walkway. Black rubbish bags were piled up by the back door of each walk-up. Ugh, probably filled with used condoms Knox thought, skirting round them gingerly. But then a pinprick red light above the back door she'd been assigned to caught her attention. Motion sensor! She froze on the spot. Too late, she saw it was attached to a camera, and even as she instinctively ducked, it pivoted in her direction.

Her voice crackled over the encrypted radio.

'Ozzy! We've been made!'

# Chapter 39: Killer Date

Matthews had never been somewhere quite so fancy. Her... man? (it was weird to think of him that way on only the second date) had invited her to an upmarket French restaurant in the middle of Holland Park. Live piano music was playing when she entered, a classical piece she didn't recognise. When the maître d' took her coat and asked for her reservation details, she suddenly felt out of place.

'My date should already be here. James, seven o'clock.'

He sniffed haughtily and consulted a ledger resting on its own little raised table. She watched nervously as he ran his finger down the reservation list filled with mostly double-barrelled names, repeating 'James, *sept heures*' over and over again as he did.

Finally, he said, 'Ah oui, madame, this way please.'

He led her through a maze of tightly packed tables to where her date was waiting. The moment he saw Matthews, he leapt to his feet to pull out her chair like a perfect gentleman.

When he took his seat, Matthews smiled. He was too perfect. That impression was reinforced further when he produced a single red rose from underneath his seat. It was the long-stemmed variety, the kind that still smelled of roses. Simple, elegant, and classy.

'How're you, James? Long day in court?'

He looked better tonight than he had on their first date. Perhaps the spark would come by the end of the evening. It wasn't that he was unattractive. He looked almost the same as on his Review My Ex profile although it had obviously been created with some rather out-of-date photographs. Matthews didn't mind that too much. The important boxes were ticked. James was tall, easily topping six foot, and almost, though not quite, as well-built as Seb Stryker. He had wrinkles and a few chicken-pox scars that hadn't been apparent in the photos. His hair had was greyer too. That was no big deal. Matthews liked the salt and pepper look. It made James look sophisticated. Her biggest concern was his age. He'd said he was in his late twenties and if he was willing to so blatantly lie about that, what else was he lying about?

He smiled, splaying his palms as if it were no big deal. 'Got a big settlement today. It was a door of the court deal.'

'What's that?' The phrase "settled on the steps of the court house," was familiar to her, but she'd never heard of that one.

'Some solicitors are cowards,' James said. 'They don't want everything coming out in court so they settle at the last second.'

'Oh, I see.' Maybe different areas used different idioms. Anyway, it would sound churlish to correct him, so she let it go. 'How exciting. What kind of case was it?'

There was a moment's hesitation.

'It's okay if you can't tell me,' Matthews said. 'I'm sure it's confidential or something.'

'I'm afraid so. Non-disclosure agreements and all that. How was your day? Making progress on catching The Lady Killer?'

He had to ask, didn't he? She shouldn't have mentioned what she was working on during their first date. It was inevitable he'd be curious. It was all over the news. 'Not much I can say on that front.'

'No closer to catching him then?' His tone was almost cheerful.

'Can we talk about something else?' Matthews said. 'This restaurant is gorgeous. Do you come here often?'

'I've wanted to for ages. I've been saving it for a special occasion... like meeting the woman of my dreams.'

It was a bit strong for a second date. To hide her discomfort, Matthews made light of the situation. She craned her neck left and then right. 'When will she be getting here then? Had I best get going?'

'Ha-ha, very funny. Don't be like that. You know I mean you and only you.' He leant forward as if expecting to be kissed.

'Look, James, I'm not meaning to be rude. I know you're buying me a very expensive dinner – thanks very much for that by the way – but you're coming off a bit desperate. You barely know me.'

James blinked, his eyes narrowing to slits for just a moment and then he laughed. 'I'm just messing with you.' He turned away to look for the waiter. 'Sommelier! Can I get a bottle of house red over here?'

As he did so, Matthews slid her chair backwards.

'You're not going... are you?'

'Yes, I am,' Matthews said firmly, 'to the ladies. I'll be right back.'

# Chapter 40: Going South

It took barely a heartbeat for Ozzy to reply. His hoarse tones crackled as he broadcasted to the entire team. 'Belay last order. Go now. I repeat. Go now.'

The whole street was abuzz with action within seconds as the teams descended on the alleyway from every direction. All pretences dropped, they were no longer tourists milling around but highly trained plain-clothes officers. From her vantage point in back garden, Knox could hear movement in the alleyway that ran along the back of the row of houses. She assumed that was one of the other teams taking up position to cut off the northern escape route. The tiny garden behind the walk-up was overgrown with rubble strewn everywhere. A rusty old pushchair took pride of place by the back door.

A crack rent the air swiftly followed by another. If Knox hadn't known better, she'd have mistaken the sound for gunfire. Crack, crack, crack. In quick succession, each of the six walk-ups were struck as door rams splintered wood.

OZZY HAD BEGUN MOVING as soon as he gave the command. His target was the hardest and the most important. Because there was no glass panel on the front door, he was going in blind. Unlike the other walk-ups, there was no fluorescent sign that read "MODELS" nor, once he had broken through the front door, was there a whiteboard with today's price list. Instead, a security door made up of thick metal bars barred his way.

It was a blessing and a curse. He wasn't getting through the door in a hurry but nor was anyone coming out this way.

'Knox!' he said. 'I've hit a barrier. Pincer movement. You're going to have to go in from the back. See if you can flush them this way.'

As he spoke, a gargantuan man came bounding down the stairs. He was unarmed but someone his size didn't need a gun to do serious damage. Behind him was a squat, older man cowering in his shadow. He had a briefcase and a laptop bundled up in his arms.

The moment they saw Ozzy, they doubled back.

'Target is fleeing the drum on foot. ARV team one, we need urgent back up. Two male IC4 are fleeing the scene unarmed,' Ozzy broadcast to everyone before switching to the private channel. 'Knox, they're probably heading your way. Be careful, the big guy's easily six five. Backup is on the way with a TOA of two minutes to your location – don't do anything stupid.'

The armed response vehicle was parked south of the alleyway just out of sight. Ozzy's estimate of two minutes was a best-case scenario. Until then, Knox was on her own.

IF OZZY WAS RIGHT, she had seconds until they headed her way. Time slowed as her heartbeat quickened. Knox kept her eyes fixed on the back door expecting the two men fleeing the scene to burst through at any moment. For that reason, she hung back – getting smacked in the face by the door would be a rookie mistake. She crouched low, ready to spring into action.

She had to stop the two men no matter what the cost. From Ozzy's brief description, she imagined a pintsize Mr Big with his freakily oversized bodyguard. The large man would be a challenge to take down especially as she couldn't afford to let the trafficker escape.

Seconds more passed. Still nothing. Her heart thundered in her chest, the adrenaline making the pain of crouching for so long tolerable. Come on, she thought. This was the worst of it – the moment before the confrontation.

Realisation dawned on her. They weren't coming out – they were going *up*.

'Ozzy! I'm going in. They're headed for the rooftop!'

His voice came back immediately. 'Don't do anything stupid. I repeat. Don't do anything I wouldn't do.'

She shut him out as she approached the door. She turned her back on it, leant forward so that her weight rested on her weaker, left leg, and then mule-kicked the door, driving her heel into a spot just below the handle which she knew was the weakest point in the door. The door cracked but didn't break. Sweat prickled her brow. Knox tried again, and again threw all her weight into the kick. Rewarded by the smallest of cracks, Knox gritted her teeth and tried a third time. The door cracked around the lock allowing Knox to shove against until it swung on its hinges to create a gap barely big enough to admit a small adult.

Once inside, the smell of weed assaulted her nostrils. The back room was a sitting room which had obviously doubled as both an office and a bedroom. A laptop lay next to a bong on a low coffee table in the middle of the room. If there hadn't been a stream of light coming in through the crack in the door, Knox would have tripped over it. Bedding lay on two sofas on either side of the room. It was damp, decrepit, and tendrils of black mould snaked up the walls.

She pressed on to find herself in a long hallway which was dimly lit at the other end where she could see a metal security door, all slatted bars running top to bottom. It was here that the natural light was creeping in, partially blocked by the shadow of a man. As she drew closer, the man came into focus. Ozzy was trapped on the other side of the security door.

'Knox!' Ozzy shouted.

She sprinted towards the end. As she reached the halfway point, it quickly became obvious that she wouldn't able to open the door without a key. She had no choice but to ignore Ozzy and press on. She nodded at him as she ran. There was no time to stop and explain. She swung right and then right again, doubling back on herself to climb the stairs running parallel to the hallway. She bounded up them two at a time while keeping her eyes peeled for people. It was quiet. Too quiet.

The first floor only had a small kitchen and was empty at a glance. No time to clear it properly, not if she wanted to catch the traffickers. The second floor had a bedroom door closed. She had to clear it. Leaving a closed door at her back would be madness.

She paused long enough to get her breath back and kicked the door open in one smooth move.

Screams erupted from inside. Two women were sprawled on mattresses. They wore rags and looked as if they hadn't seen daylight for months.

It called for Knox to make a quick decision – stop and try to help the women or carry on up the stairs in pursuit of the bastards that did this. It was no decision at all.

Once she ascended again, Knox emerged onto the roof. This building, like several of its neighbours, had undergone loft conversion to add precious square footage. The result was a flat roof which left only a small gap between it and the next one over. Eight feet, Knox could jump that far.

The men had a significant head start. Knox could see them running across a rooftop two buildings over. How on earth had they managed to get that far? The rooftops were slick with rain which slowed the big man down. The short man shuffled along behind him, clutching a briefcase in one hand.

Knox took the first jump at a run. She wanted to squeeze her eyes shut as she took the leap of faith. She made it easily. Her momentum carried her forward almost too quickly, the soles of her Merrell's only just finding purchase on the roof. Every fibre of her being told her to slow down, to stop, to find safety. She couldn't. If she slowed down, she wouldn't make the next gap. The two men had made it so she could too. Trusting to momentum to keep her from slipping, she took it at a sprint, the pavement below flashing into the periphery of her vision as she approached the edge. It was a long way down.

She leapt. In the air, time seemed to slow down. It was too far. She stretched her fingers and toes, willing herself forward. She made it. Just. She rolled as she landed. As she did, her radio crackled again.

It was Ozzy coordinating the team. 'India nine nine has visuals.'

Ahead of her, the two men were tiptoeing precariously along the next roof. This one wasn't flat, and the bigger man swayed dangerously in the wind.

'Stop! Police! You're both under arrest!' she called out.

He turned, his face a mixture of determination and terror. His hands shook as he tried to balance. The briefcase slipped from his fingers. It slid down the roof and into the gutter. He stopped and crouched down, leaning precariously with his fingers outstretched. It was just out of reach. He glanced up to see Knox closing in. If he stayed still for too long, Knox would catch him. Did he have time to retrieve it?

Her shadow loomed large over the roof as she prepared to make the leap.

She took a deep breath, eyed the gap, and fumbled with the secure radio. The damned thing wouldn't clip back onto her belt like every other police radio she'd used. She finally managed it, precious seconds wasted. She opened a direct channel to Ozzy. 'Ozzy, he's dropped a briefcase. I'm four rooftops north of the original target. Wish me luck.'

'Four *what?*' Ozzy replied. 'Knox! You're almost forty! What the hell are you doing?'

Proving I've still got it, Knox thought. She jumped. The tile split under her heel with a crack almost as loud as the door rams. She felt the tile give way throwing her forwards. She splayed her arms wide to grab hold and landed with a thud face first on the roof, her chest slamming down and a ripple of agony radiated across her chest. The gap had closed. The two men weren't far ahead. If only she could get up. A sharp pain emanated from her ribs. This was getting to be too dangerous. Desperately, she shouted again, 'Stop! You're under arrest.'

As she struggled to her feet, the tiny man hesitated, his eyes wide with fear, and then he made his decision. He left the briefcase behind.

She thumbed her radio. 'Ozzy,' she said, 'they're heading north. I can see there's a fire escape they're probably heading for.'

'On it.' With a great heave, she wrenched herself up to a sitting position. The briefcase was almost within her reach. She lay forward, her ribs objecting as she did, and then shifted left through ninety degrees so that her head and torso lay down the slope towards the briefcase. She reached forward, her arms fully extended. Inches short.

She glanced up to see the big man swaying. His centre of gravity was too high, and while the morning's hail had subsided, the strong winds had not. Gusts whipped across the rooftops as she stretched down again.

*One last try,* she thought. She let more of her weight hang forward until she was as far down the roof as possible. Her fingers clasped around the handle. She had it.

By the time she'd hauled herself back to a standing position, the men were almost out of sight, silhouetted against the sky by the bleed of streetlights.

'Ozzy,' she said. 'I've got the case. I can't keep up. Has India nine nine still got eyeballs?'

As she spoke, she saw the big man stumble again. This time, he didn't recover his balance. He slipped, falling somewhere on the other side of the building. She thought she could hear him hit the pavement, a sticky thud that sent a shiver down her spine. It had to be her imagination.

His voice came back strong. 'We've got visuals on the little man. Yohann and I are on the way to intercept. It's too dangerous, Knox,' he said.

'I think the big man fell.'

'Copy that, India nine nine confirms they saw him go. He's not moving. It's too dangerous. Don't be a hero, Knox. Abort now – we'll send India to bring you down when the winds die down if there isn't an easy way down.'

She backtracked to the edge of the fourth roof and looked for a safe way down. There was a window ledge that looked large enough to stand on approximately six feet below the roofline. She debated hanging down, kicking the window in and swinging inside so she could re-join the others in the pursuit.

Fuck that. 'I'll sort a lift down. Don't worry about me, Ozzy. Good luck! Roger.'

She was safe. Now all she had to do was wait for a lift down off the roof. Perhaps she'd even meet a nice fireman at the same time. Today was starting to look up.

KNOX REFUSED TO SEE a doctor until she knew if the chase had been worth it. One of Ozzy's team had patched her up as best he could. Her legs were lacerated and bloody but the pain was bearable so she told anyone who would listen that it wasn't nearly as bad as it looked. Within half an hour, she was back at New Scotland Yard with a cup of tea and a thermal blanket when a shadow came between her and the light.

'Ozzy!'

'Hey, heard you took a few knocks.' Ozzy beamed at his own joke.

'You're as hilarious as ever,' Knox said. 'What happened?'

From the twinkle in his eyes, it had to be good news.

'The big man's dead – the fall got him.'

'Bugger.'

'Doesn't matter,' Ozzy said. 'He was just the muscle. Call it instant justice.'

'What about the other guy?'

Ozzy paused, a shit-eating grin spreading across his face. 'His name was Xiang Min Shieh.'

He waited for the penny to drop. 'Hang on... that little old fella was the *accountant*?'

'The one and only.'

The accountant – a former accountant turned Triad leader – had been on Interpol's Red List for the better part of two decades.

'Hang on, you said was.'

Ozzy's glee subsided. 'Bastard killed himself when we cornered him. He doubled back up when I got to the stairwell and then jumped off of the roof before I could stop him. He faceplanted the pavement right in front of a bunch of tourists. It was lucky no one else got injured.'

'Fuck. Not much justice there then.'

'Au contraire, Knoxy. You got his briefcase.'

'Isn't it all in code?' Knox asked, already wondering if GCHQ would be able to crack it. The Triads were notorious for using complex codes that were unique for each operation.

'We got the Sister. She was in the third flat. Yohann spotted her trying to make a break for it. She's been watching the accountant for years now and wants to cut a deal – her help breaking his records in return for a place in the Witness Protection Programme.'

'She's getting off lightly then. You going to deal?'

'Yeah,' Ozzy said, 'if what she's got is legit, it'll be enough to bust his entire network. And don't forget, she was once a victim too. If she'd argued, they'd have killed her. She really didn't have much choice.'

Knox grumbled. There was always a choice. But it sounded as if the decision was already made. 'I want in on the bust when we find the real masterminds.'

'Me too,' Ozzy said. 'However, as you've no doubt already guessed, the National Crime Agency has seized this. There's no more imminent risk of loss of life so it's out of my jurisdiction. I'm 'fraid you'll have to get back to your murder enquiry. Your DCI has been asking after you left, right and centre. She's pretty pissed off that you went AWOL without texting her.'

'Suppose I could have dropped her a line. It was all a bit rushed,' Knox said. 'I guess I'll have to hide in my office 'til this all blows over.'

'About that...'

'What about my office?' Knox loved that office.

'On my way up here, I saw someone carrying boxes out. Sounds like Fairbanks has reassigned it to his new DI.'

'You're bloody kidding me. Why now?'

'Bad timing, I guess,' Ozzy said. 'It is technically his team's office. If you're caught short, I can spare a desk in our hot-desking area.'

'I'm going to kill him.'

'He's not worth it.'

# Chapter 41: Disaster

For Catriona, cleaning up after other people was a way of life and she'd seen it all. Or so she thought. For years she'd worked in upmarket hotels where she'd seen first-hand how quickly the apparently civilised public could become savages. She'd seen faeces smeared on walls, urine everywhere, and cleaned up more used condoms than any woman her age ought to have. She'd seen televisions smashed in a fit of rage, mattresses thrown out of windows, and even found an elderly guest dead in his bed where he'd fallen asleep but never woken up.

None of that had prepared her for Saturday morning. It was still dark when she struggled down to the house from Holland Park tube station, her cleaning trolley trundling behind her with the wheels spinning against the icy pavement.

This was supposed to be an easy job, a one-off clean for a homeowner who let their house out online on one of the sharing economy websites. Catriona didn't know which website the house was listed on. It could be Airbnb, Homestay, FlipKey or one of the many other websites to have sprung up in recent years. It didn't make a difference to her. A mess was a mess and twelve quid an hour was... well, barely enough to make ends meet, but it was all she had.

She'd never even met her client. All business was conducted by email. The landlord had told her to pick up the key from a neighbour which she'd done with no fuss despite the ungodly hour. The neighbour was a nice old chap who'd said the place hadn't been rented out for a while so she had opened the front door expecting the worst. It seemed this landlord was one of the few who respected the 'no more than ninety days per calendar year' rule that stopped landlords becoming perpetual hoteliers.

The house appeared normal at first, a beautiful Georgian townhouse in a very desirable postcode. When she opened the door and flicked on the light, she found that the interior was as nice as the exterior with an enormous hallway bedecked with parquet wood floors. The centrepiece of the hall was a grandfather clock taller than she was. She turned to grab her cleaning supplies from her wheeled trolley which was still on the front doorstep. It was a strain to lug the thing over the threshold, an effort which made her ticker thump in her chest. It was then that she thought she heard a thud at the back of the house. It was the same sound her husband often made when he fell asleep on the sofa and his arm hit the floor. She put the thought from her mind. Old houses made noises... didn't they?

The second thud followed shortly after. Perhaps the landlord was home after all. It looked as if there was a light on somewhere at the back.

'Hello?' Catriona called out.

An unnatural stillness descended. When nobody replied, Catriona called out a second time. This time, she could definitely hear something. It could just be a cat. The landlord hadn't mentioned one – it would be a bit weird to impose an animal on temporary houseguests after all – but such an omission would be far from unusual.

No. It was too loud. The thud was something – or someone – heavy. Catriona felt her breath quicken as that thought took hold. As an asthmatic, she was prone to hyperventilation.

'Calm down,' she told herself, her voice barely a murmur. 'In. And out. In. And out.'

She had just about convinced herself that the noises were a figment of her imagination or some inconsequential banging like air in the pipes when she heard a different sound. This was the sound of footsteps, growing ever louder. She imagined an intruder coming for her out of the darkness, a looming menace waiting to hurt her.

This time she couldn't control her breathing. She inhaled and exhaled, faster and faster, so quickly that she began to hyperventilate. Within seconds, Catriona began to feel lightheaded. It was the feeling that some got when they stood up too fast yet it lingered for much longer. Another sound. Someone was definitely in the house.

'Hello?' Catriona gasped for the third time. 'Help... me...'

The hallway went dark as Catriona leant heavily against her cleaning trolley for support. For a moment she thought it was her vision fading from lack of oxygen but then the shadow of a man – and it had to be a man because he was huge – barrelled past, knocking her to the floor.

XAVIER HATED THE LARKINS next door. Not only did the family rent out their townhouse, they asked him to handle the keys for them too as if he were some sort of concierge rather than a neighbour. It wasn't a friendly request for a favour either. It was a demand.

He had little choice but to comply. The Larkins family owned the whole street so they were practically royalty around

Holland Park. They even claimed to be related to the Charles John Larkins who'd built the neighbourhood. Whatever the current Mr Larkins wanted, he got. Xavier was home, he had reasoned, so what harm was there?

That was why Xavier had dragged himself out of bed just before six thirty in the morning to let their cleaner in, a woman nearly as old as he was. How strange it was for the old to wait on the young.

He heard the noise just as he was dragging himself up the stairs to bed. It sounded like it was coming from the other side of the wall. Perhaps that cleaner had taken a tumble? At her age, it could be serious.

Despite his own advancing years, Xavier was still the first to venture out into the darkness to investigate, leaning heavily on his cane as he went. He saw the neighbours on the other side of the Larkins' silhouetted against the lights inside their lounge. They must have heard something too for they were pressing their noses up against the glass of their bay window, craning their necks to see what was going on.

The Larkins' front door was banging against the frame in the wind, a light on inside. Xavier shuffled over as quickly as he could. He was about to click the door shut when he heard another yelp within. He shoved his foot inside just before the door closed and then pushed it fully open. It was then that he saw the cleaner on the floor, her trolley on its side next to her.

The urge to run to her was strong but his head knew better. He turned to lean off the porch far enough for the neighbours to see him and yelled out. He had no mobile with which to call for an ambulance.

It seemed to take an age for the neighbours to respond. Eventually, the youngest of their children sauntered out to see what was going on.

'Get your dad, boy! Tell him to call an ambulance. You got that?'

The kid nodded. He couldn't have been more than eight or nine. Was he old enough to understand? Xavier hoped so.

His leg cracked as he dragged himself back to the cleaner.

'Hello? Miss? Can you hear me?'

By now the lady was spread-eagled on the ground, her arms quivering from the effort of trying, and failing, to push herself up to a sitting position. She was taking short, shallow breaths. Xavier knelt down next to her without thinking and immediately realised that he'd have almost as much trouble getting back up as she would. Hopefully, someone would be along soon to help them both to their feet.

From here, he could grab her wrist to check her pulse. It was fast but steady. She wasn't in any immediate danger. 'What's your name, miss?' he asked. When she didn't reply, he repeated himself a little louder.

Her eyes flickered behind her eyelids and then opened just enough for her to realise someone had come to her aid. She wasn't unconscious just yet. 'Kah... tree... na...'

It was a struggle to make out what she was saying. Xavier could see her purse beside her, cards spilling out. He glanced at the top one to double-check her name before tidying them away.

'Okay, Catriona, help is on the way.' He didn't dare add "I hope".

She mumbled something he couldn't quite hear. He leant in closer again.

'What is it, Catriona?' Xavier said, his neck twisting back and forth as he looked out the front door for any sign of help. 'How can I help you?'

'Man... barge... past...'

She had to be delusional. This looked like a classic slip and trip, something Xavier was all too familiar with given the age of his friends. 'Forget about that for a moment. Tell you what, why don't I go and get you some water? Your voice is cracking.'

Satisfied that she could be left alone for a moment, Xavier heaved himself up ever so slowly, his knees crackling with pain as he rose. If the Larkins' house was laid out in the same way as his own, the kitchen would be at the back of the house adjoining the garden. He pushed the hallway door open and caught a whiff of meat, a kind he couldn't quite place. It was subtle, delicate, a little like pork.

Slow, careful steps took Xavier into the kitchen, his bones aching from having been kneeling on the floor. The kitchen was already lit which set Xavier's nerves on edge. Perhaps the woman wasn't delusional after all? If she'd fallen on the way in, why was the kitchen light on? He felt his muscles tense as if ready to fight. How ridiculous at this age. What was he supposed to do, have a heart attack in front of an intruder? He swallowed, put the thoughts of Catriona's dark stranger out of his mind, and opened the door.

He froze in the doorway. Surely the scene in front of him couldn't be real? Time seemed to unfreeze and he heard screaming, a pained sound that sounded alien to him. And yet, it was coming from him. The scene before him had unleashed a guttural reaction that he couldn't stop.

There, on the kitchen floor, was a young woman, undressed, with a knife sticking out of her chest. Behind her, a spurt of blood was splattered all over the wall like a Jackson Pollock painting.

His mind focused as he turned away from the horrors in front of him.

'Help!' he yelled, hoping that the useless neighbours next door might finally hear him. 'Help!' he yelled again and again. He could feel his heart palpitating in his chest. At this rate, Catriona might not be the only one in need of medical assistance. He forced himself to breathe. In and out. In and out.

Forget the ambulance.

This was one for the police.

# Chapter 42: An Act Interrupted

The call came in as Elsie was working up the willpower to drag herself out of bed and have a shower. The week's washing was still piled up on the bedroom floor, the dishes were in the sink unwashed, and the kitchen bin still hadn't been emptied making the stench almost unbearable. Without the adrenaline of another murder to investigate, her Saturday morning would have been a time to catch up on the rest that the hectic nature of the week had so far denied her.

She skipped the shower and brewed herself a cup of instant coffee which she knocked back with a grimace before heading out. The address which she had been summoned to was a short drive south into zone two, an upmarket place in swanky Holland Park.

Uncharacteristically, Valerie Spilsbury had beaten her to the scene. Despite the early hour, the pathologist was immaculately put together as if she'd been up and working for hours. The first thing that struck Elsie as off was that Spilsbury wasn't with the body. Instead, she met Elsie on the narrow pathway which ran through the front garden and to the house. Her expression was unusually sombre. The doc didn't usually let cases get to her.

'What've we got?' Elsie asked, fearing the worst.

'You should recuse yourself from this one.'

'Why?'

'Trust me,' Spilsbury said.

'I asked why. What's going on here? This isn't a graveyard shift case.'

Elsie looked past Spilsbury towards the front door of the house. That explained why she'd been paged and not whoever was on the morning shift. 'I'm not following you here, doc. If this is a serial killer – my serial killer – then it's my case. If you're not coming in with me, would you mind moving off the path?'

Spilsbury stayed right where she was. 'Elsie, we know the victim.'

The "we" echoed in Elsie's mind. Who on earth did both of them know? And since when had they been on a first-name basis?

'Who?'

The pathologist shuffled uncomfortably. 'It's Detective Sergeant Matthews.'

It sounded like an abstract statement, so matter of fact yet so profound. Elsie knew what Spilsbury was saying and yet it didn't register.

Confusion must have shown on her face; almost of its own accord, her head shook slowly, in denial.

'Like I said, you'll want to recuse yourself from this one,' Spilsbury said. 'Trust me. It's not worth the pain.'

It sounded as if Spilsbury had seen it all before. No doubt she had, wizened and old as she was.

There was no way Elsie was letting someone else take this one. She could just imagine Fairbanks traipsing in and lapping up the media attention. He didn't give two figs when it was a black girl from Croydon and Elsie wasn't going to let him pretend that now he did care. 'I'm not giving up on Matthews, or

Morgan or Boileau for that matter either,' Elsie said. 'Just show me where they found her.'

Spilsbury gave a "don't say I didn't try to warn you shrug". 'If you're sure,' she said and then finally stood aside to allow Elsie access to the crime scene. The pathologist followed her, keeping back a few feet. The front door was open and Annie Burke was already suited and booted.

'Gear up before you cross the threshold,' Annie said.

'Hello to you too,' Elsie muttered. But something inside told her that she'd better copy Annie's professionalism or risk fouling up. So along with a veneer of detachment, she put on the required booties and plastic clothing and made her way in.

Annie launched into a recap before Elsie could utter another word. 'At half past six this morning, a cleaner came by to clean the house ready for visitors who were due tonight. It seems that she interrupted the killer midway through his own clean-up routine. He barrelled past her, knocking her to the floor. An elderly gentleman next door heard the commotion and came to investigate. He then found the body.'

Elsie played it all back in her head, trying to make sense of it. The timeline was jarring. Why was the killer cleaning up early on a Saturday morning?

'I'm not following,' Elsie said.

'The body may help explain,' Spilsbury said. 'Let me show you.'

They left Annie and her team to continue collecting samples, and Elsie allowed herself to be led through to the kitchen where a white sheet covered the body. Matthew's body. Swallowing down the bile in her throat, Elsie asked bluntly: 'is this the Lady Killer, doc?'

Spilsbury demurred. 'Not for me to say. I can tell you that we found her on her back with a knife through her chest. She was stabbed just once. It is consistent with the Boileau and Morgan investigations.'

'How?' Elsie demanded. 'How did the Lady Killer find Matthews?'

There was a thought floating somewhere in the back of her mind, an idea that hadn't yet coalesced.

'Again, not for me to say,' Spilsbury said. 'Can we go back to the forensics?'

Elsie waved for her to carry on while she stared, transfixed, at the body under the sheet.

'Are you going to be okay if I peel back the sheet?' Spilsbury asked. 'It has to be done to put her in a bag but I can do it without you present.'

'No,' Elsie said. 'Do what you need to do.'

She looked as if she might refuse at first. At Elsie's insistence, she relented and pulled back the sheet to reveal Matthews' lifeless body. Elsie tore her gaze away.

'You okay?' Spilsbury asked. 'I can send my report or ask Fairbanks to take—'

'No,' Elsie said quickly. Not Fairbanks. He'd never get justice for Matthews. 'I can handle this.'

She wasn't sure if she were trying to convince Spilsbury or herself. When she wrenched her eyes open, she turned back to Matthews' body, her stomach churning as she tried not to puke.

Someone had closed Matthews' eyes so it looked like she had simply fallen asleep just like the other two victims. Except, the red bloom upon her chest was definitive proof she was dead.

That, and as the pathologist had forewarned Elsie while they were outside, a knife stuck straight up out of her chest.

A quick glance around the kitchen revealed a wooden knife block upon the counter. There was one knife missing. Judging from the gap in the knife block, it was the same knife that Matthews had been killed with.

'He didn't plan to kill her,' Elsie said. 'The murder weapon belongs to the homeowner. He didn't bring it with him. That doesn't fit.'

Everything they'd seen about the Lady Killer so far suggested premeditation, planning, forethought. He'd managed to get in and out of highly trafficked central London locations unseen. This was the opposite. It felt like a crime of passion using any available weapon. Then again, even that thought was contradictory – Matthews had no visible signs of defensive wounds. If she'd seen her death coming, she'd have fought tooth and nail, but there were no nicks, no cuts, and no bruises on her arms. Nor were there any signs of rope marks or restraints. If, as Elsie expected, her toxicology report was as clean as that of Layla Morgan and Leonella Boileau, then it meant Matthews willingly faced her killer and didn't see the knife coming until it was too late to defend herself.

'What doesn't?' Spilsbury asked.

'Our killer is impulsive. He lost control, grabbed a knife and stabbed Matthews. Doctor Burton Leigh—'

'You know Bertie?' Spilsbury asked.

'He's my godfather,' Elsie said. It was mindboggling to think that Spilsbury also knew Uncle Bertie, like the moment Elsie had had as a child when she first saw her primary teacher outside of school. It almost felt as if she were in a bad dream watching, dissociated, as the events of the day unfolded. She recognised her own detachment as shock, a way to avoid the inevitable feelings of anger and guilt that were no doubt lurking just beneath the surface.

'I had no idea,' Spilsbury said, snapping Elsie back to reality.

'No reason you would have,' Elsie said. 'He thought the killer was a contradiction. He's smart enough to get in and out of St Dunstan in the East and Chelsea Physic Garden without being seen. He isn't on any criminal database.'

'And,' Spilsbury added, 'He knows about anatomy. Your killer was massaging the body to break rigor when he was interrupted. That was how he was dressing and posing his victims.'

Annie had obviously been eavesdropping from the next room. She shouted out. 'He wasn't that smart!'

'Do you want to get in here and tell us why,' Elsie called back.

Annie appeared in the doorway. 'He keeps leaving trace evidence behind. He barrelled past the cleaner today – clearly in a panic – and he left transfer on her and on the doorway. I'm rushing those samples to the lab now by motorbike so we can confirm he's our serial.'

It was a catastrophic mistake. The previous bodies had been dumped in public places. This was a primary crime scene. Why had the killer chosen this house? How had he got in? It clearly wasn't his. Could he be a friend or relative of the Larkins family?

'Cover her up, doc,' Elsie said. 'Unless there's something that you need to show me.'

'Nothing new. The killer followed the same pattern of trying to pose the body. The underwear she's wearing is hers, and it's bloodstained.'

Elsie hadn't thought about what the victims had been wearing underneath the dresses they were posed in.

'Is that consistent with our previous victims?'

'It's not inconsistent,' Spilsbury said. 'Ms Burke?'

The crime scene manager hesitated. 'I haven't run DNA samples from the victims' underwear. We prioritised samples from male donors. What're you thinking, that the killer might have supplied both the dresses and the underwear?'

Elsie shuddered. That was far more intrusive than just the dresses. What was with this psycho?

'Let's find out,' Elsie said. 'Run the samples for me.'

'Rush job?'

It came back down to money. The cost of the investigation was spiralling. With three victims, the media pressure would ramp up again. No doubt Hamish Porter would call in his favour too. And they still didn't know who was leaking information to the press.

'No, standard turnaround on those. We need the lab to confirm that this is the Lady Killer first and foremost.'

'On it,' Annie said. She disappeared out of view to corral the rest of her team leaving Elsie standing with Spilsbury.

'When will you be doing the autopsy?'

'As soon as I get the body to the mortuary,' Spilsbury said. 'She was one of our own. That puts her at the front of the queue in my book.'

'Thanks, doc. I'll be attending myself so I'll meet you there as soon as I can.'

She left the doctor to it, returned to her car, and collapsed into the driver's seat, slumping over so that her head was resting on the steering wheel. Matthews deserved better than this. She deserved for her death to be investigated by someone who wasn't fighting every moment to keep her eyes from glazing over. The tiredness got worse whenever Elsie was stressed and being tired caused her more stress. It was a self-perpetuating cycle that needed several days of rest and relaxation to break. It would have to wait. Now that she was two weeks into the hunt for the Lady Killer, Elsie was overworked to the point of exhaustion, stacking "normal tired" on top of chronic fatigue. She shut her eyes. She'd be okay in a minute. She had to be. For Matthews' sake.

# Chapter 43: The Neighbours

Paramedics were keeping Xavier company when Elsie knocked on the door. A plump woman answered the door for him.

'DCI Mabey,' Elsie said. 'Is he in a fit state to be interviewed?'

'I think he ought to be okay so long as you're calm,' the plump woman said. 'Don't bring up the body, poor gent seems to have suffered a bit of a shock seeing that lady dead on the floor like that. I'll introduce you and then leave you to it, shall I?'

A silver thermal blanket covered Xavier's lap when Elsie was shown through to the living room. His skin was ashen and when he shook Elsie's hand it was clammy to the touch.

'Hi, Xavier, I'm DCI Mabey. Are you up to having a little chat?'

He nodded. 'I'm fine, lass. I don't know why everyone is making a fuss. It's nothing I haven't seen before. I was in the war, you know.'

Which war? Elsie wondered. Surely the man sitting in front of her couldn't be old enough to have served in World War Two? That would make him at least eighty.

'Then I'll crack on. I promise I won't take up too much of your time.'

'Take all the time in the world, lass. I've got nowhere to be. Can't walk too far these days.'

'Must be nice having Holland Park on your doorstep.'

He brightened up at the mention of the royal park. 'Love it. I've been here fifty-five years now. I can't imagine anywhere better to be.'

Behind Xavier's chair, there was a collection of knick-knacks and photographs on the shelf. In the very middle was a picture of a much younger Xavier with a beautiful woman.

'You were a handsome man,' Elsie said.

'Were?' he joked. 'I think you'll find I still am. That's my late wife by the way. She's been gone for twenty years now. I miss her every day.'

'I'm sorry,' Elsie said. Rattling around a big beautiful house for two decades... it had to be hell.

'But you didn't come to hear an old man ramble. What do you need from me, inspector?'

'Tell me what you saw.'

'I didn't see much,' Xavier said. 'It's what I heard. I heard a noise. I thought maybe the cleaner had suffered a fall. When I found the front door open, that's when I saw her – Catriona, I think her name is – on the floor. She said a man had barged past her.'

'Did you see him?'

'I'm afraid not. He was long gone by the time I could get next door.' Xavier gestured at his right leg. 'I'm still walking around with a bullet in there so I'm a bit slower than I was as a young man.'

'How quickly did you get there?' Elsie asked. 'Was anyone else about?'

'Two, maybe three minutes. The idiots at forty-three – the other side of the Larkins – were gawping through the window, squinting out into the darkness. I'd hazard a guess that they might have seen the back of the man as he escaped. Perhaps you ought to talk to them.'

'I will,' Elsie said. 'Before that, I want to ask you about the Larkins.'

His expression darkened. 'I don't like to speak ill of people.'

'So, you're not a fan.'

'Was that a question?'

'Merely an observation. Why don't you get on?'

He sighed. 'If I must talk, I have one condition. Not a word to the neighbours.'

'Deal.'

'The Larkins are all bullies and the husband is the worst of the bunch. His family owns virtually every house in the street. My home is rented from them. Despite being here for years, he jacks up the price every September. He never allows me to paint or refurbish. The Larkins like to control everything and everyone and they do it through money. They are rarely even here. Their house next door is rented out too on one of those online short-let websites.'

'Then the man who came running out could have rented the place out.'

'I doubt it. Before each guest, they send a cleaner. If he had booked it out, the lady I found on the floor would never have been in the house.'

'How do you know this?'

'I handle the keys for Mr Larkins. In return, he charges me a tiny bit less rent. All I have is my pension so I have no choice.'

'Can't you move?'

'This,' Xavier gestured grandly around, 'is home. It is the only place I have ever felt truly myself. My wife lived here. My son was born here. I will die here.'

By the pallid look of him, death might not be too far away. She put one of her business cards on the coffee table. 'Thank you for your time, sir. I'll let you get some rest. Call me if you think of anything.'

THE REST OF THE TEAM had arrived while Elsie was inter-viewing Xavier. Knox was sitting in the passenger seat of Stryk-er's car, seemingly unable to pull it together long enough to get out. Stryker gave a little shrug as Elsie approached. She saw him nudge Knox and point in her direction. Knox slunk down in her seat, dabbing uselessly at her smudged mascara as if a tissue would undo the flood of tears.

Stryker got out and jogged around to the pavement. 'We only heard that Matthews was the vic when we got here. Knox doesn't seem to be taking it too well. Bit of an overreaction, though isn't it?'

'Don't forget that Knox has known Matthews longer than you or me. Matthews did her placement with Fairbanks' team. Besides, emotions always run high when it's a colleague,' Elsie said. 'We all feel it when one of us gets hurt because it could be us next. Naturally, we're overprotective of our own.' The fear of death bred a level of camaraderie that those outside the force would rarely know. The Met was one big, very dysfunctional, family, and no doubt there would be a tsunami of support from that family to try and solve Matthews' murder. Elsie vaguely realised that as lead detective, all eyes and expectations would be on her. She wasn't just investigating any old murder now. One of the Met's own was dead and her colleagues would be out for blood. At any other time, that thought would have terrified her. But right now, she just felt numb.

'So, what do you want to do with her?'

'Leave her to it,' Elsie said. 'I'm going to go talk to the neighbours and then head to the autopsy. While I'm doing that, I need you to find out everything you can about the man that Matthews had dinner with last night. She was out on a date somewhere near here, somewhere posh. Find it, speak to the staff, and get me a proper description of our killer.'

'And then?'

'Go and pick up Doctor Burton Leigh.'

'You want me to babysit the shrink?' Stryker said. 'Can't we send a constable to play taxi service?'

'Go and pick him up. Brief him on developments, get him to the incident room. He predicted this killer would accelerate. The Lady Killer is down to a week between murders. If he's going to lose control and strike even faster this time, we need the best profiler we can get and Doctor Leigh is that man.'

'Fine. What about talking to the landlord?'

'I'll have Knox on that when she calms down. She's got as long as it takes you to find where Matthews had dinner last night to pull herself together.'

# Chapter 44: Blue & Black

The navel-gazing neighbours on the other side of the Larkins from Xavier were clearly enjoying their five minutes of fame. The father was quick to jump in with his story as soon as Elsie appeared as if he had been waiting for this moment his entire life.

'There we were,' he said, 'enjoying *Saturday Kitchen* as a family. We do it every weekend so we can decide what to cook. My wife, bless her, is a grand old cook when it comes to the everyday stuff but she's no sense of adventure. Why, if it weren't for James Martin, lovely chap that he is, we'd be eating meat and two veg just about every day of the year bar Christmas. He was just cooking this tarte au-'

'Ahem, I don't need to hear about your culinary plans for tonight, sir,' Elsie said. 'What was it you saw exactly?'

'Well, several things really. We heard a bit of a noise really early.'

'Before *Saturday Kitchen*?' Elsie prompted. Didn't it start at ten o'clock?

'Oh, you're confused about the time. We watch it a week behind the live show. I record it on my TiVo box so we can fast forward over all the bumph. Can't stand all that celebrity nonsense where they decide if the celeb gets their food heaven or food hell. Utter drivel. Just show me a proper chef making a proper meal and give me enough so I can go away and make it for the fam later in the day.'

'If you keep bringing up the contents of the show, I will arrest you for wasting police time. Do I make myself clear?'

'There's no need to be so snippy!' the husband said. 'I just wanted you to know when we were watching. It was over breakfast. We eat every Saturday at half past six precisely so it would have been just after then.'

'And what was it you heard?'

'The wife thought it was a scream. I told her, "Lucrezia, darling, it's just a fox." They make such a racket, you know. It's like howling banshees around here and all because that old fool Xavier has to feed them. He made such a big deal out of me threatening to shoot the little rascals. One of them had a go at my chickens!'

The man was so far up his own backside and he veered off topic so frivolously that Elsie couldn't decide if she should chide him for threatening to shoot a protected species or try and steer him back on topic.

'As sir is no doubt aware, shooting a fox is illegal,' Elsie said. 'So, if you could get back to this morning, I'd appreciate a more expeditious answer. What did you do in response to the noise?'

'Nothing,' he said proudly. 'We ignored it, didn't we, boys?'

He looked to the two young children sitting on the other sofa engrossed in an iPad. 'Didn't we, boys?' he prompted again.

This time they looked up and realised that their father was staring at them expectantly. 'Yes, Daddy,' they said in unison.

'You ignored it. What then?'

'Then that behemoth of a man came flying out of the house, his dark, greasy, mangy hair flying everywhere. He was like a whirlwind. Probably high on coke or something.'

It had still been dark when the man had escaped from the Larkins' house. How could these self-important idiots have seen anything? As Elsie couldn't be quite that rude without risking the man getting offended and shutting down the interview, she asked, 'Could you describe the man to a sketch artist?'

'Oh no, we only saw him from behind, didn't we, boys?'

Another chorus sounded. 'Yes, Daddy.'

Shocking. The husband was backtracking faster than a government minister.

'And then,' the husband continued, 'Xavier, the bloody fool, came limping out of his house. At first, I thought he'd gone to check up on the foxes or some such nonsense. It's just the sort of thing he'd do. Poor chap came back from the war with more than a dodgy leg if you ask me. But then he disappeared into the Larkins' place.'

*So obnoxious.* 'What happened next?'

'The old codger came back out and started talking to my youngest. Told him to call an ambulance. The cheek of it! Why didn't he call one himself?'

'Perhaps because he didn't have his mobile to hand.'

The husband harrumphed. 'Well, he could have trotted on back to his little pigsty of a house and called from there if he's so careless as not to grab his phone in an emergency situation.'

'Did you call an ambulance?'

'Of course,' he said. 'As soon my son said he saw that poor lady lying there in the Larkins' hallway, I got straight on the blower.'

'And then?'

'Then there were flashing lights and sirens and everything. You lot were on the scene before we knew it and we'd missed the end of Saturday Kitchen.'

'Didn't you say you'd recorded it, sir?'

'Quite right you are. When my poor dear Lucrezia recovers – she's convalescing from the shock upstairs now – we'll have to get the rest of my recipe.'

'Could I speak with her?'

'What for?' he demanded. 'No, no, no. I just told you she's recuperating. She's not fit for visitors. Now if there's nothing else that I can help you with, I shall bid you good day, madam.'

Elsie didn't move. 'Which way did the man go?'

'He got into his car, didn't he? Some nasty old black thing that was much too small for him.'

'Are you sure it was black?' Elsie jotted it down in her notebook.

'Black, blue, navy, I don't know,' he said. 'I'm not a car man per se living in London with the tube on my doorstep. What difference does it make anyway?'

Blue or black. Just like that first witness had told Stryker.

Elsie couldn't resist mocking his over the top patter. 'A great deal of difference, a great deal indeed. If I need anything else, I'll be in touch. I know where you live. Good day to you, sir.' And then she smiled at the kids as she stood up. 'Bye, little ones.'

# Chapter 45: Regrets and Recriminations

The tears had dried up and now Knox was desperately trying to remove her smudged mascara with a tissue and some saliva.

'It's my fault, Seb,' Knox said. 'I told her to go out with him.'

'Last night's date?' Stryker said. 'You couldn't have known what was going to happen. We can't even say for sure that her date was involved. For all we know, they had dinner and she was attacked on the way home.'

'Get real,' Knox said. 'This has "jilted lover" written all over it. Three dead women, three identical MOs. She was prevaricating over her date and I encouraged her to go. If I hadn't ...'

'No,' Stryker said firmly. 'She made her own choice. It isn't on you.'

'Yes, it is. She wouldn't have gone if I hadn't told her to give it a try. This was her second date with the guy – James I think his name was – and she wasn't exactly feeling it. She said he was nice but there was no spark.'

'You thought the spark might come later,' Stryker said.

'Exactly!'

'It happens. I'm sorry but you need to focus on what you can do right now, not what you did or didn't do yesterday. What exactly did she tell you about this James guy? Where did they plan on going?'

Knox closed her eyes as if trying to replay the conversation in her head. Her forehead scrunched up as she failed to pull anything concrete from her memory.

'Relax, Knox. Was it a dinner date?'

'Yes, somewhere posh, somewhere around here. French, I think? She said she'd probably never been anywhere that nice before.'

Virtually everywhere around here was posh, thought Stryker. It would have been much more useful if she'd gone to one of the handful of budget places.

'Okay, was she planning to dress up?' There was no sign of whatever Matthews had been wearing when she'd gone out. The killer must have taken her clothing with him. A trophy?

'She'd ordered something online. I'm not sure what.'

'Okay, we can check her credit card for that. What else? Did she say where they met?'

Knox's eyes opened. 'Review My Ex.'

'Of course,' Stryker said. 'Don't suppose you know her PIN number and Review My Ex password?'

Not only would they need to crack her phone, but they'd also need to get into her account. Even the company behind it couldn't see what messages she'd exchanged as everything on the app was so heavily encrypted. Trying to break Layla's phone had landed him in hot water and it didn't look like Nelly's would bear much fruit either. Perhaps this time would be different.

'Nope,' Knox said. 'There was one other thing – he wasn't as attractive as his photos. It was why she almost didn't go on the second date.'

Stryker rolled his eyes. 'We've all been there. Ten-year-old photos, Photoshop jobs. I once turned up to a blind date expecting this tiny blonde woman and it turned out she was the whale hiding in the background of the shot.'

The anecdote elicited a weak smile. 'So what does Mabey want me to do?'

'Talk to the guy who owns this house,' Stryker said. 'There's no sign of forced entry and that's a Shi-He Chi-Me U-lock on the front door.'

In other words, it was an exceptionally good lock. 'Nobody picked that then,' Knox said. 'You think our killer is known to the landlord?'

'It makes sense to me.'

'Alright. Any idea where he is?'

'Nah, 'fraid not. You're on your own there, Knox.'

# Chapter 46: The Sketch Artist

The clock read ten past ten when the man from Richmond made it to New Scotland Yard. He thundered through the revolving door and skidded to a stop at the reception. He was breathing heavily as he leant on the counter.

'Hullo,' he said. 'I'm Harry Graham. Detective Inspector Stryker asked me to come in. So sorry I'm late. There was a one-under on the District line.'

The receptionist seemed totally nonplussed. She checked the diary, found the entry, and waved at the communal seating. 'Someone will be with you shortly.'

Shortly turned out to be three-quarters of an hour. During that time, Harry saw detectives coming and going at a frenetic pace. There was no sign of Stryker.

At just gone eleven, a woman emerged. She bore no resemblance to Harry's idea of a policewoman. She was short, had neon-pink hair that was about as long as his, and so many piercings that she jingled when she walked. Sod being behind her at an airport's walk through metal detector, he thought.

'Hi, Mr Graham?'

'That's me. Where's Mr Stryker?'

'No idea, I'm afraid. I'm Flick. According to my notes, Mr Stryker wanted us to draw up a composite image of a man who frequented your charity shop. Does that sound about right?'

'Yeah, I guess,' Harry said. 'I thought he'd be here.'

'You're stuck with me,' Flick said. 'But fear not. I rarely bite. Come on, we've got a meeting room to cadge before someone else does.'

The meeting room in question was a conference suite on the first floor. It seemed it had recently been vacated by a large team as there were empty coffee cups everywhere.

Flick made a beeline for the hot water dispenser. She placed a cup underneath and plunged the handle. 'Excellent, plenty left for us. What's your poison, Mr Graham? We've got crap tea, crap coffee or hot water.'

'I'll take the coffee.'

'Good choice.' She poured a second cup and handed it to him. It was thick almost to the point of being sludge. 'The Met's speciality, coffee with enough caffeine in it to see you through a night shift. Brass are pretty good about keeping it stocked. Help yourself to milk, sugar and a biscuit, and grab a seat when you're ready.'

Under Flick's watchful eye, Harry nabbed a couple of packets of digestives to go with his coffee and then took a seat. She'd already pulled a tablet out of her bag and now took out a stylus.

'I want you to close your eyes,' Flick said. 'From my notes, you've met this guy a few times so I'm confident we can get a good profile out of this. Before we start, I want you to clear your mind as much as you can. Today isn't about getting a perfect image down. It's not a painting of our man. All we're trying to do is get down an impression that resembles him. A good impression does no more than jog people's memory. Take a deep breath and then, whenever you're ready, tell me about the first time you saw him.'

'It was a few months ago. I'm not sure when exactly...' Harry paused to think. 'The weather was still warm so maybe September. We'd just had a big pile of summer clothing come in – cocktail dresses, short-sleeved shirts, shorts and the like – which happens every year as people get ready for winter. Yeah, September would be ma best guess. Mebbe at the end. I was sorting donations out the back when I heard the bell jingle. Normally I don't pay attention to customers.'

He stopped for a while forcing Flick to prompt him again. 'Why'd you pay attention to this one?'

'It was this big, blond dude. Really muscle-bound. It was weird. He was rifling through the womenswear section.'

'And that was new?'

'Well... nah. I've seen a few of them crossdressers coming in. They're usually furtive, looking around like they're about to nick something, and they always shuffle up to the counter like a teenager buying their first condoms. It's hard not to laugh at 'em, bless 'em.'

'Not this guy?'

'Naw, he was bold as brass. He looked through the racks, seemed to spend an age feeling 'em as if he could magically divine how nice the stuff was by touch, and then he came up to the counter with a couple of fancy frocks and paid cash.'

Flick scribbled notes as he spoke, though what relevance it had to the sketch Harry didn't know. 'Was there anything that really stood out about him?'

'His eyes. Blue. One looked at you, the other stared off to the side. I'm damned if I can remember which though.'

He must have said something right because she started sketching immediately. She turned the tablet to show him a pair of oval eyes. 'Like that?'

'Nah,' Harry said. 'Squintier like. He had proper black bags under 'em too.'

'Could you see the whites of his eyes above and below the pupil?'

'Yeah, think so... With little red squiggles in the corner too. I remember he didn't blink too much.'

'Dry eyes,' Flick said. She tried sketching the eyes again and turned the tablet to Harry once more.

'Better...'

'But not perfect. It's okay to say so, I won't be offended. What's wrong with them?'

'His eyelids were a wee bit droopier.'

The third time was the charm. The moment that Flick showed him the latest sketch, his jaw dropped at just how accurate it was.

She repeated the process for the other features: jawline, eyes, wrinkles, eyebrows, even the places where the face was asymmetrical.

'How far were his lips from his nose?'

'No idea,' Harry said.

Flick held up a hand. 'Give me a few minutes.'

She pulled tracing paper out of her bag and sketched out half a dozen pairs of lips. 'Do any of these lips look close?'

'The second row in the middle.'

She cut around them and pinched her tablet so the size of the sketch was about right. With a delicate touch, Flick put the hand-drawn lips in place between the jaw (square, hairy and dimpled) and the nose (crooked, greasy and ridden with black-heads) and then moved the tracing paper up and down slowly.

'There!'

His upper lip perched just below his nose. Next, Flick ran through each section again, offering up dozens of similar photos to narrow down which the mystery man resembled the most.

'Can I pick a blend of two?'

'Of course,' Flick said. As if by magic, she combined the two photos on screen and overlaid them onto her existing sketch.

'Bigger crow's feet and they arched upwards.'

A dozen more adjustments – a quick look at clothing to match – and Flick was done.

Overall, it was almost a handsome face. It clearly belonged to a man in his mid to late thirties. A little bit more care and attention would have evened up the unruly beard and dealt with the proliferation of blackheads. The fatal flaw was the lazy eye. It unbalanced the face dreadfully.

'That's him, that's absolutely him,' Harry said.

'Sort of face only a mother could love, eh?' Flick joked. 'Thanks for coming in. If you think of anything else, give DI Stryker a bell, and my apologies again for the delay this morning. Things have been a bit manic around here – one of our own got murdered last night.'

# Chapter 47: Mistakes were Made

Retracing Matthews' steps meant knowing everything about her schedule in the days leading up to her death. Unlike the first two victims, they had a good handle on where Matthews had been. The most immediate concern was finding the restaurant.

Stryker ticked off the criteria. First, it was posh. That wasn't massively helpful. Second, it was French. Third, it was probably nearby. Matthews had used her Oyster card the night before, tapping out at Holland Park underground at ten to seven. Stryker decided to start there. He parked haphazardly next to the Boris Bikes opposite the station entrance.

The station was typical of London Underground stations. There were cameras everywhere, thirty-eight of them to be precise, a mere fraction of the four hundred and eight at King's Cross that Ian had gleefully told him was the record for any London station. It was ample for such a small station. The feeds ran to a central CCTV room hidden in the staff area at the back of the station. Stryker had radioed ahead to let them know that he was on his way so, after a cursory examination of his warrant card, he was shown through to the cramped control room. Here dozens of monitors were mounted in a semi-circle around a single desk. It was hot, cramped, and smelled of sweat.

'I need to trace the movements of Georgia Matthews. Her Oyster card number is 427848927. She tapped out at ten to seven according to the TFL logs. Can you get her up on the screen?

'Is the Pope Catholic?'

It took a while for the screen to spring to life.

'We've only just gone digital,' the tech said by way of apology. 'If ya had come last year, I'd be knee-deep in the old tape right now.'

Judging from the resolution of the feed, the cameras were older than Stryker. He could see Matthews' likeness when it popped up on the screen but if he hadn't known her then the footage would have been of little use. There was no way the quality was enough for a computer to trace her movement. The time-stamp read 18:50 which lined up perfectly with the Oyster card log. Stryker watched as she passed through the barriers alone.

'Work backwards to her arrival at the platform.'

The CCTV tech did as he was told and easily found Matthews arriving on the west-bound platform. Judging by the Oyster records, she had gone from New Scotland Yard to her bedsit off Tottenham Court Road before heading west on the Central line from nearby Oxford Circus.

The tech put her first appearance on the top left screen. She disembarked alone, walking quickly but with a certain bounce to her step. She looked happy. Another camera caught her coming up the stairs and another still saw her weave through the crowds towards the barrier. Before he could blink, Stryker was watching Matthews across five screens. Nothing untoward had happened within the station.

'Outside... which exit did she take and are there cameras out there?'

A few clicks more, a few more agonising moments waiting while time ticked away, and Matthews' likeness popped up on two more screens. The first feed showed her walking across the foyer and past the Oyster machine. The second showed her outside walking towards the park. In every shot she was alone.

'Play it all again.'

He did. Stryker watched frame by frame for any hint of someone following her, someone watching her, or even just someone acting suspiciously. There was no sign of a killer on the tapes.

'She left alone...' Stryker mumbled to himself. He turned to the tech. 'Can you email me a copy of this lot? Sebastian dot Stryker at Met Police dot co dot UK.'

'Sure.'

'Thanks.' Matthews hadn't met her date here in the station. He jogged back to the pavement. They must have met at the restaurant itself and now he knew which direction Matthews had walked. She'd crossed the road on Holland Park Avenue and gone out of the reach of the CCTV.

Stryker retraced her steps until he was standing on the pavement just beyond where Matthews had disappeared. She could have turned left to head north along the A402 towards Notting Hill or turned right to head in the direction of Shepherd's Bush.

Almost straight away, Stryker's gut said left. It looked markedly more upmarket and he could see signs for restaurants. He doubled checked with Google. There were a surprising number of French restaurants nearby.

It couldn't be anything that wasn't exceedingly posh. Matthews had boasted to Knox that she'd never been invited anywhere that posh before, and Matthews herself obviously came from a wealthy family. That took out chain restaurants like Côte Brasserie which were undeniably good quality but not the sort of once-in-a-lifetime dining experience that Stryker was imagining.

Next, he struck off all the restaurants that were closer to a different tube station than Holland Park. Matthews wouldn't have surfaced at Holland Park if either of the adjoining stations on the Central line – Shepherd's Bush to the west, Notting Hill Gate to the east – were closer. That knocked off the likes of Aubaine in Kensington and Le Gavroche near Marble Arch even further east.

Twelve remained. Google had a "£££" rating against three of them, one of which was in the park itself. It seemed as good a place as any to start so Stryker turned left to head for the park entrance which was guarded by the statue of St. Volodymyr. He turned right as soon as he saw the statute, marvelling at the number of cranes in the area. It seemed even west London was now subject to the onslaught of high-rise shoebox flats springing up across the capital.

Numerous cars were parked on the crescent-shaped road leading into the park. There were so many that he almost missed the tiny stone archway on his left that led into the park proper. Once he was inside, he could walk the narrow footpaths that joined up the various gardens. He passed by a large fountain – and another statue – before the path opened out into a more formal garden. A large sign welcomed him to the Holland Park Tulip Garden. He couldn't see any signs of life. In front of him was just a brown, icy mess and Stryker supposed that it would remain that way until spring. On the other side of the garden, he found the restaurant.

It was gorgeous. The building itself was centuries old and it was tastefully lit by chandeliers. Live piano music echoed softly from within. The menu outside was equally impressive with everything from the classic foie gras, pear chutney on brioche to the thoroughly indulgent cèpe consommé with roast chicken and truffle espuma. Google hadn't been kidding about their £££ price rating either. Even with his recent raise for transferring to the Met, Stryker would be out almost his entire disposable income for the month if he bought just a main course.

The maître d' was on the phone when Stryker entered. He seemed to be talking in an over-the-top Parisian accent that Stryker felt certain was put on. The maître d' eyed him with disdain, his lip curling upwards at the sight of Stryker's mud-stained Loake's and a thread-worn old jacket. The sneer didn't entirely disappear when he got off the phone.

From a distant kitchen, the rattle of pots and pans echoed as the day's *mise en place* prep work got underway.

'We are not open yet for lunch,' the maître d' said. 'Does monsieur wish to make a reservation?' His tone was scornful as if he knew that Stryker couldn't afford to dine there.

Stryker didn't have time to mess about. This might be his best bet, but if he drew a blank here, there were two more restaurants on his list to check out. 'Detective Inspector Stryker. I have reason to believe that one of your guests was murdered after she left these premises last night. Are you in charge?'

The maître d' turned white. His accent dropped. 'Murder? Are you serious?'

'Deadly.'

'Come through. The office is out the back.'

Once Stryker had been led through to the back, he found himself in a tiny back room on the side of the kitchen. From here he could feel the heat of the ovens and smell everything that was on offer. It was a dizzying combination.

Stryker pulled up a photograph of Matthews on his phone. It was the Met's personnel file photo and bore only a passing resemblance to the fully-made-up look of a woman ready for a night out on the town. 'Do you recognise this woman?'

The maître d' shook his head. 'I am afraid not.'

'You were working last night?'

'Oui.' The affected accent was back.

'Think harder. She was on a date. After six?'

'Oui... Hmm...' he picked up a thick leather-bound appointment diary from the desk and held it in his left hand. It fell open to today's page which was marked by a ribbon. He flicked back a page and spent what felt like an eternity running his finger down the page, pausing over each name as if trying to match his customers to the reservations. 'Ah, now I remember. This woman came in a few minutes after seven for a date. Her... partner? He was waiting for her to arrive.'

'What name is the reservation under?'

'James.'

'First name?'

'I only have the name "James". I know not if this is his first or his surname. I am afraid I did not take the reservation.'

Stryker cursed. No last name and the first name James – easily one of the most popular in the UK. A person could barely swipe past a dozen profiles on Review My Ex without running into a James. 'What about a credit card receipt?'

Once again, the maître d' turned to the big desk and rifled through his papers. Eventually, he found a stack of duplicate credit card receipts held together with an elastic band. On top was a Post-it note marked "*Friday 14$^{th}$ December*". He searched through them. 'I cannot find one for his table.'

'Look again,' Stryker demanded.

The second pass was no more fruitful. 'I am afraid he must have paid by cash.'

'CCTV,' Stryker said. 'Please tell me that the camera by the entrance is real.'

Surely, Stryker thought, such a high-end restaurant would have a working CCTV camera for security. They had to be a ripe target for robbers if they took cash.

'Of course, it is working... It records for twenty-four hours only and then we reuse the tape.'

Stryker wanted to fist-bump the air. 'Get me that footage, now.'

'Right away.'

Thirty minutes later, Stryker's elation turned to despair. Unlike the older cameras that he'd seen in use at Holland Park, the restaurant had invested in pin-sharp lenses that picked out every detail. The moment he saw the man, he knew that he knew him from somewhere. He was so familiar, so distinctive. Even so, it took Stryker a few moments to place where he'd seen the tall, broad man with the lazy eye. It was the man who lived next to St Dunstan in the East, the "witness" who said he'd seen the car. What the hell was his name? Stryker pulled his notebook from his breast pocket and riffled through, desperately trying to remember the name.

Drew Rekshun. He turned the name over in his mind. There was something strange about it. What kind of surname was Rekshun? He'd sounded vaguely northern but Stryker himself was northern and he knew nobody called Mr Rekshun. He said it aloud.

'Mr Rekshun. Mister Rekshun.'

Misdirection.

'Fuck!'

# Chapter 48: Without a Trace

Seconds after realising that Andrew Rekshun was the Lady Killer, Stryker impulsively leapt into his car and drove towards St Dunstan in the East. He called Mabey as he drove, his fingers drumming against the steering wheel. No answer. She was probably already in the mortuary or knee-deep in managing the press breathing down their necks.

'Damn it!' He didn't leave a voicemail.

The GPS indicated that it was a mere five miles from Holland Park. Back in Yorkshire that would have been a snippy five-minute drive tops. In London, it was almost quicker to walk.

The bloody satnav didn't help either. The robotic woman's voice was as unemotional as normal – machines didn't understand emergencies. "You will reach your destination in... twenty-eight minutes."

The route it had selected couldn't possibly be the most efficient. It had driven him right along the southern boundary of Hyde Park and was now telling him to head through Trafalgar Square on a Saturday morning.

Bugger. He'd forgotten that he had to pick up Doctor Burton Leigh. He couldn't ask Knox to go – she was busy chasing down the landlord – and there wasn't another detective. Desperate times called for desperate measures. He dialled Ian. He answered almost immediately as if he'd been sitting by his phone waiting for someone to call him.

'Yo, yo, Seb Stryker! You finally decided to come to Funscape today, bruh?'

'Ian, I need a favour. You drive, right?'

That would be the last thing Stryker needed, a forty-year-old tech who lived at home and didn't even own a car.

'Course, bruh, you need a lift?'

Stryker swallowed the urge to criticise his fake accent and cut to the chase. 'Doctor Burton Leigh, you know him?'

'Heard of him, yeah?' Ian asked. 'Hold up... is this a work call?'

'I'm WhatsApping you his address. Go pick him up, bring him to New Scotland Yard. Right now. Can you do that?'

Stryker fiddled with his phone as he inched past frost-covered pavements and tourists wrapped in woollen mittens to avoid the biting cold.

'Yuh, can do,' Ian said. 'It'll take me a while... you know I live in Walthamstow, right?'

*Where's that?* Stryker wondered. It didn't matter. Ian was the best – and only – option he had. 'Drive as fast as you can.'

He could hear Ian smile. 'Like a real cop? Can I speed and get away with it?'

'No, you bloody can't!' Stryker snapped. What a lunatic. Ian had worked for the police for God knows how long. Surely even he ought to realise that only highly-skilled, trained drivers were permitted to exceed the posted speed limits. Even then, it was only with permission of rapid response control. Stryker sighed heavily. 'Look, drive fast, but drive safe.' Another heavy sigh. 'And maybe we'll sort out that visit to Funland when this is all over, okay?'

'Funscape, dude, it's called Namco Funscape. Give it the respect it deserves.'

'Ian, not now. Are you doing the job or not?'

'Yuh, I'm walking to my car right this second. I'll have Doctor Whatshisface at New Scotland Yard before you know it.'

Once Ian was off the phone, the traffic worsened. Everything slowed to a crawl as he drove past Blackfriars Bridge, cars running bumper-to-bumper and only moving inches at a time. What was the hold up?

This was a disaster. The boss was going to kill him. He'd been face to face with a serial killer and he'd failed to notice a psychopath staring him right at him. He thumped his steering wheel angrily. Why hadn't he asked to see some kind of ID? It was such a ridiculous name too. Who was called Rekshun?

His old boss had told him never to take anything at face value but that was exactly what he'd done. The mere notion of being a property guardian had been enough to distract him. Stryker had spent so long thinking about how that worked and what it was like that he'd failed to see the killer standing in front of him.

No wonder "Drew's" accent had been so hard to place. It was as fake as his name. Stryker had fallen hook, line and sinker for "James'" routine. The moment he'd come close to asking a real question, the killer had distracted him by asking him to read his self-published drivel. Now he was willing to bet that the book didn't exist either.

The cars in front of him came to a complete stop in the Upper Thames Street tunnel. According to the satnav, although there was barely a mile to travel it would take twelve minutes to get there by car. *Twelve minutes!* Now it really was slower than Shanks' pony.

'Fuck it!' Stryker slung the steering wheel to the left and drove between the bollards running along the road and into the coned-off maintenance section. He motored past the traffic, cars honking him as he overtook. A familiar-looking skyscraper came into view in front of him as he emerged from the tunnel into yet more traffic. Here there were no more shortcuts.

Once his signal was back, he tried Mabey again. Still nothing.

'Siri, call Patricia Knox.'

His phone buzzed to acknowledge his command. Knox declined the call.

Stryker swore again. Nobody was helping. He called the Met's switchboard to put out an all-units call for help. Somebody ought to be backing him up. He couldn't be expected to take a serial killer down all on his own.

The GPS continued to give him stupid directions. If he followed its instructions, he would have to drive past St Dunstan and come in from Aldgate. That loop would add another half mile to his journey.

Perhaps he really should ditch the car. He stabbed the small pedestrian icon on the satnav's screen. The route changed to point straight as an arrow. The mileage showed as point seven – he could easily run that far. He jammed the brakes on, to the annoyance of the arseholes behind who'd decided to follow his lead. He killed the engine, slammed his door shut and then bolted for the pavement accompanied by a chorus of car horns. The source of the traffic jam became apparent as Stryker jogged. Two cars had collided in the Canon Street underpass. It was freezing as the rain pounded down upon him. Any colder and he'd be running through a hailstorm.

By the time he turned onto St Dunstan's Hill, he was soaking wet and had a serious stitch in his side. He slowed to a brisk walk so he could catch his breath. The entire jog, he'd kept his eyes peeled for CCTV cameras. The initial search had been fruitless because the killer hadn't needed to drive that night; he'd simply dumped Layla Morgan on his doorstep. No wonder his number plate recognition search hadn't revealed anything.

Now that he knew where James lived, the CCTV footage that he'd already seized might be useful. He'd been looking at the night of her death but the killer hadn't driven then. He was living right next door. Now he knew that, he could look at the nights either side of Layla Morgan's death to see how the killer had travelled in and out of St Dunstan.

The rain had stopped by the time he arrived at the office building. Still clutching his side, Stryker tipped back his head to survey the place. In the cold light of day, the boarded-up windows gave the place a derelict air which, without the presence of a property guardian, would be catnip for squatters and vandals.

Nobody had responded to his call for backup yet. *Why on earth was everyone being so slow? Was everyone stuck in traffic as he had been?*

'Now what?' he muttered, and wondered why he'd busted his guts to get here. Surely, he hadn't really expected to find James still hanging around? Stryker paced towards the office block entrance, trying to recall "James'" every word. He had to have said – or done – something that Stryker could use to catch him. What had they talked about?

The revolving door was locked, shutters pulled down tight over it. Next to it, the side door had an iron bar bolted across it secured in place by a massive padlock. Inwardly cursing himself for not paying more attention during that fateful meeting, Stryker pounded his fist against the door in frustration. The killer had literally been within arm's reach last time he was here. It would have taken less than an hour to pull James into the station for the purposes of a formal statement. James might even have tripped himself up. At the very least, the station's security cameras would have captured his image. If so, would Matthews have put two and two together and realised the bloke chatting her up via Review My Ex was actually the so-called "Lady Killer"?

Despite the freezing cold December air, Stryker broke into a sweat. He leaned his forehead against the door and groaned. He'd messed up big time. Again. And this time his mistake might very well have cost Matthews her life.

He squeezed his eyes shut. This was his fuck-up and he was going to fix it no matter the cost. A quick search revealed several ways in and out of the building, all seemingly barred. There was the main door on the southwest corner, but there were two fire exits too, one on the western side, one on the south. Then, to compound matters, there was the car park exit on the eastern side of the building. If the killer was here, Stryker couldn't stop him running. There was no way to guard all four exits at once. He called the switchboard again, demanded an ETA. Ten minutes. It was too long. He'd have to go in.

The main door was no good – he'd need to go back to the car for a door ram, a "Big Red Key" in police parlance. There had to be an easier way. The west side of the building ran along St Dunstan's Hill where every window was barred by metal grills to prevent vandals from getting in. The fire door was too thick to break without a ram. Stryker jogged along Cross Lane to the south. No luck there either. There were no doors, only a solid brick wall with a couple of windows at head height that were again barred by metal grills. Another fire door, again too strong to mule-kick.

There was no point looking to the north – that was where the main road was – so he turned his attention to Harp Lane which ran along the back of the building where he found a roll-down shutter hiding a vehicle entrance.

That's more like it, Stryker thought.

He was going to need the car after all. He sprinted back in record time, carried by sheer adrenaline. A traffic warden on a motorbike had already written out a ticket and was plainly waiting for a tow-truck to come and remove Stryker's car.

'Sorry!' Stryker said. He fished in his pocket. 'Police. Look, my warrant card is in the glove compartment. Let me grab it real quick.'

Before the traffic officer could object, he'd leapt into the driver's seat. He flashed the warrant card, locked all the doors to pre-empt any objections and then reversed back into traffic while honking to announce his stupidity. The cars in front parted before him like the red sea, his horn blaring continuously as he thundered towards St Dunstan in the East. His car was unmarked but still had lights built into the grill and dash. He flicked those on.

Before he knew it, he was turning back onto Harp Lane. Instead of slowing down as he approached the back of the building, he sped up. This was going to be fun. There was a fifty-foot clear stretch to use as a run-up between him and the big metal barrier guarding the car park. It wasn't possible to accelerate too much in the short distance from Cross Lane. He managed to get to sixty-two miles per hour in the seven-and-a-bit seconds it took him to traverse the space.

It was enough. His bumper crashed into the metal with an almighty sound, metal scraping against metal. The barrier tore like cheap wrapping paper, folding around his car.

He was in.

Behind the roller was a cavernous car park devoid of cars. The space stretched for a couple of hundred feet, easily enough for a few dozen cars. At the very end, there was a single dim bulb illuminating the entrance to a stairwell.

Stryker's hairs stood on end. He was alone in a car park, breaking into a suspected serial killer's abode and it was too dark to see much. He killed the engine quickly so that he didn't make any more noise than he already had. He was plunged into darkness, the light from outside only reaching a few dozen feet into the enormous garage. His eyes would take a while to adjust and until then, he was at a marked disadvantage if James was lurking in the shadows.

He crouched low as he made his way towards the stairwell. This was the ground floor. There were five more above him for a total of six. When he'd last been here, it appeared that James had chosen to make himself at home on the sixth floor.

Every few seconds, he paused, held his breath and listened. No matter how much he strained, he couldn't hear anything except for the sound of his own heart beating. Dare he risk using his mobile phone's torch to search the car park? He was torn. If James was on the premises, there was a good chance that Stryker had already been rumbled. There was no mistaking the sound of a car crashing into a barrier.

If he were the killer, what would he do? Would he flee or fight?

The murders had been clinical and efficient but they also demonstrated a lack of brute force. The stab wounds were precise, neat, and delivered to unsuspecting victims. The lack of defensive wounds was testimony to that.

It was one thing to stab an unarmed woman in cold blood and another entirely to go hand to hand with a man Stryker's size, especially one with police combat training under his belt. A sensible killer would flee. He'd seen three exits on a quick survey of the exterior of the building and there could be a way out through the adjoining building to the north too. Clearly, James had a key to the front door and the fire exits ought to be easy to open from the inside for the sake of safety. It would be child's play to flee from an army of one. Why hadn't backup arrived? The response time was abysmal and it was entirely because of the traffic in central London. This wouldn't have been a problem back in Yorkshire.

He had no choice. He couldn't see a damned thing in the darkness. He'd have to use the torch on his phone. He fumbled as he navigated his iPhone's swipe menu, eventually finding the right place to tap the screen. The light came on, blindingly bright against the pitch-black car park. His eyes slowly adjusted as he spun through three hundred and sixty degrees straining for any sign of movement.

Nothing. Nobody was waiting in the shadows to jump him. He turned the torch off. He needed his eyes to adjust to the dark.

Breathe, Stryker, breathe, he told himself. His nerves were getting the better of him. Again.

The dim light he'd seen emanating from the stairwell was just the other side of a wood and glass panel door. He passed through it, all too aware of the creak the door made as it swung inwards. Someone had been smoking in the stairwell recently. Hundreds of butts were scattered across the floor. Stryker felt them compact underfoot as he ascended. At the first-floor landing, he paused by a door. It didn't sound as if anyone were moving within. He pushed the handle slowly and was met with resistance. The door was locked.

One more flight up and he found the same thing. The door wouldn't budge.

Up and up he went, each time finding locked doors until he found himself, slightly winded, on the landing of the sixth floor. It was the same floor that he'd been on with "Drew Rekshun". He finally found an unlocked door which he nudged slowly open, its hinges creaking as he did. If the killer were here then Stryker had just announced his arrival as surely as if he'd rung a doorbell.

'James!' he shouted. 'Or whatever your name is! Come out with your hands up.'

Silence answered him.

The stairwell was positioned on the opposite side of the building from where he'd entered last time which meant that he was now in the northeast corner of the building, well away from St Dunstan's hill. The sound of the rain outside was now too distant to hear. Instead, all he could hear was the sound of his own heart thundering in his chest. Ahead of him was a corridor that ran south with half-glazed doors all along the right-hand side. Treading lightly, Stryker started along the corridor, hunching as he neared the first door. Through the upper glazed partition, the dark outline of what appeared to be a mountain of furniture was visible. Rusting metal and plastic chairs, similar to those foisted upon unlucky schoolchildren, were piled up to the ceiling.

Stryker turned his attention to the second door. If his internal compass was right, this one led through to the large room that James had been using as a bedroom and living area. He cracked the door just a smidge and peered into what appeared to be near-total darkness.

He held his breath once again, straining to hear if someone was moving within. After satisfying himself that he wasn't about to get jumped, he cautiously opened the door.

The room was much as he had remembered it. Now that there was no duvet covering it up, Stryker could see a filthy mattress, the bedding so stained that Stryker wouldn't have used it for a dog. It seemed that property guardianship didn't always include access to a washing machine. Next to it was a pile of clothing, a mix of shirts, underwear and an old pair of jeans. The suits that he'd seen on his first visit were gone. So too were the suitcases.

James had bolted.

The squalor was such that, if Stryker hadn't known that a property guardian was living here, he'd have assumed a vagrant had wandered in and then decided that they'd rather chance a nearby doorway.

Unless the whole "property guardian" spiel had been a lie too.

The more Stryker found out about this killer, the more he questioned what he thought he knew. James had seemed every bit the useless bystander. It was as if he'd been eager to help and yet the information which he'd fed Stryker had been utterly worthless. He played me like a fiddle, Stryker thought.

Several windows were covered with cardboard and duct tape. Stryker felt for the edges and pulled the cardboard free.

Light flooded into the room. Now he could see everything. Piles of the killer's stuff remained. Books, mostly anatomy and true crime, pots and pans, together with a little oil burner, and even a box full of paperwork.

He'd have to 'fess up, tell DCI Mabey everything. It was his fault. If he'd been more observant, James could have been in custody within hours of the first page. He'd have been a hero. Instead, he was standing in the gloom trying desperately to visualise what was missing from the room since his last visit. The killer had fled in a hurry – that much was obvious from the abandoned clothing and kitchenware – could he have forgotten anything in his haste? And where had he gone?

This was a dangerous killer. He had no known ties to any particular part of the capital. He could be anywhere in London. He could just as easily have checked into a hotel in Westminster or joined the tent city of homeless people under Finsbury Park Bridge. The only clue was that he flitted around central London.

He had to have a car. There was no way he'd fled this place in an Uber or an Addison Lee. Too much had been removed for James to be on foot.

*Think, Seb, think.* What had he seen the first time he'd been here? The week-and-a-bit since Layla Morgan's death seemed like a lifetime.

He shut his eyes, trying to conjure up an image of the scene. As he did, he murmured each item he could see.

'Two cases. Suits, neatly folded. Shoes, leather. A watch... a fancy watch. Breitling? The old projector. The folder with the manuscript. Gym clothes. Undies. Towels.'

He opened his eyes and went back through the checklist he'd just recalled. The projector was still there. The folder was too.

Stryker picked it up, wondering what clues James' manuscript would reveal.

'Bastard!' He'd been had again. The folder was full of printouts of end-of-year financials for the office which had occupied the space before James. *Was everything he'd said a lie?*

His old boss' voice echoed in his mind. Every good lie starts with a kernel of truth.

It was true. Few possessed the ability to make things up in a vacuum. His boss had once demonstrated it by asking them to make up a random name and facts about a person. Nearly everyone drew up those they held nearest and dearest.

So, what did Stryker actually *know*? What were the indisputable facts?

The killer had a lazy eye.

He was tall and strong enough to have carried three dead women with ease. Now that he thought about it, James had been in great physical shape.

He had access to this place. Until Stryker had rammed the car park shutters, there had been no break-in.

He was about Stryker's age, maybe a bit older. James had already begun to go grey.

He used Review My Ex to pick up women.

It begged more questions than it answered. Was he really a property guardian? What did he do for work? Where would he flee to?

Perhaps most important of all was the question that kept burning in Stryker's mind. Why did three young, attractive, desirable women agree to go out with him? It wasn't that he was ugly per se, just that James' lazy eye would be a deal-breaker for many. The dating game was superficial like that. From what Knox had said, Matthews was excited about their date – and eager to go to a nice restaurant – but hadn't felt the necessary spark. Had he fed the women lies the same way he'd deceived Stryker with such ease? It took real acting chops to appear so unassuming, so timid, and to remain so calm while face to face with a homicide detective.

There was nothing more to be gained from standing here in the gloom. Where was the nearest station? It probably belonged to the City of London Police. Stryker remembered reading the background information Mabey had sent ahead of him joining the team which explained a bit of the history of the police in London. The City boys only served the historical City, roughly a square mile, and they handled little more than financial fraud. Even though they weren't part of the Met, their officers would be able to secure the crime scene. He made the call and was given an ETA of ten minutes. He'd have to wait until they got here.

In the meantime, he dialled Annie Burke's number.

'Annie? It's Detective Inspector Stryker. I think I've found your primary crime scene.'

# Chapter 49: On the Slab

The walls of the mortuary corridor were lined by the Met's staff, many of whom had probably never even met Matthews. That didn't matter – one of their own had been murdered. They had come down to pay their respects as the body was wheeled into the mortuary.

The atmosphere was sombre and reverent. The silence which had descended upon the mortuary seemed louder than gunfire as if Matthews' death had sucked all the life, all the joy, all the laughter, from the world.

Elsie walked behind the trolley as Spilsbury's assistant pushed it down the corridor and into autopsy room one. The door shut behind them like an airlock, cutting them off from the world.

It was not unusual for a detective to die "in the line of duty" but this usually meant an older man succumbing to a weak heart, not a fit young detective being violently murdered. The pressure to solve this case was about to be ratcheted up another notch. The pathologist's assistant busied himself with transferring the body bag from the trolley to the autopsy slab while Spilsbury waited.

'Doc, I'm afraid I can't stay for the whole autopsy. The press is already howling and I need to corral all the volunteers before someone turns into a loose cannon.'

Not only had they lined the walls, the extended Met family had rushed to offer help. For once, New Scotland Yard would be packed to the rafters on a weekend. Imposing discipline on so many strong-willed detectives and support staff would take a firm hand lest a loose cannon turned the whole investigation into a vigilante witch hunt.

'You know I have to follow the Home Office guidelines,' Spilsbury said.

'I do. I also know you already know if this is the Lady Killer.' The name still rankled.

'It's forensically consistent with him,' Spilsbury said flatly. 'The stab wound is identical. She's been stabbed just the once like Boileau and Morgan. We already know that took strength and ample knowledge of anatomy as well as the ability to get close without the victim realising what was going on. None of our three victims show any defensive wounds whatsoever. Matthews' corpse—'

Elsie shuddered at the use of the word "corpse" to describe a woman who she'd been talking to just yesterday.

'Her corpse,' Spilsbury continued unperturbed, 'has been massaged to break rigor mortis as I noted at the crime scene. He hadn't finished the job. As you can see, her face is still contorted into the classic "rigor grimace".'

'Why hadn't he finished?'

'A lack of time, I assume. He only massaged the limbs as much as was required to dress up his victims. He was about halfway through posing Matthews. His work was slow, methodical, and deliberate.'

Elsie felt her nostrils flare. 'You sound like you admire him!'

'His work is diligent. There is no extraneous damage and he worked limb by limb. Presumably, if he stayed true to the pattern which he followed in the first two cases, he was going pose Matthews in a frock. Did you find a dress at the crime scene?'

Elsie had been wondering about that. Where had he kept the dresses? 'Nope.'

'It had to be nearby,' Spilsbury said. 'He was within half an hour of being ready to move the body. Whoever interrupted him did so just in time.'

The cleaner had started work in the house at half six. The Lady Killer clearly hadn't been expecting company else he'd have cleared off long before then. His date with Matthews had been at seven the previous evening. That gave him a huge window of opportunity to commit murder and pose the body before sunrise at eight o'clock. Elsie supposed that he was intending to move the body under the cover of darkness. Surely that meant that he had a car nearby to take Matthews away from Holland Park... unless he hadn't intended to move her this time?

As Elsie watched the pathologist's assistant set up an SLR to take photos of the body, her mind wandered. *How had the whole evening gone down? Matthews hadn't put up a fight at any point. That meant the date couldn't have gone too badly, could it?* Elsie could picture it now. A young, naïve, Matthews enjoying a ridiculously overpriced dinner. She probably felt like she was in James' debt if he paid. It was an easy trap to fall into. Men often used money to manipulate, coerce, and control the women around them. Presumably, he'd lured her back to the house in Holland Park somehow. Had he outright asked for sex? Or perhaps he'd simply suggested "a nightcap"? Dinner been booked for seven so it would have been natural for a good date to carry on afterwards. He'd obviously succeeded so why had it all ended in disaster? Had he planned to kill her? The use of someone else's knife said it was spur of the moment. Over and over again, Elsie kept coming back to the contrast. He'd driven to Holland Park, he'd gained illicit access to the Larkins' house, and he'd set up the dinner date. That wasn't spontaneous at all. It just didn't fit.

'He *had* to have a car,' Elsie mused aloud. 'It's the obvious place to keep the dresses, isn't it? And yet he used a knife that wasn't his. There's one missing from the knife block. Why prepare only half of the job?'

Elsie didn't expect the pathologist to venture an opinion on that. She wasn't disappointed. Spilsbury just carried on with the autopsy photography.

'It's weird, isn't it?' Elsie said. 'This whole posing malarkey. Have you seen anything like it?'

Spilsbury nodded. 'People disturb me. I much prefer the predictability of bodies. I have seen some strange things over the years. Posing a body barely registers on the scale of strange things.'

Elsie desperately wanted to ask what Spilsbury had seen. This was neither the time nor the place for such a discussion.

'How hard is it to learn how to break rigor mortis?' Elsie asked.

Spilsbury put the camera down. 'It's not something you could learn by accident. However, I dare guess that should one wish to learn how, one need look no further than YouTube.'

It was a horrendous thought. The beauty of the internet was how easy it was to find things out, to learn. Its greatest weakness was the same.

'Is there anything else I need to know right now?'

'Not from my initial investigation but I shall let you know if I find anything,' Spilsbury said. 'I presume you would like me to call with my findings.'

It was a rare offer. Spilsbury was notorious for making detectives stand and wait for her to finish before offering even the vaguest of comments. 'Yes please,' Elsie said.

'Don't look so surprised, dear. I might not know much about the living, but I am, for now, one of them. This is a courtesy any pathologist would extend to one of our own. Now go catch this bastard.'

# Chapter 50: Access

Getting in contact with the landlord, Mr Larkins, proved easier than Knox had expected. The old man next door had his emergency telephone number. When he wrote it down, Knox was convinced it was wrong.

'That's a weird format...'

The number began with "plus six four" and went on for another nine digits. It had to be an international number of some kind though Knox was damned if she could work out which country it was for.

'Mr Larkins can't stand the cold,' Xavier said, 'so he overwinters in the southern hemisphere.'

'Right... where exactly?'

'Pohara,' Xavier said. When Knox looked at him blankly, he added, 'it's in New Zealand.'

'Oh, right. Don't suppose I can borrow your landline?' That call wouldn't be included in the Met's mobile phone plan.

Xavier almost smiled. 'Not a chance, detective. I believe Mr Larkins uses WhatsApp. I do too – my grandson showed me how to use it so he could send me photos of his travels. You're welcome to use my broadband. It's the only network with a signal in here. I'll give you the room. The password is PASSWORD. That's all in upper case.'

*How secure.* Knox rolled her eyes but typed it into her phone anyway. Once she was connected to Xavier's Wi-Fi, she quickly added the number to her address book, opened WhatsApp and dialled Mr Larkins. Despite the time difference, he answered quickly.

'Who the hell are you? And how do you have my emergency number?'

'Sergeant Knox, Metropolitan Police. I obtained your number from your neighbour Xavier. I'm calling about your property in Holland Park.'

'Good lord,' Larkins said. 'Has there been a break-in?'

'No, sir,' Knox said. That was precisely why she needed to talk to him. If nobody had broken in, that meant that the killer was someone he'd directly or indirectly permitted to access the house. 'I'm calling about a murder, I'm afraid.'

Silence met her statement. 'This has to be a hoax. How dare you call me pretending there's been a murder! It is a hoax... isn't it?'

His tone switched from pleading to angry and back again so quickly it made Knox's head spin. 'If you need to verify my identity, you're welcome to call New Scotland Yard's switchboard. Give them my service number 116116 and then call me back.'

The next time he spoke, he seemed almost broken. 'No, no, just tell me what the heck happened. Who was murdered?'

She couldn't bring herself to think of Matthews as a murder victim. 'A... woman.' She left a pause long enough to let the gravity of the situation sink in. 'The killer was in the house this morning when your cleaner visited at half six. He barged past her to flee.'

'*My house*? A killer was in my house? *How?*'

'That's what we're trying to ascertain, sir. I understand you've been renting your house out online.'

'What's that got to do with anything?' Larkins demanded. 'Nobody rented the place last night, I can promise you! And if what you're saying is true, young lady, nobody ever will again! I'll be selling it in the morning, just you see. Houses in Holland Park are like gold dust.'

While homes in Holland Park were in high demand, Knox very much doubted that Larkins could sell the place without heavily discounting it. Few buyers wanted to live in a murder house even if it were beautifully appointed.

She steered the conversation back in a more useful direction. 'Mr Larkins, who has a key to your home?'

'Well, I do, of course. So does my wife, my son, and Xavier.'

'Where are your wife and son?'

'Here,' he said, 'in bed.'

'And their keys. Where would they be?' Knox prompted.

'Here too, I'm sure of it,' Larkins said. 'Shall I check?'

'Please.'

She heard footsteps followed by the sound of keys clinking against one another on a fob.

'All present and accounted for, sergeant,' Larkins said. 'That just leaves Xavier's, doesn't it? Where's his key?'

'It's also present and accounted for, sir.'

To Knox's surprise, Larkins sounded almost jovial. 'You've got him in custody then? Xavier?'

'For what purpose?'

'Aiding and abetting a killer, sergeant! If that fool let someone into my house...'

'There's no evidence that his key was compromised,' Knox said. 'What kind of key do you use?'

'Just a bog-standard one,' Larkins said. 'It's in my hand right now. What am I looking for?'

'Could you describe what it looks like?' Knox said. 'Does it have a brand name on it?'

'It's... umm... pointy. Five prong bits. Look I'm going to send you a photo okay?'

It came through. Knox reverse-image searched to find out what it was. A hit came up immediately. It was a standard British Fortress mortice key, a type which had been used for decades. Any half-decent locksmith could copy it in a minute flat, no questions asked. It wouldn't be impossible to pick either.

'Thank you, Mr Larkins. Are there any other locks?'

'Yes, of course,' he said. 'There are two deadbolts that we use whenever we're in. Do you think someone copied my key? Oh God... that explains everything.'

Knox paced back and forth in Xavier's living room. Out the window, she could see the scene of crime officers packing up. 'What does it explain, sir?'

'I thought guests were trying it on...'

Impatience got the better of her. 'Trying *what* on, Mr Larkins?'

His voice went quiet. 'I think I ought to speak to my solicitor...'

Knox swore. 'You only need a solicitor if you've committed a crime.'

'No harm just talking to them though... but it is a weekend... and with the time difference... could we chat again next week?' Larkins said. 'Say Wednesday?'

'Time is of the essence here, sir,' Knox said. 'I needn't add that if you fail to assist this murder inquiry, I would be obliged to consider arresting you for obstruction of justice.'

It was a reach especially when Larkins wasn't even in the jurisdiction. She imagined him turning pale, his hands becoming clammy at the thought of the police turning up at his door at daybreak to arrest him.

'Fine,' Larkins said. 'I had some complaints.'

'From?'

'From those individuals who rented from me. I got kicked off one of the platforms because of the reviews which is why all my recent holiday lets have been on StayAway.'

StayAway was one of the latest "rent out your home" apps to hit London. It was looser and less regulated than some of the competition. Fees were lower and so too was the quality of most of the homes listed on there. Larkins' luxury place in Holland Park would have been in hot demand.

'What sort of complaints?'

'Things going missing. A watch here, a few pounds there. One lady said that she lost a pair of diamond earrings. As I said, I thought they were trying it on. People know I've got money and they always want a part of it.'

'Do you have CCTV?'

'Absolutely not,' Larkins said. 'It would ruin the character of the area.'

An area he didn't actually live in, Knox thought scathingly. 'What did you do?'

'I told the first couple to sod off.'

'How many were there?'

'A dozen perhaps out of dozens and dozens of customers. After the first few complaints, I thought it might be my cleaner so I fired her. No big deal there. The agencies change them a lot anyway and that makes it so hard to find someone decent, reliable and affordably priced. The new girl Karina—'

'Catriona,' Knox corrected.

'Whatever her name is, her agency came highly recommended. Several of my friends use them and none have had a problem. As far as I was concerned, that was that. None of them ever actually sued me so I assumed they'd given up on extorting me, or simply found their missing things after all.'

'How long has this been going on?'

'Seven, maybe eight months. I took a break from letting for a while. It's only legal to rent out a place for ninety days per calendar year so I try and pick the days with the highest demand. People love to open their wallets around Christmas and I get another ninety days on the first of January anyway so I may as well make a few quid while we're sunning ourselves on the beach here.'

Knox paused. If someone was stealing, and it wasn't a cleaner, then this wasn't a recent problem. Could the old man Xavier have been helping himself to a trinket here and there? He clearly hated Larkins.

'What's your relationship like with Xavier?'

'Fine, I think,' Larkins said. 'He's been one of my tenants forever. Occasionally he handles the keys for the guests and the cleaner and in return, I let him stay on for well below market rent.'

'How far below?'

'Hmm... I'm not totally sure... I seem to recall he pays something in the ballpark of fifteen hundred per calendar month. I've got another unit down the road that I let out last month for four thousand two hundred. But they've got kids and a dog so they're bound to wreck the joint.'

It was a hefty discount. 'Why so much off?'

'Feel sorry for him, I suppose. He's been there forever. I can't rent it out for nothing, I am a businessman, but I'll break even in return for a bit of free admin here and there. It seems to work for both of us. Hang on... do you seriously think he's involved? At his age?'

Larkins sounded like he relished the thought. Perhaps he was keen for an excuse to evict Xavier and rent the place out at a higher price. Knox ignored him. 'How long has he been handling the keys for you?'

'Three and a bit years.'

'Doesn't seem likely then.' *Unless something changed eight months ago.* Knox made a note to check Xavier's finances for any sign that he might have started struggling more than usual around then.

'And you're sure nobody else has keys?'

'Dead certain,' Larkins said. 'Look, I have to be getting back to bed. It's GMT plus twelve here and I'm going to fall asleep on you. You're welcome to call back any time, this phone number is always on. Is there anything else you need from me in the meantime?'

'A list of everyone that stayed with you,' Knox said. 'Going back for as long as possible.'

'That might take a while. I used so many sites over the years.'

'Then, Mr Larkins, you'd best make yourself a big pot of coffee and get cracking, hadn't you?'

# Chapter 51: False Positives

For the second time, Annie was summoned to St Dunstan in the East. This time she wasn't skipping her anniversary dinner. Instead, her Saturday afternoon task – window shopping for the best divorce lawyer in town – was put on hold so that she could see the devastation Sebastian Stryker had wrought when he forced entry into the office cark park.

He was such a typical man. He'd driven straight through a metal barrier at top speed, found the crime scene empty, and then fled the moment that the local uniformed officers had secured the scene.

How he'd found this place was anyone's guess. The abandoned office block was a stone's throw from where she'd found the thread snagged on the bush. Indeed, the fire exit on the west side of the building was directly across the road. As a theory, Stryker's hypothesis that Layla Morgan was murdered here and dumped just outside made sense.

It didn't hold water for long though as the initial forensic tests didn't show any evidence of a bloodbath. Annie sprayed the place liberally with luminol. While she did see the characteristic chemiluminescent blue glow that could indicate blood, it wasn't a large quantity. If the victim had been stabbed here, she would have expected to see arterial spray as well as a pool of blood at the site of the stabbing.

Luminol didn't make things quick or easy. It reacted with any oxidising agents so that while it did flag the location of blood, it also reacted to plenty of substances that weren't blood like horseradish or hair dye.

That wasn't to say there was no blood. There were a few out-of-place drops at the end of the parking space nearest the stair-well in the garage which could indicate that the body was trans-ferred from a car before it was dumped in the lower garden of St Dunstan in the East.

What was worth the trip was the chance to prove Stryker wrong. If the killer had lived here, his DNA would be all over it. The fastest DNA test available to Annie would take around four hours plus the time to get the sample to the lab. If Stryker were wrong, she'd get to say "I told you so". If, on the off chance, he was right... well, a manhunt would be on.

Either way, they'd know by late afternoon.

STRYKER WAS ACCOSTED the moment he walked into the Yard. He had expected Elsie to ambush him, to demand to know where he'd been. He was all ready to confess everything he'd done wrong, to come clean about "Andrew Rekshun" and ram-ming the garage door when Flick the e-fit artist shouted out his name. She was legendary around the Yard for changing her hair-style on a daily basis much to the confusion of some of the less observant members of staff. Today her hair was bright pink and pixie cut.

She bounded over to him as if her feet were sprung. She had a leather satchel slung over one shoulder. 'You're Mr Stryker, aren't ya?'

'Guilty.'

'You stood me up this mornin'. I've been waiting for you to show. Your man identified your killer.'

She pulled her iPad from her satchel to show him the e-fit she'd drawn. It was unmistakably him.

'You're miles too late,' Seb said. 'Found the git on CCTV. Has anyone else seen this?'

'Nah,' Flick said.

'Then can you do me a solid? Keep it to yourself. The Lady Killer has fled. All his stuff is gone. If this leaks to the press, he'll know we're onto him. This needs to stay between us until he's in custody, okay?'

'You got it.'

Flick jogged on, leaving Stryker to make a beeline for conference room one. Elsie had sent out a group WhatsApp while he was driving back asking everyone to convene there and then sent a second message just to him asking him to take over while she finished up with Dr Spilsbury.

With any luck, his mistake wouldn't come back to haunt him. He knew he was on thin ice, but with one woman down, the team needed every available body to catch this guy. The lack of backup justified ramming the garage door, didn't it?

Now that there was an e-fit, there was no hiding the fact he'd run into the killer without suspecting a thing. It was, in many ways, a relief. He could go back to playing it straight, put his hands up and say sorry, and be damned if there were consequences. No job was worth his integrity.

He couldn't undo his mistake, but he could help catch the Lady Killer.

# Chapter 52: Told You So

Burton Leigh was proving to be an absolute pain in the backside. Surely the old duffer knew he was being picked up. Anyone else would have been waiting at the door. But oh, no, not Doctor Burton Leigh. Conscious of Stryker's need for speed, Ian had jiggled from one foot to the other as he'd waited in the hallway while Burton Leigh changed into his "lucky sweater". Next, as if aware of – and amused by – Ian's impatience, he'd made himself a thermos full of hot tea ("not that crap you lot brew at the station") and filled a tiny plastic lunchbox with cucumber sandwiches and rich tea biscuits "for dunking in the tea". By the time Ian had loaded him into his Kia, they'd wasted so much time that he felt justified in putting his foot down the entire way back into London.

The drive back had been mostly silent, punctuated by the occasional burst of music as Bertie had jabbed the pre-set button which turned on Classic FM and Ian had just as quickly switched it back to his favourite heavy metal. After three miles of this battle of the bands, Ian ejected the music system from the dashboard and stashed it under his seat.

'That, young man, was uncalled for.'

Ian shrugged. 'Sorry, old man. My ride, my rules.'

Halfway into London, Bertie piped up again. 'I take it he struck again then.'

'No idea what you're blabbering about,' Ian said. 'I'm literally just your taxi driver. You got an issue, you take it up with the boss man, 'kay?'

'Young man, I think you'll find that's "boss lady". DCI Mabey is in charge of the team after all. She's also my goddaughter and I won't tolerate rudeness.'

Suitably chastised, Ian drove in silence the rest of the way. The promised day out with Stryker would be worth it. And he'd be sure to take lots of photos of him and his bestie riding Funscape's rollercoasters, photos that would go straight onto his "Review My Ex" profile. Maybe then, he'd finally get a response to one of the many hopeful messages he sent to likely looking young ladies.

While Ian drove, Bertie busied himself with his phone. He seemed to be texting someone though when Ian leant over, Bertie turned the screen away and tutted.

Conference room one, the largest in New Scotland Yard which been designed to hold meetings of joint task forces featuring hundreds of staff, was buzzing when they arrived. News of Georgia Matthews' murder had spread like wildfire and so many colleagues had arrived to offer their assistance. Ian watched as Bertie greeted a number of them like old friends as they made their way from the back of the room to the podium at the front.

'No sign of the team,' Ian said. 'Lemme text Stryker and find out where they're at, yeah?'

Bertie wasn't even listening. Before Ian had finished talking, he'd ambled over to the podium. In the absence of DCI Mabey, DI Stryker and DS Knox, it seemed that Burton Leigh had decided to assume control.

'Mr... sorry, Doctor Leigh, you can't—'

It was too late. He'd flipped the microphone's power button to on. 'Testing... testing... can everyone hear me?'

A terrible feedback screech drew everyone's attention to the front of the room.

'Ladies and gents. If it were not in such dire circumstances, I would say that it is a pleasure to see you all once more.' Bertie's voice echoed through the auditorium.

From where Ian stood off to one side, he saw heads nod accompanied by murmurs of recognition. Many of the older detectives seemed to know Bertie. Just how long had he been "retired"?

'Alas,' Bertie said. 'Today is one of those days where the worst has happened – one of our own has been slain – and it is up to us to come together to catch her killer. I wish I could say that this is a one-off event, an unexpected and unexplainable tragedy. This is the...' he trailed off as if trying to consult a memory that was just out of reach.

'...thirty-ninth serial killer case which I've consulted on and so far the Lady Killer has followed a typical trajectory.'

A large man in the fourth row from the back stood up, his belly spilling over the, thankfully unoccupied, seat in front of him, and waved impatiently. 'If he's as predictable as you say, Doctor Leigh,' the man said. 'Where exactly is he? I'll send my team to go pick him up right now.'

A few brave souls sniggered. Bertie glared at them.

'DCI Fairbanks, thank you for joining us. The first case was yours, wasn't it? Why don't you join me at the front?'

The fat man squeezed past his team and loped up towards Bertie, all eyes in the room watching him intently. Even though social skills weren't his strongest point, Ian could see from their expressions how little respect he commanded among his colleagues.

'As I was saying before DCI Fairbanks interrupted, this serial – who the press have dubbed The Lady Killer – is a compulsive, dangerous killer.'

Fairbanks snatched the microphone off Bertie. 'Didn't you say predictable before?' He handed it back looking pleased with himself.

Bertie stepped away from Fairbanks. Ian thought he detected the glimmer of a smile around Bertie's eyes as if he were pleased to be mocked by the big man.

There were a few seconds of silence before Bertie answered. 'I said typical, not predictable. As you would have discovered, if you'd bothered to put the effort in to investigate.'

A vein in Fairbanks' temple throbbed. He was livid to have fallen for the trap. Bertie had handed him the rope and watched as he'd hung himself.

The room hung on their every word. The audience hadn't expected this war of words. 'It wasn't until the second murder that I was brought in to profile the killer. There was a lag of two weeks between the deaths of Leonella Boileau and Layla Morgan. One week later, he struck again and Georgia Matthews was found dead before she could be posed like the first two victims. Now that his preferred modus operandi has been disturbed by an interloper, it is my expectation that the killer will lose control and strike again even more quickly—'

At that moment, the back doors burst open. Stryker. He had a panicked look about him as his eyes traversed the conference room.

'Where's DCI Mabey?' he demanded, ignoring Ian's frantic waving. Instead, when Bertie beckoned him to the front and then killed the microphone, he hurried towards the stage. He just hasn't seen me yet, Ian consoled himself and trailed after him, as a good sidekick should.

He reached the stage in time to hear Stryker talking to Bertie. 'Elsie's not here,' the doc said.

'I know,' Stryker said. 'She texted to say she's at the mortuary attending Matthews' autopsy. Might be a while.'

'You should have taken over this meeting but as you weren't here...' Bertie whispered.

'I've found him,' Stryker said. 'We've got a witness who saw him buy the dresses and a sketch to match, CCTV footage of him going into and coming out of the restaurant he dined at with Matthews last night.'

'And?' Bertie prompted.

'And what?'

Ian kept quiet despite loitering close enough to hang on every word. Stryker shot him a glare to warn him off. Now wasn't the time to mention Namco Funscape. Dr Burton Leigh, oblivious to Ian's nosiness, clearly thought Stryker was about to take off without the aid of a rocket. In a calm professorial voice, he said softly, 'Young man, you're clearly about to explode. What on earth do you mean you've found him? Is he in custody?'

'He's fled. No idea where, he's a property guardian, an itinerant. He's not local to any one place. That's why we thought he was smart. We thought he was getting in and out of places like St Dunstan without being seen. He wasn't. He'd been there the whole time.'

Bertie didn't ask how Stryker knew this. His eyes narrowed. 'He fled?'

'Yep,' Stryker said. 'Seems like he left St Dunstan in a hurry. A lot of his stuff is still there but the essentials are all gone. What does that mean?'

'It means we've spooked a dangerous psychopath,' Bertie said. 'He'll feel like he's losing all control, that time is running out until we catch him.'

'Which means?'

'It means, Inspector Stryker, that when he can't assert control, he's going to lose any restraint he might have had. He'll do the only thing he knows to do when he can't control the world around him – lash out violently. Someone is about to be murdered.'

# Chapter 53: No More Amateurs

As soon as the big meeting fizzled out, Ian made a beeline for the safety of his office. He made it back unscathed and set to work on accessing Nelly's mobile. It didn't take long. Matthews' list of attempted pin codes was bundled in with the chain of custody paperwork and the last number was circled in green.

Typing in 1962 worked like a charm.

The next task wasn't so easy – finding something that DCI Mabey could use to catch the killer.

The same brick wall they'd been up against from the off had yet to be dealt with. Review My Ex was encrypted end to end and secured by a separate app-only password. There was no way Ian could break that without massive resources and a lot of luck to boot.

He flicked opened the address book and immediately swore. Nelly had *thousands* of contacts. Since she'd died, she'd had hundreds of messages, nearly all of them from men. They were split 90/10 between WhatsApp messages and iMessages.

Opening up WhatsApp to read them proved to be a schoolboy error. As soon as he did, new messages flooded in. Most of them were in the vein of "*Hey bby, wuu2?*" which Ian interpreted to mean "*hello, what are you doing?*".

He switched the phone into Airplane Mode to prevent any more messages from appearing and then began to read through the messages that Nelly had received in the days immediately preceding her death.

There were *hundreds*. One conversation was with Vito. His messages were short and to the point. He wanted Nelly back and she was having none of it. Despite the stereotypical action man poses in his profile photo, he was a complete softie. He'd already forgiven Nelly and his messages were of concern, not hate.

The others made Ian cringe. Judging by the profile photos on WhatsApp, many of the men Nelly had been chatting with were at least twice her age. Nelly had been flirting with dozens of men, demanding that they send her money in return for her affection.

It was a train wreck two years in the making. The men who said no were blocked but not before Nelly verbally abused them first. Those who said yes set themselves up for greater and greater demands until they too said no. It was a scam that relied upon Nelly finding a continuous stream of new blood.

It also explained how she'd hidden the money. It never touched her actual bank account. Nelly had solicited the money via whatever online app the men were willing to use, and Cash App was clearly her preference. Ian swiped back to Cash App to double-check that he'd read Nelly's balance correctly. It seemed she really did have tens of thousands of pounds sitting in her account. As it wasn't a bank, it hadn't been spotted by the Met's standard financial background check.

Once the money was in her account, Nelly could use the money in one of three ways. The first was to withdraw the money to her real bank. Ian discounted that. If she'd done that, one of the detectives would have found the cash by now and then he'd never have been given this task. The second use was to pay other Cash App users using their @username. If she'd spend the money that way, it ought to be easy to find from her transaction history assuming they could subpoena the right records. Third, Nelly could have used the Cash Card feature which functioned exactly the same as a debit card but without being linked to her or her personal bank account. In many ways, it was like using a prepaid VISA gift card. No wonder her real bank account's spending patterns had appeared to show such a frugal lifestyle.

Ian had to give it to her. Nelly was smart. She was also greedy. Some of the men she'd been chatting with had sent her thousands of pounds. Nearly every man eventually got blocked. Some lasted weeks, some months. It seemed that she had no intention of ever meeting up with any of them. Her messages were flirty but guarded. As far as Ian could see, she never deliberately disclosed any personal information. There were titbits here and there. Some men knew her favourite flowers were chrysanthemums. Some knew she loved the colour purple. A few big spenders had photos of an adult nature though even then Nelly had cropped out her face.

Taken together, Ian could see how joining the dots might reveal her identity. In isolation, however, it was all a bit useless. No one man held more than one or two pieces of the puzzle that was the real Nelly.

There had to be something in here that could identify the killer. DCI Mabey wouldn't give up on the idea that the killer was a man known to both of the victims. If only Stryker hadn't buggered up Layla Morgan's phone, it would be easy. See which number they'd both been in contact with and voila, one serial killer.

Now Ian had to be even smarter. He was tempted to ignore those messages from men that were still contacting her. On the other hand, the killer might have been thoughtful enough to send fake post-death messages to try and throw the police off. Would the killer have foreseen the police breaking into the victim's phone and combing through each message one by one to find him? Ian wasn't sure.

For now, he had to cut down the search some other way else he'd never get through them all. The day before her death, Nelly had sent sixty messages. That was much more manageable.

He pulled his headphones on, turned his rock music up to maximum to shut out the world and got to work starting with the earliest messages.

THE ROOM WAS DARK WHEN Elsie entered, lit only by the lights of Ian's computer. He seemed in his own little world as Elsie approached.

'Progress?' she called out. He didn't react. The blare of Avril Lavine could be heard escaping from his headphones. Elsie yanked them off of him.

'Hell, lady!' Ian said. 'Who do you think you are giving a man a heart attack like that?'

He spun around, whiter than a sheet. When he realised it was DCI Mabey that he'd just spoken rudely to, his head drooped.

'Progress?' Elsie demanded again.

'Err, sorry about that, chief,' Ian stammered. 'I've managed to crack Leonella Boileau's phone.'

'You mean Matthews managed to crack it.' Elsie glared at him accusingly as if to ask how he dared to take credit for a dead colleague's achievement.

'Right, right,' Ian said. He recapped the last half hour's work for her. 'So now I'm trying to work out which man she met on the night she disappeared.'

'I assume,' Elsie said, 'that you've considered looking to see which phone numbers have connected to the cell towers around St Dunstan in the East.'

He hung his head again. 'Well, I was just getting there...'

'Then get there,' Elsie said. 'Before I get annoyed, write down each number that sent Layla a message. Don't skip any of your sixty-message shortlist and then see which towers each connected to last.'

'Okay,' Ian said. 'Before I do that, let me see if any of these numbers are registered.'

They both knew that it was a sensible suggestion. Elsie nodded her assent and then watched like a hawk while Ian sorted the numbers into pay monthly contract numbers and pay-as-you-go numbers. The latter, anonymous numbers would be of most interest, as it was likely the killer had used a so-called burner phone.

'Hell yes!' he cried. 'That's got us down to thirty-seven.'

'Now, have any stopped being active since the murders?' Elsie asked. If she were in the killer's shoes, she'd have ditched the mobile in case it was used to trace her movements.

Precious seconds ticked by as Ian tried to find out. 'Three are currently off. One of them last connected on... the night she died.'

It had to be him. How could it not be? The killer had contacted her, killed her, and then ditched the number.

'One of the burner phones?'

'Uh-huh, chief,' Ian said. 'Lemme find the messages from him.'

He did. He turned the phone to her. His last message to Nelly had been simple. It read:

*See you at seven.*

Elsie grabbed the phone and scrolled up to see the earlier messages. The first read:

*Hi, it's J from RME. Let's cut to the chase and go for a drink.*

A few messages back and forth later, Nelly had succumbed and agreed. It seemed that she actually wanted to date J. He wasn't simply a mark to her. Either that or she'd envisioned such a big payday that he was worth the risk.

'Let's take a look at him,' Elsie said. She hit the miniature icon at the top to enlarge J's profile picture. It showed two men climbing a mountain. One man was in the foreground and he was gorgeous. Early thirties, chiselled jawline, sandy blond hair, and a six-pack that Elsie's eyes couldn't help but linger on. In the background was a man that looked a little like him. He was still in shape, but he was older with an asymmetrical face.

'Fifty quid says it's the gremlin in the background,' Ian said as he struggled to see the screen. He was too short to peer over Elsie's shoulder.

Elsie privately agreed. 'Do you not think it inappropriate to bet on the outcome of a murder investigation?'

He cowed away, sitting back down and busying himself at the computer.

'What're you pretending to do now?'

'Cars,' Ian muttered.

'What?'

'He didn't kill either woman at St Dunstan, did he?'

It was true. Annie had combed over the place today looking for any traces of blood.

'So he had to have a car, didn't he?'

It followed. 'Right, but I asked Stryker to check CCTV and the ANPR cameras. I assume he enlisted your help with that?'

'He did, yeah, but he asked me for any signs of the guy on the night of the murder,' Ian said, 'not any other time.'

'Okay,' Elsie said. 'We know it takes him time to prep his victims to pose them. We know he killed Layla Morgan well before we found her last week on Friday so go back to the days before then and get me every car that's been in the area.'

It would still be hundreds if not thousands of cars.

'I tried that. It ain't much help, but I think we can do one better,' Ian said. 'Lemme explain.' As he worked, his computer grew louder as if it were under strain. Elsie was forced to raise her voice to be heard over the fan noise.

'What're you doing?'

Ian beamed as if he had just had a stroke of genius. 'He's been careful on the nights he's committed murder, but if the body was in the car, he had to have come in and out of St Dunstan before. If he had one car, he'd show up on the same reg more than once? If I discard all the cars that only show up in the area once, I can narrow down our search. Might take me a while.'

Her phone rang. 'Ian, how long will this take?'

'An hour maybe?'

'Find me when you're done, okay? I need the killer's registration plates. Get me that and I'll order DI Stryker to go to Namco Funscape with you.'

Her phone was *still* ringing. Everyone wanted a piece of her today. 'Mabey,' she said.

The line crackled as her phone connected. This basement was awful for getting a signal. She nodded at Ian and headed towards the stairs where the line began to improve. 'It's Knox. You know the guy who owns the house, Mr Larkins, had been letting it out online? It turns out that someone had been robbing those who'd rented from him and he'd dismissed it all until now. He's not sure when it started but it was eight or nine months ago. I've got a list of everyone he's rented to. It'll be in your inbox in a mo.'

'Good work,' Elsie said, her opinion of Knox thawing considerably. 'Get yourself back here. I want a full team meeting in the incident room.'

# Chapter 54: The War Room

'Elsie, you've got to trust me on this,' Bertie said. 'Stryker and Annie's visit to the killer's abode won't just have flushed him out into the open, it's made time of the utmost essence. You've taken his sense of control and he'll get it back the only way he knows how.'

She patted his arm. 'I believe you, Uncle Bertie.'

After a long, stressful morning, Elsie's eyes were beginning to close on her. Trying to keep up with an entire conference room full of colleagues was exhausting. There was no way she could corral and coordinate that many people without any advanced planning.

To try and avoid her brain shutting down, she'd downed three cups of coffee and then retreated to the incident room. In her mind, it was now "the war room", the place where she'd plan just how she was going to find, arrest and convict the Lady Killer before he could harm anyone else. The theory was great, now she just needed to execute it before the brain fog was so strong that she couldn't function.

Only Elsie's immediate team was allowed in. If Bertie was right that the killer was about to lose control then the last thing she needed was for the press to find out. The enormous team of volunteers that had convened in conference room one could easily become a leaky sieve. For now, the most important task they could help with was protecting Matthews' family – her mum, dad and younger sister – from the inevitable media onslaught. Their house in Hampshire was about to become a camping ground for the fourth estate if it hadn't already.

True to her word the list Knox had procured from Mr Larkins was in Elsie's inbox. It contained the names of everyone he'd rented to. In early April, he'd rented to one "James Robertson". Could he be "J"? It fitted the timeline. Mr Robertson had stayed before the thefts started. It was an uncomfortably common-sounding name and could easily be fake.

The door clicked shut as Annie sidled in behind Stryker, and they were ready to plan their next move.

Elsie waited until everyone was seated and motioned for hush. 'I've just come from the Digital, Cyber and Communication Department. Ian is now working on tracking where the killer's mobile phone went before he dumped it. He's also looking for any vehicles that the killer might have used to transport the body into the office car park by St Dunstan. What progress has everyone else made?'

Annie raised a hand. 'At Stryker's request, I returned to the office building to the east of St Dunstan. I found DNA evidence that is now with the lab. There is little doubt in my mind that it belongs to the killer. I found blood drops in the car park too. Everything is consistent with the current case theory that the killer simply dumped Layla Morgan on his front doorstep.'

All eyes turned to Stryker for an explanation. He glanced down to avoid Elsie's gaze. 'And how, perchance, did you know to send Ms Burke there, Detective Inspector Stryker?'

'Boss,' Stryker said. 'I... I messed up. When I sent Flick the witness from the charity shop, I had no idea what our killer looked like. But the moment that Flick showed me the e-fit she'd drawn, I knew it was the man from St Dunstan.'

'What man?'

'The witness,' Stryker mumbled.

'The *witness*?' Elsie roared. 'The man you told me *didn't see a thing*? The man you neglected to ask for any form of ID?'

He had nothing to say that would stop her and so he merely mumbled his apologies.

'Sorry? You will be sorry. Give me one good reason you shouldn't be fired right this second.'

The rest of the room watched, mouths agape apart from Knox who looked amused.

'Don't you dare look proud of yourself, Knox,' Elsie said, turning her glare towards her sergeant. 'You didn't even bother to stay sober that night. You're on thin fucking ice too.'

'Boss,' Stryker said, 'I'm sorry. I messed up. I know that. Once. You said we all get one mistake. That was mine. We're already down one team member and if you fire me or Knox, or worse, both of us, then you'll have nobody left to help you. Let me own this mess. I didn't recognise him as the Lady Killer the first time I met him but I did find the witness and I went back to try and arrest him. We know who he is now. Fire me if you like. I deserve it. Just do it after we catch this bastard.'

She closed her eyes, shutting out his pleading puppy dog eyes. He deserved to be fired. So did Knox. But she couldn't catch the killer alone. As much as she hated it, she needed to pull this useless team of hers together to get justice for Matthews, Morgan, and Boileau.

She ignored him and turned to Bertie. 'What's the psychology at play here, doc? Why is he picking these women when they've got nothing in common?'

Bertie looked at her thoughtfully. 'Every set of victims has something in common. I have a theory about how these three are connected. Before I venture my guess, would you be so kind as to explain to an old codger just how this new-fangled Review My Ex thingamajig works?'

It hadn't occurred to Elsie that there were still people out there who hadn't used it. 'It's pretty simple. You sign up on your phone and put in your details like any dating app—'

'Can we please assume,' Bertie said slowly, 'that some of us haven't used any dating apps at all, ever.'

'You put up a nice photo of yourself, describe yourself in a paragraph, and that's it. Afterwards, all those people who you've dated in the past are allowed to leave their thoughts on your profile.'

'Even the ones that hate you?' Bertie said.

'Even them,' Elsie said, 'especially them. The whole idea is that one woman's rubbish is another's treasure and that by going in forewarned about someone's biggest flaws, we can save a lot of time and heartbreak.'

'Rather naïve,' the profiler said. 'People aren't logical like that. Unless I'm way off the mark, it would be a magnet for hate and slander.'

He wasn't wrong. Plenty of profiles were full of terrible reviews. 'You can pay to "demote" those ones,' Elsie said putting air quotes around the word demote. 'It means they go to the bottom of the list and people only see them if they scroll all the way through the good reviews... which no one does because it's a horrible interface.'

'Clever,' Bertie said. 'Unleash the worst of humanity on each other and then extort them to hide their deepest secrets. Bet it's profitable.'

Knox raised a tentative hand. 'Very profitable,' she said. 'So profitable in fact that the company behind it, Better Future Media Ltd, are about to list on the stock exchange. The sole founder, an American called Adelrick Melrose, is likely to jump into the top ten of the Times Rich List. *The Impartial* ran a feature on him last Sunday. He's going to be worth billions.'

No wonder he hadn't wanted to help Elsie out. If the press had any idea that his company was connected to a murder, no matter how tenuous that connection, his float would be dead before it started.

'And, get this,' Knox said, 'he's also the biggest shareholder in StayAway.'

It couldn't be a coincidence, could it? thought Elsie. The same man was behind two companies that cropped up in one investigation.

'Melrose will cooperate. He has to,' Elsie said confidently. 'We need his cooperation to find out every place that James Robertson ever stayed using his app. Knox, I need you to find out where Melrose lives so we can go and pay him a visit. I hope you don't mind me saying this, but you can come across as a cold-hearted bitch. We're going to need that sass. If we play it right, we can use the float to expedite things. You up for a bit good cop, bad cop? Or bad cop, worse cop?'

Knox grinned. 'Careful, you'll make me cry,' she said. 'That's the nicest thing anyone has ever said to me. Let's put his balls in a vice until he cooperates. He's got a billion-dollar float planned and we can fuck his shit up.'

'Then go get Googling. Speak to no one else. This list can't leak to the press, or any of our colleagues, until we've got a proper plan of action. I don't want a witch hunt on my hands and I don't want to spook our killer any more than necessary.'

While Knox found a quiet corner of the room to work, Elsie turned back to Bertie. 'You said you've got a theory.'

'I do,' Bertie said. 'I think the killer is acting out his rage against women.'

'Duh,' Stryker said. At Elsie's stern look he gave a subtle shrug as if to say "I could have told you that".

'He's picked women who he thought were broken in some way. Nelly grew up without a father and was trying to use men for their money.'

'And succeeding,' Stryker chimed in.

This time, Bertie glared at him. 'Young man, do you want my help or not?'

'I'm sorry, Unc-... Dr Leigh,' Elsie said, quickly correcting herself so as not to call him Uncle Bertie in public. 'Stryker is clearly an idiot. Please carry on.'

'As I was saying, broken women. Layla Morgan was an anorexic and Matthews had the self-confidence of a puddle.'

'Why would he want to date broken women?'

'Two reasons,' Bertie said. 'Firstly, these are women that he thought he could control. Secondly, they're women he thought he deserved. He thinks of himself as broken and believes he deserves to be with someone else who is also broken.'

Elsie found herself nodding along. She had tried settling once or twice. It never ended well. 'So if they then reject him...'

'It's the ultimate act of betrayal,' Bertie finished for her. 'He sees it as being rejected not by beautiful, intelligent, wonderful women who he doesn't deserve but by broken, pitiful things he has deigned to take on. Chances are he throws money around in an attempt to buy their love and affection which compounds his feeling of betrayal.'

'Sounds like a classic incel to me,' Stryker said.

'That, young man, is not a proper psychological term.'

Elsie knew what Stryker meant. The "incel" movement had been in the papers. It stood for "involuntarily celibate", a man so obsessed with – and corrupted by – the desire for carnal relations that he demeaned women in order to avoid his own insecurity becoming unbearable. They lurked on the internet where they insulted and threatened violence against women as if doing so might actually get them laid.

Stryker piped up again, his tone dubious. 'How did he get so close that they didn't see him with a dirty great knife then, doc?'

'Simple. He surprised them. This is a man who would appear to be perfectly lovely, respectful, even kind,' Bertie said. 'Right up until he flipped a switch. Going back to this app thing, can you see everyone in London on it?

'Just those who've registered, naturally,' Elsie said. 'In theory, you can see all who match your sexual and dating preferences.'

'So if I put in "straight male",' Stryker said, 'it shows all the women. I can then narrow them down by age and proximity.'

Bertie sat upright. 'Proximity? My God... When did he get in contact with Matthews?'

Nobody moved. When had Matthews started talking about her "new man"? It couldn't have been long after they were called to St Dunstan in the East.

'Are you saying what I think you're saying?' Elsie asked.

'If you think I'm suggesting that the killer digitally "met" Matthews because he was at the crime scene then, yes, I'm saying what you think I'm saying.'

It took Elsie a moment to parse his round-about statement. She swore. Matthews had been killed not because of random chance but because she'd been near enough to the killer to be a "Proximity Match" on the app. Her attempt to come to work after a couple of drinks had cost Matthews her life.

A knock at the door made every head turn. It cracked open a little and Ian peeked in.

'Come in,' Elsie said. He took an empty seat and gave Stryker a thumbs-up. 'What've you got for us, Ian?'

'Found the car. It was last seen passing an ANPR camera out by White City.'

White City was out past Holland Park, a couple of miles north of Layla Morgan's home. 'Where?'

'Heading west into Acton but he didn't hit any of the cameras out that way. Half ten this morning.'

Two hours ago. If he hadn't flashed past any other ANPR cameras, he might still be around. 'Stryker, go scope out the area around the camera.'

He looked dubious. He must have seen Elsie was biting back a scathing remark because his doubt vanished a split-second later. 'On it,' he said.

'And check in with the DVLA while you're on the way,' she added. 'The car's probably been nicked or driven on cloned plates but check anyway.'

With Stryker gone in search of the car, the race was on to find the killer.

She turned to Knox. 'Where are we with the owner of the office building?'

'I pulled the land reg stuff no probs,' Knox said, 'and a quick squizz on Google found me an advert for property guardians. There are loadsa companies doing it and I don't know which the office owners used.'

'Called them?'

'Place is owned by a hedge fund,' Knox said. 'They're closed on weekends.'

'Find out who the directors are, send the local police to find out in person if necessary. The sooner we know which property guardian agency was managing the office, the sooner we know who they let to. That ought to get us the killer's real name.'

The net was finally closing in. Elsie said as much.

'And that,' Bertie said, 'is why he's going to be dangerous. He knows the game is up. This will force his hand.'

'Why, though, is he so angry?' Elsie asked.

'He's been hurt,' Bertie said. 'By a woman, of course. It was something so traumatic to his ego that it made him snap. It was almost certainly a rejection of some kind. He didn't directly confront that rage.'

'The women were proxy victims,' Elsie said, recalling his first profile of the Lady Killer. 'Doesn't that mean there's a real victim out there somewhere?'

She imagined some poor woman dead in her flat, unfound for months, the first victim of the Lady Killer but nobody knew about it. She wondered how long it would take for someone to find her if she were murdered. She had no close friends who visited, no family except her dad, so it could take a while.

'The opposite,' Bertie said. 'If he'd killed the woman who spurned him, he wouldn't be taking it out on proxy victims.'

'By that logic, if you're right about him losing control now we're close to catching him, he'll go after the women he loves, won't he?'

'I'm afraid he will. If you can't find her before he does, you'll have a fourth victim on your hands.'

# Chapter 55: Lawyers and Jam

White City was rammed on Saturday afternoon. According to his TomTom, traffic was running bumper to bumper from Shepherd's Bush roundabout all the way up to the A40. Once again, Stryker found himself cursing the realities of London living. He was crawling along and couldn't see a damned thing.

How on earth was he supposed to find one car among thousands?

'Siri, call Ian.'

His phone, which lay in the passenger seat, sprang to life.

'Yo.'

'Ian, I need you to run down a number plate for me. Can you do that right now?'

'The boss lady's way ahead of ya,' he said. 'She had me email you everything the DVLA's got on him.'

He leant over and opened his email while keeping Ian on the line. A loud honk sounded from behind him.

'Read me it, will you, Ian?' Stryker said. 'Can't afford to get done for using my mobile while driving.'

'Awright,' Ian said. 'Get this, the car hasn't been reported stolen and it ain't a cloned plate either. The registration is in the name of some law firm in Pimlico. I'm texting you the address. The DVLA's records say that the car is an Audi A8, last year's model, very swish and plenty of room in the boot too. It is black after all.'

The address flashed up on Stryker's phone as Ian was speaking. 'How far's that from me?'

'Dunno,' Ian said. 'Half hour?'

'Look it up for me?'

Stryker heard the telltale click-clack of Ian's mechanical keyboard. 'Yep, twenty-five ish mins in traffic.'

'This firm – they open?' It was, after all, Saturday afternoon.

Ian laughed. 'You think lawyers get Saturdays off? They wish. Someone will be in even if it's some poor sod of a paralegal.'

HALF AN HOUR LATER, Stryker found himself in a marble-bedecked foyer where a smartly attired young lady sat in front of a large wooden desk. Behind her, stencilled on the wall in gold, was the name Faulkland & Robertson LLP. To her right was a security door. The firm was based in a grand old townhouse nestled between two embassies. It was the sort of well-heeled firm that dealt with the posh Sloanie types who lived in the area. Their website advertised them as "specialists in advising high net worth clients". Stryker had no idea what that really meant but he imagined a lot of zeros.

The receptionist was polite enough.

'I'm afraid there's nobody here to speak to you, Mr Stryker,' she said. 'I wish we could help.'

'Look,' Stryker said, his eyes darting down to a name badge pinned to her chest, 'Deborah, I'm not here to waste time. One of your cars was used in the commission of a crime. I know there's someone here who can help with my inquiry.'

She glanced over her shoulder at the door that led through to the back. 'I can't, inspector. I'd be fired.'

'For helping with a murder inquiry?' Stryker said. 'Surely keeping the name Faulkland & Robertson out of the press here is invaluable.'

'Murder?' Her eyes went wide. 'Wait here for a moment, okay?'

She leapt up out of her seat and turned to the security door. Stryker watched as she typed 8678 into the keypad. She swung right after she entered and the door slammed shut behind her. He gave her thirty seconds head start and followed her in.

The other side of the door led through to an open-plan office area. A few people were working though none paid much heed to Stryker. Judging by the cheap desks, they were paralegals or secretaries, the unimportant kind of replaceable staff that no law firm would allocate a company car.

He turned right, following the path he thought that the receptionist had taken, and found himself in a stairwell. If, he reasoned, he was a partner in this firm, he'd have his office on the highest floor with the best views, well away from the noise and traffic. He climbed quickly, keeping his eyes peeled for anyone else in the building. As he had expected, the top floor was much better appointed than the ground floor. It was divided into two halves with a central corridor down the middle. On the left was a door with a brass name plaque which read "Faulkland" and on the right there was an identical door with an identical plaque which read "Robertson". The left-hand door was closed while the right was ajar. Mr Robertson was in.

As he approached, he heard voices. One belonged to the receptionist he'd spoken to not two minutes earlier.

'I'll get rid of him then, Mr Robertson,' she said. She walked out into the hallway with head bowed, not paying attention, and collided with Stryker.

'I see you've found a partner for me to speak to,' Stryker said. 'Thanks for being so accommodating, Deborah.'

He left her in the hallway and walked into the solicitor's office without knocking.

'Mr Robertson, I presume?'

The solicitor looked up. He was wearing a suit without a tie. His top button was undone and his jacket was slung over the back of his chair. He looked the spitting image of the killer but for the lack of a lazy eye. In front of him was a nameplate that read "Joshua Robertson". James and Joshua. Surely they had to be brothers?

'Who let you in here?' he demanded.

He even sounded like the man from St Dunstan in the East. 'Your car,' Stryker said. He reeled off the registration plate. 'Where is it?'

'What car?'

'Don't play games with me, Mr Robertson,' Stryker said. 'The Audi A8 your firm leased. It's yours, isn't it?'

'No.'

'Then if I subpoena your insurer, they're not going to tell me you're the insured driver?' Stryker smiled sweetly.

'I don't own it.'

It was, Stryker thought, a subtle distinction. Of course, Robertson didn't *own* the car per se. His firm leased it. 'But your firm leases it.'

'Get out.'

No denial this time. Just faux outrage. 'I'll happily go, Mr Robertson, but if I do then I'm coming back with half of Scotland Yard and we'll examine every inch of this place and we won't be quiet about it. Can't imagine it'll stay quiet for long if a big shot Pimlico solicitor like yourself is under investigation for murder.'

Robertson set his jaw, his lower lip protruding. 'What is it that you want?'

'Your cooperation,' Stryker said simply. 'I know it's your car, I know you don't want me crawling all over your business, and you certainly don't want the press involved so let's make things nice and easy, eh? Who's got the keys to your Audi? Your brother?'

As soon as he said "brother", Stryker knew he was right.

The lawyer seemed to deflate. 'I sometimes let James borrow my car.'

The Lady Killer really was called James Robertson. It had sounded almost as made up as Drew Rekshun. 'Then you know why I'm here.'

'What's he done this time?'

His receptionist clearly hadn't told him. Nor had Stryker mentioned why he was here yet. '*This* time? What did he do *last* time?'

Robertson looked at him, exhaled deeply and gestured at the still-open door. 'Close the door. The walls have ears around here.'

No harm in humouring him. Once the door was shut, Stryker helped himself to a seat. 'Siblings, eh? Always a pain in the arse.'

'No kidding.'

'Mine got arrested once for selling crack,' Stryker said. 'The week before my passing out parade.'

It was a total lie. Stryker was an only child. Robertson fell for it hook, line and sinker.

'Right,' he said. 'James has always been a thorn in my side. First, he dropped out of university – it was only Loughborough mind you – and then he decided that his life calling was as a personal trainer cum sports physiotherapist. Not much money in that, I can tell you!'

That explained his knowledge of anatomy. If James had spent years giving sports massages then it was only natural that he would know how to break rigor mortis. The personal training explained his strength too. What it didn't explain was the "last time" which Joshua Robertson had referred to.

'Sounds like he's drifted,' Stryker said. 'How's he managed to live off that sort of money?'

'He doesn't,' Robertson said. 'He's always in my pocket now that Mum and Dad are gone. Good job I earn well! You'd think I was the older one the way he goes on about supporting the family. He's thirty-four and still hasn't got a proper job.'

'That must be frustrating. What's also got to hurt is having a criminal for a brother especially when you've got such similar names.'

From the derision evident on Robertson's face, Stryker knew he'd overstepped the mark. It was one thing to listen to a man rant about his family, another thing entirely to join in with the insults.

'Woah, woah, woah,' Robertson said. 'He hasn't been convicted of a crime yet.'

'Yet,' Stryker agreed. 'But I imagine if someone were to Google "J Robertson" and find a crime report, it'd be pretty damaging for your businesses.'

His eyes flashed angrily. 'You're in dangerous territory, inspector. Don't you dare threaten me.'

Stryker gave a languorous shrug. 'No threats, Mr J Robertson, merely an observation. Perhaps you and I can work together to prevent that sort of confusion. Tell me what it was that James did "last time".'

'He's a thief, okay?' Robertson said. 'He's been pinching things for years. I can't control his kleptomania any more than he can.'

'But you can cover it up,' Stryker said, filling in the blanks.

Robertson swore. 'I'm not admitting to that.'

'I don't expect you to. Can I assume though, for the sake of this discussion only, that your brother has somehow avoided entanglement with the law?'

The solicitor hesitated and then gave an almost imperceptible nod.

That explained how James Robertson had managed to avoid being in the system. He'd never had a record because his brother had always bailed him out. It also explained why Dr Leigh was so surprised that the Lady Killer had managed to escalate so quickly from having no record to full-blown murder. Most criminals started out small and grew over time as they got their sea legs. The police might have noticed as James followed the same pattern of escalating criminality had his brother not somehow hidden it.

'It's more serious than theft,' Stryker said flatly.

'I'm not following.'

'Your brother is wanted in connection with a murder inquiry.'

Stryker's dramatic pronouncement didn't faze Robertson in the slightest. The shocked expression which he had now assumed took him far too long to conjure.

'You knew,' Stryker said quietly. The accusation lingered in the air. Robertson knew or strongly suspected his brother's involvement. He wasn't even angry. If Stryker had been accused of being related to a murderer, well, he'd probably have laughed at the absurdity of it all. To be so damned calm in the face of a murder accusation was unnerving. It made Stryker wonder if the man in front of him also harboured dark and violent fantasies.

'No,' Robertson said firmly. 'I didn't know a thing, and frankly, I don't believe you. This interview is over. I'm going to have to ask you to leave.'

'It's an interview now?' Stryker mocked. 'I thought we were having a friendly chit-chat. Where's the car, Josh?'

'I said leave,' Robertson demanded. 'And don't come back.'

'I shan't,' Stryker said and then mentally added: *without a warrant.*

What he would do is have Robertson watched like a hawk in case he got in contact with his brother.

# Chapter 56: The Aspiring Billionaire

Knox and Elsie had come to New Pinnacle Plaza, the latest super skyscraper to pop up in Mayfair. It was home to Mr Adelrick Melrose, the brainchild of the StayAway site that Mr Larkins used. He was the same Mr Melrose who had foisted Review My Ex upon the world and who had been as evasive as possible when Elsie had visited him in Old Street.

Yesterday's visit to the American had gone terribly because she'd gone in blind with no warrant, no plan. This time, she came prepared.

A white-gloved footman was in the lobby when they arrived. He tried to stop them making a beeline for the lift to the penthouse but soon acquiesced when Elsie flashed her warrant card. Given the lack of protest, it was fair to assume that Adelrick hadn't made himself popular with the domestic help.

'Swish lift,' Knox said, looking around. The lift, which was on the western side of New Pinnacle Plaza, ran up the outside of the building offering sweeping views of the south, west and north through floor-to-ceiling windows. The building was in the perfect spot. To the south, Elsie could see Green Park and Buckingham Palace. To the west, Hyde Park and Holland Park beyond that. To the north, Regent's Park and Primrose Hill.

'I heard a flat in this building costs over half a billion. That's billion with a *b*,' Elsie said as they ascended so smoothly that it didn't feel like they were moving at all. 'And Adelrick Melrose has got the penthouse.'

'Nobody makes that sort of wonga without stepping on a few toes,' Knox said. 'Bet he don't sleep too well no matter how many silk pillows he lays his head on.'

From her last encounter with him, Elsie doubted that Adelrick had any moral qualms. He seemed only too happy to take his money and laugh all the way to the bank.

He was waiting for them when the lift doors pinged open.

'Detective, how nice of you to visit,' Adelrick said. 'To what do I owe the displeasure this time? Come to serve me with a pointless warrant?'

'No,' Elsie said firmly. 'We just want to chat. This is my colleague, Detective Sergeant Knox. Nice place you've got here.'

It was. The ceilings were double height while all-glass walls ran from floor to ceiling which made the enormous space feel even bigger. Because it was open plan except for a few glass-walls which divided up the living room and the kitchen, Elsie could see the London skyline in every direction. It was like being on the viewing deck at the Shard except there were no tourists and exquisite, minimalist furniture filled the apartment. The sheer volume of empty space was testimony to Adelrick's wealth. Where Elsie's own flat was crammed with storage solutions in every nook and cranny to make use of all the available space, Adelrick's home was vast and cavernous in the manner usually reserved for stately homes out in the countryside.

Adelrick looked at her curiously. 'Would you care for a tour as we "chat", detectives?'

If it got him talking, there was no harm in having a nose around. She gestured for him to lead on.

'Been here long?' Knox asked. 'It don't looked lived in, see.'

'It shouldn't,' Adelrick said. 'I redecorate every other month. I like my home to change with the seasons. When Hyde Park turns icy and desolate, I make the flat warm and inviting. When it's spring out and I see the bluebells appearing like magic all over St James' Park, I like to opt for cool, neutral tones that don't detract from what's around me. In fall, when leaves tumble to the ground, I like reds and oranges to match. But you didn't come here to admire my interior design skills.'

'I'm here about StayAway.'

'Ah, you are all over my business interests this week, detective,' Adelrick said as he walked them through the living room. 'What precisely do you want?'

'I need a list of where one of your clients has stayed over the last year. He's wanted in connection with a murder inquiry.'

'Got a warrant?' Adelrick taunted. He knew the answer.

'No, but I can get one,' Elsie said. 'I thought I'd give you the professional courtesy of asking nicely first.' *And save myself the time and risk of going to court.*

He laughed. It was a derisive, nasty sound. 'I'm going to have to call your bluff, detective. But thanks for dropping by.'

There was no mention of the "end to end encryption" that he'd used for Review My Ex. This time a warrant would get them the right information. If only they had time.

Knox plonked herself down on a nearby sofa which faced out to the west. 'I think what my boss means, pretty boy, is that we're doing you a favour. We know you've got a stock market float coming up, don't we, boss? Wouldn't it be a shame if the media heard that poor Adelrick here had been arrested for obstructing a murder inquiry just when he was due to ring the opening bell?'

Adelrick's face dropped. 'That's blackmail!'

His outrage elicited a nod from Knox. 'Effective too in my mind. Two major companies, one billionaire arsehole. Bound to make the front page, ain't it? Can't see this going too well for you. I've got every major newspaper editor in my phone book. Want to risk it?'

Elsie tried not to mirror the smile spreading across Knox's face. 'It would be very helpful if you cooperated with us, Mr Melrose. Let's not get into allegations of wrongdoing here. We're all sensible adults, aren't we?'

He paced the room, one hand in his pocket as if he were fishing for a mobile phone with which to call his lawyers. Knox continued to smile at him.

Finally, he stopped and turned to Elsie. 'If, and I mean if, I give you what you want, you'll keep my involvement totally confidential? No leaks to the press, no accidentally telling the information commissioner's office, nada.'

'I think we could manage that,' Elsie said carefully to avoid saying that she *would* do so, just an assertion that she *could* do so if she so chose. The subtlety was lost on a now-mollified Adelrick.

'And no arrest?'

'No arrests,' Elsie said, unable to avoid a direct reply this time. Not that she could bind herself with such an outrageous promise.

'What's the name?'

'James Robertson. I've got his profile link so we can find the right James.'

'Give me half an hour, I'll make some calls.'

# Chapter 57: The List

Half an hour later they had the list. Elsie and Knox left New Pinnacle Plaza with a printed copy in hand and a digital version in Elsie's email inbox. On the way out, she flicked through eight pages of printouts detailing everywhere that James Robertson had stayed. He'd been a busy boy. He'd organised several dozen stays via StayAway and it was entirely possible that he'd used other websites too.

Knox drove on the way back to New Scotland Yard. For the first time since Elsie had met the older woman, she finally felt like they could have a conversation. The list shook in Elsie's hand as they drove over a pothole. Until they had a chance to assess it properly, there wasn't much to be gained in obsessing over it. The office was a smidge under two miles away but in traffic, it would take them just over fifteen minutes. With a bit of luck, Stryker, Ian, Annie and Uncle Bertie would be waiting for their arrival in the incident room. Elsie had also put out a general call for assistance to everyone who'd previously volunteered to help with the investigation. She could imagine conference room one filling up once again with the Met's finest, all eager to assist.

'Knox,' Elsie said tentatively, the elephant in the car looming large. 'When you said you deserved to have got my job... why was that?'

The question elicited a sigh. For a moment, Elsie thought Knox was about to be combative once again, that the breakthrough of the day was temporary, but then Knox did something that Elsie recognised as one of her own bad habits – she chewed over the edge of her bottom lip with her front incisors.

'I haven't told anyone this.'

'You can tell me – as long as it isn't illegal, I'll keep it to my-self.'

'It ain't illegal. You prob know this but I started with the force when I was eighteen,' Knox said, her hands still perfectly steady at ten and two. 'I worked well hard for the first few years and I earned my place on Fairbanks' murder investigation team..'

'I saw.' Elsie had been given Knox's service record. Until only a short while ago, it had been exemplary. 'Are the rumours true?'

'The "I'm a lush" rumours?' Knox said, her eyes still fixed on the road. 'I guess a bit. I like a drink every now and then. It's a hard job. But the booze isn't why I got demoted if that's what yer getting at.'

'Then why were you demoted?'

'I changed my mind.'

If Elsie had been curious before, she was the proverbial cat walking headfirst into traffic now. 'About...?'

'About fucking Fairbanks.'

'What did he do?'

'This is still between us, right?' Knox said. 'Swear it on your old man's life?'

'Sure.'

'That's closer to the truth than you might like,' Knox said darkly. 'I was ... well... I made a mistake. Once. I drank too much at the Met's Christmas shindig, one thing led to another and...'

Elsie put two and two together. 'Yuck!' she pulled a face. 'Fairbanks?!'

'Yep,' Knox said. 'One drunken blowie last Xmas. I was feeling sorry for myself – my husband died at Xmas a few years back – and he offered me a bit of affection. Part of me craved it.'

'And that's why he fired you?'

'Nah,' Knox said. 'Like I said before. I changed my mind. He kept pestering, said if I fucked him, he'd give me the recommendation I needed to make DCI. Until the day before you got offered it, I was a shoo-in. When I didn't follow through, he trumped up misconduct charges and said that if I disputed it, he'd tell the whole fucking force about Christmas.'

No wonder she'd been raw the first time they met. She'd been sextorted and blackmailed by the slimiest man either of them had ever met. 'Knox... I'm so sorry.'

There was a tear forming at the corner of Knox's eye. 'Look, we're almost back. Don't tell anyone else this, 'kay?'

After another two minutes, this time in silence, Knox parked up in Mabey's spot and threw her the keys. 'Come on, boss. Time to catch a killer and get justice for Matthews.'

AS ELSIE HAD HOPED, the whole team was on-site and waiting in the incident room. A large pot of coffee was on a warming mat, steam gently rising off of it. When he saw her looking, Stryker poured her a mug and then went back to whatever he had been doing. She was half-asleep and her head felt like someone had thwacked it with a sledgehammer. Shame the caffeine didn't actually help with the chronic fatigue. She didn't have the heart to tell Stryker that as it was nice of him to try.

Everybody rushed to sit down when Elsie did except for Bertie who had already assumed the seat nearest the door. He was deep in thought, his eyes peering over the top of his glasses which were perched on the very end of his nose. It appeared that he had been reviewing pages upon pages of his own handwritten notes.

To his left, Ian and Annie sat side by side looking like chalk and cheese with a sharp contrast between Annie's powder blue power suit and Ian's heavy metal T-shirt. Stryker now sat alone staring at the screen as Flick's e-fit of the killer loomed large on the projector.

'Is that our man?' Elsie said. He looked less dangerous than she had expected. She had imagined the sort of man who could kill with a single stab wound would be scary, shaven-headed, perhaps even ex-military. The man Flick had sketched looked more like a gym rat facing down a mid-life crisis with a slightly hooked nose – it had to have been broken at least once, but not in a charming Owen Wilson way – which combined with an off-kilter eye to make his face look decidedly unbalanced.

'It's him,' Stryker confirmed.

'I have,' Elsie said, 'attained a list of everywhere that our killer has rented using the StayAway website. Ian, I emailed it to you before I got here. Any patterns showing up for you?'

He nodded, gulped, and raised a hand.

'You don't need permission to speak, Ian.'

'Right... right... can I borrow that projector please, Seb?' Ian asked. 'Sorry, Detective Inspector Stryker.'

Stryker grinned, unplugged the HDMI cable plugged into his laptop and passed it over.

'I took your list, looked 'em up on Google Maps. First up, he's picked nice places. We're talking big townhouses, luxury flats, the kind of places that rich people live in.'

'How's he affording that?' Stryker asked.

'Easy, he's a thief,' Ian said. 'Not all but many of these places have been subject to police complaints over the last eight months. Guests who stayed in these rentals invariably found that their stuff disappeared while they were out. It's usually really common stuff such as jewellery, mobile phones, laptops, passports, cash, cards and the like. Things a thief can get rid of without being noticed. The common denominator is really obvious when you spot it. No thefts before James Robertson rented the place, lots of thefts after.'

It was such an obvious scam – find where rich people live, get access once and make a copy of the key to make it easy to return later. 'He's been copying keys,' Elsie said to a murmur of assent.

'Yep,' Ian said. 'Probably. He's also smart. The places he's robbed have crap security. I had a look on Google Maps, zoomed in on Street View to check out the frontage, and the ones where thefts have occurred don't show any obvious signs of CCTV cameras or other security. I reckon he's been using his StayAway bookings to scope the places out.'

Elsie swore. It was so out of character that it elicited a "young lady!" from Uncle Bertie who, until just then, had been quietly nursing a mug of coffee.

'Don't you lot see it?' Elsie said. 'He's not just been renting these places to steal – the money is secondary. He's been using these homes to lure women to their deaths. Who would suspect that he's dangerous when he takes women to Michelin-standard restaurants, drives an Audi A8 – any news on that by the way? – and takes them home to multi-million-pound townhouses?'

'About the car,' Ian said, 'it's registered alright but to someone else. Looks like a corporate lease. Can I ask you detective types a question though? About the website?'

'Go on,' Elsie said.

'The dates he's bin out robbin',' Ian said. 'How's he know when to go?'

The obvious answer was that he didn't. Just that morning he'd been interrupted by the cleaner.

'Relevance?'

'This morning, he got seen, right? But none of the crime reports for the burglaries mention seeing someone. He can't be that lucky.'

Elsie looked around the room. How had the killer managed to get in and out without being seen? It was the same question she'd been asking since St Dunstan in the East and the answer was staring her right in the face.

'He's pulled the same trick twice! Why didn't we see it?'

Confused expressions met her gaze.

'Think about it,' Elsie said. 'At St Dunstan in the East, we wasted forever looking for his car but he didn't drive it there because he lived next door. It was Occam's razor all along. The simplest explanation is the best. We couldn't find a car coming or going from the crime scene because he his car was safely tucked up in the parking garage a hundred yards to the east of the crime scene. No wonder he wasn't seen if he could drive into an abandoned car park and then dump the body when nobody was looking. The same probably applies to Chelsea Physic Garden. Someone find out if there are any properties that were vacant nearby –

I'm betting he was a property guardian near there as he used it as a dump site.'

'Right,' Stryker said. 'I can do that... but how's that help us now?'

'He committed murder in a StayAway rental last night. It likely wasn't his first time. What if he's using one of them now?'

Even Bertie swore. It was so simple, so elegant. Rent a house with an integral garage, scope it out and check for CCTV on the first visit, and come back with a car, presumably with the body in the boot. Simple.

'How's that fit with your theory, Dr Leigh?' It still felt weird calling Uncle Bertie that. She'd heard him talk to Dad over the years but this was the first time that he was working for her rather than with her.

Bertie looked around the room, his eyes big and doleful. He pushed his glasses further up his nose. 'It explains the contradiction, I suppose. Our killer is not the sophisticated genius who could get in and out of St Dunstan in the East unseen. Instead, he is simply following the path of least resistance in that regard and dumping the body on the doorstep... or close enough to the doorstep while still satisfying his compulsion.'

'Conscious?' Elsie prompted.

'Perhaps not,' Bertie said. 'It may be that he is choosing dump sites that mirror a place of trauma for him, somewhere he was rejected by a woman. There is something I am curious about. How did he choose *when* to visit those particular properties? If they were actively being rented out, surely it was a risk to break in and steal?'

A light bulb went off in Elsie's brain. 'Ian, get up the Stay-Away website for me.'

He did. The home page flashed up a registration screen. In the top right, it read *"Already signed up? Login here"* in tiny grey text.

'Now, login,' Elsie said.

'Can't, don't have an account.'

'We'll use mine then. Pass your laptop down.'

Sixty seconds later, Ian's Alienware laptop was flashing its LEDs in front of Elsie, and they were in. She clicked through to find a random London property and smiled.

'See?' she said.

They didn't. Blank looks met her excitement.

'Look,' she said, this time using the mouse to drag the cursor around and around the box marked "select a date". It was more than simply a space for her desired dates. When she clicked on it, coloured boxes came to life. A key underneath indicated that the cheapest dates for the month were illuminated in green. The midrange prices were in yellow through to orange. The most in demand – and therefore the priciest – were in red. She read out that explanation.

'And,' she added, 'the greyed-out boxes show when the place isn't available. He knows when properties are empty because StayAway actually tells him. The dates show up as available for rental, ergo, the property is empty.'

'So,' Knox said, 'he's found a way to break into houses to steal and kill. How do we find him?'

'He's a creature of a habit,' Elsie said. 'Isn't he, Dr Leigh?'

The profiler nodded. 'He does exhibit a consistent and well-defined modus operandi.'

'So, he'll probably go back to one of these rental properties. He'll pick one where he can park his car, one without CCTV, and probably one he hasn't been back to. That sound likely?'

'Highly,' Bertie said. 'He's taken a few risks but he's careful with it. Hitting the same properties repeatedly would expose him to the chance that the locks had been changed or cameras added in response to his last break-in.'

'Locks!' Stryker said. 'How's he been copying the keys? Surely that's how we can find him?'

It wasn't a bad shout. It was just too slow. According to Bertie, now the killer had been forced to abandon St Dunstan in the East, he'd lose the last of his self-control and lash out well before Stryker could trawl every locksmith in London with a copy of Flick's e-fit.

'Keep it on the back burner,' Elsie said diplomatically. 'For now, we've got more pressing things to think about. What happened with the car you tried to track down?'

'It belongs to a law firm which is co-owned by one Joshua Robertson.'

'Got to be a relative.'

'No doubt about it,' Stryker said. 'Joshua Robertson is his younger brother. While he admitted to knowing that James is a habitual thief, he denied everything else. I think we should get a warrant to tap his phones. In the meantime, Knox did me a favour and asked her friend Ozzy to tail him while we concentrate on finding the brother. So far, Robertson is sitting tight in his office.'

'Good work, both of you. The warrant is a good shout but be quick. I'm mindful that time is getting away from us. James is out there somewhere and we need to find him pronto.'

'So what's the plan?'

What was the plan? So much information had come to light in the last few minutes that it was almost overwhelming. Elsie could feel the fatigue creeping in at the edge of her periphery. If she wasn't careful, she'd crash and be of no use.

'Ian, Stryker, I want you two to analyse the list of all the rental properties he's been in. Get me the details for every last one. I want to know the type of property, how visible the front door is from the road, how many crime reports there are associated with the place. Plot 'em on the map. Mark those properties where a burglary's been reported in red. Those he's less likely to go back to.'

The two men shuffled to the end of the conference room table and set to work to translate the list that she and Knox had obtained from Adelrick Melrose into a plotted map.

'What next?' She looked around the room. The list would be over eighty strong before the robbery crime reports eliminated some. They couldn't keep an eye on every one of those.

'CCTV?' Annie volunteered. 'If he's been avoiding places with security as you said, we can knock off anywhere he rented but decided not to return to.'

Those were the lucky ones, the homes that he'd scoped out and never robbed. 'Good. More. We need more. What else?'

'Garages,' Knox said. 'If there's cover for his car, we bump it to the top of the list.'

It was a solid thought. He'd had access to a garage at St Dunstan and that had undoubtedly made his job easier. 'He didn't have a garage in Holland Park. He's not totally risk-averse. I like your idea but let's try and rate the properties based on exposure risk rather than a binary division based on garage status. We need to be holistic here. If he can dart ten feet under the cover of darkness in Holland Park, he's willing to take even bigger risks now.'

Bertie raised a hand politely. 'Perhaps,' he said, 'the Lady Killer will become less picky. He's not had to deal with this sort of pressure before. He can't go back and rent more properties – he's got to know we know his name so everything here on out has to be strictly off that grid which means he's going to be spending cash not cards – so he's only got the selection he already knows about. He may be choosing the "least bad option" rather than a property which ticks all his boxes.'

Compromise. The killer would have to compromise. 'Then what,' Elsie asked, 'would the killer prioritise? Is he going to be efficient and look for the most logical places to commit a murder? Or is he going to be smart and try to guess what we think he's doing so that he can do the opposite?'

'Neither,' Bertie said. 'He's driven by compulsion. It's not an entirely conscious, logical choice on his part.'

Elsie felt herself getting annoyed at how vague that was. 'But practically, what does that mean?'

'He's likely to stay in the same comfort zone, geographically and logistically.'

Every single property that James Robertson had rented was in the same vein – big, posh houses in zones one and two. Nothing he'd stayed in was cheap. One of the girls had suggested geographic profiling of the victims right at the start of the investigation. That seemed like an eternity ago. Perhaps it would be possible to apply the same approach to profiling the rental properties?

'Can we build that into a profile of the places he might go?'

Knox raised a hand. 'It was Matthews who suggested geographic profiling way back. I looked into it a bit when you dismissed it out of hand. Aren't we going to come up against the same brick wall that we've got an itinerant killer with no permanent fixed abode?'

It was true. The Lady Killer had hopped from rental to property guardianship and back again. They had no known history of everywhere he'd stayed. Yet. But he had to call somewhere home.

'Where does his brother live?' she asked, thinking of the lawyer that Stryker had just interviewed. 'If his brother is his closest family, it stands to reason that anywhere they've lived together could be home. Where did he grow up? Ian, can you pull up the census and electoral roll records? Look for any overlap between Joshua Robertson and James Robertson.'

He looked annoyed at having to switch tasks so quickly. The map which he'd been busy building was minimised to the system tray. In its place, he opened the necessary databases. She waited, her fingers drumming impatiently against the desk. Minutes ticked by, nobody daring to make small talk, all eyes fixed on the screen.

'Chelsea,' Ian announced. 'Beaufort Road. That's the poor bit, isn't it? Looks like our two "J"s lived there with their parents for a while.'

Elsie knew it well. It was a road that bisected the Kings Road, half a mile or so west of Sloane Square Underground Station.

Ian kept tapping away, cross-referencing the address against the Land Registry's ownership database. 'It seems to have been inherited by the brother, Joshua, and I'd guess it's not a rental.'

'That had to hurt,' Elsie said. One brother a successful solicitor and property baron, the other an itinerant wanderer with no proper job.

'Right,' she continued. 'Here's the plan. We're going to prioritise the list. Ian can carry on mapping it – I assume that'll take a while – and then we'll divvy it up. If we call in enough volunteers, we can cover most if not all of the properties. We need to be careful that this doesn't leak to the press.'

She looked around the room. Someone with access to the incident room had already leaked once. Was one of the people in this room responsible? If she couldn't figure out who the leak was – assuming it wasn't Matthews anyway – then sooner or later, she'd have to pass the issue to the Directorate of Professional Standards. That would have to wait until after this case was resolved, one way or another.

'Dr Leigh, I want you to come with me. I've got hundreds of volunteers to corral and you know most of them. Is that okay?'

He nodded. 'Consider me your personal assistant for the afternoon.'

'Boss?' Stryker said. 'What about the warrant for Robertson?'

Elsie's headache flared up. There were too many little things in motion, too much to keep track of. 'Right, yes, we need one.'

'I know but you asked me to help Ian with the map. Which do you want me to do?'

'The warrant. Go get the warrant. Then come back, put the surveillance in place and then see how Ian is progressing.'

She could see the afternoon melting away before her. Before she could corral the extended family that was the Metropolitan Police, she needed to give Knox a task.

'Knox,' she said. 'I want you out on patrol. As Ian maps the properties, drive past them. Have a quick look. See what the state of play is. Anything that looks suspicious, call me and I'll send out a volunteer team.'

She would, in effect, act as the advance recon team to scope out the StayAway properties.

'Got it, boss.'

'Then move. Stay in contact. If you've got anything, WhatsApp the entire team in case one of us is occupied. Play it smart, play it by the book.'

# Chapter 58: All on Deck

The volunteers trickled back in over the course of the afternoon. There were far too many of them to effectively make use of. Working out who was there, what they were capable of doing, and managing them was turning into a nightmare. Annie's team was on-site and raring to go but had nothing new to examine so they had taken up residence at the back of conference room one to review and re-review the existing evidence. Confirmation had come back from the lab that the blood drops Annie recovered from the car park by St Dunstan in the East did belong to Layla Morgan which meant they were on the right track.

How infuriating it was to know the killer's name, have his DNA on file, and know where he had been mere hours earlier, but not be able to arrest him. He was simply out of reach.

Elsie had Ozzy's team keeping tabs on the brother. He'd made a phone call to a criminal barrister in King's Bench Walk but their warrant didn't cover eavesdropping on that as it was a privileged conversation. It seemed that Joshua knew that the situation was a car crash in motion and he was keen to ensure that the best Queen's Counsel in London was onside and ready to represent the Robertsons.

'How do you want to play this?' Bertie asked.

'How about I go have a nap while you catch the killer?'

She was only half-joking. In the state she was in, she didn't feel fit to organise hundreds of the Met's finest.

'Can I be honest with you, Bertie? I'm feeling a bit overwhelmed here. How do I organise everyone? How do I stop the killer realising we're onto him if hundreds of us flood the streets of London to look for him? Won't the press notice?'

Bertie took her to one side. 'Lass, you've got this. This isn't going to be easy or straightforward. It never is. Your father—'

'He'd be in his element,' Elsie said. 'He always made everything look so easy.'

The profiler laughed. 'Not when he was with me. Your old man talks a good game and he knows his stuff. That doesn't mean he didn't fret about getting things wrong. He's made his fair share of mistakes, he just doesn't talk about them.'

'He's proud man,' she said. There was no doubt about that. Elsie could just imagine him sweeping his failures under the carpet.

'Do your best, Elsie. That's all you can ever do.'

She knew that. 'I'm just so damned tired. It's so unfair.'

'I know,' he said. 'I know. The chronic fatigue syndrome has cost you so much. You know I've been best friends with your father for your entire life and most of mine so I'm going to give you the advice I wish I'd given you years ago. Life is too short to spend it dwelling on what's fair instead of what is. You need to grieve for the woman you think you ought to be and accept the woman you are because the woman you are is spectacular and I'm so proud to call you my goddaughter. Now go get in front of that lectern and tell these folks what you need.'

'Come with me.'

'No,' Bertie said. 'It's time for you to be the leader you were born to be. Go and prove the doubters wrong. Find the Lady Killer. Solve the impossible case. I'll be watching from right here.'

Alone, she traipsed down the stairs to the front of conference room one. Her back straightened as she walked past colleagues, a shiver running down her spine. This was it. This was the moment she put everything on the table.

She descended towards the front of the conference room, her confidence faltering with every step. A sea of heads turned in her direction. She ignored the lot of them, focused on Uncle Bertie hiding in the back row, and turned on the microphone.

'Good evening, ladies and gents, thank you for coming in. You all know why you're here. This is, simply put, a manhunt. The Lady Killer has been identified and his residence at St Dunstan raided. He is on the run. I have a list of places that we believe he may go to this evening. Those of you who have undergone surveillance training will each be assigned a location to watch. Those who have not will remain here to assist in coordinating our efforts. If there are no questions, can I please ask you to come to the front if you're in the surveillance group.'

Hands shot up.

'Who is he?' one woman asked.

'I'm afraid that until we have our suspect in custody, we are operating on the basis of an e-fit only.'

'But if you know who he is, why can't you tell us?' she asked again.

'Operational security,' Elsie said ominously. The leak was probably in this room. There had been a continuous stream of support staff in and out of the incident room since the start of the investigation. Elsie stared around, wondering which familiar face had leaked information to the press.

A few more mundane questions later, everyone was on the same page. Bertie walked up to the front and handed her a folder.

'The list, hot off the printer. Ian and Stryker did as you asked and ranked the rentals by priority. Those top of the list tick all the boxes. They're allegedly empty tonight according to Stay-Away, they've got garages, they haven't been robbed yet, and, perhaps most importantly, there isn't any sign of visible security on Google Street View.'

She perused the list which had been printed out as a giant table. Each property had a score in each column. Proximity to the Robertson family home in Mayfair, presence of CCTV, garage, crime reports on file, and availability this evening. Twelve targets met all the criteria that Bertie had outlined. Another twenty-six met all but one of the criteria. That gave them thirty-eight plausible targets and those were only properties they knew about. It was entirely possible that James Robertson had also been using other short-term rental websites, other profiles on StayAway, or even sites like Gumtree or Facebook to find places.

Even with her team of volunteers, it was a daunting task to cover them all. She made a quick call. The top twelve would go to her core team, Knox, Stryker and her. Ozzy's team would take any they couldn't cover. Yohann was coordinating for them while Ozzy ran point on keeping tabs on Joshua Robertson.

Fairbanks – who until now Elsie hadn't seen loitering by the door – would get the least likely properties. She couldn't exclude him entirely from the operation without seeming petty, but she'd be damned if she was going to trust that muppet with her case. If his entire team came in, they could easily cover twenty of those low priority properties on their own.

Stryker came up to her. 'Got a plan?'

'Yep, I think so.' She'd have to make arbitrary allocations of the properties in the middle, and they'd have to be totally on it to manage to cover all twelve of the top tier properties themselves. She'd then have to make sure everyone was properly kitted out with radio, door ram, stab proof vests and everything else they might need to confront a violent serial killer.

'Then let's do this thing.'

# Chapter 59: Him Again

Life in the West End suited Tara Davenport except when she lost her weekends trying to cajole yet another uptight actor or actress into doing the work they'd already agreed to do. Despite working all day Saturday, the New Years' production of *A Life in Ravensburg* was proving the worst thing that she had ever project managed. They were two weeks away from press night and every second was precious.

The latest snafu was with an actor who was well past his sell-by date. He'd spent years on the telly and had brought his ego with him to the theatre. Her boss, the theatre's creative director, was on the phone as she tried to wrap up after the evening show.

'He's just going to ask again,' she said. This particular actor kept asking for "favours". One minute it was a simple rider addition asking for a bowlful of Skittles with all the yellow ones removed. Then he wanted to tweak a line of dialogue. Pushing it, but still doable. Tonight, he wanted extra money for a taxi to work because it was icy out. It was mid-December in England. What did he expect?

By the time she was off the phone – and the actor had his complimentary taxi in the bag thanks to a pushover of a creative director – she was knackered and in dire need of a cigarette.

The fire exit on the other side of the corridor from her office led out to the theatre's tiny staff car park. It felt like a stretch calling it that. Really it was a space big enough for two cars and the mix of recycling and refuse bins that the theatre filled to the brim every night during the post-show clean-up. An alleyway ran down the side of the building so the council could wheel the bins away before morning.

The door clicked shut behind her. She was finally done for the day. Once she had parked herself in a dry corner away from the drizzle of the rain and the smell of the bins, she lit her cigarette and took a long drag.

'Hard day?' a voice said out of the darkness.

She knew that voice. Ice ran through her veins. It was *him*.

He appeared from the pitch-black darkness of the alleyway, his broad frame blocking off any possibility of simply walking away.

It was impossible to stop her voice trembling as she replied. 'What are you doing here?'

'I came to win you back,' he said simply without a trace of irony in his tone. 'I love you, Tara. You know that.'

He's crazy, she thought. Her mobile phone weighed heavily in her pocket. She wished she could call the police, her parents, anyone. Should she yell or scream? Would he be the nice, kind man she'd first met? Or the psychopath he'd proved himself to be? Was he Dr Jekyll or Mr Hyde tonight?

'I...'

'Shh,' he said, stepping closer. 'Don't say anything yet. Please just hear me out, okay? You owe me that.'

Inwardly she chanted, leave me alone, leave me alone, leave me alone. Outwardly she nodded. What choice did she have? 'I know you've had it tough, Tara. Depression... well, it's a black hole. I know you pushed me away because of it. I'm here because I want you to know that I still care, that you're my everything.'

'Three weeks, James,' Tara said. 'That's how long we dated. You don't even know me.'

'I do know you. I know that I love you, that we're meant to be,' James said.

He really had lost it – if he'd ever had it to begin with. The superficial charm had lasted no more than a week. It seemed like everything she knew about him was a lie. The big beautiful house he'd showed her on their third date had been his brother's, the car likewise, and as for his "degree from Oxford", surely nobody counted a foundation degree from Oxford Brookes.

James reached out to touch her lightly on the arm. She recoiled. 'Don't be scared. I know. I know you, Tara. I know you hide in the theatre late every night so you don't have to go home to an empty flat. I know you're throwing yourself into your morning gym sessions to fill every waking so you don't have to spend a moment alone – without me – and I'm here to tell you that you don't have to be alone ever again. I'm going to be with you for the rest of your life.'

She had backed away so far that her back was now pressed firmly against solid brick. He inched ever closer, so close that she could feel the warmth of his rank breath.

'Stop, James, stop!' Tara said. 'We've been broken up now for two months. Why are you coming back now?'

'Because nobody compares to you. Come with me. Just to talk somewhere private.'

A scream caught in her throat. Though she'd never seen it first-hand, she knew he was capable of turning violent. He got this cold, glazed-over and detached look in his eyes whenever he was angry. It was a quiet, burning rage that simmered just beneath the surface.

'I can't,' Tara said. 'Not tonight, okay? This can wait 'til the morning, can't it?'

He pressed closer still, so close that she could almost feel the stiffness of his beard as it grazed her skin. His breath hung in the cold winter air, tepid and foul.

With a long, slow shake of his head, he laughed. 'No, it can't wait, Tara. I'm done with waiting. The rest of our lives together starts here and now. Come with me. My car is parked up around the corner.'

She knew exactly where he meant. There was a small car parking space at the end of the alleyway between the buildings. She needed to get past him to reach civilisation so that she could signal her distress to a passer-by.

Before she could protest, he had seized her arm and begun to steer her down the alleyway.

Despite every fibre of her being yelling that she should run, should flee, should fight, she seized up. She meekly allowed herself to be marched towards his car, the scream still caught in her throat. She knew that one misstep, one word in anger, one failed attempt to flee, and she'd be a goner.

For the last time in her life, she climbed into his car.

# Chapter 60: Downfall

As Elsie drove past the homes which she'd assigned herself, a cluster of three properties in zone one centred on King's Cross, her mind ran in circles. The logistics of this manhunt were proving problematic. There were too many targets, too many teams, and she had no way of keeping on top of what everyone was doing at any given moment.

Warrants were another massive obstacle. She had the right, in law, to enter a property in "close pursuit" of someone she believed had committed, or attempted to commit, a serious crime.

While "close pursuit" wasn't quite as narrow as it sounded, Elsie couldn't possibly argue that she was in pursuit of the same suspect at dozens of residences. She had support staff trying to find the homeowners' contact details so they could simply ask permission to enter the properties but without that, she'd find it hard to justify taking a big red key to the front doors of dozens of very posh homes. No doubt she'd be dealing with the compensation claim fallout for months.

Sometimes the rules had to be bent.

The twelve most likely targets were those she was keen to focus on. These were the grandiose homes that the Lady Killer hadn't yet robbed. Or so they thought. It was entirely possible that some of these thefts had gone unnoticed, that others had been noticed but not reported, or that the report was, for whatever reason, not on the system. Police records were imperfect and smart criminals knew that they could ride the border between police boroughs to stay under the radar. A burglary in Chesham at the end of the Metropolitan Line would only be reported to the Thames Valley Police. Elsie hoped that wasn't the case here. The Lady Killer seemed to operate in a very small geographic area that primarily covered zone one and nibbled at the edges of zone two.

She pulled over and grabbed her phone. 'Knox, any sign of him your end?'

'Nothing,' Knox said. 'This feels like a waste of time.'

It did. Knox was assigned to four high-priority properties. One of those was near St Paul's, the other just to the east in Aldgate. Hers were the nearest to St Dunstan. They were also the busiest roads with ANPR cameras everywhere. Assuming the killer kept his car, he'd probably be avoiding the cameras.

'Stick with it, Knox. We can't afford to have a single property unwatched.'

'I know...'

There was an unspoken "but" hanging in the air. Stick too close to the properties, the killer would never show. Too far away, they'd never see him. It was a delicate balancing act.

'He's got to be out there somewhere,' Elsie said. 'He's been forced from his home. We know he has to find somewhere to lay low and these rental properties make the most sense.'

'What if he's gone to ground in a hotel?' Knox said. 'Or he's sleeping in his car? Or he's ditched everything and started begging on the streets? We'd never find him if he did that.'

'He can't hide forever. We're watching his brother after all. Nobody can stay away from family indefinitely.'

As she said it, she thought of the infamous case of Lord Lucan who had done just that. Could James Robertson also disappear without a trace?

'Okay,' Knox said. She sounded sceptical.

'I'm going to check in with the others. Call me if you find anything.'

She hung up, exhaled, and looked once more at the big house in Argyle Square. To her right was a public garden, lit only by a couple of dim streetlights. It was a similar scene to that of St Dunstan. The only security was a metal fence that barely came up to chest height. There were even benches arrayed haphazardly around the garden, reminiscent of those at both crime scenes.

As she waited, a traffic warden ambled along, checking the cars ahead of her for parking permits. She was about to drive off, circle back around, and head for the other house once again when the thought struck her – *Benches. Both the dump sites had benches.*

Is that what they'd been missing? Why had the killer chosen places with wooden benches? It couldn't just be coincidence and it couldn't be something as simple as a bad back. The killer had lugged bodies around seemingly without breaking stride.

She dialled Uncle Bertie.

'Elsie, how's it going?'

'Benches. Could they be a big part of his compulsion?'

She could just picture his wizened old face blinking as he carefully considered. When he spoke, he did so in a plodding voice. It sounded like he was carefully choosing each and every word one at a time, deliberating over every syllable. Elsie knew better. It meant that he was trying to think and talk at the same time, his mind racing one sentence ahead of his brain.

'We did discuss they might be a part of the compulsion, didn't we?' Bertie said. He seemed to be straining to recall the crime scene photos. Unlike Elsie, he hadn't personally visited either of them. 'Hmm... I had come to the conclusion that the benches were probably just incidental to dumping the bodies in gardens. They're everywhere after all.'

It was true that London had an enormous number of benches. All along the Thames, there were benches. In every park, there were benches. A brainwave came to her. Could it be that simple?

'Uncle, could the *layout* of the benches have significance?'

'Remind an old man how they were arranged?'

'They were laid out in a circle, all facing each other like the numerals on a clock. They weren't identical though. In Chelsea, there were three while St Dunstan in the East had a total of eight benches in the lower garden.'

'What about the would-be dump site, the nearest garden to the Holland Park crime scene?' Bertie asked. 'Are there benches arranged in a circle there?'

Elsie strained to think. An image of the Lord Holland memorial flashed into her mind. It was a tiny corner of a very large park but she was pretty sure there were benches laid out around it. A quick Google confirmed they were *sort of* laid out in a circle. It was an imperfect shape but it was enough to fit the pattern. Bertie kept on the line, waiting with bated breath.

'Just checked,' she said. 'Yep, another circle of benches.'

Three crime scenes, three instances of benches in a circle.

'And did the benches have anything else in common?'

'Now that you mention it, he always picked benches on the western side of the crime scene, the one placed at roughly nine on the clock face.'

'Then I think,' Bertie said cautiously, 'you're onto something. We thought before that it was gardens that mattered, that a garden somewhere had particular significance for the Lady Killer. What if we were erroneous in that assumption? What if it's the benches that matter and they just happen to most commonly be found inside London's gardens? Which of your possible Stay-Away rentals has such a formation nearby?'

That was the million-dollar question, one which required an outstanding knowledge of London to answer. There were far too many possibilities to look for on Google Maps.

With time running out, she needed to ask someone who knew better than she did. She needed to swallow her pride and call Dad.

THE BOSS HAD THEM DRIVING around all evening. The later it got, the less hopeful Stryker became. It was one thing to keep an eye out for a man in broad daylight. It was another to try and find a black car in the dark of winter. Several times since sunset, he'd pulled a black car over only to realise on closer inspection that it wasn't even an Audi A8. He could forgive himself not being able to catch a number plate from a quick glance in the darkness but mistaking a Fiat hatchback for a luxury sedan was an error born of tiredness. Every time, he'd waved the driver off after the briefest of chats, his eyes darting around in case the Lady Killer had appeared in the meantime and seen Stryker. The drivers he'd stopped probably thought he was a lunatic.

The boss had come to the conclusion that benches were the key. She'd started listing places close to gardens with benches arranged in circles, cross-referencing them against the full eighty-odd strong list of StayAway properties. Places which had previously been top priority were demoted as benches became the defining characteristic. It was, in Stryker's mind, madness. Why would the killer be driven by the need to leave the body on a bench? He'd never heard of anything like it.

Nevertheless, an order was an order, and the boss had told him to prioritise places with benches. It was gone six when he found the first circle of benches near one of the StayAway properties. It wasn't a property that he'd have paid much attention to before. For a start, it was a flat. The killer hadn't ever used a flat as a crime scene, presumably because noises carried through the paper-thin walls of most London rabbit hutches.

It was in Kennington Park. He'd picked it by trawling Street View on Google Maps and looking for anywhere that might fit the pattern. While Google had been right that there were benches, Stryker had neglected to check the perimeter carefully enough. It was only when he was standing in front of the five-foot-tall fence running around the outside of Kennington Park that he ruled it out. There was no easy way to get there from the flat being rented out on StayAway in nearby St Agnes Place. Doing it while carrying a body would be difficult and doing it without being seen would be a million to one shot. Dozens of flats overlooked the route.

Strike one. He hoped the rest of the team was doing better.

# Chapter 61: Going Around in Circles

Like the others, Knox was driving around in circles. Throughout the evening, she'd been in contact with everyone. Ozzy's team were watching the killer's brother. It seemed that he was too smart to make a move straight away. He'd spent most of Saturday in his office, made no calls as far as they were aware, and headed home by cab as evening approached.

The team was beginning to tire. Despite DCI Mabey's insistence, aided and abetted by the old profiler, that the killer was losing control and would strike again imminently, the volunteers thought it unlikely. Fairbanks' team had long since knocked off after a few hours of driving around in circles and, as eight o'clock was fast approaching, Knox was tempted to join them. This whole manhunt was an exercise in futility.

Forget benches. It couldn't be something that simple. Knox's first thought had been of St Paul's Cathedral. On the southern edge, by St Paul's Churchyard, there was a tiny raised dais behind the fence. Did that count as a garden? Knox had dismissed it almost instantly – the killer wasn't some sort of ninja. He had been lucky at Chelsea Physic Garden and St Dunstan in the East. Even on this grey, drab, gloomy evening, someone would see him if he attempted to dump a body at St Paul's.

And weren't they a bit *early* anyway? If he were going to kill tonight then surely he'd need until morning to dump the body? Unless Mabey thought she could catch him sneaking in or out of one of the StayAway properties? That seemed about as likely as Fairbanks going on a diet.

Her own assigned properties included two that were far too public for the Lady Killer to risk, one which appeared to have had a CCTV camera added to the exterior since the last time Google's Street View van had been past, and one which Knox had been watching almost non-stop. The others were reporting the same. Everyone was getting tired, everyone was bored, and nobody could see a damned thing in the darkness.

She called Stryker.

'Still nothing?' he said immediately.

'Zip,' Knox said. 'Diddly bloody squat. This is a waste of time. Mabey's got us chasing a ghost here. When do we call it?'

'When she tells us.'

'Since when were you teacher's pet, Seb?' Knox teased. 'Or is it because you've got a bit of a thing for DCI Mabey? Don't think I ain't seen you looking. Those furtive little glances ain't subtle. You know she's taken right?'

Stryker didn't say anything for a moment. Then: 'No, she's not... is she?'

'Afraid so, Seb. I hear she's reconciled with that Hamish fella, you know, the handsome journo who gave her the tip-off about Vito?'

'How'd you know that?'

'I know things, Seb, I know things. That and I saw her texting him earlier. Three kisses. Must be serious.'

'You're lying.'

Knox grinned. Winding Stryker up made this whole charade of a stakeout worthwhile. 'Keep dreaming, Seb, keep dreaming.'

# Chapter 62: Benches & Benchmarks

As half past nine approached, Elsie felt her eyes closing once more. She'd come close to inadvertently taking a power nap several times since starting the stake-out and so she had reluctantly asked her volunteers for help covering her properties for a while. For an hour, Fairbanks' team had taken over her watch so could have a quick nap and pee in an actual bathroom rather than resort to using the Shewee she had stashed in the glove compartment. That break was now a distant memory.

Maybe the team were right. Maybe it was time to call it a night.

Something told her to hang on in a little longer. The killer had taken Matthews out for dinner before he'd killed her. Somehow, during that night, he'd flipped a switch and killed her. There had to be a reason why he was wining and dining Matthews. Was it so he could keep an eye on the investigation? He had certainly kept a close eye on Mabey's team throughout. Daring to confront Stryker was a reckless move. Taking Matthews out even more so. The killer still seemed like an enigma. Why was he stealing money from StayAway's renters to fund lavish Michelin-starred dinner dates if his intention was to kill them afterwards?

Uncle Bertie had said that he was a creature of habit driven by compulsion rather than logic. Elsie could relate to that. She knew that her own mind was far from perfect. Many nights she lay awake, ruminating, running in circles, wondering if, in fact, she really did deserve the top job.

Perhaps the killer was the same. Perhaps he was a broken man possessed of a diseased mind, simply craving love and attention like everyone else. Perhaps that's why he always picked women as his victims. They were all objectively attractive though not of a single type. They were all in their twenties.

Perhaps he'd been rejected. That would fit with his profile. An anxious, compulsive man snapping when he is – or believes he is about to be – rejected. It would explain why he had taken Matthews out for dinner. As Elsie understood it, the fatal date was their second. Why hadn't he killed her on the first? Had she been pliant, willing, interested? Is that what had bought her a stay of execution. Or was it simply that the second date had led to the killer tripping up, giving Matthews the chance to guess his true identity and thus necessarily, from his point of view, her death?

Her phone buzzed again. Another volunteer clocking off for the night. At this rate, she would be the last woman standing.

She turned the engine back on. Time for another circuit. She couldn't watch them all at once and so had concentrated on a house in Heathcote Street. It was set over five storeys, had a parking bay out front, and was a mere two minutes from St George's Gardens in Handel Street. Elsie had done a recce on foot and there was a small semi-circle of benches that might be close enough to what the killer needed. Then again, perhaps it wasn't.

Where else could fit? Russell Square? Bloomsbury Square Garden? Brunswick Square? No, no and no. They were all too public. That was half the battle. The killer wasn't going to dump a body in an exceptionally busy place. He might chance somewhere semi-public if he had to, but there was a difference between "might be seen under the cover of darkness" and "so close to the theatre district that he would definitely be seen by someone". Could he be getting reckless now that he had fled?

It came back to the compulsion. If he needed a garden and benches, there was no choice about it. There were easier ways to dispose of a body, even in central London. He could have thrown the bodies into the Thames, left them in one of the many lay-bys that fly-tippers hit on a nightly basis, or even just left them in the StayAway property. He was taking a risk for a reason.

Elsie scanned the list on her phone. This time, she didn't apply her "crime report" filter. The places which had been the subject of a crime report were now back on the list so that she could cast a wider net in the hope of finding a place with benches. Perhaps he would sooner risk returning to the scene of a crime than forgo his needs. Several properties jumped out at her. One was in Northampton Square, the home of London's City University. Knox was the nearest. Elsie texted her. She called back two minutes later.

'Boss, I'm here in Sebastian Street. I can see the square. There are students everywhere. This one's a bust too. Can we call it a night? I'm knackered.'

*Knox* was knackered? That was ironic. Elsie's brain had kicked into overdrive – one of her rare alert moments – just as her team was flagging.

'Nope,' Elsie said. 'Keep driving.'

Further down and down the list she went. There was one near her – Percy Circus. It was a funny little road just southeast of King's Cross, a short hop from her present position. The house had been the subject of a crime report filed by a tourist just over six months ago alleging that her engagement ring had disappeared while she was staying at the property. The homeowner had disagreed, forcing the woman to go to the police. Eventually, the complaint had been dropped. Presumably, the homeowner had paid her off to avoid a bad review. What was it Larkins had said? *People know I've got money and they always want a part of it.* No wonder if had been swept under the carpet. Homeowners would sooner pay up than risk negative reviews shutting down their business.

The moment she turned onto Vernon Rise, the road leading up to Percy Circus, a chill ran down her spine. The road climbed steeply away from the bustling A road and nobody was in sight. Here, unlike the other sites that she'd visited this evening, it was possible to find momentary solitude.

Percy Circus came into view as she inched past a row of recycling bins guarding a trio of parking spaces behind a rusty old metal fence. She paused at the top, killed her engine, and plunged herself into near darkness. This was what he needed.

In the middle of the roundabout was Percy Circus Gardens, a tiny patch of grass with a little walled garden at its epicentre complete with a circle of benches just how the Lady Killer liked it. It reminded Elsie strongly of St Dunstan, eerily beautiful, un-naturally quiet, and not a soul in sight.

After a few minutes of watching the square, the first car came past. It was red, didn't stop, and paid no heed to Elsie who had slunk down in her seat.

Elsie carried on watching, trying to ascertain if this was a plausible spot for the killer to choose as a dump site. Every few minutes or so, a car drove past. It would be risky to dump a body here but nowhere near impossible. She stayed in her car to call Uncle Bertie.

'Bertie?' she said. 'I'm at Percy Circus Gardens. Get it up on Street View, tell me what you think.'

'Just a minute,' Uncle Bertie replied groggily. 'What am I looking at?'

'Benches, garden, big grand houses,' she said. 'Bit exposed. Does it fit in your mind?'

'It isn't dissimilar.'

He didn't sound very certain. 'What's putting you off?'

'There's no parking.'

Elsie swore. He was right. The whole circle was double-yellows. Any car that parked would be ticketed and towed by the next passing traffic warden. It was too big a risk.

Her mind flashed back to the cars parked behind the bins.

'Bertie, stay on the line for me.'

She emerged from her car, doubled back down away from the house, and quickly came upon the little parking area. Four cars, all fenced off. The lock on the vehicle gate was broken.

There it was – the Audi A8 that belonged to Faulkner & Robertson.

'Bertie! I've found it. The Audi! Call Stryker, call Knox, send *everyone* to my location. Now!'

She hung up. She couldn't risk the killer seeing her mobile phone lighting up in the darkness. Percy Circus Gardens came back into view as she passed her own Audi.

There, on the other side of the roundabout, was the Stay-Away property. It was a gorgeous house, towering four storeys above ground level on top of a basement. Despite being almost identical to half a dozen of its neighbours, all with black doors and gold-trimmed handles, it was alone in still being a single residential dwelling. Most of the neighbouring homes had been carved up into flats as evidenced by the number of doorbells by the front door.

A light was on inside.

Elsie could only imagine what was going on. Had the killer already killed tonight's victim? Or was she inside right now, terrified and unable to escape?

There was nothing for it. She'd have to go in.

# Chapter 63: The Big Red Key

While back up was on its way, Elsie found herself in the same dilemma that Stryker had faced only yesterday. If she waited, she risked the life of the woman that the Lady Killer had taken home this evening. If she didn't, she risked her own.

No choice at all.

She fetched her Big Red Key from the car and then shut the boot as quietly as she could.

The light was still on when she returned less than three minutes later. She was on shaky legal ground. If anyone asked, she'd have to argue that she was in close pursuit or pretend that she'd heard someone cry out for help. It didn't matter. This was her chance to catch a killer, save a life, and keep her career on the straight and narrow. She had to take it.

The hallway light was on. There was no way to creep in unseen.

She paused on the doorstep, ram in hand, and held her breath. She couldn't hear anything going on inside. Three. Two. One.

With every fibre of her being, she swung the door ram back and then forward. It landed hard on the door, a loud crack emanating around Percy Circus Gardens. Straight away, she swung back again, letting the momentum of the first swing carry her higher than before. The metal collided with the door, splintering it inwards.

'James Robertson!' she shouted. 'Police!'

She heard a scuffle within as if someone had started moving very suddenly. Her adrenaline levels spiked, her senses becoming heightened. The sound of her heart thundering against her ribcage pounded in her ears and her hands began to shake with unbridled fear. She felt as if a lump had caught in her throat. Though she had only just crossed the threshold, time dilated so much that the walls inched by her in slow motion as she ran forward towards the door.

It was now or never.

She made her way down the corridor, keeping her body low to the ground and moving quickly.

The door was slightly ajar, a seam of light escaping through the crack to illuminate the hall. It wasn't enough for Elsie to see shadows that might give away the killer's location.

Where was that back up? She had yet to hear the scream of sirens as the Armed Response Unit arrived on the scene. She prayed they were smart enough to arrive without announcing themselves in that manner.

Her heartbeat reached its peak and her mind raced with it. Was she too late? Had the Lady Killer already struck again?

She kicked the door wide open to reveal two figures stood against the far wall. One was James Robertson, a near-perfect likeness for the e-fit that Flick had drawn. He was wearing jeans and a skinny T-shirt as if he were simply relaxing at home of an evening.

It wasn't his height that scared Elsie, it was his expression. He wore a sneer of derision, the face of a man who knew that this was the end of the road. There was no fear in his eyes. He had made no attempt to flee.

Instead, he had simply pressed a knife to the throat of his victim and wrapped an arm around her chest, binding her tightly to him. Elsie wanted to speak to her, to tell the woman – and herself – that it was all going to be alright.

'Don't take another step,' James demanded.

Elsie held her hands up. She was unarmed and outmatched. While Elsie was tall and strong, James had a bodybuilder's physique with veins popping out of his bare forearms.

Though Elsie did have her stab proof vest on underneath, she knew that fighting would be a disaster. The only way the woman he was holding hostage might live was if she could somehow talk him down and manipulate him into releasing his hostage.

'James, I'm Elsie. Can we talk?'

His jaw jutted out as he sneered. 'Fuck you,' he spat. Elsie felt her contempt for him well up. This man, this bastard, had killed three women in cold blood including a colleague and she would not give him the satisfaction of showing him just how scared and angry she was.

Elsie ignored him, turned her attention to the woman, and said gently. 'What's your name?'

'T-T-Tara,' she stammered.

'Hi, Tara,' Elsie said. She searched her mind, desperately trying to recall the very brief hostage negotiation training day that she'd undertaken years ago. How exactly was she supposed to talk down a psychopath? James had nothing to lose here. He was facing three charges of murder and one attempt no matter what. Adding a fourth murder charge wouldn't make a difference. Should she appease him? Flatter him? Let him think that he'd won? There had to be a way for Tara to make it out of here alive.

'Are you hurt?' Elsie asked.

Almost imperceptibly, Tara shook her head. The knife quivered in James' hand, the blade mere millimetres from her throat.

'Okay,' Elsie said. She spoke much more calmly than she felt. Inside, her heart continued to beat ten to the dozen. 'How about someone tells me what happened this evening? James?'

He looked at her as if he might snarl. 'Fuck you,' he said again.

'That's not very productive, is it, James? Why don't you start by putting down that knife? I know you don't want to hurt Tara here, do you?'

For a second, the sneer broke. 'Why do you think that?' he demanded.

'Simple,' Elsie said. 'If you wanted to kill her, you'd have done it. There are more than ten feet between us. I couldn't stop you if I wanted to.'

Behind her back, she crossed her fingers that James wouldn't simply call her bluff.

He didn't. Yet.

Why hadn't he slit her throat? Something was stopping him.

Perhaps Uncle Bertie was right. His voice echoed in her mind: *If you can't find her before he does, you'll have a fourth victim on your hands.*

Was Tara the intended victim all along? Had James forsaken his proxies and sought out the woman who had inspired all this rage?

Elsie took a leap and made an educated guess. The Lady Killer had been acting out his violent fantasies against proxies from the beginning but this was the end game. He was homeless, he knew the police were closing in. This victim had to be the intended victim, the one who had inspired his killing spree. Tara had to be the woman he hated to love. This was the Lady Killer's last stand. He wouldn't waste it.

Tara looked so normal, so boring, and so innocent. Elsie couldn't believe this petite redhead could be the cause of such all-encompassing rage and yet she had to be.

'You love Tara, don't you James?'

He hesitated, his lip quivering. 'I did.'

'You still do,' Elsie said. 'Isn't that why you're together tonight? So you two can reconcile?'

She shot a look at Tara, hoping the redhead would understand to play along, that it was her best chance of getting out of here alive. Elsie thought she saw a flash of recognition as Tara slowly blinked at her. Her eyes said it all. James really was a lunatic.

'What happened before? When you broke up?' Elsie asked. 'When did you two struggle?'

'We didn't!' he said. 'We were fine until... until...'

'Until he proposed to me,' Tara finished for him, her voice a mix of fear and anger. 'Outside St Paul's.... just *two weeks* after we started dating.'

St Paul's Cathedral was on the list of public gardens with circles of benches and Knox had swung by at least twice this evening only to find it was far too busy for anyone to dump a body. No wonder. It was where this all started, where James Robertson's hatred of women began. He had asked for Tara's hand in marriage and, when he was rejected, he had resorted to violence.

'When you know, you know,' Elsie said. 'Isn't that right, James?'

'Yes!' he said. 'I knew. I knew the moment I saw you at the theatre. I knew you were the one for me, Tara. Why'd you have to go and ruin everything?'

He stared at the top of Tara's head, his jaw set, his sneer more pronounced than ever. Hate and lust, two sides of one coin, and James was spinning between the two.

'Perhaps,' Elsie said reasonably, 'she just needed a bit more time to realise what a wonderful man you are, James. Look at you, you're in incredible shape.'

It was the first thing that Elsie had said to him which was true. He was in almost as good shape as Inspector Stryker.

As he spoke, Elsie's ears prickled. She could hear engines outside. Was backup here? Would they burst in before she could talk him down and cause him to draw the knife across Tara's throat? As much as the thought turned Elsie's stomach queasy, she needed time to build rapport with James.

'I'm a personal trainer,' James said proudly.

'And it shows,' Elsie said. 'How about I make us all a cup of tea and we sit down and talk about this? You can tell Tara how you feel without scaring her. You'd like that, wouldn't you, Tara?'

'Y-yes,' Tara stuttered. 'James... I... I'd like to talk about us. How can we move forward from this?'

Elsie wasn't convinced by Tara's abysmal acting skills but James was. It was if he believed it because it was what he needed to hear. The knife quivered again, his hand dropping a tiny bit as if he were about to acquiesce. At just the wrong moment, blue lights flashed outside the window.

'What the hell?' he yelled, his arm tightening up. The knife pressed against Tara's neck, too close this time, drawing a trickle of blood.

'Stop!' Elsie yelled. If his hand moved even half a centimetre, he'd cut Tara's carotid artery and she'd bleed out in less than a minute. 'James, those are my colleagues outside. I called them. You're getting angry at me, but you're hurting Tara. Look at her, James. Look at the woman you love. You're hurting her right now. That's not what a good man does, is it? Don't you want to protect her? Put down the knife, James.'

His eyes flicked to the window and then back again to Elsie. 'I can't.'

'Why not?'

'You'll arrest me.'

Had he only just realised that? There wasn't any point trying to lie to him. He wasn't thick enough to believe that everything was going to be fine and that he'd get to go home.

'I will, yes.'

His hand tightened again.

'If I don't arrest you, my colleagues will. Or worse, they'll shoot you and they'll aim to kill. That's what we're ordered to do in these situations. If you want to live, I'm your ticket out of here. Think about it. There's hope for you and Tara as long as you're both still breathing. You can call a lawyer the moment you're out-side, tell them your side of the story. Isn't your brother a hotshot lawyer?'

He could even call a shrink. Elsie was willing to believe he was insane. Right now, she didn't care if he spent the next twenty years in HMP Belmarsh or locked up in a straitjacket in Broad-moor.

'No!' he said. 'I'd rather die.'

Despite his words, Elsie knew it wasn't true. He didn't want to die. Nor did he want to kill Tara. He couldn't. He needed to strike without the blow being expected. That was how he'd killed the other three. Why would he break that pattern now? If he was as compulsive as Uncle Bertie thought, he was much less likely to kill in a different way.

'No, James, you wouldn't. Look at Tara. Really look at Tara. She loves you, James. Don't you Tara?'

'Uh-huh,' she murmured.

Elsie's shot her a glowering look. Play along, woman! She turned her attention back to James.

'If you're dead, you can't be together. But if you surrender, Tara can visit you in jail, wait for you to get out. Isn't that better than a bullet, James?'

Footsteps sounded outside. An Armed Response Unit was about to descend on the scene.

'Stop!' Elsie yelled. 'DCI Mabey! I'm in here with Mr Robertson and one hostage. Do not come in. Repeat, do not come in.'

After a moment's pause, the sound of footsteps receded as the Armed Response Unit beat a retreat. They wouldn't have gone far, and they wouldn't be gone for long.

'James, I'm going to reach into my pocket and get out my phone. I need to tell them not to shoot you. Do you understand me? I'm not going for a gun. I'm unarmed.'

He nodded so she slowly delved into her pocket, pulled out her phone, held it aloft so James could see that she was telling the truth, and then called Stryker.

'Boss!' he said. 'I'm outside. What's going on?'

'Stryker,' she said cautiously. 'You're on speaker. Everything is okay in here. We're just having a chat, James, Tara and I. I need you to tell them to stand down.'

'Right. I'll do that,' Stryker said. 'Our good friend DCI Fairbanks is out here giving orders. I'll go speak to him now.'

Elsie hung up. Fairbanks. If he was the one calling the shots, James Robertson would be dead in five minutes flat. Fairbanks would shoot right through Tara before he let James get away.

'James, you have to listen to me. My colleagues will have snipers with them. You see that window at the front of the house?'

She gestured to the windows where curtains were tightly drawn.

'Those curtains won't protect us,' she said. 'They'll be using thermal imaging technology to search for body heat. They can aim through the curtains just fine. We need to go out there, okay?'

He bit his lip. 'I... I can't. I can't live without Tara.'

His left arm – the one which wasn't holding the knife – pulled Tara tighter against him, a human shield.

'James, no one is asking you to live without Tara. But Tara's bleeding. She needs to see a doctor, okay? If you put the knife down, we can walk out of here together.'

'Will you still love me, Tara?' he whispered.

She looked at Elsie, terrified. Elsie wanted to yell at her. For fuck's sake woman, say yes. Instead, she gave her an imperceptible nod, her eyebrows arching just a touch.

'Yes, James, I'll still love you.'

'Will you... will you marry me?'

If ever a man had picked a worse time and place, Elsie had never heard of it. James had a knife to her throat and yet he was proposing marriage.

All went silent. Tara's eyes went wide, her expression meek. Finally, she said 'Yes.'

The knife fell to the floor with a clang. Elsie sprang into action, running forward to kick it out of the way. James spun Tara around and then leant in as if to kiss her.

Just as his beard had come into contact with her cheeks, her knee had come into contact with his balls.

He doubled over, howling in pain.

'James Robertson, you do not have to say anything. But it may harm your defence if you do not mention when questioned something which you later rely on in court. Anything you do say may be given in evidence.'

She slapped her cuffs on him as she cautioned him. Before Elsie could stop her, Tara kicked him.

'Enough!' Elsie said. 'Before I have to arrest you too.'

She hauled James to his feet, yelled to her colleagues outside that they were coming out, and emerged into the night to find floodlights pointing in her direction. The unmistakable red glow of sniper rifles fell on them the moment they appeared in the doorway.

'Don't shoot! He's in custody!'

# Chapter 64: The Career Killer

The next morning, thanks to the mountain of DNA and other evidence as well as having been caught in the middle of an attempted murder, James Robertson confessed everything.

A press conference was hastily arranged, and by midday, conference room one was full again, this time filled to the brim with London's finest journalists and newscasters, all desperate to find out if it were really all over. The whole team had come to bask in the glory of having caught the Lady Killer. Annie sat at the back where she cast a beady eye at DCI Fairbanks. She looked as if she hated his guts. Just behind Fairbanks sat Hamish Porter. He grinned at Elsie, flashing two thumbs-up. Elsie smiled back. Without Hamish, she wouldn't have found Vito and so might never have broken the case.

As she passed journalist after journalist, she wondered which of these people had managed to secure pictures of her incident room and who they'd bribed to get them. Had Matthews fallen prey to the lure of money? With her gone, it was possible that they'd never know who the leak was.

Stryker sat on the left. He was scowling when she glanced over but began to smile when their eyes met. He too had been invaluable throughout the investigation. Without him, she'd have given up and thrown in the towel.

She made it almost to the front before Ian appeared in front of her. One minute to the hour. The press conference would start at any moment. Ian miked her up so that she could talk to the whole auditorium. Out of the corner of her eye, she saw that Fairbanks had a microphone on too.

'What's that about?' she asked Ian.

He shrugged. 'Dunno. Just do as I'm told, don't I?' Fairbanks stood as Ian was talking, shuffling past Hamish Porter.

Once miked up, she approached the lectern. Fairbanks beat her to it. Cameras flashed in his direction as he began to talk.

'Ladies and gentlemen, thank you for coming today,' he said. 'It is with great pride that I can tell you the Lady Killer has been brought to justice. Thanks to my team's valiant efforts, aided and abetted by the lovely Detective Chief Inspector Mabey,' he nodded in her direction, the cameras turning on her as he did, 'we managed to prevent a fourth murder late last night.'

*We?* Elsie's jaw dropped. Fairbanks was claiming credit for the bust? What on earth had he done?

'The killer,' he continued, 'is a mentally ill young man. He was one of the so-called "incels", driven by rage against women and society. He felt it was his right to have any woman of his choosing. Now he will spend the rest of his life behind bars with only men for company.'

He laughed, his belly jiggling.

Elsie was going to kill him. She wanted to wrap her hands around his pudgy little throat and squeeze the life out of him. How dare he take credit for her investigation? He hadn't even bothered to properly investigate Leonella Boileau's death and now he was taking credit for the lot?

Knox beat her to it. She appeared like a blur from the side of the conference room, all eyes turning on her as she leapt at Fairbanks, her hand colliding with his face so firmly that the slap reverberated throughout the room.

'You bastard!' she screamed. She yanked his microphone from him, held it up to her mouth and walked right on past him.

'This piece of shit,' Knox gesticulated in his direction, 'has never investigated a case properly in his life. He has had nothing to do with the investigation. Every bit of success we've had is down to DCI Mabey.'

Elsie flashed her a grateful smile.

'And while I've got your attention,' Knox continued. 'I need to get something off my chest. This useless fat fuck demanded sexual favours from me. In return, he promised me the promotion to DCI that he held me back from for years. When I wouldn't sleep with him for the promotion that I earned, he trumped up disciplinary charges against me and had me demoted to sergeant.'

At the sight of the shocked, yet delighted, journalists, she added, 'The first of you to come up with fifty grand can have an exclusive. Boss, the floor is yours.'

Knox stormed out, several journos running after her to try and strike a deal. They'd come for one morning's news reports and scooped a much more scintillating and scandalous story.

Elsie took centre stage, 'Well, that was eventful.'

A chuckle went around the room.

She wanted to pay tribute to Knox for her work rescuing Sumiko and breaking the back of a trafficking ring but the encrypted records from the accountant were still being deciphered and so it all had to stay hush-hush for now.

'As Sergeant Knox said, this was nothing to do with Chief Inspector Fairbanks. This was a team effort. I'd like to pay tribute to all those involved but especially my own team. Stryker, Annie, Ian, I'm proud to work with you. I'd also like to thank Doctor

Burton Leigh for coming out of retirement to assist with this case. Finally, I'd like to thank all our colleagues who joined us for yesterday's operation, especially Ozzy Calder and his team who were an integral part of coordinating the efforts. I'd like to pay tribute to my father, the now-retired Chief Inspector Peter Mabey, without whom I'd never have joined the force.'

It was odd. Despite the crowds, she couldn't see any sign of dear old Dad. Perhaps he didn't want to steal the limelight. She did spot a teary-eyed Beya Boileau hiding at the back of the auditorium.

'I also want to pay particular tribute to the late Georgia Matthews. In the short time that she was part of my team, she proved herself an enormous asset. Her loss will be felt for some time to come. My heart and sympathy go out to her family at this difficult time.'

She paused for breath and looked around the room, seeking out the eyes of those who'd previously doubted her. Today wasn't about her, it was about her team, and so she kept it short and sweet. She resisted the urge to pre-empt the inevitable questions about whether she deserved to lead her team. She knew she did. She'd caught the bastard, and she'd saved a life into the bargain.

'Thank you all. I'll take your questions now.'

As the cameras flashed, the crowd applauded.

I'm proud to be a detective, Elsie thought, but I'm prouder still to be my father's daughter.

# From the Author

The biggest challenge in writing this novel was depicting ME/CFS fairly. Ultimately, Elsie's symptoms are relatively minor when compared to many real-life sufferers, a necessity borne out of the need to solve murders.

Elsie can't represent every person with ME/CFS and so she is only intended to represent the one woman who she is (loosely) based upon. I'd like to thank that person for helping to craft a unique, plausible and relatable character.

I'd also like to thank my team of 'Advance Readers' who gave me feedback along the way: Alyson, Tina, Laura, Cinta, Felice, and Martha. You rock, ladies!

Elsie and the team will return in 2020 for another case. To find out more, visit GunnCrime.com[1] or search Ali Gunn online.

---

1.   https://www.GunnCrime.com

Printed in Great Britain
by Amazon